Blood and Fireflies

B.M. HOWARD

BLOOD

& Fireflies

CANELO

First published in the United Kingdom in 2023 by

Canelo
Unit 9, 5th Floor
Cargo Works, 1–2 Hatfields
London SE1 9PG
United Kingdom

A CIP catalogue record for this book is available from the British Library.

Print ISBN 978 1 80436 270 9
Ebook ISBN 978 1 80436 269 3

Look for more great books at www.canelo.co

Printed and bound in Great Britain by Clays Ltd, Elcograf S.p.A.

1

In memory of Dorothy Carrington (1910 – 2002) to whom all English-speaking students of Corsican history and lore owe so much

Dramatis Personae

In 1797 the French republic still maintained the revolutionary terms *citoyen* and *citoyenne* as alternatives to *monsieur/madam*, or titles of nobility. In the army, and in the fledgling republics of north Italy, these terms were used simultaneously, hence *Citoyen* general, or *Citoyen le Comte*.

The Investigators

Felix Gracchus Retired Commissaire of police and disillusioned revolutionary

Lieutenant Dermide Vanderville Aide-de-camp of General Dumas

The Bonaparte family

Letizia Buonaparte Widowed matriarch of the family

Napoleon Bonaparte Commander-in-chief of the French Army of Italy

Josephine Bonaparte Scion of Parisian society. Recently married to Napoleon

Fortune Josephine's pug dog

Joseph Fesch Commissary officer in the Army of Italy. Half-brother of Letizia

Elisa Bonaparte Eldest daughter of Letizia

Paolette Bonaparte Second daughter of Letizia

The Army of Italy

General Alexandre Berthier Chief of Staff to the Army of Italy, second-in-command to Napoleon

General Alexandre Dumas General of the Army of Italy

General Leclerc General of the Army of Italy. Fiancé of Paolette

Captain Pasquale Bacciochi Officer of the Army of Italy. Fiancé of Elisa

Lieutenant Hippolyte Charles Officer attached to the staff of the Army of Italy

Lieutenant Pietro Piotr Officer in the Polish Legion

Lieutenant Joseph Damingué Hercule Officer of Guides de Bonaparte

The Mombello Household

Comte René Mombello Franco-Italian noble. Friend of the Bonaparte family and their host at Mombello

Lieutenant Alexandre Marbeuf Officer of Guides de Bonaparte. Nephew of Comte Mombello

Francesco Leonardi Comte Mombello's cook and head of kitchen

Supporting characters

Fortunée Hamelin Friend of Josephine

Comtessa Francesca Gheradi Friend of Josephine

Marquesa Giuseppa Visconti Friend of Josephine

Antoine-Jean Gros Painter patronised by Josephine

Prologue

20 August 1794, Year three of the Republic

The magistrate hauled himself up the tower staircase of the citadel in Fort Carrè. He was struggling with his leg despite the walking cane and regretted having brought the bundle of files containing his research on the prisoner. The climb proving troublesome, he stopped at one of the casement windows to rest and admire the view over the bay. A finer day never shone over Antibes.

The fortress walls falling away below were dotted with pink rose leaves and yellow broom blossoms, but their smell could not reach the heights. Beyond the walls, the surrounding sea lapped on white sand where soldiers were bathing. As the sun struck the surface, it was refracted through the water, lending the waves a blue tinge as of the lambent flame of burning spirit. The effect of the sunlight was that the swimmers in the water appeared clad, as it were, in glistening silver scales.

The magistrate blinked and pushed his green spectacles further up his nose. He was surprised the prisoner was entitled to enjoy such a view. Condemned men were more often made to sit starving in the lower cells while the smells of the fort kitchen wafted cruelly past, as was so common for French fortresses in those days.

Sucking the sauce from a chicken leg retrieved from that very kitchen, he regarded the spiralling stair ruefully. The sympathies of the garrison for the prisoner were apparent; he was confined not in a cell, but an eyrie. The magistrate sighed, tucked the

I

greasy chicken leg carefully into the paper files, put those under his arm, and continued the climb upwards.

The sentry outside the cell was on the verge of open rebellion and trod heavily on the magistrate's foot with his nailed boots while opening the door. The calculated discourtesy was amplified by their disparity in footwear. The magistrate's opinion was that the best passport to the south was a pair of canvas hemp-soled shoes. Not only were they of extreme utility and comfort upon the stony footpaths which are found between the vineyards, but they inspired the inhabitants with respect for the wearer as not a stranger at least to one of their customs. Gingerly assessing his insulted foot for injury, he ducked into the cell.

The prisoner's room was sparsely furnished with a low bed and rude table spread with maps and half-finished appeals. The only ornaments on the walls were the three windows which drenched the fore part of the room in converging shafts of light. The prisoner sat on the single chair behind the table so that the only shadow was over him, his face partially concealed behind the lank curtains of long dark hair that hung over his temples in the prevailing Muscadin style currently favoured by the young firebrands of the Revolution.

The magistrate tossed his bundle of papers on the table and, as an afterthought, topped them with his magistrate's hat and rubbed his cropped head with relief. The greasy portion of chicken plopped unceremoniously onto the maps that littered the table. As he stood for the visitor the prisoner moved the ink well carefully aside, and they surveyed one another warily.

The cell's inhabitant was emaciated, ill looking and decidedly ugly, as if he had been confined for years, not mere weeks. He hardly seemed to grow as he came to his feet, which he accomplished just slowly enough to convey disrespect. By contrast, the magistrate was tall and well-fleshed, his waistcoat buttons straining for pre-eminence against the evidence of good living. He was not a good-looking man either, and behind his spectacles, his eyes betrayed a glint of intellectual vanity.

As each performed the slightest of bows, the prisoner's a mere inclination of the chin, the magistrate's foot encountered the edge of an uncollected night bucket under the table. Deploying a handkerchief to his nose he moved towards the nearest window. From it, he observed that across the bay the flag on the telegrafo still sagged at half-mast. Whether it marked the end of the Committee of Public Safety's iron reign, the death of Robespierre, or an anticipation of the fate he conveyed for the prisoner confined here he did not know, but it was decidedly unorthodox and would have to be addressed.

He blinked through his spectacles as he swivelled back to the prisoner, who had morosely lowered his meagre frame back into the chair and was trying to conceal the fact that he was reading the visitor's topmost file upside down.

The magistrate cleared his throat, uncertain how to begin. He indicated the remains of a loaf on the table. 'I passed the kitchen on entering the citadel and borrowed proof of their ability to cater better than this. I will arrange for the supply of superior viands.'

'That will not be necessary,' said the prisoner, with ill grace, 'I prefer plain soldier's fare.'

The magistrate, who deplored the implied virtue of asceticism, turned his face aside to smile before continuing. 'I come bearing news for you, General.'

'My rank has been suspended, I am afraid you are culpable of an error,' said the prisoner. He waved at the pile of files. 'Despite your grubbing you remain poorly informed. And you enter my quarters like Madame Guillotine's handmaiden without even introducing yourself.'

'My name is not important.'

'Nonetheless, I know it,' replied the prisoner. 'I know who you are. I know what you have done.'

'Then we understand one another,' said the magistrate simply, and he began again. 'You are a creature of Robespierre, which is a sure route to the gallows this morning. Your patron has fallen.'

3

'And so the wheel of fortune turns, and destinies are corrupted. Two weeks ago, it was another story.' The prisoner unbent his legs as he spoke. They were so thin as to be ridiculous, disappearing into his gaping boot tops like two broomsticks.

'Republics are subject to all of the same sort of problems as monarchies,' the magistrate began to lecture, instantly regretting it but unable to extract himself. 'They are not a panacea for fighting nepotism, corruption, greed, crime, or injustice. A republic must be eternally vigilant against insurrection within, those who will corrupt their ideals, as well as the exterior forces that seek their destruction and subversion.'

The prisoner considered him scathingly. 'Was that a comfort to you when they came for *her*?'

The question landed like a fizzing bomb shell spinning on the cell floor between them. The magistrate removed his spectacles and polished them carefully on one end of his neck cloth. When he raised his eyes again the prisoner met his stare without blinking, and neither spoke for some time as they probed one another's gaze, waiting for the fuse to ignite or splutter out.

Eventually, with a conciliatory shrug the prisoner said, 'It is you then, *citoyen*, who represents the purity of the Revolution this week? May the supreme being take pity on us. Well, my congratulations, fortune has brought you high, and I find myself spun to the wheel's bottom, barely clinging on by the mercy of my fingertips.'

'Say, by your pen, rather,' suggested the magistrate.

The prisoner affected indifference, but the magistrate detected a flash of keen interest blaze in the intelligent sunken eyes.

He removed a letter from his coat pocket. 'The incriminating material that links you to the Robespierre plot bears several curious features. It is written partially in dialect, which appears to be an attempt to convey your patterns of speech. It is badly done though, this expression for instance is pure

Marseilles port slang. I do not believe you would use such a phrase.'

The prisoner eagerly seized the document and scanned it. 'You are right, this is not something a Corsican would say. Our equivalent reads rather, "The friend on the piazza is worth more than gold in the bank."'

He handed back the letter, glancing at the other documents deposited by the visitor on the table. The magistrate noticed that the prisoner's position had softened and so he waited for him to continue.

'It was fortunate for both of us that you were here. I shall not forget this. You have done the Republic a service in releasing me.'

The magistrate frowned. 'Do you think so? Although this evidence is flawed,' he tapped the letter, 'that does not imply your innocence.' He moved back to stare out the window and the wheeling gulls. He spoke softly to them rather than the prisoner. 'You are a Robespierrist. If we were at my tribunal in Paris, rather than amongst your partisans in the army, your neck would already be locked in the guillotine's wooden collar, alongside Robespierre and all his other creatures so drenched in the blood of innocents.'

The prisoner's mask flickered, and his glittering eyes beheld the magistrate with new attention. 'I will remember that too, *citoyen*, when the wheel turns again.'

The magistrate nodded, and turned to walk to the cell door, on which he rapped sharply. 'They will bury you in a backwater, you know. Your career is over,' he said over his shoulder as the sentry let him out. 'Nonetheless, welcome back to the active list, General Bonaparte.'

Chapter One

9 June 1797

The twenty-first day of Prairal, Year five of the Republic

The front courtyard of the Villa Mombello had been pressed into use by the headquarters of the French Army of Italy as a waiting room. By means of a striped canvas awning drawn out from the wings of the house the space was transformed into a vast salon. Beneath this blue and white roof, defended from sun or sudden rain alike, was a circular fortress of tables staffed by harassed military clerks, their bare heads agreeably tinted with soft colours by the light filtering through the canvas. The front was open to the June morning, and this was welcome as the day already promised great heat, and because the wafting wraiths of tobacco fumes mingled with the scent of wool-clad soldiers, far from fresh after days in the saddle, had a tendency to linger. The greater number of those waiting were there to conduct business with the headquarters staff, but there were also idlers and passers-of-time cluttering the place up, while a constant stream of dusty horse-borne couriers mounted and dismounted before the awning, some striving to enter, some impatient to be away.

Sagging on a rough bench against the wall of the villa trying to eavesdrop through an adjacent window was a man enveloped in a voluminous pilgrim's travelling cloak that shadowed his face. He packed a long clay pipe stubbornly and appeared to be having difficulty with it from the curious way he kept peering into the bowl, poking it forlornly with a twist of paper. But the business of the pipe, together with the cloak, sufficed to insulate him from the bustle and hum of the soldiers who surrounded him.

He kept one sour eye on the flustered clerks holding the jumble of tables against all comers. Those tables, requisitioned from the villa, echoed the house's faded gilt dignity, while others were gimcrack tavern cast-offs, and at least one had the particular marks of having been but lately installed in a chicken house. The clerks were on their feet, all the seats having been commandeered by the idlers who lined the walls and windows of the villa's interior flanks. It was on one of these that the pilgrim had taken refuge from the cluster of cavalry officers who had escorted him in, under protest, two hours previously. They stood near the beleaguered clerks talking animatedly among themselves and their faces shone with confidence and certainty – and the other things he had lost. Observing their world he despised himself as one afloat in a sea of self-loathing, disappointment, and disillusioned hopes. An ardent lieutenant was holding forth to the others on the advantages the Revolution had brought to Italy, and the pride on his face seemed to be diffused throughout his companions like some golden haze. Since they had intercepted him early that morning near Milan, he had suffered their zeal in bad humour. Their enthusiasm, and his temper, had only increased as they neared headquarters.

Abandoned, or at least temporarily ignored by the young revolutionaries, he peered once more past the clerks to the yearned-for freedom of the carriage drive. The villa's marble colonnades were guarded by dark sentinel cypresses, and its grounds of magnolias, fountains and rockeries, ilex groves and statuary were infested with scurrying martial figures in the blue and white uniforms of the French Republic, imparting a foreign sense of purpose to the villa's stolid timelessness.

He rested his head on the windowsill again. This enabled him to overhear more of the conversation within, which satisfied both his habitual inquisitiveness, and his curiosity as to his own immediate and uncertain future. Two voices could be made out.

'The point is, General Berthier,' said the first voice, 'that the men are unhappy here. They associate the villa with unnatural events and Comte Mombello going missing has only made matters worse.'

The reply came in a reedy tone, 'These rumours of a ghoul are nonsense, and need to be stopped. Superstition affects only weaker minds. In any case, all the soldiers not here on headquarters business are strictly denied the grounds of the villa—'

A gale of laughter drowned out the rest of the reply and the irritated pilgrim flicked his eyes up. The culprits were the group who had brought him in, and he surveyed them with distaste. The stage was held by their commanding officer, who wore a preposterously magnificent cavalry uniform of tight breeches, coloured boots, and short dolman jacket. He packed his breeches like a carthorse, with huge straining sinews and a rudely protuberant bulge of maleness. Tight Hungarian *pantalons* were experiencing a vogue and his figure suited these to perfection, while the colourful cockerel plumes of his cap lent him the air of the lord of the farmyard. Squinting, the pilgrim imagined him tethered by one leg to prevent him from annoying the hens. As the officer concluded his tedious anecdote the group laughed heartily again, except for one young lieutenant, whose bored face was turned away from his peers. The cockerel was a type, he concluded. His entourage was the same. They could have walked straight off the stage of a Racine play. Slack-jawed toadies and place-filling curs. Except that one. Here was a man apart. Something in the expression of his face was cut from an uncommon cloth. That face was what was commonly called fine, but it was not that which made him appear different. Eavesdropping at the window forgotten, the pilgrim studied him with interest.

Their eyes met, and a spark of unexpected complicity flared between them, but he dulled it with a scowl that the lieutenant received with a perplexed frown.

Ignoring him pointedly, he stretched out one aching leg to admire its hemp-soled sandal. If not in the height of fashion, it was practical at least. Past the tip of his toes, his eyes found the young officer still observing him, wincing at this sartorial innovation. Mercifully at that moment the villa doors clattered open and a liveried messenger hurried out, his eyes scanning the company purposefully.

'Lieutenant Vanderville. *Now*, if you please.' Then as an afterthought he turned to the pilgrim. 'You too, *citoyen*.'

The young lieutenant who had been staring at him fell in dutifully behind the lackey's back. The pilgrim followed their business-like pace through hallways of faded splendour before fetching up abruptly in front of a pair of tired wooden doors. The lackey knocked, and spinning seamlessly on his heels he addressed the pilgrim, who had been struggling to keep up.

'General Bonaparte is absent. You will meet with Berthier – a general, but not *the* General. The next best thing, in fact. Do you understand?'

He nodded carelessly, and the messenger broke open the doors, bellowing, 'Lieutenant Vanderville and the *citoyen*-prisoner!' before waving them impatiently inside.

Lieutenant Vanderville strode boldly into the grand salon, clattering his sabre on the floor, while the pilgrim ambled in behind him more slowly, looking around carefully at his surroundings. It was stiflingly warm and on each flank of the entry portal twin secretaries scribbled furiously at their desks while fanning themselves with stray papers. The gracious frescos were at odds with the ranks of battered wooden boxes of files arrayed in ad hoc fashion around the walls. Shafts of light streaming through the tall windows illuminated the centre of the floor where Vanderville came to an abrupt stop and stood at attention, sweeping his hat under his arm. The pilgrim shuffled to an uncertain stop next to him in the pool of sunlight and uncovered his own head.

Beyond were two men in senior general's uniforms conversing over a billiard table, smothered in files and papers.

The generals were intent on their exchange and ignored the new arrivals. The room smelt of overheated leather armchairs and floor polishing wax. A clock chimed on the mantlepiece over the embers of an entirely unnecessary fire.

The pilgrim was hungry and tired and felt the shaft of sun from the window uncomfortably hot on the back of his head. This was his first encounter with General Berthier, the second in command of the Army of Italy. The other general at the billiard table he was more familiar with. Everyone knew of General Dumas, dubbed Horatius Cocles by the more literate soldiers after a hero of the Roman Republic. Bald on the top, with bushy dark hair and conjoined whiskers, tall and well made with the dark skin of his native Saint-Domingo, he was instantly recognisable.

Berthier was less immediately impressive: by comparison he was small, and no Apollo. His hair was long, a billowing yellowish powdered mane that framed his well-fed face in startling fashion. It was as if a large loaf had been cut into three portions and attached to his head, one part on the top, and one on each side. Traces of hair powder stuck to his glistening, overheated cheeks. The overall effect in the close room was that of a baker's lunch abandoned in a hot kitchen, and made the hungry pilgrim feel faint.

The generals being in no hurry to acknowledge their presence, the pilgrim reflected on the circumstances that had brought him here. Squinting through dancing dust motes, he retrieved a pair of spectacles from his pocket and, perching them on his nose, took the opportunity to examine his companion again. Good looking, he thought. Probably French rather than Italian. He knew that the colours of the blue uniform coat, as well as the gold buttons and the markings on the epaulettes, signified a specific role, but remembering these details had always exhausted him and the uniforms changed so quickly nowadays. He sighed wearily. He had been so close to escaping, to avoiding any further entanglement with the Republic, but now here he was, in the belly of the revolutionary beast's Italian adventure.

He was recalled to his senses by a loud crash as the lieutenant beside him fainted. As the secretaries helped the protesting officer to a nearby sofa, watched by the disapproving generals, he winced in sympathy. He was sufficiently distracted by the discomfited young officer as to lack his customary composure when General Berthier finally deigned to take notice of him, and smiling like a fox in a chicken pen he barked out his opening salvo. 'Good day to you, *Citoyen* Gracchus, if that is the name you are going under today?'

'Never mind that now, General,' he responded, meeting Berthier's stare. 'What am I doing here?'

'Congratulations are due. The Army of Italy have directed you to be attached to headquarters. You have been summoned to take an oath of loyalty and obedience to the Republic before taking up your post.'

Gracchus held up one hand to stop him continuing. 'General, I am on the verge of being honoured by your choice, but as I know nothing about the army's business, I cannot fulfil any such responsibilities, nor take any oath. Deepest regrets and so on.'

He turned and hobbled towards the doors. Lieutenant Vanderville's pale face popped up from the sofa in anticipation, momentarily revived by this novel approach to the total authority of the Army of Italy. One of the secretaries smirked, and as Gracchus approached the open door, stretched out an elegantly booted leg, and kicked it shut. Gracchus paused, regarding the floor thoughtfully under the secretary's icy stare. 'I must insist…' he began, turning back to the billiard table.

Before he could finish, General Dumas addressed him in a thundering voice. 'How *dare* you *citoyen*? No Frenchman may refuse to serve the Republic! It is not possible.'

Gracchus whirled around, his eyes flashing with irritation. 'Why do you need *me*? To advise on stationary?' He strode forward to the billiard table and grasped a sheet of paper. 'The Journal of Bonaparte and the Virtuous Men,' he read aloud and tossed it down. 'The style is as execrable as the letterheads. Who writes this nonsense?'

Berthier regarded him impassively. '*That* is our internal army news sheet. It doesn't meet with your approval?'

'It is mediocre; nobody wants this ultra-republican nonsense anymore.'

'I agree,' said Berthier. 'You will be taking control of its modern replacement, *The Courier of the Army of Italy*, while you find your feet here with us.'

'I can see where this is going. For the record, I refuse.' Gracchus dropped the papers back onto the table. 'How did you even know I was here, anyway?'

Berthier summoned a secretary. 'Bring me the files on *Citoyens* Gracchus and Vanderville,' he ordered, and he waited for them to arrive before speaking again.

'Unfortunately for you, your papers were recognised as forgeries at a posting house in Piedmont, drawing the attention of an alert official.' He waved imperiously at the secretary arriving with the files. 'Make out an order for the arrest of this *citoyen* on the grounds of treachery against the Republic, and the dissemination of false information.' He pointed to a second secretary. 'Prepare a temporary twenty-day commission for an editor of army communiques. Place both documents on file.' He turned back to Gracchus, 'Now, which of these two is more to your taste: the commission, or the arrest?'

'Look, by your own account I am a corrupted republican of dubious, if not downright illegal politics. Paris will not confirm my appointment.'

'Take a seat and calm yourself down.' As Gracchus moved towards the nearest chair, Berthier added, 'Not that one, it suffers, as you do, from a weakness of the leg. Now, instead of us wasting any more time on pleasantries, let me make your position clear to you.

'The Commander-in-chief does not like you, but he has a high opinion of your abilities. I don't much like you either and I have no conception of what your value is here. I'm busy and you don't have much time to convince me that you are worth a ration allowance. So I advise you to start at a gallop. Do you have anything to say? Please confine yourself to brief responses.'

'Yes… and no, General Berthier.'

Berthier took up a pen. 'I am at a loss to make out whether it is me or the Republic's service that you are mocking, but I can assure you that the consequences either way are not something you want to contemplate.' He waved a handful of printed forms, scored heavily in red. 'These are personnel returns for a demi-brigade from the front. We grind men here, and our mill is always hungry. Do you understand me?' He put down his pen and glared. His bureaucrat's disguise slipped to reveal eyes of steel forged under fire and Gracchus realised he had erred in mentally filing Berthier as a desk-mounted swinger of paper sabres.

'Very well. That's understood then. You have a week to convince me not to have you sent to the front. You might not be much use in an assault, but you are built like a mule and ours drop like stones the way we work them.'

'He looks like a mule to me,' agreed General Dumas. 'A stubborn good for nothing idler of a mule.'

Berthier nodded. 'Do you know the average lifespan of a mule in the army of Italy, *citoyen*? Three weeks. We work them like slaves, and they drop inside the month from work and scant forage if a stray ball doesn't open their bellies or carry off one of their legs.'

He nodded to the other general. 'Dumas, do the creed.' The general duly performed a republican oath to which Gracchus acquiesced with bad grace.

'Don't worry about Paris,' said Berthier, 'we are not so particular here. And in any case, by the time your proposed appointment reaches them, and they decide it's just the Army

13

of Italy exceeding their authority again, you will be finished and have leave to travel on as an itinerant bookseller, or whatever you are posing as. Sign here, and here,' he continued, pushing a form across the table. 'As a sop to your principles we have attached you to the Army of Italy as a civilian rather than as a staff officer, but you still need an official representative of the occupying power to assist you. And there he is, recovering on that sofa. Lieutenant Vanderville! Your commanding officer has indicated that you can be spared for a few days. Is that right, General Dumas?'

Dumas nodded his assent. 'For a few months if needed, I shan't miss one *aide-de-camp* who can't keep his feet.'

Berthier tapped the papers in front of him. 'Lieutenant, your service file is littered with superlatives and commendations, yet I see that you have applied twice now to be transferred from an enviable position on the staff of General Dumas to General Bonaparte's Guides?'

Vanderville, somewhat recovered now, coloured visibly under Dumas's stern gaze.

'Well,' continued Berthier, 'since your present duties clearly displease you, you can have no objection to being employed as a nursemaid to *Citoyen* Gracchus during his sojourn here. You want to be a Guide? You can be his guide to staff headquarters. Afford him every assistance, while ensuring he does not run afoul of any regulations, especially those relating to unauthorised absence. The latest *ordonnances* are detailed here,' he slid a large file across the desk. 'In addition, you will need these.' He added two more folders to the pile.

'I still cannot believe you had me brought here just to edit your newsletter.'

Ignoring this, Berthier continued, 'Gracchus, you are required to take charge of the printing operations at headquarters and use your particular talents to organise and produce a newspaper, or rather two newspapers, which will reflect dual opposing views of the beneficial effect of the French operations here in Italy. Opposing is a relative term here. One of your sheets will be extremely enthusiastic, and the other merely highly so. Your first issue might pay particular attention to countering the present unsettling rumours regarding hobgoblins and *bashi-bazouks* roaming the villa grounds at night. Shine the light of republican reason into those shadows haunted by superstition.'

Gracchus fanned himself with one of the newspapers. He sensed that Berthier was about to arrive at the real point. 'That's not all, is it? You don't just want me to edit your propaganda rags.'

Berthier lowered his voice. 'That is merely your ostensible purpose here. While you marshal your resources on the news prints you will exert your particular and well-attested investigatory powers to uncovering the mystery of the disappearance of our host here, *Citoyen* the Comte Mombello. His absence is morally inconvenient at a moment when we are expecting to celebrate marriages in the commander-in-chief's family, to which a set of important Italian and Austrian peace negotiators have been invited.' He sighed. 'Uncovering the present whereabouts of our noble host, whose unexplained absence has contributed in no small regard to the ridiculous rumours circulating, will ensure your subsequent soonest departure.'

Berthier settled back in a chair and pointed an imaginary pistol at one of the secretaries who was scuttling about behind the bookcase with one ear cocked. 'General Bonaparte returns this afternoon, and it would be as well for Mombello to be found by then. The General has mixed views regarding your usefulness, and very unmixed views regarding your presence in Italy without the correct forms of authorisation for travel. I would begin with a success if I were in your shoes... or whatever those things are,' he corrected himself, eying Gracchus's sandals with distaste. He closed the files before him and waved an arm. 'Welcome to the Army of Italy, *Citoyen* Gracchus. *Salut* and Fraternity.' To Vanderville he said, 'Introduce

Gracchus to the Hetairoi, and find someone to sort out quarters for both of you. Dismissed.'

As the doors of the bureau slammed behind them Vanderville set out confidently across a great hall dominated by a massive stone staircase, saluting as they passed other officers, and nodding to the clerks. As they walked, he said over his shoulder, 'May I ask, *Citoyen* Gracchus, what the service was that you rendered to General Berthier's brother?'

Gracchus held up his hand, imploring the younger man to slow his pace. 'Certainly, you may,' he answered. 'But would you care to sit down? Are you feeling quite well now?'

'Thank you. I am quite recovered,' responded Vanderville, his face colouring, but he paused and leant against the hall staircase in the approved light cavalry manner while Gracchus caught up, cleared his throat, and said, 'The general's brother was lodged at an inn where another traveller was robbed of a considerable sum. I was able to supply some proof of his innocence, and so my fellow magistrate's case collapsed, and the general's brother regained his freedom.'

Vanderville set off across the hall again to hide his smile. 'You are an investigating magistrate then, *Citoyen* Gracchus. Now I understand why Berthier tasked you with finding Comte Mombello.'

'I was once,' said Gracchus. 'Now tell me, who or what on earth are these Hetairoi you are taking me to meet?' he asked, struggling to match Vanderville's stride.

'You must forgive the army its flight of fancy,' smiled Vanderville. 'We are all republican heroes now and must have appropriate names to match, so the Guides, General Bonaparte's bodyguard, have been named after the chosen companion cavalry of Alexander the Great.' He frowned. 'They even wanted to dress them in outlandish helmets. At least no one has suggested yet that we adopt the Persian heroic identity, or we would all be dolled up as the sultan's catamites in an instant.'

Chuckling at his own wit, Vanderville eased open two tall glass doors that led onto a stone terrace running the full width of the rear of the villa. Leading the way between potted trees and decorative Grecian urns to the balustrade on the far side he indicated the view with a proprietorial sweep of his arm. It had not been apparent to Gracchus from the front of the villa quite how dramatically the ground fell away behind it. The wooded eminence on which the house perched tumbled away dramatically below, and from the sweeping terrace could be seen the full extent of the gardens. In the distance they gradually merged into the hazy Lombard plains, whose verdant monotony was interrupted only by the pinnacles of village belltowers.

'I can see now why the General chose this place. It feels as if we were looking down on half of Italy. It's enough to make anyone feel like a god.'

'Breathtaking, isn't it?' said Vanderville dreamily. 'On a clear day the dome of Milan's cathedral can be seen from the upper windows. With a telescope you can watch what passes below for a remarkable distance. I do wonder why they call it *Villa* Mombello though; it's big enough to be a castle.'

They both turned to look back at the house, which was indeed enormous. The looming face of the building was still in shadow, and Gracchus was unexpectedly struck by the impression that the house was a malignant petrified toad peering out over the world from its crag. He frowned at his flight of fancy and turned back to the view.

At each end of the terrace twin flights of steps swept down to a second smaller terrace, from which in turn two further flights reached the villa's gardens. The flight to the right was obscured at the bottom by a stand of overgrown asphodels, grown wild like sugarcanes, which were being cut and laid up in bundles by a group of gardeners.

'They seem to be very busy,' said Gracchus.

'Some of these overgrown thickets can't have been touched for years. Since the headquarters was installed here Bonaparte has been adamant that everything be cleared tidily so that his wife has the full fairy-tale Lombardy villa experience.'

17

'Is it customary for the Republic's generals to bring their wives to war?' asked Gracchus.

'Oh, she hasn't been anywhere near the front. And now that the French and Austrian armies have paused hostilities for an armistice, Bonaparte has arranged for his sisters to be married here, so we are under siege from his family.'

He waved at another officer who was sauntering along the terrace towards them. The wiry figure of the new arrival bore the still fresh uniform of the Guides. He was ridiculously young, thought Gracchus, even in this army of children, and his serious eyes were a soft brown. Two gold rings glinted gayly among his hair's dark curls, striking an incongruous martial contrast to his shy glance. Vanderville introduced him as Alexandre Marbeuf. The young man bowed and said politely, 'We will be happy to welcome you to our select company of Mombello, *Citoyen* Gracchus.'

'We?' said Gracchus, observing that under the sparse whiskers that he appeared to have been cultivating since at least breakfast, his face was lined by fatigue.

'Ah yes, I'm sorry. You did not know of course. My name is Marbeuf, but my uncle, the Comte Mombello, has been in possession of these estates, for, oh, three years now. It was at his suggestion that General Bonaparte assumed residence here during the pause in hostilities.'

'An expensive invitation, one imagines,' said Gracchus.

Alexandre smiled. 'Uncle wasn't very keen on all the work in the gardens at first, because he has to pay for it, but he said it would be worth it in the long run, whatever he meant by that. Anyway the General is an old friend of the family, so he gets what he wants. When Uncle gets back from wherever he has gone, I hope you can meet him. He is quite old now, but very entertaining, and can tell you all sorts of stories about when the General was young in Corsica. Will you come and join the party?'

He led the way towards a large gathering at the other end of the terrace, where some twenty staff officers were assembled.

As they approached various of them greeted Vanderville and Alexandre cordially. They were all clad in blue uniforms and Gracchus was at his usual loss to tell them apart. The French Republic allowed leeway in the matter of hats, and it should therefore have been possible to identify the different men by their taste, or lack of it. On this occasion however, the great felt cocked hats had been abandoned in a pile together on a table selected for that purpose, giving the effect of an indiscriminate orgy of black tortoises spewing coloured feathers.

'Ah,' said Alexandre, 'you are lucky this morning, Gracchus, you can meet both the Hetairoi and their queen at the same time.'

Gracchus saw the officers were grouped around a woman in a reclining terrace chair, a dog skipping at her feet, and it was to her that Alexandre effected the first introductions.

'*Citoyenne* Bonaparte, may I introduce a newcomer to our little assembly. *Citoyen* Gracchus, the General's wife, our lady of Victory.'

Gracchus adjusted his spectacles to peer at the reclining celebrity curiously. She was swathed in a white dress in the *à la mode* classical style, and on her chestnut hair was arranged a garland of ivy that harmonised with the potted foliage of the terrace garden so that she seemed at one with the plants and statues found there. Her voice had the fashionably musical Parisian lilt, and her face, merely comfortable in repose, took on loveliness when she spoke. 'My husband has told me so much about you,' she said, hiding her smile behind her fan. 'He says you are one of the cleverest men in Paris.'

'We are a long way from Paris, *citoyenne*. Fortunately my reputation has yet to reach these parts.'

'We have another taste of Paris here,' she replied. 'Perhaps you know each other? Lieutenant Charles, come and meet Bonaparte's funny friend.'

An officer detached himself from the throng, bobbing from foot to foot as if he were bubbling over with good humour and *joie de vivre*. He was small, and his face was too fine for his own good, but it was hard not to warm to his pleasing expression. There were other striking men with good figures on the headquarters staff – hardly one of them seemed above thirty years of age – but it was to Lieutenant Charles that *Citoyenne* Bonaparte paid the most attention. She seemed determined to present herself as a relentlessly silly woman, an under-accomplishment that Gracchus did not find in the least convincing.

The new arrivals did not hold her attention for long, and Gracchus found himself at liberty among the company. As a group, they emitted the confident comradeship of victors, and their conversation gave the impression of a thorough acquaintance with the professions of both war and pleasure. Gracchus reflected that the Hetairoi were well named.

After the first nods of acquaintance and polite enquiries had subsided, Lieutenant Charles disengaged himself from *Citoyenne* Bonaparte and grasped Vanderville's arm in a friendly way. 'As junior lieutenants in a sea of generals, we must stick together,' he said with an easy smile. 'Let us show you our quarters in the Champ de Mars.'

Lieutenant Alexandre stood with a scrape of his chair. 'I'll join you if I may. You will find it a grand name for squalid digs,' he promised, taking post on Gracchus's free flank as they squeezed through the forest of uniforms. But as they made their way across the terrace a terrible scream rose from somewhere below in the gardens, followed by a mingled cries of terror and consternation. The terrace assembly rushed to the balustrade to survey the scene below.

Carried along with them, Gracchus was spun around in the crowd. In the bustle his spectacles fell and so on reaching the edge he could make out nothing but the indistinct cluster of gardeners at the bottom of the stairs who appeared to be agitated. Behind him, the General's wife was deserted on her chair, and in the space surrounding her he spied his mislaid spectacles.

As he retrieved them, bruised but intact, she implored him, 'Do go and find out what's happening, Gracchus, I abhor surprises and commotion.'

Returning to the balustrade with his glasses restored he could better make out the scene below. Among the thicket of asphodel bushes, the gardeners had erected a wooden tripod over an excavation in the ground to dredge debris out from the depths, and a sodden mound of refuse ringed their works. A hook was drawn to the top of the poles and dangling from its grip was a distorted human figure bowed in the obscene posture of the lifeless. It was the body of a half-dressed elderly man, his features pale and bloodless, his white hair dripping loose, his wet shirt shrunken back upon his body.

Chapter Two

Gracchus clutched the balustrade grimly as jostling uniforms pinned him in place. Someone kicked him in the back of the knees and his body craned perilously out over the waist-high parapet until he thought he too would form part of the unwinding tragedy. He was rescued by Alexandre, who elbowed in next to him, relieving the pressure of bodies. The boy was pale, his gamin smile gone. A violent shiver gripped him and as the convulsion passed a limpness replaced it, as if the grease of life had been sucked from him. 'Like a discarded prawn case,' Gracchus muttered to himself. Thoughts of food, never far from his mind, came most fervently at that hour of the day.

'Have the enemy come?' came the plaintive voice of *Citoyenne* Bonaparte, who had been abandoned by her admirers, her languid charms eclipsed by the brutal spectacle. Gracchus's eye passed uneasily over her pettish face before coming to rest on General Berthier, who had burst out of the villa and was directing General Dumas to remove a shutter from one of the windows. 'Not that window; that is the General's cabinet. Take one from the ballroom.'

The released shutter was borne across the terrace and Gracchus hobbled down to the gardens behind Berthier's party, stumbling his way over soggy mounds of debris to the front of the circle of spectators. The gardeners' tripod was erected over an exposed well shaft. Parts of the rough brick lining had been dislodged by roots, and its yawning mouth lay flush with the ground. The corpse was suspended so that it swung gently just at the height of the eyes of the onlookers, and the body's bare head and gawky shoeless legs flopped gracelessly on each side of the hook snagged in the breeches. The lifeless form was swathed in sodden asphodel stalks, their leafless stems topped with star-shaped pink-white flowers. The formal black breeches of the deceased man were crumpled and dripping, and around the stomach they were awry. As the body slowly revolved on its rope that part came better into view, exposing a long gash from which the inner parts protruded rudely. General Dumas grunted and pushed a bare, dripping foot away from his head. 'A sabre cut,' he muttered uncomfortably.

Berthier answered peevishly, 'Everything is a sabre cut to you. He might equally well have struck something on the way down.' He peered down the hole gingerly.

'Possibly,' concurred Dumas. 'Old ones burst, the meat is less connected, and the skin isn't elastic at all. They open up more easily. Sometimes they just sort of pop, and everything comes out like a frog.'

'Thank you for that,' said Berthier, placing himself officiously between the arriving Alexandre and the gruesome scene. To a gardener he said, 'Can you tidy him up a bit for his nephew?'

But Alexandre pushed past him, flung aside his hat, and pulled at the ropes in a vain attempt to lower the body. Finding the attempt fruitless, he staggered to his knees in the mud and gazed up in despair at his uncle. Dumas swung an avuncular arm around Alexandre's shoulder and drew the young man to his feet while the other officers huddled in a respectful hush.

Alexandre looked tearfully around at the house squatting on the hill behind them. 'I wish we had never come here,' he said, and his face crumpled into itself. Dumas grunted, his meagre store of sympathy expended, as he directed the gaping onlookers to recover the dead man and lay him upon the window shutter.

'General Berthier!' commanded Gracchus, taking him by one arm. 'Is there a surgeon in the villa? I need help to examine the body.'

'What? *Surgeon*? There is no surgeon here,' snapped Berthier. 'They are all with the army field hospitals.'

'Take the comte to the kitchen cellars,' interrupted Dumas. 'It's cool, and the cook is the nearest thing to a saw-bones we have here.'

'The gardeners can carry him,' agreed Gracchus. 'General Berthier, be good enough to remove these people from the well and post a sentry on it until I return.' He turned to Vanderville, who was hovering behind them, and said quietly to him so that they could not be overheard, 'Listen to me. Quickly now. Take Alexandre to the stables as arranged. It is of the foremost importance that you observe him and everyone else closely as the news of what has passed spreads. I shall ask you later to recount to me the reactions of everyone you have met. I want to know what you hear them say, and what you see in their faces. I will go with the body to the kitchens. You understand me? Then go!'

Following the sad cortege across the terrace, Gracchus was detained by *Citoyenne* Bonaparte to relate the details of the tragedy. She was being consoled for the absence of her escort of officers by a gaggle of fashionable women who, he learnt, had travelled with her variously from Milan and Paris. They watched the party carrying the body disappear around the far end of the villa sombrely before indulging their horror in a frisson of excitement and fluttering handkerchiefs. Finding himself at a loss among these *élégants*, Gracchus made his excuses to the General's wife at the first opportunity and found his way to the kitchen gardens which adjoined one side of the villa and could be accessed from the terrace at that end.

Passing through the gardens he found the kitchen door ajar. It opened onto a ramshackle stair clinging to one wall of the subterranean kitchen complex. The walls were black with ancient soot, in contrast to the battery of bright-bottomed copper pots and gleaming pans which hung upon them. More of these tin-lined pots were sizzling at a great open hearth that dominated one wall, and the cupboards and tables cluttering the kitchen hall were hung and strewn with every sort of food, plant, and animal. Several people were at work there, but the head cook was immediately apparent. Although shorter than the other two, he stood in an easy manner before the fire in his shirtsleeves, with his long red waistcoat worn open. His grey hair was neatly queued with a bright red ribbon in the small of his back; his breeches were a vibrant blue, unbuckled at the knee, and his stockings were askance over carpet slippers. At his feet was an immense apricot-coloured bandog with a quiet and lowering expression. His merry and ruddy face glistened as he fretted over his pans, and as he worked he remonstrated loudly over his shoulder with an imposing woman in a dark round gown with a cream lace fichu loosely knotted around her shoulders.

Their conversation ambled to a close on Gracchus's close approach, and they turned to him curiously. The cook introduced himself as Francesco Leonardi and named his tall assistant as Piotr. Gracchus was surprised to see that he wore an officer's uniform under his grease-stained apron, and a red bonnet over his short crop of hair. The woman was Madame, *not Citoyenne*, Buonaparte, mother of the commander-in-chief. As Gracchus bowed to her, he realised that she was not tall, as he had first thought. She was slight, and it was her upright posture that commanded attention, as well as her imperious voice, which now asked him abruptly, 'The Comte de Mombello is no more then?'

'His remains were found in an abandoned well shaft in the asphodel grove the gardeners were cutting below the terrace.'

'Ah. He had forgotten the asphodels, that one,' she turned the words over in her mouth deliberately as if tasting each one. Her French was heavily larded with an Italian accent. She was a person of the middle age, and Gracchus strongly suspected that her first language was not Italian either.

'And so, not seeing them in the dark, he mistook his way and fell into the well?' prompted Gracchus. She did not answer but waved her hand dismissively as she inspected him critically. He returned her scrutiny. She wore a cap with a crest of pendent feathers that shaded her face so that it was possible for her to reveal or conceal her eyes with the slightest inclination of her head. She exposed those eyes now and they were immense, and deep sunken, blue like a cloudless sky. She knew their power, he realised, even as he quailed under her gaze. Gracchus broke the unnerving effect by addressing Leonardi. 'If the Comte Mombello has been living here for some time, surely he would have been aware of the old well?'

Leonardi considered this as he pinched salt into his pan. 'No one could have known it was there. Maybe the gardeners. Most of the staff came here with the comte, and certainly the asphodel was there before we arrived. We have beautiful water here in the villa's own wells, we don't need another. Bonaparte, he ordered the asphodel cleared because he wants the gardens just so for his wife.'

'How sad that this tragedy should be owed to Parisian vanity and the love of novelty,' observed Madame Buonaparte dryly. 'This is the consequence of the modern mania for turning everything upside down. Some things are better left unchanged.' Piotr laid a cup of tisane on the table next to her and paused attentively at her elbow. 'I don't want to discuss this business in front of the staff,' snapped *Citoyenne* Buonaparte.

'Because he has a strange accent and the dark beard, he is a spy?' suggested Leonardi.

'No,' she said coldly, 'that point hadn't occurred to me yet. But I shan't contradict you.'

Piotr rolled his eyes and stepped away from her, grinning. 'I was just on my way to the stables to get those geese anyway,' he said, taking his leave. He left the kitchen by a door perched in the centre of the wall opposite that from which Gracchus had entered and reached by a staircase no less rickety.

'A shame. He is the natural anatomist, that one,' said Leonardi, watching him go. 'His help we could have used.' He peered reproachfully at Madame Buonaparte, who ignored him. 'The Comte is down here. In the cold.' He led the way to a larder slightly below the main kitchen. Gracchus and Madame Buonaparte followed him, Gracchus taking care to step shy of the slumbering mastiff as they passed.

The remains of the Comte Mombello were laid out on a table and Gracchus performed a perfunctory inspection of the body while the other two watched intently. He moved methodically over the body with practised hands.

'It appears you have done this before,' commented Madame Buonaparte wanly.

'Your son didn't call me in for my prowess with a garden trowel,' agreed Gracchus. He found that the corpse was spare-limbed and devoid of both fat and muscle. Much as one would expect of an elderly *ci-devant* aristocrat the hands were fine and well groomed. His lips were pulled back over good teeth in a grimace, and peering inside it Gracchus saw that an asphodel head blocked the throat. While directing the attentions of the others to the body's missing shoes he discreetly secreted the seed pod in his handkerchief. When he arrived at the rude opening in the stomach, he had to brace himself, and he heard Madame Buonaparte's intake of breath as he pulled the shirt of the dead man apart to inspect the gaping wound. Leonardi leant forward to help him, and as they laid the body bare, there was a crawling movement inside the corpse, and they both recoiled. With a hard swallow, Gracchus looked again. Nestled in the stomach cavity were writhing, chitinous brown objects the size and colour of small apples. They squirmed and wormed against each other as he exposed them further. Gracchus gingerly forced himself to grasp one and extracted it. Smothered in the mucus of the intestines and wriggling its sharp legs against his grip was a brown crab.

Leonardi examined it curiously. '*Potamon fluviatile*, the river crab,' he breathed in wonder. 'Fried – as good eating as you will find. I had better see this garden well.' With a stifled yelp of disgust, Madame Buonaparte excused herself and hurried up the steps, her hand to her mouth. 'The crab won't hurt you,' called out Leonardi after her as the door slammed. He smirked. 'Unless you are dead already, in which case he might nibble you a bit.'

'Does this wound appear to you made by the crabs? Or by the body catching on some object in falling?' asked Gracchus, bent over the body.

'Don't ask me, I am not a butcher of men, nor an anatomist, but I know well the mark a knife makes, and this opening looks to me something like that of a blade in meat. If the crabs had not begun the feast, I could be more sure. If I had seen it before the crabs began… but now I cannot make you an answer.'

'I need to see inside this well,' said Gracchus. 'Let us go up to the kitchen. I need to think, and perhaps… if you have such an excellent article as a bottle of brandy?'

'With pleasure,' answered the cook, 'the comte, he is in no position to stint us the Armagnac now. But first let me place the rest of these formidable little cuirassiers where they cannot scuttle away.' He scooped the remaining crabs from the body into a bucket which he placed beside the stairs. As they went up, he explained, 'You can't eat him today, but in water, nice and fresh, he will be ready within three days. No dirt, no dirt at all, I do assure you.'

Gracchus found himself in sympathy with Madame Buonaparte's queasiness. 'Does the commander-in-chief's mother often frequent the kitchen?'

'She wanted me to find for her the teeth of the hedgehog,' explained Leonardi, leading the way back to the kitchen. 'For making an amulet to protect her son, she said. She is another for these ghost stories they are so crazy of upstairs.' In answer to Gracchus's questioning look he explained, 'Me, I have a curiosity perpetual for the art of all types of food. She is more interested in the household economy than gastronomy, but she recognises my use in obtaining the ingredients more obscure. Which is more than you can say for her son.' He sighed. 'Everyone wants to work for the modern Alexander, but he has a most plebian and deadly approach to the table. He finds no joy there.'

'Excuse me, *citoyen*,' said Gracchus, his face rosy with a dawning revelation, 'but you said your name was Leonardi? Might you be that *Francesco* Leonardi, author of *The Modern Apicius, or the Art of Preparing all Types of Food* in six volumes?'

Leonardi beamed at Gracchus, 'Your servant,' he said, and gave a deep bow, which Gracchus returned profoundly. 'I find you a gourmand, *Citoyen* Gracchus.'

Gracchus wormed his way past the great table, avoiding the dog, and paused by a wall cabinet. 'What are these flies in the jar? A delicacy?'

'He is the glow worm, I gathered him last night. He arrives with the heat, usually in June, and only displays his light on the warmer evenings. It is a beautiful festival for the country people when he comes, but this year he seems to have passed unnoticed, so many people have been dislocated by the war that the observance of traditions, they are all astray. The spectacle is beautiful, extraordinary. Of course those fools upstairs missed it, shut up in the salons with the shutters closed talking their nonsense. Regard also the *grilli*, in the jar to your left. He is the cricket who produces music to accompany the light show of the worms. I am sorry that the worm, he will tear your stomach up if you eat him. I had hoped we might do something with him by way of making the table beautiful, but he will not perform to order.'

'And in these bottles are tomatoes,' said Gracchus, lifting a jar, 'but isn't it a little early in the season?'

'We make a little system of experimentation with Piotr's method. We boil him before sealing. Thus, he is preserved without vinegar, without sugar or salt. In this way, on opening the bottle, he passes for fresh, the flavour not corrupted. But you shall try him at once with a dish of macaroni, please take the chair by our table.'

'You have been with the Comte Mombello for many years?' asked Gracchus as he drew up a seat. Leonardi nodded and stirred his pans. 'The question is vulgar I know,' he continued, 'but tell me... what was he like as a master?'

Leonardi cocked his head to one side, and scratched his ear with a spoon. 'If you are here to do what I suspect you are here to do, then you will find no better way to knock your investigation than by hearing the servant's tattle. Then of course, you know your work as I know mine, and you are right to think that I am no ordinary servant. Me, I am here by choice, not by necessity.'

Gracchus waited patiently and Leonardi continued, 'The Comte was a great fork as we say, a *buon gustaio*. The table was beautiful and important to him and became more so as age curbed the pursuit of love that was his other dearest pleasure. Indeed, under the most careful tutelage, he was in the foothills of the mountain range of knowledge that comprises the true beauty of the gastronomic art. Away from the table he was full of grey-brained republican ideas and sometimes, him and the young master, Alexandre, they had the blowout. The young one, he is the regular firebrand Jacobin, but they saw eye to eye as many days as not. Of course, when the master was in his cups he could be a regular tyrant, but this failing is not uncommon in men of his age and class.'

'Had Mombello and his nephew argued recently?'

'Most of what goes on upstairs of my apparatus,' said Leonardi, gesturing at a system of little wooden trays and ropes in a channel cut into the wall of the kitchen, 'is so far obscured from me that it may as well occur ten leagues up in the clouds as ten feet above the head.'

'What is this curious system?' asked Gracchus, plucking at its cords speculatively.

'An innovation of beauty, all mine,' boasted Leonardi. 'I am prouder of him than is right. The set of wooden shelves are so contrived in the channel, that on pulling this cord they ascend into the room above loaded with the dishes placed on them and by the same process the removed dishes are conveyed out of the room.'

'It is a prodigy of invention,' observed Gracchus. 'I confess I am agog to witness its operation. How have you named this innovative apparatus?'

'I call him the *serviteur apparatus* – *roulante* for the imperceptible and silent delivery and removal of plates.'

'That has the benefit of precision, to be sure,' began Gracchus cautiously.

'You have strayed into verbosity, Gracchus,' interrupted Leonardi. 'Forgive me, but you must allow me to arrive at the point. Piotr, he serves at table most of the time now, a soldier being more acceptable to the General than any of our old table servants. Not that most of them did not flee when the French arrived, excepting some of the more forward maids who went to join the soldiers in the camp when they found they wouldn't be all eaten alive. Anyway,' he made a strange croaking noise which Gracchus presumed was a laugh, 'Piotr, he knows what passes above, and he relays to me the choice *bon mot*.' He blinked, and tasted his sauce with prinked lips. 'Not that I have any interest in gossip.'

'Naturally,' agreed Gracchus. 'And yet I cannot imagine much gets past you.'

'Sometimes one simply cannot help overhearing, no matter how discreetly one conducts oneself. For instance, I assure you, if you climb up onto the casement of that small window above the back door, extraordinarily little of what transpires in the kitchen garden will escape you.' Gracchus tried the ascent and found he needed a box to manage it. Leonardi continued, 'I myself, I heard the Comte Mombello the other day remonstrating with Madame Buonaparte in the kitchen garden. Sorry,

I should say *La Citoyenne*, but old ways die hard with me. The comte had the hard words to say about fashionable Parisian parlour games. The gist was that they had changed since his time, and he did not find stimulating the new variety in his house. She took offence to the effect that she was a *ci-devant* aristocrat too, and at least as *ancien regime* as him, and would not take dictation from him. He flung a few unkind words at her. It was his failing as a man when he had taken drink, as I have mentioned earlier, and he may have exceeded the bounds of propriety.'

'Most illuminating,' said Gracchus. 'I do hope soon to view your rotating apparatus in full flow. I had better talk to the rest of the villa staff as soon as possible, though.'

Leonardi slapped a bowl in front of him. 'First, you eat!'

Gracchus privately considered tomato eaten with macaroni to be an abomination that would never catch on. What was certain was that Leonardi's sauce, made by simmering seedless tomatoes with onions, celery, garlic, and basil, was a wonder, and Gracchus found some of his antipathy to the enforced stay at Villa Mombello dissolving in its vapour.

–

Lieutenant Vanderville was traipsing a well-trodden path across the villa's ruined lawns to the stable complex, which was screened from the house proper by a stand of prosperous elms. 'My father left those trees up to hide the stables when he bought the house,' said Alexandre morosely.

'Don't ride across the lawn,' advised Lieutenant Charles, who was at his other elbow, 'it's against Berthier's regulations, which you will find pinned on yellow paper everywhere you look.'

As they grew closer to the elms, the familiar hum of a barrack yard reached them, and they passed under a collapsed stone arch whose remaining columns were garnished with little tidily hooded noticeboards bearing copious examples of the aforementioned notepaper. The stables were ranged around a yard which abutted a house or inn on the far side. That building leant out over the road outside which was glimpsed through an arch corresponding to that through which they had just passed. The inn was a semi-fortified traveller's rest of a type that seemed so solid and eternal that it may as well have sprung from the road in the time of Caesar and stood ever since without improvement or further decline. Vanderville considered that it must have watched no end of armies coming and going since it was raised, and it had waited in vain since that day for an end to thirsty soldiers – or for a second coat of paint. The four sides of the yard were composed of tumble-down stables, overloaded storerooms that had been full a quarter century ago, and carefully tended tack rooms, with living space above that opened onto a wooden roofed gallery running most of the length of each side. Laundry lines were strung from the gallery to a noble pine that dominated and shaded half of the yard, and soldiers lounged under these.

'Stables under, rooms for the officers over,' said Charles. 'The men are in huts camped behind the high road. The Polish Legion you might know, the Guides are all new but most of them are away this week. The word is that they ravished all of the ladies in Milan and are in disgrace.'

'Camp gossip,' said Alexandre, 'the Poles are always jealous of the Guides because they never leave the General.'

'Hercule!' shouted Charles to a black man in shirtsleeves who was beating a coat of the Guides with a carpet duster.

'Not bad, eh?' said Hercule with an impulsive smile, indicating the battered green coat.

'It's a manifest disaster,' replied Alexandre, seizing a brush and applying it to the sleeve. 'If you can't get it better than that, ask your betters to teach you.'

'Thank god for the idle sons of itinerant aristocrats,' responded Hercule with a mock bow, '*Salut et fraternitie*,' he added to Vanderville with a polite nod.

'Is there any space with us?' Charles asked Hercule. 'Vanderville needs a bunk.'

33

'Junot moved out this morning, so I've taken the window bed while you were on duty,' grinned the Guide. 'You had better take him up, I'm on duty in ten minutes. Alexandre, I beg of you to help me finish this coat.'

Kicking a rowdy gaggle of geese away from the foot of an open staircase, Charles pointed. 'Right at the top, names on the door, add yours later. We wash at the well, or at the pumps behind there,' he indicated the further range of stables with an airy wave, 'when it's busy. And it is always busy here. Who are you with, anyway?'

'It was General Dumas until this morning,' said Vanderville, following him up the stairs.

'That's everything then,' said Charles. 'Shitters past the camp, we collect food from the villa kitchen rather than the camp kitchen most of the time, but otherwise don't go to the villa unless you are on duty. Or asked for,' he added, grimacing. 'We eat here, men eat in the camp. You will know when,' he added, gesturing at the jumble of tables in the yard. 'Bring your own things; crockery is just for the house. If you have a servant, send him away, there isn't any space. Same for your horses, stables are just for the generals and their aides. There's space in the village, ask Hercule to show you. If you have a girl, meet her in the village too, Berthier is particular about that as well.'

Vanderville wondered inwardly how he would reconcile the abundant regulations of Berthier with his role herding the profoundly civilian Gracchus, who he imagined would be on business at the house exclusively. He resolved to solve this dilemma at the first opportunity before getting on the wrong side of the testy second in command. He asked Charles, 'If this is Alexandre's uncle's house, why does he mess here with us?'

'He says the villa brings on his sickness. Not that he sleeps quietly where we are.'

Vanderville raised an eyebrow.

'Alexandre is a little delicate, and different from the rest of us in a few ways. Nothing against that of course, he does his duty, and insulates us from his uncle. Up and down all night, that's why we put him in with Piotr. I think he just prefers being with us, and the house is full of the Bonaparte family now. The tone up there is markedly less like a barrack room now we are all banished to the horse stalls.'

Charles showed him the view from the gallery that ran above the courtyard. Under the venerable Roman pine, there were storytellers improvising verses to a rapt audience of soldiers. Some officers were amusing themselves at the ball game called pallacorda, their wooden mittens clacking as they clouted the ball against the walls and off the roofs of the gallery. The yard seemed a jumble of every nationality on earth. There were French hussars in their conical caps, and wild-looking Polish levies of the Legion who looked as if they had come from the ends of the earth. Italian soldiers of the new Transpadane Republic were wandering vacantly around saluting the officers uncertainly. By the road at the end of the courtyard, half-naked children of the camp were dancing in front of a barrel organ and a kind of mountebank was whipping up an impromptu lottery for a fat plucked goose, which he dangled at the end of a stick. Vanderville commented on the air of prosperity, unusual in a barracks.

'The General paid off the army's back pay with a levy raised on the city of Milan. What a debauch we had,' said Charles in happy recollection.

'The watchmakers and jewellers saw their shops emptied in twenty-four hours,' came a voice from below, and looking over the low gallery balustrade, Vanderville saw Hercule being helped into his coat by Alexandre. 'Everyone strutted around with two watches dangling halfway down their thighs, in the Paris fashion!'

'Speaking of Paris, the inn end is full of generals and their bints,' said Charles, 'off limits to us. There aren't more than twenty of us jumbled into the stable rooms. Lieutenant this, captain that. Ah! This is Piotr,' he announced, as a fine-looking soldier in a Polish uniform and an apron sauntered into the yard. He called down from the gallery, 'What are you Piotr, anyway, still a mere lieutenant?'

The new arrival smiled. His hair was so dark that the day's growth on his chin was almost a beard.

'He isn't a staff officer yet,' rumbled Hercule, 'but he is a damn good fellow and makes iced creams, so we keep him here with us anyway. It is inevitable Bonaparte will make him a great man if he lives another year, and then we'll all be cleaning his boots.'

'So long as he doesn't force me to join the Guides,' smiled Piotr.

Hercule guffawed, 'Spoken like a true foot-warbler!'

'I had better get up to the villa and collect my civilian charge before he gets into trouble,' said Vanderville, as Charles settled onto a ramshackle chair and produced his pipe.

'You are lucky,' said Charles, 'everyone wants access to the villa, but it is strictly controlled now. Berthier used the arrival of the General's family to impose order. That is why this present trouble is driving him spare. He is supposed to insulate the great man from minor problems for a few weeks while he deals with his family. The first thing that happens is the ghoul starts killing the farm animals in the night and because Berthier hasn't squashed them, the General has brought your man in. That makes Berthier look bad, so he takes it out on us. They are putting a proper cordon round the house now, and a curfew in the evenings, so no going out of bounds anymore. Of course, it is not the Guides who are the problem, but the Poles are a superstitious bunch, and the Italians, by your leave, Alexandre, aren't much better.'

He looked around, but Alexandre had disappeared. Charles laughed. 'Scared of their own shadows, and what with the talk of the ghoul and vampire-owls and whatnot, the camp is full of quivering wrecks.'

Vanderville was about to take his leave when a mumbled cheer erupted in the yard. Three riders mounted on Arabian horses had clattered under the inn arch, and their gambolling mounts drew the attention of the Poles there, who were expressing their appreciation noisily. As the first rider's horse pirouetted below their vantage post, Vanderville was surprised to see that despite alone of the three riding astride, the rider was a young woman. Tendrils of dark hair had escaped the jockey cap that framed her face, and she bit her lip with concentration as she mastered her mount. She was aware of the admiration she evoked, and laughed as the sun shone on her face. Her eyes flickered over the ranks before passing to the gallery where they met his. A thrill suffused him, and he felt the sun suddenly hotter on his face.

'*Citoyenne* Paolina Bonaparte to you. Paolette to her family,' commented Charles through his pipestem. 'Is she not the most wonderful thing imaginable? And the greatest coquette in the Army of Italy against some pretty stiff competition.'

Hercule grunted appreciatively, and made an anatomical observation inadmissible in company.

'Which is one more reason why you aren't invited to the salons at the villa,' said Charles.

Vanderville was unable to tear his eyes away from her. She was not a beauty. Not yet at least, but every line of her urged potential in a way that none of the officers could ignore. After a hard campaign of sleepless nights in rain-drenched bivouacs followed by sun scorched snatched naps, she was the dream of spring to supplant uncomfortable memories of desperate raddled *cantinières* and shameful snatched encounters with peasant girls. She made them feel like lions again.

'What is she doing here?' wondered Vanderville. 'Here with the army, I mean?'

'All of Bonaparte's family are here, half of his sisters are being married off,' said Charles. 'Paolette is to be the undeserving General Leclerc's wife.'

'It makes no sense, but there it is,' agreed Hercule. 'They will be married next week, along with her sister over there

37

who is marrying dear, useless Captain Baciocchi. He has already moved his kit into the general's quarters in anticipation of his promotion.'

'Are they all like her?' asked Vanderville.

'Nobody is like Paolette. The other one is closer to Bonaparte in looks,' said Charles with a smile, 'but neither is going to make a husband happy if you ask me.'

'Give her five years, it will all be over,' opined Hercule, as they watched Paolette. 'These southern beauties go off in the sun.' Hercule shrugged, but another hubbub was beginning as the thrumming of hooves outside the inn arch increased to a din.

A frisson of anticipation swept the yard. As the soldiers turned away from the girls, their murmurs swelled to a roar as a cavalcade of mounted men burst into the courtyard, their green and gold uniforms sparkling, their officers all in red pantalons. 'The Guides, the Guides,' cried the children's voices, their kites forgotten, and to the waving of handkerchiefs and the soldiers' throaty roars, the escort parted to reveal the conqueror of Italy himself on his grey horse. His pale face was shining, his hat in one hand as he saluted the cheers. 'Bonaparte! Bonaparte!' urged the voices of the throng, surging forward as the commander-in-chief and his staff forced their horses through the crowd into the courtyard.

'Well, there he is,' said Charles with a nonchalant air, 'and now the birds can sing in the trees again, the bees resume flight. Life has returned to Mombello.'

Chapter Three

Having finished talking to the villa staff, Gracchus was in the villa garden poking about in the well disconsolately with a dried asphodel stem. The shaft was too deep to see the water below, although he thought he had detected the glistening of metal jutting out part of the way down. As Gracchus pondered the depths, he mulled over an unexpected conversation. As General Berthier had passed on his way to the stables, he had paused to discuss the villa's water system, the quality of its water, and the events leading up to Mombello's disappearance. Berthier had issued an invitation to an audience with Bonaparte that evening, something Gracchus did not look forward to with any pleasure.

'He will be busy for some hours after he returns, we have much work to do,' Berthier had said. 'We could really have done without this inconvenience. Be ready by eight. Don't expect him to be very interested or give you much time. Frankly all of this is going to be an immense irritation to him.'

'I can imagine,' said Gracchus, who felt much the same way himself. 'Forgive me, *Citoyen* Berthier, but I must observe that tedious mortality raises its head with distressing frequency in these times and around your... around armies, that is. What is one carcass more or less on the lawn?'

Berthier said peevishly, 'You might consider keeping such remarks to yourself when you meet the General. This is a remarkably inconvenient death. One of the leading citizens of the Transpadane Republic and a personal friend of the commander-in-chief goes out for a midnight walk, slips down a well in his own garden, and ends up with his insides outside.

An innocent accident, but now half of the villa's occupants have seen that nasty wound in his stomach, tongues are wagging.'

Gracchus looked keenly at Berthier, but met only his bland bureaucratic mask. 'You mean this story about a ghoul who stalks the villa at night killing animals?' he asked, sitting down on the last terrace step.

'The soldiers' fevered imaginations are the least of it. Comte Mombello was at the heart of the new Transpadane Republic government, and we do not need a lot of speculation that he didn't tumble but was helped into that well. The Italian delegates have already hinted that Bonaparte was annoyed with Mombello because he had made some unauthorised changes in the new constitution. Others have insinuated that Mombello was using his position in the new government to award the lucrative army supply contracts to his friends.' He glanced sharply at Gracchus. 'None of this goes further, by the way. Mere gossip of course, but of the provoking kind, and until it has been conclusively proved that no one else was present when the accident occurred, it will continue.' He sighed. 'I suggest you find your escorting officer now. He is supposed to be keeping an eye on you, and already appears to be utterly unreliable, like everyone else recommended by that fool Dumas.'

As Berthier strode off Gracchus watched him meet a rider near the stables. The other man spurred his horse through the trees to meet him. He leant from the saddle to speak for a moment, and then he dismounted abruptly, throwing his reins to a groom, and the two strode off towards the villa. As they conferred, the new arrival was swinging his riding crop angrily.

Gracchus returned to staring into the well, pondering how the dead man might have arrived there. In the popular print sheets, an investigator would have reconstructed Mombello's movements by means of footprints left in the mud. But although the newly cleared ground was ideal for recording tracks, any chance of reading them had been obscured by the passage of the gardeners, and the subsequent stampede of gawkers. Peering down the well shaft, he was fairly sure the glint of metal in the shadowy depths was a stanchion. It certainly stuck out far enough to snag a falling body.

His deliberations were interrupted by the arrival of the young popinjay assigned as his military escort. He cast a disgruntled eye over the officer, who was standing at attention in the middle of the mud-trodden stalks around the well as if awaiting orders. Gracchus considered him from feathered hat to soiled calfskin boots, and decided to take a high hand.

'Lieutenant Vanderville, this association will work best for both of us if you follow my instructions to the letter, otherwise, when I have no instructions for you, stay out of my way. Above all, you must not do anything under your own initiative. You are a soldier, so that oughtn't to be so difficult for you.'

'General Berthier has detailed me to preserve your person from harm,' observed Vanderville. 'Even though I may be preserving you from mere ghosts and phantasms, he doubtless has good reason for issuing his orders, and I shall insist on following them, by the application of apron strings if need be.' To Gracchus's frustration, Vanderville was systematically trampling the asphodel stalks that had escaped the cull of the gardeners, scowling as he did so.

'The only harm that I foresee will come from you blundering around trying to be useful. In an investigation of this sort, having no assistant is better than having one who does not understand the nature of the business in hand.'

Vanderville circled the well, and peered down into its shadows. 'You don't much like the Army of Italy, do you?' he asked.

'You have passed through this country like a march of locusts. The old systems of government in this benighted peninsula were not perfect, but they had the advantage that familiarity had weathered both rulers and subjects into mutual tolerance.'

Vanderville kicked a few stems down the well and watched them fall thoughtfully. 'If by mutual toleration you mean the moral abjection in which the people formerly lived, then the present evils of the war of liberation frighten me less. Of these two conditions neither is to be recommended, but the latter is more to my taste. It at least holds out the possibility of improvement.'

Gracchus rubbed his brow sorrowfully. 'I can see that I have to put up with a mere automaton, a clockwork soldier, and I may as well reason with the sky. Very well, I shall outline my campaign of attack, and the strategy that I intend to follow.' He paused, savouring his martial turn of phrase. 'And how to deploy my forces, as you might say.' Or rather deploy you where you can do the least damage, he thought to himself.

'I am at your disposal, *citoyen*,' said Vanderville. He was accustomed to suffering the indignities inflicted on him by superior officers, and a few barbs from this new manifestation of authority were nothing to him.

'Well then, here is the situation; the lay of the ground,' Gracchus suggested, looking up to make sure that the young lieutenant had grasped his allusion. 'This place has fallen under the spell of wild supernatural rumours. Our role is to dampen the hysteria, so that the Army of Italy can continue terrorising and molesting the province secure in the apprehension that fear of wild apparitions will not impede their impositions on the inhabitants.'

'I was under the impression,' said Vanderville, resuming his trampling, 'that your business here was with newspapers?'

Gracchus waved a hand, 'A mere sop to divert curiosity. My real business is here in the well.' He kicked the remains of the stone well head for emphasis and regretted it instantly, regarding his sandalled foot with distress.

Vanderville wrinkled his brow. 'So your investigation is intended to apprehend the murderer of Mombello?'

Seeing his contented expression Gracchus hastily added, 'I expect to find nothing of the sort. My impression is that Mombello was intoxicated, and that taking the air to clear the

42

wine fumes from his head, he strolled out to the stables and lost his footing here at the well head. In these matters, the simplest explanation that fits the facts is usually all that we need. And, more importantly, is all that is required of us.'

'I had imagined from your instructions to me when the body was found that you harboured suspicions concerning his death,' said Vanderville, baffled, but lest he be thought dull, he nodded carefully in what he hoped was a sage manner. But Gracchus was busy regarding the villa. The sun had reached its zenith and crept over its roof to bathe it in light.

'A sense of foreboding is not convincing as a logical explanation,' said Gracchus, 'though in my personal case I admit it is often borne out as correct.' He straightened up, throwing away his asphodel stalk. 'I have already been able to start reconstructing the events of the evening that Mombello disappeared from talking to Berthier, and the cook, Leonardi. It was habitual for the other kitchen servants to be dismissed after dinner in the late afternoon, and the kitchen staff served the light refreshments needed for the evening.'

He pointed at the terrace above them. 'Picture the scene: the evenings after supper are generally informal affairs reserved for a small circle, and invitations are cherished, so the company was select. They were assembled at the back of the house, in the grand reception rooms that open onto the terrace. The rear of the house was shuttered because the commander-in-chief often retreated to his cabinet which adjoined the salons to work in the middle of the night, or when he bored of the ghost stories and games the family played in the evening. Bonaparte and Mombello were expressing their differences about the work underway in the garden. The General had ordered the tangled grove below these steps cleared. This exposed the disused well shaft.'

He swivelled and directed Vanderville's attention back to that gaping hole with one imperious finger. 'Mombello was against the clearing of the shrubs, which appears contrary, as the steps on that side were obscured by the overgrowth, rendering passage impossible. We must assume he had a fondness for the asphodel bushes. He may also have been concerned that the overgrown grove had damaged the masonry of the steps, which indeed does appear to be the case, a circumstance which may have contributed to the ensuing tragic accident.

'After the party concluded, Mombello did not go up to bed with the rest of the company at the usual hour. He was inebriated, which was unusual for him according to Leonardi, and he worked in his library until two. His valet said that he was called at that hour, and his master stated that he was going to the stables to see his nephew about a tree. He bundled up some papers on the desk and left. The valet said his master was agitated, but disagreed with Leonardi's assertion that he was drunk. He was perhaps concerned because the boy had been upset and left the salon halfway through the ghost story he told that evening.'

Vanderville wrinkled his brow. 'What tree did he want to discuss with his nephew?'

'Presumably the liberty tree that is to be erected in the stables. Everyone heard them arguing about it at the party.'

'But if Mombello was going to the stables as he told his valet, he would have taken the staircase from the terrace on the left. Why did he use this one instead? It's all muddy from clearing the asphodels, and doesn't seem to lead anywhere except the lawn. Unless…' He shaded his eyes and peered into the grove edging that side of the lawn. Amid the trees there was just visible the tip of a bell tower. 'What's that, a chapel?'

Gracchus cleared a space of discarded plant debris with his foot and sat down on the terrace steps. Vanderville's conclusion had already occurred to him. He removed his hat and squinted up at the sun. 'In falling into the well, Mombello struck a metal stanchion set in the wall of the shaft, which caused a wound sufficient to kill him, had he not inevitably drowned. The crabs living in the walls of the well sufficiently explain

44

the further mutilation of the remains. The asphodel discovered in his mouth can be explained by the gardener's lazy habit of dumping debris into the well. In the absence of any compelling evidence to the contrary, I am inclined to declare this an accident occasioned by a drunken gentleman stumbling around in the dark. There was no moon due that night, so without a lamp a misstep would have been almost inevitable. Add to those circumstances the natural overconfidence of an inebriated man traversing his own park and the ingredients of a tragedy are all present.' He stood up, and brushed off his seat absentmindedly. 'I am reassured that this matter can be brought to a swift and precise conclusion. It was an accident, death by misadventure. Berthier will reprimand the gardeners and have the work fenced off until the well can be cleared or reconstructed, and the stair repaired.'

Vanderville protested, 'But what compelled him to set off in the middle of the night? Surely any business with his son could wait 'til the morning?'

Gracchus answered wearily, 'Berthier says that his valet was questioned and revealed that the comte had the old man's weakness of rising at all hours of the night, and that he was in the habit of walking outside. The valet said that he normally accompanied him on his walks with a lamp, but on this occasion, he was not required, perhaps because he had private business to discuss with his nephew.'

'But he would take the other stairs,' insisted Vanderville stubbornly. 'In order to encounter the recently uncovered well, he must have traversed the entire length of the terrace and taken this stair which leads over there. So, did he have business in the chapel? Was he going to meet somebody there?'

'We do not know, and it is probably irrelevant,' said Gracchus. He placed his hat back on his head.

Vanderville persisted, 'If Mombello was indeed hurrying to meet somebody, his haste may have contributed to the accident, so that a well shaft that no one would have missed by daylight swallowed him up. If that is so, why didn't whoever he was going to meet raise the alarm when he didn't arrive?'

Gracchus waved an arm dismissively, 'When he didn't turn up for the assignation, whoever he was hypothetically meeting would have assumed he had gone to bed drunk, and in fact he wasn't missed until the morning. When he did not appear for breakfast, the valet was questioned. Mombello said that he had sent a housemaid to call him, at eight, but not having come down, he said he would go again: he did so, and presently returned, saying, with a look of terror, that the Comte Mombello was not in his room. He was quite positive he could not have walked out before breakfast, because the shutters of his chamber, which he always opened himself when he began to dress, were still closed; and because another housemaid, who had been washing the stairs, the hall, and the hall steps, must have seen him pass, and would have mentioned it. His evening clothes from the night before had not been put out and were not in his room.'

'Are you not curious to know who he might have been meeting in the gardens?'

'I repeat, it is irrelevant if he merely fell because he could not see his way,' said Gracchus. 'The commander-in-chief wants calm to be restored. That does not necessarily imply that a thorough explication of the circumstances is desirable or required. Especially,' he continued, stroking his waistcoat neatly down over his belly, 'especially if exposing the truth inflames the febrile atmosphere of the headquarters rather than soothing it. Naturally, we shall arrive at a version of the truth, and present it to Bonaparte, but he will decide what we do with that truth, and whether to declare it real, or not.'

Vanderville shook his head. This was not the sort of thing he had expected from the investigator.

Gracchus uneasily turned matters over in his head. The needling from Vanderville was compounding his sense of guilt over the tidy version of events he had decided to present to

Berthier. The sooner he cleared this up, the sooner he could leave Mombello. But there was something that had been said in the kitchen that worried him, gnawing away at the back of his mind. 'I will meet you in the villa for a supper party tonight, Lieutenant. In the meantime, your first task for me is to discover whether there is indeed a chapel in the trees. My legs are tired, and I have business in the villa.'

Vanderville soon found the chapel nestled in the trees to the west of the lawns. It was a plain little yellow building disfigured by a fussy rococo facade and surmounted by a pinnacle with a single bell. Someone had recently swathed the door pediment with long festoons of magnolia and laurel. As Vanderville sprang up the steps the door banged open, and the end of a stepladder was propelled outwards with some force. His evasive manoeuvre was complicated by the entanglement of his sabre in the ladder. Apologising as he disengaged himself clumsily, he looked up into the face of the ladder's bearer and was startled to find it was the rider from the stable yard. Close up, she was even more striking than when he had seen her earlier. Her hair was disordered, and a flush of exertion lit her eyes and cheeks. She must have been about eighteen years old.

'Oh, hullo,' she said, pulling her skirts aside deftly and placing down the stepladder. She considered him critically, her head on one side. 'You were with Charles and that Guides officer in the stables.'

'Yes, *Citoyenne* Paolette— I mean *Citoyenne* Bonaparte,' managed Vanderville.

'You can call me Paolette if you like. You know then that I am the General's sister, Lieutenant?'

He nodded, uncomfortably.

'So why do you keep staring at me like that?'

Vanderville was still stunned by her proximity and found himself embarrassed, lost for words.

'Oh, come on! I'm just teasing you. Watch me if you want. I don't mind,' she surveyed the laurel festoons seriously, her chin in one hand. 'What do you think of all this? I'm doing it all myself,' she said, her words tumbling over each other. 'God knows my sister Elisa isn't interested.'

He recovered himself sufficiently to admire the decorations, and while she pointed out the highlights of her scheme of garlands, he looked sideways at her. Her large dark eyes had a tender expression which did not appear to belong to her character. He observed with delight the delicate loveliness of her chin and mouth as she spoke.

'It's nice for Alexandre as well, because he has to bury his uncle later, and now the chapel isn't so gloomy.' She clapped her hand to her mouth in mock horror. 'I shouldn't have said that! Do you find it in bad taste to have the same decorations for a funeral and a wedding? Mamma says so, but she is *very* superstitious and old fashioned about these things. Dear Alexandre… is he very upset, do you know?' Before he could answer, she nudged him with her elbow. 'Are you going to help? You are quite tall, and I can't reach everything.'

Vanderville nodded apprehensively. 'Delighted,' he said.

'Hmm? Hold this,' she said, propping the stepladder. Grasping the tottering frame, he found himself rewardingly level with her slim ankles, which were encased in high Greek sandals closed with an acorn. 'Thanks,' she said, laying a hand on his shoulder as she hopped down. 'Are you really just a lieutenant? You look brave enough to be a general, or a colonel at least.'

'A mere staff lieutenant, I'm afraid,' said Vanderville, 'and detached to look after a civilian, what's worse.'

'You mean that funny fat man on the lawns? He's new isn't he, what is he doing here?'

'Berthier asked him to work in the printing office, but really I think he is a failed *gendarme*.'

'How thrilling, will you be helping him to catch the phantom?'

'I suppose so. He doesn't seem very interested in ghouls though. I think I will be mainly keeping him out of trouble.'

She frowned. 'I suppose they will want to put Mombello in the chapel until he can be buried. I hope he doesn't get in the way of my decorations.' She brightened. 'But of course, he will go in the crypt. It's just been opened up. Have a look, the entrance is behind the altar.'

He followed her advice gratefully with a tinge of regret at leaving her. She didn't bother moving aside for him, forcing him to squeeze awkwardly past her to enter the chapel as she fiddled with the laurel above the door. He walked down the nave towards an altar under the central dome.

'I regret that my niece is a mercilessly frivolous person,' came a disembodied voice from behind the altar. Stepping closer, Vanderville saw a long man emerging from a hole in the floor, pushing a large oil skin bundle ahead of him. Vanderville recognised his uniform coat as that granted to the army commissaries. It was not displayed to advantage, being covered in cobwebs and dust.

'Good morning to you, young man,' he saluted Vanderville affably as he stood up. His face was smooth, and calm with the sleekness of good humour. 'You must forgive me for one moment *citoyen*,' he said, pulling a pocketknife from his coat skirts. 'If I am not wrong, this humble shroud conceals a remarkable aesthetic discovery.'

'I am a collector of Italian primitives,' he explained, kneeling to cut open the oilskin parcel. 'Some heathen has updated this chapel sometime in the last forty years, and a little bird whispered to me that the original quattrocento polyptychs were stashed down there.'

'In the crypt?' said Vanderville.

'Nymphaeum, you mean,' smiled the commissary. 'Anyway, forgive me, and pardon my maudawort appearance. I am Commissary Fesch,' he bowed in a flourish of old-fashioned good manners.

'I understand you are helping the good *Citoyen* Gracchus to construct the story of our unfortunate host. He will be rather in the way today, I'm afraid,' apologised Fesch. 'Have you got to the bottom of it?'

'News travels at a cock's stride,' said Vanderville, shaking his head bemusedly.

Fesch crossed himself and he too shook his head sadly. 'I fear that you needn't look too far for an explanation as to how he reached the bottom of the well. The poor man was as fuddled as an ape the night he disappeared.'

In answer to Vanderville's astonished face, Fesch smothered a laugh. 'Cup struck! Bosky! Oh, don't look so shocked, young man. Our Good Lord was a bibber of wine himself, and he was never shy of a home truth, either.'

'You were there that night?' asked Gracchus.

'Me? No, I was despatched to the village after supper to help General Dumas with some supply waggons I needed. A curious fellow, Dumas.'

'Overdressed? Bedaubed all over with tinsel like a shop girl's dream?' suggested Vanderville.

'Precisely! Now speaking of tinsel, look at this.' He held up one of the wood panels. 'Unless I am very much mistaken, these are some of the lost panels of the Griffoni polyptych.'

Vanderville regarded an anaemic lisping Madonna, whose pert swan's neck curved in ungainly fashion over a bulbous-headed child swaddled in an elaborate gold basket that was somewhat at odds with the humble stable setting. A donkey peered disconsolately at a pair of myopic monsters flanking the crib. They may well have been chickens.

'Old Mombello may not have had much of a head for wine, but I congratulate him on preserving these. If you knew the price I have been asked for similar ones recently... last year they couldn't give them away quickly enough.' He rewrapped the picture and thrust it away. 'Anyway, do you want to see the nymphaeum? It is quite remarkable.' He eased himself into the hole let into the floor. 'Careful, I only had the flags taken up last week. All of this was sealed off when the chapel was restored, I suppose.'

As Vanderville followed him down the ladder, Fesch waved his arm effusively. 'The word nymphaeum originally denoted a natural grotto with springs and streams, of course, traditionally considered the only proper habitat of nymphs. But this one is artificial. It could have served as a sanctuary, a reservoir, and an assembly chamber where weddings were held. I did think it would be remarkably appropriate to hold the wedding of our little Paganetta upstairs here, but her mother, my sister Letizia, doesn't approve, and Paolette's sister Elisa doesn't care for classical allusions. Have you met my other niece, young man?'

'Just the one of them upstairs, sir,' Vanderville said, and Fesch eyed him with a smile. 'To our ancestors a nymph might appear in a whirlwind,' he said. 'Such encounters could be dangerous, striking the besotted individual dumb. The infatuation could lead to madness or a stroke to the unfortunate human. Better be careful, eh?'

Vanderville peered about. Most of the grotto had been tamed by classical stonework but the springhead at one end under the chapel entrance was still unimproved. There was an accretion of withered moss around the basin like a shaggy brown fringe, showing where water had dripped interminably over eons of damp afternoons. The walls were all lined with niches, and the whole place felt forlorn and cold, except for the two niches nearest the spring which were surmounted by curious colourful silk urns. It struck Vanderville as not at all the sort of place for a wedding, even a republican one, and especially not for a Christian blessing, and he said so.

'Jesus Christ never pronounced in favour of any particular form of government,' responded Fesch. 'Christianity has prospered in the centre of republics, as well as in the bosom of the monarchy. Although the gospels are lamentably reticent on the matter of architecture, I see no reason for our Lord to be shy of sharing his space with a nymph or two.

'Originally there would have been statues in all of these niches,' continued Fesch, 'in fact, some of the sculpture in the gardens might have come from here. I ought to check, but unfortunately, I sent the best ones to Paris just after we arrived.' He looked for a moment as if he might blush, but it must have been a trick of the light, and he continued effortlessly, 'The line of demarcation between a nymphaeum and a grotto is not always clear, but the nymphaeum puts greater emphasis on the presence of a supposed semi-deity. Presumably this place was dedicated to some aspect of the greater nymphs: Juturna or Egeria, by what I can make out of the inscriptions. I had hoped the village priest would have known a bit more about the local tutelary naiads, but he is astonishingly ignorant.' He contemplated the dry remains of the grotto spring. 'It isn't working anymore. I think it has all been diverted to the cisterns under the house at some point. Good for us, having the incalculable benefit of warm piped water, but sad for this forgotten little relic... I had better be getting back, would you be good enough to help me carry my prizes up to the villa?'

They went back up to the chapel proper and Fesch contemplated the hole behind the altar. 'I suppose I had better have this resealed before the wedding; unattended holes are proving most problematic on this estate.'

'I'm sure the priest would appreciate that,' said Vanderville. 'You were acquainted with the Comte Mombello then, Commissary Fesch?'

Fesch genuflected before the altar before answering, 'The principal virtues of our faith are kindness, love, faith, hope, and charity. They say that small acts of kindness are the greatest virtue, and his acts of kindness were so very small that he must be counted among the truly blessed. He loved often, and briefly, had faith in the king on whom his hopes for riches rested, and relied heavily upon charity for his sustenance.'

'I see,' replied Vanderville, smiling.

'I should have remained a priest. It's often said,' mused Fesch, brushing down his uniform. At that moment, a tocsin sounded, and Fesch said wearily, 'What fresh hell is this? This place seems to run on bells and call of drums.'

'It's the fall-in,' said Vanderville, helping him with the painting. 'Either the troops are rioting again, or the supply convoy has arrived from Milan.' He hefted the bundle onto his shoulder.

As they walked through the pine trees to the villa, Paolette reappeared beside them carrying a basket of ribbons in the crook of her arm. She linked her spare arm with Vanderville's and matched his stride. 'Will you come to the party at the villa tonight?' she asked. 'They are discussing arrangements for the wedding, and the ball.'

'We are on our way there now,' he replied, and with a happy inspiration he added, 'Can we walk you there?'

'Aren't you already doing that?' she wrinkled her nose at him. 'Slow down a bit though, I'm sore from riding.'

'You are too old to ride astride now,' said Fesch, disapprovingly. 'You know your brother has commanded you and your sisters to ride side-saddle.'

'Oh, we never bothered with any of that in Ajaccio.'

'But you were children then!'

She ignored Fesch, and said to Vanderville, 'Do you know what? I can help you to catch the ghoul. You need help in talking to women.'

'I'm not sure I understand, *citoyenne*.'

She smiled. 'For your *gendarme* work. Won't you be talking to everyone, isn't that what they do?'

'I'm not a *gendarme*!'

'I'm serious, Lieutenant Vanderville, try to understand. We have one face for you men,' she said, 'and another one when we are amongst ourselves. They will tell me things and say things in front of me that you would never hear.'

Vanderville considered her for a moment. 'I had better ask Gracchus first.'

She sighed and disengaged her arm from him, bringing him to a halt while Fesch walked on ahead. 'How disappointing you are, Lieutenant. I had better go and join my sisters.' She leant in to whisper conspiratorially, 'I *will* help you though, and just think, I will let you watch me sometimes… if you insist,' and with a mocking laugh, she disappeared into the trees.

Chapter Four

They were in Gracchus's makeshift room in the attic, which he had been grudgingly allowed to occupy in the period before the wedding guests arrived, which was the span of time Berthier considered sufficient for him to accomplish his business at Mombello. Gracchus had looked up when Vanderville entered and greeted him affably, with a pointed glance at his pocket watch. 'At last. I spent the afternoon in the kitchens,' he said. 'The cook is a remarkable man. Did I see you talking with that flibbertigibbet outside?'

'I helped her with a ladder,' offered Vanderville.

'That young woman is a head turner on a prodigious scale,' considered Gracchus. 'Actually you can cultivate her, she could be useful in telling us about the Bonaparte family.'

'If you insist,' muttered Vanderville evasively.

'She makes you sweat, eh? Anyway, her brother and uncle are here, so keep your barrack room banter to yourself. The uncle, Fesch, says that he is a commissary. Can you explain what is meant by that title?'

Vanderville removed his hat and tucked it under his arm. 'They contract the army's supplies, food, forage, uniforms and so on, a role in which many turn a tidy profit for themselves. They are here in a military capacity, although not really what we consider proper army officers.'

Gracchus commenced unpacking his clothes and dressing, and he ushered Vanderville to the bed, for the cramped space was hardly sufficient for both. 'You must be looking forward to meeting General Bonaparte,' said Vanderville, trying the bed springs.

'Not at all,' said Gracchus, noting with annoyance that his luggage had been searched, and insulted that it had been done obviously, with no intention of concealing the search. 'Tell me who will be at the reception tonight.'

'The Bonapartes?' said Vanderville, sitting down.

'Not just them. Mombello and his nephew; all the people who were in the villa the night the comte disappeared.'

Vanderville shrugged. 'There were hundreds, half the army is here.'

'Not that night. The cook has informed me of the numbers of how many ate. The villa and its gardens were closed, part of Berthier's new ordinances to stop people wandering in and out at will. The servants are housed in the village because their rooms are to be used for the wedding guests. Some rooms are set aside for the negotiators and diplomats who will arrive any day. Bonaparte likes a small staff so the servants are generally dismissed before the evening, leaving the kitchen staff to serve coffee and kickshaws. There were sentries outside the villa's gardens, so if anyone entered from outside, or departed, there will be a record of who and when. Your first task is to obtain that record for me. The salon was at the back of the house, and the shutters on the doors and windows to the terrace were closed because the General likes it like that. There couldn't have been more than twenty people there, and one of them must have seen or heard something related to the disappearance of Mombello.'

'Now you are talking as if he was murdered by the ghoul. It was a dark night, and you said he fell down a well shaft nobody knew was there.'

Gracchus was rummaging in his travelling bags and laying out clothes. 'There is something I cannot quite put my finger upon. I shall rule nothing out at this stage.'

'I can get the sentry reports easily enough. But how do we find out about these people? Ask the servants?'

Gracchus blinked down at him. 'That, I have already done.'
Vanderville shrugged exasperatedly, and Gracchus continued,
'What did I say to you by the well earlier about watching
people? This evening talk to the guests, sympathise with them,
let them know you are interested in them and what they think,
and within ten minutes they will tell you what they think of
the others around them.'

'And then report everything back to you in triplicate?' said
Vanderville, yawning. He had been hoping there would be less
paperwork in this new role.

'Naturally you write nothing down,' said Gracchus testily.
He was irritable because his clothes were fighting against his
stomach. His waistcoat popped a button, and when he bent to
pick it up, another followed suit. He fumbled for the buttons,
and almost tripped over Vanderville's sabre. 'Don't you ever take
that damn cheese toaster off?'

'This?' said Vanderville, regarding his trailing sabre fondly.
'I've never really considered it. Generally, we are so proud to
put them on that we don't give much of a fig for taking them
off.' He picked up the buttons on the floor. 'At least you get
to sleep here in the house,' he said. 'We are three or four to a
room at the stables.'

'The proximity will encourage intimacy,' said Gracchus, 'and
the quicker you get to know your fellow officers the better.
What did you think of young Alexandre?'

Vanderville produced a needle and thread from the interior
of his uniform. In his seated position he was perfectly placed
to sew Gracchus's waistcoat buttons back on. While he busied
himself with the needle Gracchus swallowed his dignity and
prayed fervently that the servant bringing hot water should not
enter at that moment.

'He has charming *ancien regime* manners, but the other
officers keep him at a distance. At first I thought it was because
he was too *enragé* – too Jacobin, that is,' he added, avoiding
Gracchus's eye. 'Overt revolutionary zeal is considered undesirable by the general officers.'

'I know what *they* think,' interrupted Gracchus. 'What were his relations with his uncle like?'

'Everyone says they were devoted. They lived together with hardly any servants and adored one another,' said Vanderville. He turned off the thread behind the last button, and snapped it with a deft twist. 'You saw him today at the well. Anyway, he had no motive to wish him out of the way, if that's what you mean. Old Mombello must have been eighty if he were a day, and Alexandre could afford to wait for his money.'

'A regular *pas de deux*,' mused Gracchus. 'The young man's mother must have been much younger?'

'His uncle adopted him when his father died, and the mother found herself unable to maintain him. She lives in France, hasn't been seen for years, and anyway there is some hint that Alexandre was born the wrong side of the matrimonial blanket. I also heard that apparently the Bonaparte family, Comte Mombello and the Marbeufs go all the way back to Corsica.'

'Yes, there might be something there,' said Gracchus. 'The Bonapartes are refugees from Corsica, although all of them except for the mother are desperately trying to forget it. When the anti-French party sold the island out to the British, the Bonapartes left at a fair old clip. Only got out by the skin of their teeth apparently and lost everything in the process. Perhaps that is why they are so hungry for distinction now. Whatever the reason we need to find out about that family connection. We must ask General Bonaparte about it.' He broke off on catching sight of Vanderville's horrified face.

'Oh, don't worry, I'm not going to ask you to beard your god in his lair tonight. I will speak to him myself if I get the chance.' Gracchus realised that the youngster was nervous at the thought of attending a salon bristling with the army's generals, and the cream of Milanese and Parisian society. To distract him, he asked, 'What about Lieutenant Charles? He was there last night, isn't that unusual for a junior officer?'

'Neither his social nor his military rank qualifies him for the top table, even in these times of fraternity and so on. But

Charles is socially known to the General's wife from Paris. In fact, they travelled here from Paris together. Although we are in the middle of the army headquarters, the society in the evenings here is much more concerned with the General's wife's friends and the Bonaparte family wedding party than with military hierarchy.' He brushed down Gracchus's coat and handed it to him.

'So, *Citoyen* Hippolyte Charles is a friend of the family?' Gracchus shrugged on his coat.

Vanderville shifted himself awkwardly on the bed. 'Yes, I think you could say so… certainly yes.'

Gracchus adjusted his necktie in the inadequate glass and surveyed his own face. It was pleasantly plump, he considered. Nothing like that of Lieutenant Charles, with his jet-black hair, brown complexion, and dimpled chin. Women would like Charles; he was sure of that. Charles was a man of the kind most dangerous to a married woman who is rather bored, and who does not love her husband. He smoothed down his clothes. There was no trace of the dusty, careworn, and sandalled pilgrim of the morning. He now looked as if he would be quite at ease in the salon with the generals and their women. 'Are you wearing that?' he asked Vanderville, who was still in his faded uniform coat.

'Yes,' said Vanderville who had also been pondering the alteration wrought in Gracchus's appearance. He wondered which of the two versions of this man was the disguise, and which the truth. 'A lieutenant's pay doesn't run to many coats I'm afraid.'

'Let us go down now,' said Gracchus complacently. 'I'm sure they are all agog to admire our toilette.'

The company was gathered in the grand reception rooms at the rear of the villa. The principal room was a long broad gallery, divided by pillars into three unequal compartments, like the foyer of the opera house in Paris. The ranks of glass doors giving onto the terrace were shuttered and the room was brilliantly lit by candles.

In the main compartment, *Citoyenne* Josephine Bonaparte was sitting on a sofa with three other women in evening dresses fussing over a fat little pug dog, who was absorbing their adoration from his own cushion on the floor. Standing before them, occupying the other part of their attention, was an animated Lieutenant Charles. He greeted them. 'Welcome to Little Paris! *Citoyen* Gracchus, Lieutenant Vanderville, may I introduce *Citoyennes* Hamelin, and Visconti. Our paragon Josephine, I believe you have already met, Gracchus, and this is the famous Fortune,' he indicated the dog.

Gracchus nudged the pug's attentions aside with his shoe and made his bow. Charles was effortlessly chatting of this and that, riding a wave of verbose froth. He saw Vanderville's consternation. 'You must forgive us,' he said, 'we are all of us the merest slaves to novelty, and unfortunately the fashion in conversation is frivolous. It must at all odds avoid serious matters, as a gravid mother flees a black cat crossing her path.'

'Not at all,' Gracchus answered for both of them, 'we can recognise a master at work when we see one, and I for one can appreciate artistry, while being utterly unable to emulate it.'

'Prettily turned, Gracchus,' smiled Josephine. 'Perhaps, like dear Charles here, you will amuse us on our eternal peregrinations after these bloodthirsty generals.'

Before Gracchus could reply, General Dumas sidled elegantly up and made his obeisance to *Citoyenne* Bonaparte. Her little dog bridled as he addressed its mistress and drowned his words with a rising sequence of shrill yaps. Defeated for once, Dumas retired under the onslaught, muttering to Vanderville, 'A fig for these aristocrat lap dogs, they should all be sliced up to make haversacks for the army. He guards her like a sentry.'

As he retreated Charles casually scooped up the pug and smoothed his head. The creature screwed up its eyes, convulsing with delight. A squeak from one end of the dog heralded an odious emission, and Charles swiftly slid him back to the floor, where he snuffled with great business around the feet of his mistress, who wrinkled her nose prettily.

While Vanderville attempted to make himself agreeable in the elevated company, Gracchus wandered off at the first opportunity to survey the rest of the company. Framed by the arch forming an entrance to the next compartment was Bonaparte. He was standing by himself; or rather, he was surrounded by numerous staff who all stood at a distance from him. He was a sparse man under the middle height, and his lank unpowdered hair fell to his shoulders. Gracchus recalled instantly his invincible self-possession. Everything else was changed: the grandeur of the surroundings, the circle of respectful generals and admiring women. Nothing could have been more unlike the scruffy prisoner he remembered.

When Bonaparte noticed Gracchus, he beckoned him over. 'What have you been up to since we last met… in Paris wasn't it?' asked Bonaparte abruptly. Gracchus frowned, unimpressed by this feigned ignorance. The nature of their last encounter was not one that admitted of a failure of recollection. Bonaparte breezed on, 'Ah, you rightly keep your cards close when questioned by a servant of the Republic.'

Gracchus found that Bonaparte still expressed himself curtly, and occasionally incorrectly, in French, but the familiarity of their earlier acquaintance had dissipated with Bonaparte's success and Gracchus made with reluctance the sacrifice of familiarity, the use of *tu*, and other conversational freedoms.

'It is a shame that your own services to the Republic have not been recognised as they deserved,' observed Bonaparte.

'Your talents, on the other hand, General, appear to have been amply recompensed.' It was strongly rumoured that Bonaparte had received his command of the Army of Italy in exchange for two astute manoeuvres: the whiff of cannon fire that had slaughtered a rioting Paris mob, and the adoption of his political patron's discarded mistress as his wife. A dowry, the Paris wits had called it.

Bonaparte allowed himself a wry smile. 'Gracchus, you have fallen into the error of believing that virtue is the source of advancement. I cannot declare that I owe my good fortune to my own sinews or to my virtue: no, *destiny* is the force driving me.'

Gracchus managed to maintain the composure of his eyebrows, and congratulated him on his marriage, and leading him down to the salon, Bonaparte was effusive on the joys of his changed condition. 'Do you see that gentleman?' he asked, as they approached his wife, where a sparkling Charles still held court on the sofa with the dog in his arms. 'That's my rival. He was in possession of madame's bed when I married her. I tried to turn him out. Vain pretension. I was notified that I could either make up my mind to sleep elsewhere or consent to go halves. I found that vexatious, but it was all or nothing. I resigned myself.'

Gracchus again concealed his consternation. He had heard that Bonaparte was in the full ecstasy of his recent marriage. *Citoyenne* Bonaparte was charming, and all the anxieties of command, all the cares of the government of Italy, could not prevent her husband from giving free rein to his domestic happiness. Was the General now hinting at an improper liaison between his wife and Lieutenant Charles? He covered his embarrassment by accepting a glass of fragrant wine from Piotr, who passed by with a tray and a wink.

Josephine looked up at her husband and smiled as she caught his remarks, stroking her pug dog. 'Fortune was not so accommodating; Bonaparte has a proof of it on his leg.'

Gracchus breathed out slowly with relief. Bonaparte snorted, and took a mock swipe at the creature.

'Be kind to poor Fortune,' chided Josephine, 'he is the last survivor of the phantom's ravages.' As they strolled on, Bonaparte observed in a confidential whisper, 'The story Josephine is amused to tell about the dog is a fabrication she invented to show that I was not master in my house. The truth is that the dog drove me from his mistress's bed chamber not with his teeth, but with the other end. I don't know from what he derives his power, but he is absolutely foul. When he emits, it is like the breath of a grave digger. I don't know how she stands it. She says she doesn't notice, but then she is used to high society.'

Gracchus nodded; his interest in the mundane aspects of other people's marriages was marginal at the best of times.

Instead, he watched Vanderville under siege from two of Josephine's friends. They were both modishly swathed, and wonderfully scented, and the effect of their combined proximity was clearly a heady one to the young lieutenant. One spoke a mixed jargon of French and Italian, all her own, by which she profited to make the most outrageous remarks and the most disgraceful confidences. Vanderville mutely appealed to Gracchus to rescue him, but he affected to study the frescoed ceiling instead.

After Piotr had served the company with iced lemonade, card tables were placed, and the room gradually separated into small groups playing *Écarté*. As Gracchus did not care for the game, he strolled around the room with others who were not inclined to play. Bonaparte sat apart and alone, with a board game set out before him. He looked up as Gracchus approached. 'I hear from my mother that you have been snuffling around the kitchens. I hope it was my business that took you there, and not merely your nose?'

Gracchus paused by the table. 'During my incarceration I developed a fondness for the apparatus and personnel of the kitchen. I made something of a study of it. The mind of an imprisoned man atrophies without nourishment, don't you find?'

Bonaparte stiffened; he was no stranger to internment either but resented the reminder. 'You do not appear to be lacking in nourishment. Did you find anything, or have you wasted all your time gathering recipes?'

Gracchus looked down at the game board. He was suddenly sick at heart of the gilded verbal fencing of the elaborate reception. It was an unwelcome reminder of the life he had been trying to evade. 'I may have discovered something relevant to the investigation.'

'Good,' replied Bonaparte, 'sit down and tell me about it.'

Gracchus took the vacant chair and examined the board. It was the children's game, 'Game of the Goose', in which dice are used to move counters around a spiral track towards the centre where the winner claims the goose. The painted board was littered with revolutionary emblems and slogans, so that the usual obstacle squares were represented not by snakes or ladders, but by liberty trees and the guillotine.

'I am normally forced to play with my mother or sisters,' said Bonaparte. 'The Parisians won't play with me. They erroneously think this is a children's game because they do not understand its subtleties.'

Paolette wandered up to their table and bent over Gracchus to see the board. The warmth of her body grazed his shoulder and he flinched. She laughed. 'Be careful *Citoyen* Gracchus, he doesn't play fairly.'

Gracchus chose a playing piece, aware the general was scrutinising him. Bonaparte began to talk again; the habit of lecturing had become second nature to him since they last met. 'There is a sonnet that describes the game, "From one door depart many pilgrims." Each pilgrim leaves by the same gate, but they do not travel together. They are driven by the bones in whose eyes is fate, here represented by the dice. The poem refers to the perils of wine at the inn, and the waters in the well, the danger of incarceration and of losing the way and ending up lifeless. Of the several pilgrims, only one will reach salvation at the winning space.'

Gracchus spun the carved bone dice. He promptly landed on a square representing the tribunal of the Committee of Public Safety and was immobilised while Bonaparte smugly surged

64

ahead. 'Can you enlighten me a little as to the politics of the deceased Comte Mombello?' he asked politely.

Bonaparte rolled again and landed on death, represented by a skull sporting a Phrygian cap. He pushed the board back in disgust and fixed Gracchus with his eyes. 'Mombello was that rare thing, a man acceptable to both the radical Jacobin element, and to the moderates forming the useful part of the liberal aristocracy. His wide experience of French and Italian modes of government qualified him to be employed in the senate of the new Republic I have created. All political men have enemies, naturally, but none of his are to be found here. Everyone here is in favour of the Republic, a rosy dawn for these territories liberated from the Austrian tyranny. Although his personal fortunes had sunk very low in recent years, they were rising again. He had everything to live for, even at his age.' He pulled the board back towards him, replacing his piece on the beginning square. 'Ultimately one can still triumph, even after apparent disaster.'

Gracchus's attention was drawn by Josephine leaving her table and swaying towards them. When he looked back to the board it was just in time to see an ambiguous movement of the General's hand revealing a five and a four on the dice, a peculiarly fortuitous gambit that instantly impelled Bonaparte's piece forward to an advanced position on the board, one considerably in advance of that occupied by Gracchus. Josephine placed a hand lightly on her husband's shoulder, and Bonaparte encircled her waist clumsily with one arm. 'Bonaparte,' she trilled in her musical voice, 'your mother is beginning her story. It is her turn tonight.'

Bonaparte rose from his chair. 'We can continue our game another evening,' he said, 'or perhaps just assume that this one goes to me.'

'I thought we decided that Lieutenant Marbeuf would take his turn tonight?' Bonaparte asked his wife, as they walked to the far salon.

'We did, but because of his uncle's accident I thought we would excuse him. I did suggest we suspend the whole thing, but he very graciously insisted it goes ahead. Letizia will stand in and tell a ghost story from your island.'

'*Cacafuoco!*' exclaimed Bonaparte. 'Not again. I told you to put a stop to any more nonsense.'

'Bonaparte,' she said winningly, 'I would sooner try to milk a pigeon than persuade your mother to alter a course she has set her head upon, and besides, she has begun.'

Gracchus followed them to where Letizia was holding forth from a dais, surrounded by draped curtains to produce the effect of a forest. Candles were on the floor below her, casting her amplified shadow onto the painted sylvan scene behind the dais. She looked at the floor as she incanted in a low voice.

> *'Twas in bright forest, on a bitter cold night*
> *Where laid young Amleth beyond all delight*
> *Stricken by bitter times and privy broken passion*
> *To recall phantom speech in terms too ashen*
> *Wond'ring was the black robed penitent vision sent*
> *To immure him to sinister practices, or merely lent*
> *Voice to slain Father's flickering shade*
> *Offering taper from limbs of children made.*
> *To scape this self-made purgatory*
> *Amleth fain feigned listless lunacy*
> *Wallowing in listless reprisal-bent lunacy,*
> *Did pale face obscured with refuse smeared*
> *And fickle spittle coat'd beard*
> *Prove that in time his scheme'd vengeance fraught might leaven*
> *Nor let his soul contrive against the mother aught – leave her to heaven.'*

It continued in this vein for some time. Vanderville nodded off, but Gracchus was utterly intent on the performance. He nudged Vanderville. 'Are you asleep?'

'Not at all. Damnably tired — just resting my eyes.'

Two swaying mute figures joined her on the stage, concealed in dark robes and carrying candles. From their elegantly sandalled feet, Gracchus recognised the Bonaparte sisters. One mimed pushing the other, who fell to the ground.

As Letizia mimed facing the wall, behind the two robed figures Alexandre sharply drew back his chair, which clattered to the floor at Gracchus's feet, and stalked out of the room. His demonstration drew gasps from one or two of the company, and there followed one of those silences commonly termed awkward. Gracchus wrinkled his brow in contemplation, while Vanderville wondered whether by the usual standards this story was a little dull, and the presentation uninspired. *Citoyenne* Hamelin tittered, and Josephine attempted an arch encouragement. 'Ah yes, tales in barbarous countries often assume very strange and fantastic forms.'

'And even more barbaric iambic metres,' smiled Charles, who was hurriedly convinced by his friends that now was the time for him to demonstrate his declamatory talents, and taking Letizia's place he began to sing.

'O thou who from us flyest to the lonely hermit cell
as from the eagle's talon flies the dove
involuntary exile there to dwell—
thus sacrificing heavenly to an earthly love'

He looked at Paolette as he sang, and Gracchus saw that she coloured at his words, but he missed the rest, as Bonaparte kicked his chair back with a snort of impatience, and left the assembly, beckoning to Gracchus to follow him. 'If there's one thing worse than my mother disobeying orders, it's bad poetry,' he snarled, stopping at a pair of doors a few paces down a corridor from the salon, and fumbling in his pocket for a key. 'Yet what man, even with all of thirty thousand ready to march and die at his command, can still sway his own mother to his bidding?'

'In these times of disturbance and disruption, harassed and overexcited by the conditions amid which they find themselves, people turn by a seemingly inevitable impulse to the supernatural,' observed Gracchus. 'Phantom horrors and blood-curdling stories are all the rage.'

'Even my own wife thinks it fashionable to consult fortune-tellers. Superstitious like all Creoles, she even brought one here with her. *Citoyenne* Hamelin is her oracle.'

'Do you not find these ghost stories unhelpful in suppressing the febrile atmosphere here in the villa?' asked Gracchus.

'It's harmless enough in the salons, but when it spreads to the army it becomes a problem. Charlatans find thousands of credulous victims in the soldiers. Now they have this story of a ghoul, which is nonsense, but the killings of animals are real enough.'

'General Berthier mentioned it. It may be that someone is stirring up trouble deliberately and playing on the superstitions of the people here. I have seen it done before.'

'The evocation of shades, the apparition of spectres, water reflected in a mirror, ashes thrown to the north wind, a cock nourished on special grains and placed among the letters of the alphabet,' Bonaparte counted off the fallacies on his fingers. 'There is no nonsense in which the army will not indulge. You may be right, I should suppress it, but you aren't here to talk about that. Give me an account of your investigation.'

'May I suggest that since the missing comte has now been found – in regrettable condition but found nonetheless – my task here can be considered at an end. My remit was, after all, to discover his whereabouts. I am eager to continue my journey and require only your permission to depart tomorrow.'

'Done with the business already? That's damnably sharp practice even for an old hack,' said Bonaparte. 'And your report? Is that complete and written up?'

Gracchus raised his voice a notch. 'If you want a formal investigation of Mombello's death you need to remember that it is usual to begin by interrogation: first the spouse, then the heirs, then the family, then close friends or acquaintances.'

'But there is nothing here except the story of a frail old man who fell down a well in the dark,' said Bonaparte calmly. 'Write me up that report. You are famous for your rational methods. Your word that this was just a misfortunate accident will be the antidote to cure the malaise in the Army of Italy.'

'I would write it up,' said Gracchus, pacing up and down before the desk. 'Believe me, if you think I care one way or another what happened here, you are much mistaken. But I cannot.'

'Why not?' said Bonaparte, throwing up his arms with exasperation.

'Mombello didn't fall down that well. He could not have,' replied Gracchus more quietly.

'So, you do not consider this matter closed after all?'

Gracchus replied, 'Voltaire said we owe respect to the living; to the dead we owe only the truth. That was my professional adage. I am no longer possessed by such delusions and wish simply to continue my travels without further interruption.'

'Whereas what you owe to the General in Chief of the Army of Italy seems obscure to you by comparison.'

They were now raising their voices at each other with the familiarity of old adversaries. Gracchus became aware that they were starting to attract attention from the salon behind. The General finally inserted the key and opened the doors into his cabinet. It was ablaze with lamps and uncomfortably stuffy. Gracchus pulled the doors to, bristling with impatience, 'General, if you think nobody had reason to kill him, and you think there was no supernatural intervention, why did you call me in?'

When the General finally replied, his voice was subdued. 'You have heard about the *citoyennes'* dogs going missing?'

Gracchus shrugged, and Bonaparte paused before this mask of composure that betrayed nothing, then he changed tack.

'Sometimes I think it is this villa. I chose it because of my wife, because of the hot springs, but no one is sleeping, and then these horrors began.'

'Why don't you just change house?' said Gracchus. 'You have all the palaces in Milan at your disposal.'

'I cannot be seen to back down before a ghost, it is too ridiculous. I, the conqueror of Italy, driven out of my headquarters by a ghoul! The marriages are arranged, the guests invited, my wife, my family... I would be a laughingstock.'

This is getting to him, thought Gracchus. Perhaps Bonaparte had not left Corsican superstition as far behind as he imagined he had. His meditation was broken as the door opened, letting in the noise from the salon.

'Excuse me General,' said Berthier, 'do you need me?'

Bonaparte sat down suddenly. 'It's hot in here, Berthier. Turn the lamps out. You are too warm too, Gracchus, you forget yourself. Open the terrace doors and let the night into the room.'

As Gracchus pulled open the shutters, his face was bathed in a flickering light. The terrace was illuminated by countless scintillating sequins dancing in the air. Berthier and Bonaparte joined Gracchus at the window to wonder at the sight. A grim-faced Bonaparte surveyed the scene. 'Don't stand there all betwattled, Berthier,' he said, 'go and tell the children.' He opened the doors and walked out onto the terrace with Gracchus behind him.

At Berthier's announcement Vanderville saw Paolette exclaim in delight.

'Look everyone!' she cried, gleefully, and she started throwing the shutters and doors open, then ran laughing onto the terrace. In anyone else it would have been ridiculous, but half a dozen of the admiring officers flocked after her, and then the rest of the salon rose to their feet. Vanderville saw that Josephine was among the most prominent striving to outdo Paolette in flirtatiousness.

'Ridiculous,' said Letizia, just loud enough for Josephine to hear. 'Women of our age should leave the gadding to the children.'

Vanderville, embarrassed, followed the company outside. The spectacle was extraordinary. Not only the terrace, but the gardens too, were lit by a million phosphorescent specks dancing under the awestruck gaze of the enchanted company. The phenomenon stretched out to the horizon, fascinating the eyes, and compelling the onlookers into the realm of faerie. He paused slightly behind the crowd, and he saw Gracchus and General Bonaparte talking further down the terrace. Loath to approach Bonaparte uninvited, he nonetheless took several steps closer to overhear,

'The cook, Leonardi showed me some of the insects he had captured this afternoon,' Gracchus was explaining, 'he told me that last night was their first appearance of the year. So, you see, General, with the darkness lit by these marvellous dancing lamps, only a blind man could have fallen down that well shaft by accident.'

Chapter Five

The next morning's schedule had been plotted in some detail by Gracchus, who was now keen to advance their enquiries into what had become a murder investigation under what he had called a proper scientific basis. He had not planned for Vanderville's day starting with a riot.

The lieutenant woke after a turbulent night of bad dreams to find the bed chamber in the stables empty of companions. Muffled sounds led him outside onto the gallery, where he found Hercule and Charles peering over the edge of the railings in front of General Dumas, who was sat in his nightshirt loading pistols with ball at the table.

'Sleep well?' said Charles over his shoulder.

'I had the strangest dream about the ghoul,' Vanderville began, trying to pass Dumas, who cut him short. 'Nobody gives a damn. Get your eyes on the brawl with the others.'

Wiping the haze from his eyes, Vanderville did as he was told. Amid the carts and tables cluttering the stable court-yard a seething skirmish of bareheaded men in various states of undress were furiously belabouring their neighbours with sticks, fists, chair-legs, and bottles. Flashes of coloured clothes revealed the identity of the opposing tribes. Here there was a scarlet waistcoat of the Guides, and there, the blue culottes of a long-haired Pole. One corner of the yard was defended by a phalanx of the Guides, who were outnumbered. Ensconced behind overturned tables, they suffered the onslaught of Poles determined to remove them from their fastness. Some Poles were on the stable roofs and had opened a most destructive fire upon the heads of the Guides with roof tiles. It threatened to get out of hand.

'General Dumas,' drawled Charles, 'are we not going to stop this?'

'Not I,' said the general. 'The Guides are Bonaparte's spoiled children; I would not interfere with their entertainments. Only a fool would trail his sabre through that puddle.' He slapped a loaded pistol down on the table. 'As for the Poles, I have a principle when training dogs, never call a mutt who is not ready to come, for he will become accustomed to ignore your voice instead of hearkening to it. Let them burn themselves out, they will be more biddable when exhausted.'

Hercule was hopping on one leg struggling to get into his boots. 'I'm for the Guides,' he announced, and clad in mere nightshirt and open waistcoat as he was, he swung himself over the gallery railing with an exultant war cry and hurled himself naked onto the heads of two onrushing Poles.

Charles grinned wryly at Vanderville. 'One day he is going to hurt himself.'

In the clock tower above the stable entrance, a Guide was being dangled by his feet far above the heaving throng, while a Pole had started beating a drum enthusiastically, summoning yet more of his compatriots from the camp beyond the arch.

'Oh, very well. Let us at least do this fairly,' said Dumas, and brandishing his pistols over the railings, he loosed both into the fray. The first shot was close enough to discomfort a Pole on the roof, who promptly lost his feet and tumbled off, while the second was directed at a Guide, whom he scored across the leg.

Hercule, meanwhile, was amid the very heart of the brawl, belabouring the Pole's drummer with a mop. Dumas rushed down the gallery stair and vaulted onto a watering horse. Using his steed as a ram, he forced his way in between the two factions. He was the only one among the combatants mounted, and like some looming greasy centaur he raised his nightcap to release his shining head, stood in his stirrups and bellowed, 'There is

73

a fucking funeral today!' He clouted one of the Guides with a pistol butt. 'Show some respect, you louts.' As he chastised them in this vein, Vanderville asked Charles, 'What the hell is going on?'

Charles spread his hands. 'Take your pick. The Polish Legion are mutinous because they suspect the Guides of killing a pampered goose they were saving for the wedding feast. The Guides said the ghoul killed the goose. But the Poles are also furious because the Guides have new uniforms before them. This inequality in personal magnificence has been considered by the local village girls when distributing their favours, but I think it's the goose thing that is the real grievance.'

'All this for a goose!' marvelled Vanderville.

'It is the manner of the business. The goose was not merely stolen for the pot but ripped up and left scattered about the place in the night. Words were exchanged over the water pump this morning, and honour was invoked.' Charles picked up his pipe. 'Never mind, Dumas has them in hand. What's for breakfast? And has anyone seen Alexandre?'

In the yard the soldiers were now hanging their heads muttering. Having cowed them thoroughly with his harangue, Dumas now held up his hand and appeased them. 'Soldiers of the Polish Legion, you had cause. I will be the first to admit it. But you will have your uniforms, the supply convoy was seen this morning on the road from Milan and will arrive today. Be patient a little longer.'

'And the ghoul, general?' shouted one brave Guide, from a position of obscurity behind a gallery pillar.

'Look, by my bald pate I have no more idea about the bleeding ghoul than anyone else,' confided Dumas, standing in his stirrups. 'I promise you this. You will have a goose tomorrow and a party before the wedding. There will be feasting and climbing greased poles under the liberty tree. You will compete for prizes with each other like good comrades instead of barn-yard oafs.'

The yard was filled with Polish cheers, and even the Guides looked mollified, although a few faces looked confusedly at each other.

'He promises them a party,' muttered Charles. 'Tomorrow! It will kick off again. Typical Dumas. Opens the mill gates without engaging the drive wheel.'

Hercule's head and bruised fists appeared over the edge of the gallery. 'Doesn't matter, we'll eat goose anyway,' he said cheerfully, clambering up. 'Best thing to do with them, before they all get pulled to pieces by the ghoul.'

'Be a good fellow,' said Charles to Hercule, 'and hide these pistols away while I go to have a word with Dumas.'

Vanderville trailed Charles down the stairs. 'Why are you looking for Alexandre?'

'He was gone when we woke up to all this,' said Charles, 'and although he seems balanced since his uncle died, you never quite know where you are with him. Not that the old man was a great loss, he never quite took to me, I must say. I think Alexandre went off with Piotr. Frankly, I'm worried about him too. He has been having some trouble with the other Poles, and I think it's bothering him more than he lets on. If you see him, tell him I will be in the camp all morning. Got to arrange the cloth allocations with the quartermasters. Bonaparte seems suddenly keen for me to have something to fill my days with.' He sighed. 'Women and generals; no point in hoping for reason from either.'

Vanderville shrugged himself into his coat. 'I'm for the villa, got to meet Gracchus in the library before he goes to the chapel for another sniff of the comte's carcass.'

–

'Berthier,' Bonaparte was saying, 'take this down. From next week, the rooms in the villa are to be reorganised as follows: General Leclerc and *Citoyenne* Paolette to the Red room, Major Baciocchi and *Citoyenne* Elisa to the Green room...'

'Baciocchi is a captain, General,' interjected Berthier.

'My sisters cannot marry captains. Make out the papers for his promotion. Major Baciocchi and *Citoyenne* Elisa to the Green room – no, that's too close to me – better change them around and add a note that it is forbidden to play the violin inside the villa for the benefit of the new major.'

'I was hoping to take over the Green room myself, General, the view of the gardens is beneficial to my health,' began Berthier.

'I imagine you would prefer the view, yes,' said Bonaparte. 'Anyway, I think it is better if you bunk down in the cabinet anteroom in case I need you in the night. We are not here on a rest cure, my friend.'

'Indeed, General,' smarted Berthier, 'let us be neither a coffee house, nor a knocking shop for all pity.'

Dumas laughed. Bonaparte reproved him. 'As for you, your behaviour is quite scandalous, Dumas. A certain *citoyenne*'s husband is asking after her all over Milan. If you want to play the whoremonger, you can do it just as well outside the villa.'

'I warrant you have a cheese in your larder, Bonaparte,' replied Dumas. 'Pray, brother, does that one cheese make you a cheesemonger?'

Bonaparte ignored him, and continued speaking to Berthier. 'No more chuntering about the room changes. I am not interested. We will do the other reallocations later, except for Lieutenant Marbeuf. He cannot return to the villa now. We need the space, and it is ridiculous for a lieutenant to maintain various residences at his leisure when some of my generals are still lodged in the stable inn.'

'Technically, this *is* his house now, General,' offered Berthier.

'If he objects, he can lodge a complaint through the usual channels.'

Gracchus chuckled to himself, however his eavesdropping was interrupted as Vanderville barged into the room. 'I thought you said the library…' he began, before being brought up short by the sight of Gracchus's stout arse elevated in the air. His head was inverted under the floor, from which he had removed several floorboards. Gracchus sat up, his hair mired by a net of cobwebs, and raised a finger to his lips.

'What are you doing?' whispered Vanderville, spying an odd brass nozzle poking out from underneath the floorboards.

'I had hoped to have the apartment over the cabinet of Bonaparte. I do not, instead being over Berthier's. Not the bonanza, but close enough.'

Vanderville picked up some clothes from the pile discarded on the bed, and began arranging them in the wardrobe. 'Do you dismantle all of your quarters in this way, or is this some novel scheme?'

Gracchus indicated the cone-shaped contraption in the crawl space with a dusty hand. 'This,' he said proudly, 'is my listening apparatus.'

Vanderville knelt and examined the thing uncertainly. The brass nozzle for the ear was attached to seven writhing tortoise-shell cones. 'It's a hearing trumpet,' he eventually concluded triumphantly.

'Exactly so,' said Gracchus, 'and I am using it to *hear* what is passing in the room below, which in this case is Berthier's quarters. I have hollowed out the back of the plasterwork in the ceiling below and pierced it several times with a darning needle. The trumpet is remarkably effective. The only conversations below that escape me are the sweet nothings that Berthier occasionally whispers to *Citoyenne* Visconti on the divan.'

Vanderville was impressed despite himself. 'You are spying on the second in command of the Army of Italy,' he whispered.

'Your perspicacity is astonishing,' approved Gracchus. 'I can see why they consider you the cream of the light cavalry. Are all of the imps of that horned devil Bonaparte as astute as yourself?'

'Do you have the faintest idea what they will do to you if they catch you?' asked Vanderville.

'Bill me for the floorboards? Throw me out? It may have escaped your notice, young man, that I have been trying to leave since before I even arrived here!'

'It could be much worse than that,' said Vanderville cautiously. 'Martial law applies to the occupied Italian territories. Would you like a list of the many capital offences that Berthier recognises? I assure you they are quite comprehensive.' He began listing them on his fingers. 'Armed resistance against the forces of the Army of Italy – death; assisting enemies of the French Republic – death; interfering with the mail or couriers of the Army of Italy – death. And did I mention, supplying or causing to be supplied information contrary to the interests of the Army of Italy to her enemies – you guessed it, death.'

'It is all one to me,' said Gracchus.

Vanderville gave up. 'Have you discovered anything of interest?' he asked.

'Certainly. I have learnt that Bonaparte is sitting for the painter Gros, who is staying in the village. Quite literally, because Josephine must confine him to her lap to persuade him to stay still long enough. Gros has finished his portrait of her and started one of Paolette. He might also paint the rest of the family if there is sufficient time.'

'Well worth risking your neck for, Gracchus. Anything of use to the investigation?'

'I did overhear Berthier and Bonaparte. They talk sometimes of love.'

Vanderville considered this. It seemed highly improbable.

'Berthier is in love. This is a common occurrence amongst human beings and is generally regarded with indifference except by those directly concerned. He is prone to sudden fits of intemperate gaiety when she arrives. And this has not gone unremarked by Bonaparte.' He sat down on the bed, and Vanderville offered him a hairbrush. Gracchus ignored it, and continued his account. 'With the ignorance of youth, Bonaparte told Berthier to act his age and get married and start a family before it is too late. "Look at my father! Dead before his time!" he said, "He never had the opportunity to know his children grown.'"

'What did Berthier say?' asked Vanderville, hanging the last of the clothes up.

Gracchus thought for a moment. 'His opinion was that Bonaparte's father was at least spared too many years of *Citoyenne* Letizia Buonaparte.'

'Shall we go to the library now? I thought you wanted to go over Mombello's papers?'

'There is no point, Bonaparte just told Berthier to remove them all to his study, and it's off limits.'

'Apart from the danger involved, spying on the generals seems a bit like listening to an old married couple bickering. Is it really useful?' said Vanderville, his head inside the wardrobe, but when he turned around, he saw that Gracchus had slid his head back under the floorboards and nestled the tube of the hearing trumpet back into his ear. Vanderville shrugged and left him to it.

More baffled by Gracchus's idea of making sense of the comte's death than when they began, Vanderville strolled out onto the terrace. Josephine was there, sitting for her portrait, surrounded by her strutting coterie. The modistes of Paris having declared that they must evoke the antique, they were sweeping the terrace with their flowing Greek-inspired costumes, and fallen leaves followed each around trapped under the dresses' transparent trains. Paolette and Hamelin were topped with the little military caps Josephine was so fond of, from the back of which tails of their thick hair escaped, imitating the helmet of a dragoon. How quickly good taste becomes vitiated by preposterous fashions, thought Vanderville. The eye long accustomed to a certain costume is offended at first by any change; nevertheless it soon becomes reconciled, and then, however ridiculous the dress may be, it is deemed the thing. At the balustrade Alexandre was using a telescope to survey the gardens, but as Vanderville went to join him, he was waylaid by the high-spirited *citoyennes*.

Josephine railed him gently. 'You look so stern today, Lieutenant, you would make a perfect study for Gros, as a republican hero of Rome. What do you think girls, can you see the lieutenant posing in the heroic mode for our little monkey of an artist?'

This question made it impossible for him to ignore the near presence of Paolette, and although he thought he could feel her eyes occasionally on him, he kept his respectfully ahead, daring a glance at her only when her attention was attracted elsewhere.

Hamelin said tartly, 'I can see him as Romulus rescuing the Sabine women,' and the *citoyennes* all laughed. Paolette examined Vanderville from under her cap peak, and his legs went so weak that he had to lean on a chair. 'I don't think Romulus was rescuing anybody, was he Lieutenant Vanderville?' she said, pouting, savouring his bemused reaction.

The painter Gros was a remarkably bohemian-looking young man, with untidy long hair escaping from beneath a curious travelling cap. In one hand he held a large portfolio in which he was sketching with utter absorption. Behind him several canvases were propped against the balustrade and Letizia was rifling through these. 'It seems expensive,' she said to Gros over her shoulder as she flipped through the stack of canvases. 'What are these? Your failures? Can't you reuse them?'

Gros answered her without taking his eyes from his sitter or stopping his rapid sketching. 'I could, I suppose. There is some danger of cracking, if the overpainting isn't done correctly.'

'So the painting won't last very long?' she mused. 'Well neither will I, so it doesn't matter.' She selected one of the panels. 'This is the best canvas, and you won't finish it now.' She held up a bust-length portrait of Comte Mombello. The face was completed, but the rest of the figure and the background was merely sketched. 'Use this,' she said, 'and what you save in materials I expect to see reflected in the price.'

Watching her dispose of the comte's portrait in this cavalier way Vanderville felt a pang of sympathy for Alexandre, and he slipped away to join him at the balustrade. 'Gracchus wants your permission to go through your uncle's papers,' he said. 'He is interested in what he was working on recently. You wouldn't happen to know anything about it?'

Alexandre did not have much to say in answer to Vanderville's enquiry. After thinking a bit, he offered, 'I wish I could help. When my uncle and I came here he thought it would be good for my health to have a distraction, and he suggested I helped him with his memoirs. He lost interest after a bit, and I suspect he didn't really care and just wanted me to amuse myself. I have got as far as his life in Corsica, when he was secretary to my father who was governor of the island for years, and frankly I was finding it hard going. There is a lot of stuff about Corsican society and history, and it is boring at times.

'Actually, I needed a bit of help making sense of some of the cultural oddities, and so the Corsican ghost story Uncle told the night he disappeared would have been fascinating to me. Unfortunately, I missed that part of the evening, as I went to Uncle's room to fetch his hearing trumpet and came back when they were already arguing. It's a shame, because I understand the General banned any more talk of Corsican traditions, and I was hoping his mother would have given me some help with making it all out; she promised she would, but she is reticent now. And I still can't find that damnable trumpet.'

'Perhaps things will be less strained after the funeral,' said Vanderville. 'It must be a terrible time for you all.'

Gracchus found the portico of the chapel door swathed in draped green cloth, overwrought with briar flowers and myrtle boughs. In deference to the military there were also the inevitable trophies of arms. There is nothing, he thought, as deplorable as the custom of dressing churches for special occasions. It makes them as tawdry as a rag seller's barrow. He spent some time poking about inside. The chapel was simple enough once one got past the facade: rectangular and plain, with the altar well-lit from the windows that pierced the dome above it. Apart from the entrance there was a narrow door opening onto a narrower spiral stair that serviced the bell pinnacle.

Descending through the hole behind the altar, he found the nymphaeum much as Vanderville had described it to him, with one difference – work on the comte's final resting place had begun. Each long side was lined with alcoves, a few of which contained tomb altars, and two of these also contained the bridal corbeilles for the weddings. These were shaped like classical urns, and each was some two feet high, one covered in smooth-grained blue leather, and its twin in pink Naples straw work lined with pinker silk that bubbled out from under the lid in a vaguely obscene manner. Shaking off an illogical feeling of impropriety, he lifted the lid of the blue one tentatively and peered inside at the trousseau contents. He was assailed by the scent of rose water in such profusion that he drew back his hand sharply, replacing the lid. As he did so he realised that a fine hairline crack ran down the body of the corbeille. He traced its curve with his finger to the base of the urn, which rested on an effigy of a disgruntled-looking bishop sculpted in relief. The last of the ledges that lined the wall on the side nearest the house showed signs of recent work. A pile of rubble testified to the workmen's activity, and they had doubled the size of the aperture, which was now some seven feet long. The workers had discarded their tools – shovel, crowbar, and a pickaxe – beside the space, and one of them had forgotten his red revolutionary cap. Gracchus picked this up and put it in his pocket. A rude wooden plinth formed the new floor of the alcove; it appeared that this place, rather the chapel above, was destined for Mombello's interment. Appropriate, he thought, for the first republican master of Mombello to choose the pagan crypt rather than the chapel for his resting place.

Driven by the same heathen impulse that had led him to look inside the bridal corbeille he sat down on the ledge, and swinging his legs up tried it out for size. He was of a height with the dead comte, but a more substantial man, and found it cramped. What made him more uncomfortable was a stone under his head that must have been dislodged by the work. He went to brush it out onto the rubble pile, but it was stuck. He examined it. The dust-covered, grey-brown bulbous object was not stone, but not wood either. It looked vaguely familiar. He tried to prise it out, and as he prodded, it dropped down the crack between the side of the alcove and the wooden plinth, settling out of reach. Shrugging, he found that the position of a corpse was admirably suited to meditation, and he closed his eyes to think.

He must have slept, because he was woken by voices in the chapel above. He scampered out of the alcove guiltily and brushed himself down. He was about to ease himself up the ladder when he realised that the voices had been replaced by the profound murmurs common to lovers, and he froze halfway up the ladder in mute embarrassment. He coughed theatrically and rattled the ladder as loudly as he could. His efforts were rewarded, and he heard the chapel door bounce shut.

'Ah, good morning Gracchus, you have risen early I see,' said Charles, as Gracchus's head emerged.

Gracchus grunted, and took in the picturesque decorations of the chapel with a sweep of his arm. 'This ambiance has been aptly created for those about to be wed. The very air in this chapel lends itself to intimate confidences and half-whispered blandishments, so it should not surprise to me to come across a pair of lovers here.'

He hauled himself out of the crypt. Charles leant forward to help him, without speaking, and Gracchus continued, 'Naturally, I do not wish to disturb anyone in a compromising position. I am glad that your companion has fled, but I cannot pretend not to have recognised her voice.' He leant on the altar, and adjusted his spectacles before meeting Charles's gaze. 'You place me in a most sensitive position, Lieutenant Charles. I am required to observe and report upon the movements of everyone to General Bonaparte himself. If witness has placed you and the General's wife together in this chapel, I am bound to report this. Yet I am loathe to do so until I am aware that there is a simple, innocent explanation.'

Charles returned his stare calmly. 'You are mistaken if you consider the *citoyenne* in any way compromised, Gracchus. Oh, I am aware of the rumours, it is always like that when a married woman has a friend.' He joined Gracchus at the altar and stared around the chapel. 'The fact of the matter is that we share certain business interests. The *citoyenne* is actually compromised in one respect. She has debts. She needs money, and together we have the opportunity to make a little. What you must understand is that this is not something along the lines of Fesch, who is plundering this country raw. Or any of the other generals if it comes to that. We are modest in our enterprise.'

Gracchus interrupted. 'Tell me Lieutenant, and I urge you for your own sake to continue in the spirit of candour you have just displayed – this wasn't the first time you have enjoyed meetings of this kind, was it?'

Charles examined his fingernails, and Gracchus persisted, 'I recall that you sang these words last night at the party:

> O thou who from us flyest to the lonely hermit cell
> as from the eagle's talon flies the dove
> involuntary exile there to dwell—
> thus sacrificing heavenly to an earthly love.

'You were singing them directly to Paolette, weren't you? And your meaning was that she was in the habit of trysting here in the chapel. Perhaps even on the night of Mombello's disappearance. No, don't try to blather me, I saw her reaction, which made sense only with that added significance.'

'Perhaps I have seen her here, what of it?'

'That is mischievous of you. But one thing interests me more than your mischief-making. How could you have known she was in the chapel that evening unless you too were outside?'

Charles picked up his hat, and turned it in his hands. 'You can hardly think that I am the ghoul, Gracchus.'

'I do not. I think you came here for a clandestine meeting with *Citoyenne* Josephine Bonaparte. Perhaps it was a meeting of the same nature as the one today.'

Charles replaced his hat on the altar. 'This chapel has the advantage of being outside the villa itself, but *inside* the cordon of sentries placed to prevent the ghoul's predations. As such it is suitable for meetings of a sensitive nature, and we adopted it after the cordon was instituted by Berthier.'

'How many times?'

'More than once...' prevaricated Charles, mortified by the turn of conversation, but unable to fashion an escape.

'I imagine you were not the only ones?'

Charles hesitated. 'We were not, but you can scarcely expect me to provide a list, to inform on my fellow officers...'

'I expect you to do just that, in order to keep the details of your own movements private.'

Charles sighed. 'There were others. Doubtless you are aware that Berthier is conducting an intrigue with one of Josephine's friends?'

'So, you are asking me to believe that the chapel is a trysting point for half the officers on the staff, and assorted sky-clad naiads?'

Charles scraped back his heels. 'You may consider me a poor figure, but I hope that you will not find me betraying my companions. Isn't it enough that you have a sword over the head of us all, must you persecute the women too?' He stalked up and down the nave testily. 'Oh very well, if Josephine has to take her pug out before she retires, she naturally requires an escort, especially after what happened to the other dogs.'

'What did happen to the other dogs?' asked Gracchus.

'The ghoul took them one by one. Their bodies were never found, only Fortune survives. Do you want to hear this or not?'

'Go on,' said Gracchus, watching him closely. Charles paused and made a show of admiring a funeral memorial. 'I arrived at the chapel about two, but trying the door, for the first time I found it locked. Initially I thought it was for security because these wedding corbeilles had been installed that day, but then I heard voices inside.'

'A man and a woman?'

'I don't know, they spoke indistinctly, or perhaps in Italian… I suppose so. I was curious and I remembered the ladders that had been used for decorating the chapel were left outside, so I went round to find one so that I could look through one of the windows in the dome to see who had taken possession of my bower, but…' he turned back to Gracchus, 'imagine my surprise to find one of the ladders already propped up, with a peeping tom at the top of it, looking through the self-same window I had intended to exploit.'

'What did you do?'

'I moved closer to try and see who it was, but all I could make out was that he wore a uniform.'

'That describes most of the men here.'

'I know, but he was distinctive in one way. It sounds strange to me saying it now, but I had the impression he was not a man at first. Josephine called me at that moment. She had arrived at the front of the chapel and was nervous she might be seen because the fireflies were out. She called softly, but it was enough to scare off the peeping tom. He scuttled down the ladder and off into the bushes in a trice. Again it unnerved me, something in the way he moved was not quite right; for a moment I thought he must be the ghoul. Ridiculous, I know. Anyway, I headed in the opposite direction, to warn Josephine that the chapel was locked and take her back to the villa.'

'And you saw nobody else outside the villa? You mentioned Paolette.'

Charles smiled. 'Mere malice, I'm afraid. Me and the villa coquette don't quite hit it off, and anyway, if she weren't one of the parties locked in the chapel, I would be amazed. She has a hand in every intrigue here, which I presume is why the General wants her married off as soon as possible – before she gets caught in much worse trouble.'

Chapter Six

Vanderville met Piotr outside the stable complex. He was limping, and his face was swollen and bruised. 'Honourable wounds?' Vanderville asked him. 'Were you scragged by the Guides?'

'The Guides? Christ, no. A Pole of the Legion did this to me.' Piotr tenderly touched his battered head.

'Your own men? But why?'

'Well, that's a long story,' Piotr sighed. 'Look, being the headquarters guard is ostensibly an honour. The pampered praetorians in the Guides are spoilt by having their new uniforms cut in Milan. The Polish Legion, on the other hand, are marching on their uppers, and it's humiliating to be on display in rags.' He scratched his bare head. 'It's all that idiot Fesch's fault.'

'Commissary Fesch? But he is a Bonaparte,' said Vanderville.

'Fesch will happily put temporary family loyalties aside to establish a permanent position of profitability.'

'I thought the commissary officers were forbidden to invest personally in the army supply contracts?' said Vanderville. 'I know they take backhanders from the bidders of course.'

'You didn't know? Everyone except the General seems to. Or they at least suspect that his uncle competes with his wife as a speculator. They borrow money to buy the materials and then award themselves the contracts. The General is oblivious to his wife's faults, of course.'

'But what does this have to do with the Polish Legion?'

'Fesch and the General's wife have each had some small success with clothing contracts, and now want to expand their operations to take in the rest of the army. The Guides contract brought in peanuts, so they are setting their sights a little higher. Can you imagine? The profits on supplying cloth to thirty thousand men would be worth having. The sort of money people kill for...' said Piotr darkly.

'And they are beginning with the Polish Legion contracts?' prompted Vanderville.

Piotr held up his hand to slow Vanderville down. 'They both tried. Fesch took payment from the Polish Legion officers to pull the same trick on the Milanese merchants as Josephine did with the Guides. He had to use different merchants this time after Josephine swindled the last lot, but the influence of the General's family means that there is no shortage of willing dupes. Anyway, these dupes took time to find, and in the meantime the real supplies are about to arrive by convoy, rendering the Fesch contract unnecessary, and when the Poles asked for their money back, they were told they will have to wait for it.'

'You seem to know a lot about it,' said Vanderville.

Piotr shrugged. 'I don't want to be a pâtissier forever. Anyway, that's not the only reason there is bad feeling between me and the other Poles. They don't like me working in the kitchens, they think it's undignified and reflects badly on the Legion, and then they all go whoring together in the village, and that's not to my taste either. Our disagreements are of the longstanding kind I'm afraid.'

Gracchus bustled up behind them. 'Come here you two, I need you. There is a cacophony of Bonapartes here and I cannot untangle the members of this family. Piotr, you have been here since they arrived? Good. And your position in the household allows you to observe everybody, so you can be of great help to us.'

He gathered them around a table that had been dragged out of the courtyard into the sun, and commandeered chairs for them all. 'Wait, use these,' he said. 'Here is the table, covered in crumbs,' he swept them into a pile, 'and this pepper-pot represents General Bonaparte.' He crunched that article down on top of the crumbs. 'Now, this villa was the General's choice for a family reunion. Why? Because of the hot water from the springs. He likes a bath, and god knows he must have needed one after two hard seasons of campaigning. The Villa Mombello is an idyllic location for his new wife to play at being mistress of an Italian kingdom, so she is happy to have their much delayed honeymoon here. Two of his sisters need to be married, and his family need to meet his new wife Josephine for the first time. Because he is a man of affairs, he is also using the occasion to shore up his power by a display of martial splendour, while he organises the new political situation in Italy. A peace with the Austrian Empire needs to be cobbled together, and the Italian states the Austrians have been sucking the juice out of need to be reorganised into proper republics so that the French can take their turn as bloodsuckers instead.'

Ignoring Vanderville's protest at his last remarks, he smiled at a passing servant girl, '*Citoyenne*, please allow me some of your excellent cherries.' Espying her other full basket of apricots, he added, 'On second thoughts leave both baskets here, Piotr will carry them to the kitchens for you later.' He took two generous handfuls of fruit and spilled them onto the table. 'We can consider all of these fruit as the people in the villa. The fruit are trying to reach the crumbs that are all piled up here around General Bonaparte.'

'What is that?' said Vanderville, pointing at a green object.

'That is a dried goose shit,' said Gracchus, stuffing some cherries into his mouth. 'It will serve to represent Fesch. He is the half-brother of Letizia, the General's mother, which also makes him the General's uncle.' He sat back complacently and jettisoned a cherry stone over his shoulder. 'Here are the Bonaparte family, they are all cherries. Describe the rest of the Bonapartes to us, Piotr.'

'The eldest is Joseph, the demagogue, who is going to be sent to Rome to bicker with the Pope; he isn't here.'

'Yes, I think you may safely exclude those who are not present, thank you Piotr,' interjected Gracchus.

'Then there is our General Bonaparte,' continued Piotr. 'Next is Elisa, who is marrying Captain Baciocchi, and Paolette,' he darted a quick glance at Vanderville, 'who we all know about, then Caroline and Jerome, who are children. There are others, but they aren't here. Then there is Madame Letizia Buonaparte, their mother, who is not even that old.'

'The General has a mother, an uncle, and lots of hungry brothers and sisters then,' said Gracchus. 'To the children we can add Josephine's two children from her first marriage, but they are too young to be of much interest to us. All of these people control access to General Bonaparte.'

'In fact,' said Piotr, 'the Bonaparte family form two opposing camps, Josephine by marriage on one side, and the family under Letizia on the other. Whereas when Josephine arrived here, she held the coveted promise of access to Bonaparte, a matter of great importance to military and political figures, she has fumbled it, and got herself involved with diverse Italian contract speculators, so her partisans are sliding towards the family. And the family have a secret weapon, Paolette, who is seducing the military household to her service.'

Gracchus started arranging the apricots in ranks. 'These apricots are the Josephine Bonaparte faction, made up of her French and Italian friends. The French include General Leclerc, Lieutenant Charles, and *Citoyenne* Hamelin and her other friend, who both have their admirers among the officers and diplomats. Her new Italian circle consists most immediately of women, backed by powerful supporters. The subjects of the affection of Berthier and Dumas are found there, so we can consider those two influential generals as also being Josephine's partisans. Mingled with the family circle you have the speculators made up of contractors and commissaries; we have also the diplomats. And then there are the rest of the army officers, whose affiliations are presently unknown, all scrabbling for crumbs from the General's table.'

'A fascinating exercise in power politics,' said Vanderville. 'Where does this get us in the investigation of Mombello's disappearance?'

'I'm coming to that,' said Gracchus, turning his ruminative attentions to the basket of apricots. 'The Comte Mombello is connected to the Bonaparte family through the position he held in Corsica twenty-odd years ago. We could assume that his relations at that time were mainly with Carlo Bonaparte, the General's father. His immediate concern here was with General Bonaparte in connection with the new Transpadane Republic, and presumably persuading Bonaparte to leave Milan and set up his headquarters at Mombello was a diplomatic coup of sorts.'

'I still can't see who had a sufficient motive to wish him harm,' said Vanderville.

Gracchus shovelled a few more cherries into his mouth. 'I suspect that the answer may lie in the events of the night of the comte's disappearance. It seems to me that our friends in the villa are a little reticent about that evening. Something embarrassing happened that we need to know about. I broached the subject in the salon yesterday, and as soon as I invited the company to dwell on the incident, they reacted like a gaggle of nuns who'd had an interesting experience viewing the secret cabinet frescoes at Pompeii. I want to know what happened at that party.'

He leant over the table to reach more cherries, and Vanderville saw him slip something under the basket. 'Piotr, you and Leonardi were the only two from the kitchens present during or after supper that evening. Why was that?'

'Bonaparte relishes the opportunity to shed the tiresome etiquette that he is subjected to all the day long. He complains that he begins to be bound by the strictures of a court. The evenings are for the family and the favourite officers of his military household, and recall to him the easy bonhomie that is already starting to elude him as he becomes an important man. He guards these moments jealously, and in fact that is why he invited Leonardi upstairs, to congratulate him on the success of his dining experiment. This was the first occasion on which it was applied here, and it was successful.'

'I have seen his kitchen serving rotating apparatus,' said Gracchus. 'How does it relate to the service upstairs?'

'Leonardi is a devotee of the Russian service, where one course is served at a time, to stop the food from getting cold. Bonaparte was not initially in favour of this because he does not care to stay that long at table. However, the other innovation adopted by Leonardi is the almost total absence of servants at table. The food is delivered by the rotating apparatus from the kitchen, and I alone serve it from there to the table, which speeds things up. Orders are conveyed to the kitchen by a speaking tube. The tube is decorated with the head of a cook upstairs, and an ass's backside in the kitchen end. Sometimes Leonardi asks me to leave the cap off the speaking tube upstairs, so that he can hear what passes in the salon above. He loves ghost stories.'

'We had a sample of them from the General's mother yesterday. I cannot say it is my idea of entertainment,' said Vanderville.

'That was a brief one last night, probably because the one the comte told on the night he went missing caused so much trouble.' Piotr sighed. 'On that evening there was a ghost play where some of the *citoyennes* acted parts. Even the General participates sometimes,' he said, smiling. 'He asks the company's leave to take off his coat and gathers up napkins and tablecloths to make costumes. I like it best when the young *citoyennes* go behind armchairs to deck themselves out and emerge suddenly in grotesque disguises.'

'Why was there trouble that night?' asked Gracchus.

'It was Comte Mombello's turn to suggest a ghost theme. He came out with some Corsican traditional folklore; I missed part of his speech because I had to get my ices from the cellar. I made something special that evening, so I remember it well: a sorbetto of pears and scorched lemon with ratafia biscuits. The comte ate three,' he said contentedly.

'Think now, Piotr,' said Gracchus, 'anything you can remember of the party might be very important in solving the mystery of the comte's death.'

'I can't recall any details of the play,' said Piotr, 'all I can remember is that Comte Mombello's story must have shown the islanders in a bad light, because the General was angry with the parts given to his sisters, and instantly banned any more Corsican stories. His wife pretended to be upset at this misunderstanding, but I think she was maliciously pleased to see Madame Buonaparte also annoyed by the theme. That's how you tell them apart, by the way: the mother uses the Italian spelling and pronunciation, and the wife the French. Anyway, then the Comte Mombello tried to cheer them all up, but he said something to Madame Buonaparte that made her more angry, and then Alexandre started on his uncle, and there was an atmosphere, so I made an excuse to go back to the kitchen.'

'Thank you, Piotr,' said Gracchus. He looked at his pocket watch. 'I think I had better go to the press office now, before Berthier has the opportunity to reprimand me again. Vanderville, I will be asleep under my desk, so if you feel the need to check up on me, please do it quietly.'

'Will you be safe with the Poles now?' Vanderville asked Piotr.

'Don't worry about me,' said Piotr, standing up and taking the fruit baskets with a yawn. He picked up the red cap that was on the table where the baskets had been. 'I have to sleep too, I'm exhausted. I'll see you both later, at the funeral.'

–

After supper, the men gathered in the covered courtyard for the funeral. There, hatbands, gloves, and cloaks were supplied, and torches lit. Vanderville could not help but notice the grace with which Fesch donned his cloak. The dignity suited him. 'I used to be a priest, you see,' he explained. 'Today I am assisting too, on account of this being such a small parish, and time being short.'

'It seems there is some haste to inter the Comte Mombello,' said Vanderville.

'You are from the north I believe,' smiled Fesch. 'Funerals follow quickly in warm countries, and in this case, the weddings cannot be delayed, so Mombello's mortal remains must be interred with no delay. The remarkable Berthier has arranged everything with Alexandre. He is just the man for this sort of work.'

'Burying people?' asked Gracchus, who was finishing an apple.

'Military organisation,' replied Fesch primly.

'Are night funerals common here?' asked Vanderville.

'Not at all, it was Alexandre's wish. It is remarkably picturesque though, isn't it?'

Under the awning was a bier cart, harnessed to four horses with nodding plumes. In the distance the chapel bell was tolling to announce the dead comte's last journey and the carriage drive was lined with the Polish Legion, sombre with inverted muskets. There were mourning veils on their standards, and the black-swathed drums rolled deeply as the bier set off. The route to the chapel would leave the estate and pass through the village, heading through the chestnut woods to arrive at the chapel by means of a gentler descent.

Alexandre led the procession, alone and bareheaded. Gracchus walked behind the bier in the procession with Fesch and Vanderville. 'Super priestcraft, this republican carnival,' purred Fesch out of the side of his mouth.

'Conspicuous display as a balm to the bereaved?' said Gracchus.

'The art of aweing the laity, managing their consciences, and diving into their pockets,' chuckled Fesch.

'Leonardi says it will rain,' grunted Gracchus as they set off. His face was gleaming under the torches. 'The fireflies have stayed away, and as a barometer they are infallible.'

It continued fine however, and on the pathway through the woods there were mourners from the village and the villa, bearing cypress branches, and on the approach to the final resting place the village girls scattered flowers from baskets before the cortege. Their flimsy attire attracted the appreciation of those officers not personally concerned with the grave occasion.

'In Corsica,' explained Fesch to Gracchus, 'I once presided at a funeral where the widow dreamed that the coffin contained the still living body of her husband. She stopped the procession, broke open the coffin, and tore the shroud from the corpse.'

'The story is universal,' said Piotr behind them, 'My mother told a version where the coffin contained the spirit of one who refused to die. He could be saved if released from the coffin before the procession crossed a river.'

'Let us hope nobody tries that today,' said Fesch, 'our dear General is quite intent on making a good impression on the locals with a bit of spectacle.'

'Corsican Christianity appears to suffer little from orthodoxy,' commented Gracchus.

'Downright heretical, I do assure you,' said Fesch earnestly.

The chapel was wreathed in tendrils of smoke from odiferous woods and incense burned on two makeshift altars before the door. Under the lowering sky the trapped smoke cast a pall in the gathering dusk, filling the clearing with its musk. 'Admirable,' whispered Gracchus through a cough, moved by a mixture of fascination and repulsion, 'the whole ceremony looted wholesale from the ancients.'

The coffin was carried inside by the principal mourners, crunching strewn flowers underfoot. They heaved the thing onto the table that awaited it inside the chapel, where the *citoyennes* were waiting to recite a rosario over the bier. The addition of burning torches to the incense and fuming candles inside the pokey space brought water to Fesch's eyes as he pronounced blessings and prayers for the soul of the dead man.

The bell tolled again and the lid of the coffin was removed, exposing the shrouded form of the comte. Alexandre kissed his uncle, and then he was closed over. A great catafalque shroud was drawn over the coffin. The heavily painted cloth depicted a sepulchre, raised like a table tomb. The base of the tomb was rent asunder, and a mazy mass of skeletons tumbled out, clawing and biting at each other. All were agrin, and some retained a shrivelled part of their flesh and hair on their stony crania. One of the dead clutched a dead child to its remaining breast, in fear of its ravening brethren. Above all this grotesquery swooped a winged death's angel, bearing a scythe, and sounding the last trumpet. 'What the hell is that?' whispered Vanderville.

'Alexandre found it in the chapel,' murmured Charles at his side.

'It is quite horrible,' said Paolette too loudly, 'it reminds me of the stories Mamma used to tell us when we were children.'

What on earth or below all this signified was beyond Gracchus. It seemed an inversion of the sounding of the trumpet, the risen dead not restored to life, as the gospels promised, but clawing desperately at each other and preserved in their rags and foulness for all eternity. 'Grotesque,' he commented to Vanderville, 'better to have gone without.'

The republican funeral orator, who in an admirable spirit of compromise was the local priest transformed by a tricolour sash around his ample girth and a cockade in his hat, delivered his patter. Then honey was poured around the coffin in homage to the dead man's sweetness of character, milk in virtue of his candour, wine to commemorate his strength, and lastly incense that his good actions might fill the tableau of his life like smoke.

The bell tolled a third time. This was the signal for the funeral journey to end. The coffin would be consigned later to the prepared vault in the nymphaeum after the departure of the mourners; nobody fancying manhandling it through the hole in the floor in the presence of witnesses. As the party exited the chapel there was an untimely clap of thunder and before they could assemble correctly for the passage to the villa the funeral was ended by the onset of a torrential rainstorm. All the mourners and the curious fled away for cover as if a great broom had passed through the gardens. Only a bareheaded Alexandre and his friend Piotr stayed, drenched by the rain, to bid the Comte Mombello goodbye.

Chapter Seven

The next morning Gracchus began examining the sentry reports Vanderville had supplied in the stable room he had commandeered as his print office. They were inconclusive. The sentries had seen a number of officers passing outside the house by the light of the fireflies, some said three and some four, but they could not identify them. They had been astonished at the number breaking curfew, not having been able to see anyone on previous nights owing to the dark. They were adamant on one point, however; none had seen a woman, or an elderly civilian who might have been Mombello. Gracchus shoved the reports away impatiently. Through the window he saw Berthier marching purposefully through the stable yard towards him. Berthier stuck his glowering head through the window and brandished a news sheet at Gracchus, who was resting with his feet up on his desk, amid the debris of his profession.

'Gracchus, I've been reading your first issue – your allegory of the Transpadane Republic as a goose turd that France just stepped in is unacceptable. Pulp the run and begin again. And Gracchus? Once more, just once more…'

Gracchus casually took the news sheet from Berthier's outstretched hand and glanced at it without interest. Outside, Berthier had commenced a vigorous circumnavigation of the courtyard, scattering nervous soldiers and somnambulant chickens alike, and Gracchus went to catch him up. Limping up to him, he tucked the sheet under his arm and asked, 'What's all the fuss about?' gesturing at the carpenters who were setting up wooden scaffolding around the sides of the yard.

'Thanks to General Dumas's unique conception of crowd control we are committed to providing a wedding festival for the soldiers,' moaned Berthier. He stopped walking and turned to face Gracchus. 'I have even more work to do as a result. But since you are here to annoy me, give me the results of your investigation. Bonaparte wants them now.'

Gracchus stared at the carpenters with a constrained and artificial sense of interest and said, 'It is essential to my investigation that we start a more rigorous approach. This morning I went to Mombello's library to see his personal papers, I am particularly interested in those documents he was working on prior to his disappearance, but his desk has been cleared. The valet says he was working on the genealogy section of his memoirs, but those papers are all missing.'

Berthier considered him carefully. 'All of his personal papers will have been secured, as is customary when a death occurs. They are in the General's study waiting for the advocates who will need them to arrange the transfer of patrimony.'

Gracchus ground his teeth. The byzantine inheritance laws by which property transferred from the deceased generation to the warmer, more ambulant one could not be accomplished without the interested intervention of a legion of advocates and archivistae. These bow-legged be-wigged bloodsuckers could be seen emerging from their dusty premises at the time of funerals, brandishing bundles of documents on land law, and croaking about precedent and primogeniture. They were like so many creaky old fleas crawling from an old bed's crevices, roused from dormancy by the sanguine prospect of warm bodies to feed upon. 'That process could take years, I need to see the papers now.'

'I presume you are aware of what you are requesting. Bonaparte will not want to be seen to interfere.'

Gracchus stared back at him blandly. 'I have done this sort of thing once or twice before. If you give me the keys, I will be discreet and quick.'

Berthier interrupted their progress to instruct a carpenter working underneath some temporary seating stands in some point of detail. His instructions given, he straightened up and said, 'Oh, very well, Gracchus. Do what you must, in your own way, but certainly do it quickly. The General and his wife are in Milan this morning and may be absent some hours. What is most essential is that you report developments immediately to me alone, and do not allow any more rumours or conjecture to flow. It obstructs the work we are doing here. Do you understand? Good, now play the game discreetly, and at least pretend to edit this wretched news sheet.'

He walked off to remonstrate with another of the workmen, and Gracchus grunted happily, screwing up the newspaper and letting it fall carelessly to the ground. He had omitted to mention to Berthier his intention to question General Bonaparte himself at the first opportunity. It suddenly occurred to him that Berthier had not actually given him the key to Bonaparte's study. He gazed around the stable yard. He would only be in the way there, and having been disturbed from repose at his desk, he could see no better use of his time now than to make his way to the kitchen to beg a snack from Leonardi.

—

Vanderville was walking with Paolette in the garden. They had been talking of this and that inconsequentially as they strolled, and Vanderville had been commenting on the very pleasant gardens when she stopped short before a statue of some cavorting strumpet, leaning on it as if to emphasise the contrast between the cold stone figure and herself. 'Pretty gardens are all very well, but I would rather be in Milan. Why are we all locked up here in this villa, Vanderville?'

He leant on his sabre, and attempted a jocular, worldly tone. 'To arrange the affairs of Italy, make peace with the Austrian Empire, and save the world by installing a new republic on each street corner.'

'That might be why you are here,' she said. 'Know why we Bonapartes are here? Elisa is becoming too round in the middle for her many dresses. She is twenty now and must marry the first person who asks her, who happens to be Baciocchi. I must marry General Leclerc, a complete stranger, because my brother likes him, and he has beaten lots of Austrians. But you know what Mamma says? The real reason we all had to come here is for my brother's new wife to confront her new relatives, his family. Which actually means Mamma, who is the only one who counts. He made no attempt to win us over before his marriage, knowing that it was hopeless. He forced Mamma and Giuseppe – sorry *Joseph* – to write to her saying how pleased we all were by the marriage and how we were dying to meet her, and Joseph also had to go to meet her in Paris. He told me afterwards that she was old and not pretty, which seemed unfair to me. Do you think she is pretty?'

'Certainly, she is charming,' began Vanderville and then, seeing Paolette's pout, 'Not to my taste though.' Vanderville found himself adjusting his posture to incline himself more in her direction, and in an effort to correct the overfamiliarity he lurched awkwardly backwards, nearly tripping over his sabre.

'Well, she certainly is ancient,' said Paolette, who appeared not to have noticed his clumsiness. 'She is nearly forty. Do you think some men like that? Charles seems to. I think I will vomit if I hear one more remark about Creole grace.' She sighed heavily.

It was hard, Vanderville thought, to imagine a prettier sigh, and he was overcome with voluptuous thoughts. He allowed his boot to graze her exquisite foot and she did not move away immediately. Pulling himself together with an effort, he decided to steer the conversation towards safer ground. 'And how is the blending of the Bonapartes and Josephine's family preceding now that you have got to know each other?' he asked.

'Before we came here, Mamma said that Josephine's character was damaged, like all of these Parisian ladies, but now she doesn't say anything, and Josephine is sucking up to her anyway.'

'Your mother did not take the news of your brother's marriage well then?'

She looked directly at him. 'Like a death in the family.'

'And do *you* find the Parisienne to your taste?'

Paolette considered, her head cocked. 'She gave me some of her old dresses, which was mean. She could have brought me new ones from Paris, she has hundreds, and I have to wear these old things.' She gestured at the elegant scraps of cloth she wore. The statue above her was more heavily clothed. 'The Italian food is making me put on weight, and I need new things,' she said, and nudged Vanderville with her toe.

Vanderville eyed her with what he hoped was a non-partisan eye and muttered about the benefits to health of the Italian climate and diet. A string of geese wandered up to them and formed a circle at his feet.

'These Parisiennes,' she continued, 'her and Hamelin. They all have many special *friends*. And they are always having ruptures with their *friends*. It's so tiring. Will you be my friend here? I need somebody on my side to look after me.'

Vanderville found himself agreeing effusively before he quite knew what he was agreeing to. 'Actually, my dear Paolette, I do have a few questions about some of our fellow guests here,' he began. His voice sounded wretched, and as usual his stomach quivered in her presence. He frowned at the geese. He was aware of cutting a poor figure, and the feeling was compounded as Charles rounded the corner of a hedge with his habitual debonair swagger, and spotting them with a friendly wave, sauntered up.

'Ah, good morning *citoyenne*,' he said to Paolette with a graceful sweep of his hat. 'What do you think of the preparations for the wedding festival?'

'Hello Lieutenant Charles. I haven't seen them; we aren't supposed to linger with the soldiers in the stable yard.' She frowned and pointed at his sabre hilt. 'Oh! What a pretty new sword you have, may I see it?'

Charles drew his weapon with an elegant flourish and handed it to her mock bashfully. Paolette held it in both hands, and turned it from side to side to admire it. It was a little light for Vanderville's taste but he admired the ebony wood hilt finely worked in silver. Both hilt and blade were copiously engraved with entwined republican motifs.

Paolette said, 'I suppose you are going to chase the poor ghoul with this silly little sword?' She swiped it at a goose playfully.

Charles mused, 'That reminds me of our Piedmont campaign. They have a marvellous method of sweeping chimneys there. They place a goose on the chimney with a string tied around her feet, and then draw her down the chimney to the hearth. Better than a brush I assure you.'

Paolette spluttered, 'You ugly bandit Charles! How cruel that would be. Poor goose.'

'You are right,' said Charles, 'a duck would do as well.'

Paolette handed Charles back his sabre. 'You are an idiot, I can't see what my aunt sees in you.'

–

By the afternoon, Berthier's swarm of engineers had entirely transformed the stable courtyard. Along the two sides not pierced by gateways they had erected wooden stands with stepped seating that rose to the first-floor gallery. Swags of bunting came from all corners of the rooftops to the central great pine, which had been garlanded and laden with republican imagery. The trunk was swaddled in bundled fascines that rose from wooden trophies of arms roughly crafted and painted for the wedding festival. From Gracchus's vantage point in the galleries, it seemed that every soldier of the Poles and Guides not immediately on duty had crammed into the space, and they were mixed indiscriminately with the women of the camp, the gardeners, servants of the villa, and some of the braver or more curious village people. The effect was picturesque; with the

Poles in their blue and yellow uniforms, and the Guides in their green and red, it had the feeling of sporting colours at the horse races. The fraught atmosphere of the morning was entirely dissipated in the intense and joyful anticipation of good things to come.

With the General and his wife away in Milan with the Parisian faction, some of the tension in the villa had evaporated. Vanderville craned his head forward to peer at the quality seats below them. Elisa Bonaparte was laughing good-humouredly with the younger children, but there was no sign of Paolette. Lieutenant Charles was talking animatedly with Captain Baciocchi, and Generals Dumas and Leclerc were waiting attendance upon Letizia Buonaparte, who was almost smiling as she chatted with Commissary Fesch, her customary dignity momentarily set aside.

Charles had abandoned his spot in the galleries to Gracchus, with the excuse that Josephine had begged him to reserve a spot in the stands in case she returned earlier than expected from Milan, so Vanderville and Gracchus stood companionably together at the parapet, looking down on the scene with Hercule and Alexandre. The young lieutenants were discussing the relative merits of their generals.

Alexandre was teasing Hercule. 'Charles said earlier that he dislikes your General Bonaparte because he is the sort of general who sends men across a river on a rickety collapsing bridge.'

'There is something in that,' mused Hercule. 'Yet it strikes me that *his* General Leclerc is the sort of general who calls out to men almost across a river on that collapsing bridge to "come back".'

'Whereas Berthier,' smiled Vanderville, 'sends both orders simultaneously, "Go on... come back."'

'In triplicate, mind!' laughed Hercule.

'And General Dumas?' Gracchus asked Vanderville, and the lieutenants smirked knowingly at each other.

'Him?' said Hercule. 'He would lead the cavalry over the bridge at a gallop as it falls under him of course.'

'But he would set fire to it first because it looks more dramatic,' replied Vanderville, deadpan.

Content with this analysis of their superiors, they turned their attention to the events in the yard. Following the affray between the Poles and the Guides, there had been an agreement that the fencing masters of each faction would do battle together in display duels to dispel the rancour. General Berthier had turned a temporary blind eye to this demonstration of *esprit de corps*, duelling being banned in his ordinances. In an unusual display of discretion, he had also arranged to arrive after these contests, having pled pressures of work. The duels went off creditably, with honours equally distributed, even if they were not as bloodless as advertised, and preparations for the goose running commenced. When a messenger arrived, bearing news that the supply convoys were passing the nearest village, the acclaim was universal. Vanderville peered at the seats below them again. There was still no sign of Paolette.

'Why, it's a regular vaudeville,' Gracchus was expostulating to someone, as the soldiers cheered rowdily. 'Who ever heard of a goose festival in June?'

'Does it matter?' asked Hercule, who had just returned bloody from his part in the duels, his head bandaged. 'The wedding is as good a reason to celebrate as any other, and it takes their mind off the ghoul.'

Gracchus considered this and fretted, 'But the geese will not eat well, taken too young. Gastronomy respects the calendar with good reason, and Leonardi is right in being opposed to eating goose before St Martin's day in principle. Reasons of digestion alone require...'

'Calendar?' interrupted Hercule good-naturedly. 'What does it matter? We have a new calendar anyway thanks to the French Republic, and doubtless the Transpadane Republic will gift us another variant, just to show they are capable of comparable idiocy. The Polish Legion are crazy about their geese, they have been fattening them since we got here, it's like a religion to them, and the Poles are right. The geese are here. We are here. Let us have a party. By October we could all be dead anyway if the Austrians come again.'

Alexandre added, 'The soldiers want the supply train. Green cloth for the Guides arrived last week, today brings blue for the Poles. The *citoyennes* await their promised ball dresses so that the Italians can vie with the Parisians in elegance and novelty. The officers want to be presentable for the ladies at the ball. Charles has been seen practising in his buskin boots and they all mocked him, and then immediately went out and ordered their own pairs. Paolette and Elisa desperately want their trousseaus.'

Gracchus sighed at these demonstrations of military logic and turned his attention to the goose-running preparations. A path from one stable gate to the other had been marked out the length of the stable yard; over the centre line of this, at a distance of about three metres from the ground, stretched a rope, by which a protesting goose was tied by a cord from the legs. The rope hung slack, so as to allow it to vibrate in an arc, bringing the breast of the creature within bare reach of a rider upon a horse of common size. Hercule, who had served with the Poles, described the rules of the game to the others. 'The rope is agitated by the men at the sides, so that the goose bobs up and down, and rotates in a circle. As the goose swings in the air, the champions ride one after another, full speed, under the rope, and rising in the stirrups, catch at the animal's head. He who keeps his seat in his saddle and his hold of the bird's head, carries it off in his hand, and takes the victor's palm.'

'They are smearing the goose's throat with oil so that the animal is harder to grasp,' said Alexandre.

'This is a curious barbarism,' pondered Gracchus. 'So the more the poor goose cries, the more she gets tortured, and the bigger the satisfaction for the spectators.'

Hercule shrugged. 'It is nothing, a bagatelle. In Holland they perform this game on skates. In Corsica they perform octopus wrestling. Now that is a sport.' He smacked his lips with relish.

Berthier arrived in the stands with *Citoyenne* Visconti in a bustle of haste, dictating to a secretary trailing behind him. Everyone stood as he pushed his way along the seats to the place of honour by Letizia. As it became apparent that there was insufficient room, and nobody had saved him a space, Charles rose, and proffered his seat. 'I had better go and get ready,' he announced.

'Are you in the running then?' asked *Citoyenne* Visconti.

'Some of the champions were injured in the duels, and I have been roped in to help the Polish Legion,' he explained ruefully. 'We will still beat the Guides – their best men are with the General in Milan.'

'Not all of them,' came the voice of Hercule from above. He vaulted from the gallery and landed on the stands beside Charles with a considerable thump. The impact from the leap caused his duelling wound to open, and a trickle of blood escaped his bandage. Visconti shrieked affectedly and clutched at Berthier.

'But you must have a favour,' exclaimed *Citoyenne* Hamelin to Charles. 'Josephine, Our Lady of Victory is not here, but will you accept something from me?' and to the general appreciation of the officers, she raised her leg on the back of the bench below her and unrolled a superb garter from her stocking. 'A little bit of Paris to carry on your lance,' she explained, handing it to Charles, who raised it to his lips with a smiling salute. Letizia sniffed impatiently and Elisa snorted with scorn. Hercule bowed extravagantly to Visconti. 'May I too beg some mark of your favour, fair *citoyenne*?'

'No, you may not. Get moving, Lieutenant,' said Berthier. 'You are obstructing the view for the *citoyennes*.' Charles contrived to clank his silver sabre over Berthier's toe as he shuffled out.

Vanderville made his excuses and went to join the assembling riders. Gracchus turned to smile at Alexandre, who was alone beside him on the gallery, and said, 'It is a great shame your uncle is not here to enjoy all of this.'

'What do you mean by that?' said Alexandre, through clenched teeth, and Gracchus was astonished to see that he was almost angry. He tried again, 'As a dedicated republican, he would surely have enjoyed seeing the stables decorated for the common soldiers enjoying the hospitality of the villa, the liberty tree...'

'In my opinion the creation of a liberty tree was already long overdue on this estate,' said Alexandre, not taking his eyes off the revelry below. 'It was *my* suggestion that we install it in the courtyard of the stables, where the soldiers congregate. The Comte decided it would be sufficient to put a Phrygian bonnet on top of the tree already here, rather than erect a proper one. He was also not in favour of trimming it to a naked pole, which is the established mode. I urged him to consider the beneficial effect on the troops and servants that a correct and vivid expression of his republican feelings would have; he asserted his authority rather abruptly, and we parted in disagreement. That was to be the last conversation we ever had.'

Gracchus considered this. The conversation had already been recounted to him by Piotr, whose rendition rendered it a virtual screaming match over whether removing boughs of the tree represented an homage or an insult to the tree as an incarnation of Liberty, concluding with Alexandre asking his uncle, 'What sort of a republican are you?' to which the old man answered, 'The sort with good taste. I *am* a republican; I just don't want to be an infernal nuisance about it.'

The two accounts tallied, thought Gracchus. 'So you never laid eyes on him again after that?'

Alexandre hesitated. 'No, I suppose I didn't. We were disturbing the company with our row, and he suggested that we meet later to continue our discussion in privacy. I walked in the gardens for a while but he didn't arrive, so I went to bed.'

'But this is of the greatest importance. Why didn't you mention it before? If you were outside the house that evening you may have seen something. Did you encounter anyone else? Think very carefully, the smallest detail may be important.'

'No one. I saw no one,' said Alexandre, and then testily, 'Doesn't it bother you, grubbing around in the private lives of your acquaintance? Surely you must see how strongly any feeling person must resent such enquiries?'

'I can't say honestly that it does,' replied Gracchus. 'Nor do I take my honour lightly enough to involve it in such trivial matters. If you are inclined to take offence, I will desist.'

Alexandre glanced at him sideways. 'You are in the right of it, I believe,' he said. 'Forgive me, Gracchus, these past days have been a great strain on me.'

'Every stone raised runs the risk of revealing crawling things beneath,' Gracchus replied gruffly, 'but without turning stones I cannot bring light to hidden things.'

'I think I understand,' said Alexandre. He rubbed his chin thoughtfully. 'My uncle and I clashing over the soup about his lukewarm principles regarding the new Transpadane Republic was not unusual. By the time Piotr brought ices rounds, we had progressed to arguing about the colour of the uniforms for the new army. Hardly grounds for patricide, even on a bad day.' He frowned. 'We are missing rather a lot of the races, Gracchus, would you mind awfully if we watched them now?'

Gracchus sighed, and a roar from the crowd dragged his attention back to the spectacle. The decrease in the size of the groups of mounted men at opposing ends of the courtyard announced that the spectacle was reaching the climatic stages.

'Hercule was the last rider and has taken one goose for the Guides, and now it stands at one goose for the Polish Legion and one for the Guides,' said Alexandre. 'He has withdrawn injured. If the Guides can scratch up a substitute there will be one more pass for each team, and because the game is drawn, the last passes will be repeated simultaneously until the goose is snatched. The first team to take it will win.'

Outside the courtyard, Vanderville helped Hercule to sit on a grassy bank. He was limping, and it was apparent that his bridle arm was injured as well as his head. 'It is nothing,' he said hoarsely, 'the arm is jarred, that's all.' It was obvious to Vanderville that he would be forced to withdraw despite his protestations, and already another rider for the Guides cantered up. He circled his mount impatiently as they waited for the debris of the collision to be moved away, and for the third goose to be strung. Despite the warmth of the day, the rider was swathed in a white cloak drawn up about his face. As the horse passed, the back of the cloak rode up, revealing a flash of the Guides' cherry red *pantalons*, and Vanderville noticed with a start that they were filled with an emphatically female form. He stood to speak to the rider, but before he could confirm his suspicions the bugle sounded the signal for Lieutenant Charles, riding for the Polish Legion, to start his run from the far end of the yard. At the same time the cloaked Guide put spurs to mount and hurtled through the archway and down the course with a spattering of muddy gobbets.

The crowd roared with anticipation as Lieutenant Charles and the cloaked Guide converged on the dangling goose. Charles looked as if he would reach the goose first, and stood higher in his stirrups to wave the interloper off, but the cloaked figure was grimly intent on the prize and ignored him. Charles hunkered down, touching spurs to his mount to make up the ground. His horsemanship was better, and as he approached the goose, he was off his saddle, reaching up, and out, and his gloved hand closed around the unfortunate bird's neck, bending the rope as his momentum carried him past. His grip was true, and the taut line parted from the goose's feet with a snap. At that moment, the onrushing Guide drove a shoulder hard into Charles's flank under his raised arm. The shock was terrible, and Charles was dashed to the ground. The Guide's horse stumbled, and it appeared the rider would be thrown, but the horse somehow kept its feet, and in the confusion the Guide lurched back into the saddle, and rode clear, brandishing the feathered trophy aloft.

A huge cheer went up from one half of the stable yard, and a roar of protestations from the other. The Guide circled the yard once in triumph, before dashing back out through the garden arch with a clatter of hooves, goose in hand.

There was no shortage of hands to help the fallen rider and recover his mount. Gracchus craned forward in the stands to watch. It appeared that Charles was badly shaken but not irrevocably broken, and between the attentions of the Polish team-hands and the hovering ministrations of *Citoyennes* Hamelin and Visconti he was able to put a brave face upon it. Some of the Poles were urging him to protest, and hotly indicating that Berthier should declare the run void, but a pale-faced Charles inched painfully to a seated posture and declared, 'No, no, it was bravely done, and a fitting result. I salute our mystery rider.' His graceful concession defused the disputing team's ardour, and Berthier rose to signal the running closed and salute the victors.

–

'Right, let us get this Jack-at-the-fair show organised,' growled General Dumas, as the first of the supply waggons pulled up outside the inn arch, and he pushed through the crowd to the carts. With the help of a quartermaster, he isolated the cart holding the supplies for the villa and sent the others for the soldiers on to the camp.

Momentarily that great waggon cleared the inn arch, clattered past the tables under the giant pine and trundled towards the rear of the courtyard where the little boy driving slid adroitly from his seat, which was at least as high as his head, ducked under the traces, freed the hairy nags from their shackles and led them off to stand near the trough. Another lad chocked the cart with stones from a convenient mossy pile under the trough and Dumas posted two sentries to usher the mob away from the cart.

At the inn end, half a dozen women of the camp had commenced furiously plucking away at some geese. The light breeze was swooping up the feathers and they danced around the yard like a snowstorm while the camp children danced and shrieked in the make-believe blizzard. Dumas took post to watch the goose-plucking contest and time the contestants with his pocket watch. He was mouthing to himself like a slow reader and as Vanderville came up to him he said, 'I thought there was something rather good to say. It is on the tip of my tongue, but it won't quite come. Never mind.' He clapped Vanderville on the back, and handed him his watch. 'You are in charge here, make sure they clean up afterwards. I'm going to supervise the unloading.'

From the gallery Gracchus was also intent on the frenzied goose plucking. The women were singing a work shanty as they laboured and he found the rhythmic motions of their arms in the billowing feather storm most picturesque. He was surprised to see that Letizia had commandeered a work apron, and she and Elisa were marshalling the younger Bonaparte children to join the contest. They proved unexpectedly skilled at the plebian pursuit, which won the crowd over to their team. Gracchus was intrigued by this example of condescension, at odds with the usual dignity of the Bonaparte household. Letizia and Elisa were smiling, enjoying themselves, and Gracchus wondered what the General's response would be to this sacrifice of dignity for the sake of popular esteem. He did not have long to wait for his answer, because his musings were interrupted when the carriages of Bonaparte and Josephine's party returned from their excursion to Milan.

The first carriage to pull up in the yard contained the General and his wife. It was one of the fashionable Milanese open carriages, set low on its axles so that those within could easily converse with pedestrians. It bore neither crest nor device and was lined in white padded upholstery picked out with green on which Josephine's perfumed and coiffed pug Fortune sprawled. The coachman sported a well-brushed white hat, and a tight coat decorated with pearl buttons and a posy in the buttonhole. The effect was refined in the extreme, and the second carriage, crowded with the coterie of Josephine in their plumed martial casques, was no less tasteful.

The visions of elegance who descended daintily from the carriages in white kidskin boots, as if they had arrived from the rarefied world of the cloud dwelling deities sported on the frescos of the Villa Mombello, contrasted rudely with the Bonaparte women in aprons and with feather-matted fingers. The effect was too clear to escape the General, and his brow knitted as his mother and sisters rose anxiously to greet him. Gracchus could not hear the brief words that passed, but as the General left his mother, her crestfallen face told the story. The aloof Milanese and Parisienne goddesses fluttered past the feather-sodden party with not even a glance, and the crowd followed them.

Arriving at the supply waggon Bonaparte was flanked by General Leclerc and Captain Baciocchi, the men betrothed to his sisters. Berthier joined them clutching inventory sheets. Two soldiers scaled the mountain towering atop the vehicle and began stripping its canvas cover, and the Parisiennes dissolved into a jostling swarm, clamouring and reaching up for the exposed bundles. 'Bonaparte!' Josephine rallied her husband, 'I am in command here!' and she directed one of her friends to take over from the beleaguered men stationed on top of the supplies. Hamelin shrugged off her shawl to the cheers of the laughing soldiers, and two Guides lifted her onto the waggon where she commenced delving among the packages and occasionally tossing one to the *citoyennes* below. Two of them, seizing upon one unloaded package, together tumbled it open by accident.

Hamelin mock-saluted the General's wife from her commanding position, and said, 'Josephine! We have a parcel of dancing boots, all according to the taste of the officer and labelled with their names. What shall we do with them?'

'Open it, and let us judge the men by their boots,' commanded Josephine. Berthier began to remonstrate, but Bonaparte shushed him. He was evidently in a mood to indulge his wife. Berthier shuffled discreetly to one side. Hamelin had snatched a soldier's hat and perched it jauntily on her abundant mass of hair. It suited her well; she was dark skinned, and her black eyes sparkled as she held the watching soldiers rapt.

'*Citoyens!*' she bellowed, 'The Army of Italy dances in its hobnailed shoes. However, Paris has decreed that the officers will wear buskins when they see fit to shake a shoe. The cordwainers of Milan, never shy of a challenge, have delivered with panache.' She rummaged in the parcel. 'Well, in some cases at least.'

The crowd laughed good-naturedly as she pulled out the first pair of boots. They were of the finest green Moroccan leather, peaked fore and aft with gold lace, with a pointed toe. Gracchus wondered if such a frothy confection would survive an hour in a ballroom, let alone the walk from the carriage to the door.

'The boots of General Dumas! Nothing too flashy,' announced Hamelin, and Dumas came forward sheepishly to receive them. Next were Bonaparte's buskins, which had surely been chosen by Josephine. They were flesh coloured and adorned with gold lace in the style of a heroic Roman sandal. The General rejected them with a shake of his head, and Hamelin tossed them into the air. They landed in the mud, splashing some on Charles, who picked them up, and Hamelin screamed with laughter as she held up a fine pair in red, white, and green, the colours of the Transpadane republic, for Alexandre, and a modest blue set, 'Regimental by the book!' for Berthier. The biggest cheer was for those of Hercule, which were ornamented with detachable gossamer wings.

There was a sudden roar from the scene below. Charles had climbed painfully up on the waggon and was cavorting there in Bonaparte's discarded buskin boots, to the appreciation of the *citoyennes*, and the displeasure of Bonaparte. 'This label reads Colonel Baciocchi?' read Charles. 'Do we have a *Colonel* Baciocchi? Perhaps *Captain* Baciocchi knows him?' This was met with screams of laughter from the women and jeering from the men. Baciocchi made a great play of whispering in Berthier's ear. Gracchus watched Hamelin and Charles work the crowd. The audience liked her, but they adored him. Josephine's eyes were rivetted to Charles. *Was there a genuine affection there, behind all the froth and playacting?* he pondered.

Berthier approached the waggon and beckoned to Charles, who smiled blithely down at him, and Gracchus hung over the gallery balustrade to hear. 'Lieutenant Charles, I have had occasion to talk to you about your sabre before,' Berthier was saying, pointing at the offending article. 'You will discontinue this unauthorised bagatelle, or I will have it thrown into the lake.' He stomped off. Charles's smile did not waver as he clambered off the waggon and saluted Berthier's back ironically. Gracchus considered him with worried eyes, and he saw that as he removed the silver sabre and its belt panoply and laid them on the benches, his mask of urbanity slipped for a moment, and his contorted face displayed the desperate vehemence of a cornered fox.

Chapter Eight

After the goose-plucking, Vanderville hastened through the flurries of flying feathers to re-join Gracchus. Through the confusion in the yard he caught sight of an elegant shape in a pair of red *pantalons* slipping behind the rear of the stands. Diverted from his course, he followed stealthily. Underneath the seating was a shadowed warren of wooden scaffolding that his eyes could not penetrate, but reaching the juncture of the stands with the stable walls he found himself in a dark narrow channel running along the wall of the stable stores. With an unfamiliar lurch of his stomach, he saw illuminated in a shaft of light two figures fervently embracing against a pillar supporting the stands above. Their faces were obscured, and he stopped short, torn between guilty curiosity and a fear of what he might discover. Motes of dust dislodged by the people above in the stands swirled in the light that bathed the lovers, rendering the details of the man's uniform indistinct. They disengaged, panting, their faces intent on one another. The girlish shape in Guide's uniform suddenly slid adroitly away and was lost to Vanderville's view behind the far end of the stands. The other figure straightened and adjusted his cravat. It was Piotr, and for an instant, his eyes met and challenged Vanderville, before he too melted away into the flurry of goose feathers, and Vanderville was left alone with his hollow stomach, feeling the hot mortification of the trespasser.

The benches in the wooden stands were emptying now, except for General Bonaparte, who sat on the upper tier with his boots on the one below, which was occupied by Berthier who was talking up at him earnestly. Gracchus sidled unobtrusively along the gallery into hearing range.

'There is a problem with the *armes d'honneur* ordered to award to soldiers for acts of bravery and exceptional service,' Berthier was saying, waving a letter he held. 'As you know, despite their sanction against them, Paris has winked at the reintroduction of what is officially still designated a pernicious *ancien regime* practice.'

'Hence those made in Milan have fascines, Phrygian bonnets and other republican garnishes,' said Bonaparte impatiently, 'and are termed *Armes de Recompense Nationale*. They are a motivational trapping for the soldiers, do they not understand that?'

Berthier was pacing to and fro. 'They have noticed that those given in Italy bear the name of General Bonaparte, which was bound to attract attention.'

'Ignore them.'

Berthier shrugged. 'As you wish,' and he crumpled the letter ostentatiously before tossing it away. Despite this cavalier gesture, Gracchus suspected that he would recover and file the letter from Paris later in his obsessive way. 'The other problem,' continued Berthier, 'is the new trumpets and drumsticks of honour awarded, not to mention the sashes of honour proposed for mayors. The soldiers are joking about spoons of honour for cooks, and even more vulgar variants for the camp women…'

Bonaparte stared fixedly at Berthier. 'Is that so? Send the manufacturer an order to cancel the contract. Rarity will restore their value. Anything else?'

'There is one thing. Lieutenant Charles wears a silver sabre inscribed, "For loyalty to the Republic."'

'Suppress the unofficial efforts,' snapped Bonaparte. 'Inform Charles that unauthorised sabres of honour are not to be carried by officers of the Army of Italy, and any seen in public from now on will be seized and smelted down for their metal with the proceeds going to the army coffers. Anything more?'

'It appears,' purred Berthier, 'that *Citoyen* Gracchus is eager to report to you in person,' and he turned round to fix his gimlet eye on the eavesdropper.

Bonaparte looked up sharply at Gracchus. 'Really? I thought you were dealing with him, Berthier. Very well, five minutes then.' He fixed Gracchus with his grey eyes. 'Yes?'

'General, I am aware that you value brevity, so I will come straight to the point. I understand that there is a history, or rather a prior relationship, between your family and the Comte Mombello.'

'Relationship is an unfortunate choice of words given rumour. I will be utterly frank with you because I want to put the gossip to rest.'

Gracchus arranged his features to conceal his conviction that frankness would not be a feature of the imminent remarks. Bonaparte invited Gracchus to join him on the stands, pointing out a bench below his own, and Gracchus cautiously clambered down.

'The Comte Mombello was a friend of our family on his first sojourn in Corsica,' began Bonaparte. 'His brother, Marbeuf, was an important man and governor of the island, and Mombello was his brother's secretary. In Ajaccio, our capital, there are not many families that matter, but our family mattered to the French, because my father made sure that it did. As a recognition of some of his services Marbeuf was to be godfather to both me and my sister Maria-Anna – not one of my sisters here. Maria-Anna died very young. It was usual in those days to baptise two children at once, to save money on the party. The baptism was at home, but business called Marbeuf away, and Mombello stood in for him. Nonetheless, Marbeuf became my father's patron, and took an interest in his children. It was Marbeuf who later secured my scholarship at the military school in France. Scurrilous talk in Ajaccio connected the comte's interest exerted on behalf of our family with the name of my mother.'

The General paused and suggested to Berthier that he precede him to the villa to begin work while he finished with Gracchus. Agreeable to this, Berthier left them, and Bonaparte continued, 'My mother was the most agreeable, the most beautiful woman in Ajaccio. Nothing could be more natural than that Marbeuf should show a preference for her and take an interest in the education of her children. As for the rumour of my admission to Brienne being owed to an illicit connection, well, do you know how many Corsicans were admitted to military school in France? You would find in my yearbook the names of an Abbatucci, an Arrighi de Casanova, a Bontini, a Casabianca. Marbeuf did at least as much for those other little boys from Corsica. However, their subsequent careers have proved too obscure to cast doubt upon their mothers' morals.'

He paused to reflect and flicked at his boots idly. 'Marbeuf's social engagement with our family was a mutually advantageous alliance. The Comte was developing supporters in Ajaccio, and we were influential adherents to the new French regime. My father was fluent in French, had knowledge of the law, was eloquent in speech and writing, and had experience of Corsican public life. These were not inconsiderable talents, and anyway Marbeuf and Mombello enjoyed his company. Corsicans are a forbidding lot, or so they can seem to the French. They are suspicious, secretive, vindictive, deceitful, arrogant, sombre, and melancholy as only a needy, war-hardened, disenchanted people can be.'

Gracchus nodded. 'It must have come as a pleasant surprise to you to renew your acquaintance with the Comte Mombello here in Italy?'

'Not at all.' He was unclasping and closing a penknife as he spoke now. 'You must realise that I was a child when I left Corsica, and a Frenchman when I returned. The name Marbeuf meant nothing to me except as a stick that my classmates had used to belabour my mother's reputation. Our present recent acquaintance was based entirely for my part on my perception of the comte's significance in Milanese political matters. Actually, that significance was vastly over-represented by Mombello himself, and I rather regret my decision to accept his hospitality, and the attendant revival of improper speculation concerning my mother's friendship with his brother in the distant past. Better for my plans that this rotten corpse had not washed up on the shore again now...'

He sighed and doodled on the bench seat with the knife. 'Let me tell you a story of my childhood. In the summer we would go to stay at my uncle's farm near the coast and play on the beach under one of the old watch towers that have long guarded our island against pirates. One day my brothers and I found the body of an immense turtle laid up on the beach. It stank too terribly for any of us to approach it, except for me, because then, as now, I was the boldest of my brothers and playmates. I gazed into the rheumy eye of that venerable old man of the sea and marvelled to imagine what wonders he had lived. That evening he must have been washed out to sea again, because in the morning he was gone. However, every week for the next month the tides of the bay returned him to the beach to our delight and disgust, because every time he washed up again, he was more and more decomposed and offensive to the nose.' He folded his knife carefully and placed it in his coat pocket.

'You see, Gracchus, the family of Marbeuf and Mombello remind me of that turtle. Every time he raises his head, the odour of rumour assaults my nostrils again, so it is natural that I view Mombello's passing with less disfavour than some. You understand me? But naturally I did not have him made away with, because I am not a fool! Observe that once again, even now he is dead, that stinking corpse makes a worse stench than when he was alive.'

'What happened to him, the turtle on the beach?' asked Gracchus.

'The National Guard came to the beach one day and blew him up with gunpowder because he had become a public nuisance.'

'This present nuisance is not something that can be removed by the application of powder, General,' observed Gracchus.

'A good general does not wage war solely through force of arms, *citoyen*,' replied Bonaparte, 'do you know what the most important consideration for waging war is?'

Gracchus assumed what he fondly imagined was his sagacious and receptive face.

'Strategy, supply, force of arms, all of these are important, but the most vital requirement is health. Health and morale,' continued the General.

That is two things, thought Gracchus, but he remained attentive and mute. His eye must have wandered involuntarily over Bonaparte's malnourished and sickly figure.

'I know what you are thinking,' Bonaparte said, and Gracchus thought, yes, you probably do, or more to the point you are convinced that you do, which is perhaps even better in some respects, and certainly more useful to you, but again he retained the silence he judged necessary to encourage further confidences.

'Although my own health is not absolutely perfect,' continued Bonaparte, 'I have the energy and the willpower to overcome nature's deficiencies. But morale... well, mine is indomitable because it is based on a thorough study of men and war, but that of the men, and of their leaders, is more fragile, and an event like this goose-killing ghoul rumour makes them susceptible. It can sap them of the spirit that is essential for carrying out my plans. So, I, as the embodiment of the Republic, require a rapid resolution to this matter. Something you have not yet accomplished.'

'There are certain papers I need to consult, and interviews to conduct,' said Gracchus.

Bonaparte stood up and dismissed Gracchus. 'There are two days until the weddings of my sisters, and then we leave here for Como and the honeymoon. I do not want anything to disrupt those weddings. I have granted you unusually broad powers, and I expect results. I shall hold you responsible for failure. *Salut, citoyen.*'

He strode off down the seating, the steps bouncing under his boots, and Vanderville, who had been waiting for him to leave, approached.

'Good news?' he asked.

'No,' said Gracchus, removing his hat and scratching his head. He considered how far he could stretch the definition of broad powers that Bonaparte had granted him, and weighed this against the possibility of failure. 'I rather think it is the other sort. Listen, Vanderville, let us imagine the scene that evening when Mombello made his fateful trip outside. He was working in his library, and then instead of turning in, he decided to go outside.'

'To speak to his nephew? Do you think he found something in the papers he was working on?'

'It is a possibility. But just because he told the valet he was going to the stables to see Alexandre, doesn't mean that he did. Instead, he took himself off to the chapel.'

'Perhaps he knew Alexandre was there?'

'Young Marbeuf has said that he wasn't anywhere near it. Charles, however, who admits to being in the vicinity, says that he heard two people talking in the chapel.'

'You think that could have been Mombello?'

'Yes. But there is a further complication. The eavesdropper on the ladder. Who was that? Did they overhear or see who Mombello was conversing with? Did they witness a murder?'

Vanderville frowned. 'You think Mombello was killed in the chapel? But then how did he end up in the well?'

'Say why, rather. It was meant to look like an accident. However, the murderer must have dragged him all the way there. Rather dangerous when the fireflies provided enough light for him to be spotted.'

'Certainly, there were enough people outside that someone must have seen something. Charles, Josephine, the eavesdropper. Besides which, it is a fair way. Our killer must be strong, and reckless. A reckless or a desperate man.'

'Or not a man at all.'

'The ghoul? But why would the ghoul hide a body? Doesn't it usually hang the animal corpses around the place in grisly fashion?' Vanderville shuddered.

'That is the wrong question. Ask rather does our murderer disguise himself as a ghoul? And if so, is it him who commits the depredations here, or is that merely a convenient cover for a murder committed for more venal motives?' Gracchus shook his head. 'From the hiding of the body, we can conclude that the killer did not want it to be found. And it would have lain hidden for weeks or even months if not for the fortuitous dredging of the well, something our sinister friend could not reasonably have foreseen. That is not the action of a creature or a madman. We need a motive for a rational being to do away with our host, and love or money are the motives most common to this crime. I think we can reasonably discount the former, the comte was a man of advanced years, and Leonardi has suggested that his sensual appetites were concentrated on the pleasures of the table. So the question remains, who profits from Mombello's death?'

Vanderville shivered. 'That is not the only mystery. If the killer is not the ghoul, then we still have to deal with the fact that something else is out there every night, tearing apart anything it comes across.'

Chapter Nine

The next morning the young officers breakfasted as usual on the gallery in the stables. Hercule had brought a pan of sauteed calves' liver with lemon and some toasted bread from the kitchens, and was portioning them out, while Charles smoked companionably. Hercule had been mounting the night guard. 'Never again let me drink before duty,' he moaned, rubbing his temples dolefully. 'Not a drop shall pass my lips today.' He helped himself to a plateful of breakfast. 'I don't know why you all complain about sleeping badly, at least you are in bed. I've been up all night making my rounds of the villa while half the sentries dozed at their posts. I'm counting the days until this week is over and it's the Polish Legion's turn to mount guard.'

'Who is on guard duty for the weddings?' asked Vanderville through a mouthful of hot juicy crumbs.

'They haven't decided yet,' said Charles. 'I'm inclined to think that both will be involved. Before the fight in the stables, I would have said the Guides were a sure thing, they are the praetorian after all, but now the Polish Legion have their new uniform they are back in the running. On the other hand, the Guides won the battle of the stables, so...'

'That reminds me, the story going round this morning is that you were unseated by a girl yesterday,' smiled Hercule.

'I think I have cracked some ribs,' said Charles, wincing. 'The Guide I fell on must have been made from solid stone.'

'Perhaps it was a statue from the garden come to life. It wouldn't be the first antique female to be unnaturally drawn to your presence,' suggested Hercule.

'Thank you for that characteristically witless insinuation,' said Charles. 'The last thing I need is Bonaparte adding me to his list of undesirables.'

'Where's our young Alexandre, or should I call him Mombello now?' asked Hercule. 'Isn't he going to inherit?'

'He is with Piotr,' said Charles. 'As for the estate, there is some complication with the paperwork. It appears that a lot of Mombello's papers have been mislaid. Most of his estate goes to his family in France of course, but he had always promised that Villa Mombello would be Alexandre's. Unfortunately, until the advocates get their claws on the papers, he will remain a mere penniless lieutenant, much the same as the rest of us.'

'Piotr is not so penniless, now,' mused Hercule. 'He must be turning a pretty penny selling those ices, he has a sack of coin under his bed that must weigh as much as his girlfriend in the Guides.'

'I suppose he gets his army pay supplemented by a second wage from the kitchens?' asked Vanderville.

'He has a finger in every pie that one. Making the most of his time here, we should all do the same and we'd be rich before the snows come,' said Hercule, picking his teeth with his pocketknife.

'No point getting the tin if you can't shift it back to France safely,' said Charles. 'For that you need waggons and cattle. Only the generals have access to that sort of muscle. Anything Piotr makes, he will lose as soon as the army moves. The transport train doesn't care about Poles trying to make their way in the world.'

'Speaking of which, we have a short arm inspection to conduct in the camp,' said Hercule. 'Come and help, Vanderville. It is high time you stopped being a flowerpot and learned the finer points of your trade.'

'Can't. Busy with Gracchus,' said Vanderville. 'Anyway, wasn't Berthier moaning that the soldiers all sold their pistols in Milan?'

'Exchanged them for bad wine and worse drabs,' said Hercule, 'but it is not that sort of weapon we need to inspect I'm afraid. Listen to this from Berthier's latest ordinance, "The Guides and the Legion will parade for bathing tomorrow at quarter before nine, after which the surgeon and his two assistants will inspect every man stark naked, the former making a written report as to the state in which he found them. The inspection for the venereal disorder to be continued every second day by his assistants until further orders."'

'Well, there's a plum situation,' said Charles with a smile.

After the others had left, Charles had a confidence for Vanderville. 'It *was* a girl who set me on the stable ground yesterday,' he said sourly, mopping up the last of the calves' livers with a slipper of bread. 'Didn't you see anything from the galleries?'

'I had an idea of it,' said Vanderville, 'but I wasn't sure, and later I thought I saw her again, but I couldn't make out her face.'

'I think I did,' said Charles, 'just before she ran away, I caught a glimpse. It was your Paolette, the General's troublesome sister. Trouble is about right for her. Everyone gets into trouble sooner or later.'

'I think you are wrong about her,' began Vanderville, stacking plates, and Charles fixed him with a thoughtfully cynical eye.

'Listen to me, Vanderville. I have the utmost liking for you, and I will only say this once, because unsolicited advice always provokes offence in the recipient. Put your honour aside and listen to me as a brother. You are aiming too high with that one. The Bonaparte girls are reserved for generals now. You are riding for a fall, my friend.'

Vanderville felt his scalp prickle. He chose his next words carefully, for he liked Charles too, and did not want to argue. 'It seems to me that some are aiming higher still. If the General's sisters are forbidden to us, then how much more must be the General's own…'

'Careful Vanderville,' said Charles, 'I do not dispute your aim, or resent your remark, but some things are better unvoiced, even among friends. It is safer for all involved that way.'

There was an awkward pause, and then Charles added, 'The material facts of my situation differ in that I did not choose to place myself in the state you have observed. Rather, I was chosen. A refusal often offends, and thus I find myself trapped between a rock and a hard place. My perspective is not an enviable one, I assure you. It will take all my luck to extract myself, and were I not possessed with the excellent weapons of wit and perspicacity I would not give a fig for my chances. Do not tread in my steps, my friend.'

He patted Vanderville's hand companionably. 'Now I must go to the kitchen and beg Leonardi for some magic balm for these ribs,' he paused. 'Think about what I have said, brother. That mysterious person did me a bad turn yesterday. If you want to know her better, ask her what *she* does outside in the middle of the summer nights.'

Gracchus was already in the kitchens listening to Leonardi tell him about the ancient bath complex under the villa. The chef was fraying herbs with a knife and training a supplemented staff from the village who would assist in preparations for the weddings, and so Gracchus had perched himself out of the way on the ledge of the casement window that opened onto the kitchen garden. From this vantage point he could watch both the kitchen and the garden, and occasionally sample delicacies that Leonardi passed up to him.

'I don't go down there. Never,' said Leonardi. 'Honestly it unnerves. It's too dark, for a start, and the cistern water distorts sound in a way most peculiar.' He paused in his chopping and sucked a spot of blood from his finger vigorously. 'There are several levels where the old baths were, but at some point modern plumbing was installed and bypassed the old basins, and now, it is all ruined and pell-mell. I'm no connoisseur of the dusty ruins and antiquities. The modern world of light and the science of the kitchen table, it is enough for me.'

Gracchus nodded sagely; he only had half an ear on Leonardi.

Piotr banged through the cool larder door. 'The ices come along well. I'm turning in,' he said.

'I have a job for you first,' said Gracchus. 'Berthier needs coffee delivered to the commander-in-chief's study now.'

'I only just removed the last tray!' grumbled Piotr.

'He wants it ready for when he gets back, you had better hurry. Oh, and there are some papers of Comte Mombello there he has asked me to go through, journals, diaries, that sort of thing.'

Piotr nodded. 'I know the ones. I removed them from the library.'

'Excellent. Take them all to the print office please.'

'Now?'

'Unless you can manage it sooner.'

–

As Piotr left, Gracchus peered outside the casement window to keep an eye on Bonaparte and Berthier. He could just make them out, walking into the kitchen garden, talking with their usual animation. Josephine and Hamelin trailed behind them, admiring the soft fruit trees. Then Berthier unexpectedly stopped dead over a herb bed, and Bonaparte stifled a curse. Craning his head, Gracchus saw that Berthier stood over something on the ground. Bonaparte swivelled quickly to try and head off the *citoyennes*, covering Berthier with his body, his face stricken with trepidation. 'Go back, Josephine, instantly!' he commanded, but instead she froze, her face collapsing into terror. Berthier dropped to one knee and scooped something up. Gracchus saw that it was the pathetic lifeless form of Josephine's little Fortune. The pug dog's wretched body was scored deeply, and the torn neck finished abruptly in a raw stump.

Josephine screamed, and Hamelin dissolved into consternation and vaporing. 'But when will all this stop?' sobbed Josephine, insinuating herself into Bonaparte's arms. 'First little Victory, and now Fortune. It's all too… too ghastly for words. What did this? Some wild animals?'

'It was the ghoul!' howled Hamelin.

'Nonsense,' said Berthier, 'this is the work of a boar.'

'Or the cook's dog,' said the General, leading his wife away from the dog's body, while Berthier kicked its detached head discreetly under a bush. 'I regret that Fortune had an impertinent disposition entirely at odds with his size and capabilities, and often teased the mastiff.'

'Oh Bonaparte, how horrible. I don't know what to do, I feel weak,' said Josephine, allowing herself to be comforted on a rustic garden seat. 'I shall miss looking out of my window and seeing him play in the garden.'

She leant her head on her husband's shoulder. 'Perhaps you had better share my room for the time being then,' he said, 'the view of the chapel is also good, and the air is better there. I will have them make the arrangements.' He tenderly disengaged his wife from his arms and offered her his handkerchief. 'Berthier, I will take the *citoyennes* upstairs. Speak to the cook about his dog.'

Gracchus removed his head from the window and eased himself back down onto his ledge just in time to affect nonchalance as Berthier barged open the kitchen garden door, and almost collided with a dishevelled servant carrying a huge pan full of hot water up the stairs. There was no room for either to pass the other, so Berthier contented himself with hanging over the railing at the top of the steps to bellow over the bustle of the kitchen.

He pointed one quivering finger at the dog who was as usual more or less asleep by the hearth. 'Leonardi!' he barked. 'That unspeakable creature has struck again, and I shall have him shot.'

'What are you talking about?' said Leonardi, not looking up from his work. 'I told you last time. The dog, he doesn't leave the kitchen at night. He sleeps here. If you are looking for an assassin, Berthier, you have come to the wrong kitchen.'

'That's enough, Leonardi,' ordered Berthier. 'You and the dog can go to lodge in the stables for the time being.'

Leonardi threw up his hands. 'If there is no place for a cook in the villa, there is none for generals in my kitchen. Please remove yourself and allow my staff the working space.' With that he turned to a complicated list he was discussing with one of his assistants.

From his perch Gracchus's feet were dangling on a level with Berthier's head, and noticing them for the first time, Berthier remonstrated with him, 'This practice of treating cooks as great men, indulging and pampering them, is quite unmerited. Just because someone can throw eggs and flour together in a novel combination is not sufficient to idolise them as if they were some great seer. We shall soon be awarding them spoons of honour and enrolling them as knights in the Order of the Golden Egg Whisk.'

'Nonetheless,' reasoned Gracchus, 'if the mastiff did not kill the pug, then we have another malicious incident to explain. Tell me, Berthier,' he continued with a lowered voice, sliding down from the window beside the general, 'when was the other dog, Victory, killed?'

'I don't remember,' mused Berthier, nonplussed. 'Certainly before you arrived. Perhaps two days before?'

'The night before Comte Mombello was discovered, in fact?'

'I suppose so, yes.'

'And that dog, too, was found in the kitchen garden?'

'No, on the contrary, by the stables. I was forced to turn her out at night, so she did not disturb me— err, that is to say, to disturb the Marquesa Visconti's sleep. She was in the habit of visiting the stable dogs, and she was found outside there outside the archway, in much the same state as the pug just now.'

Gracchus observed Berthier's unusual state of agitation. The gruesome discovery had affected him. The moment was ripe, he decided, to pierce the bureaucrat's reserve. He pressed on. 'It would have been useful if you had told me of this before. It may have some bearing on this puzzle. Tell me now, the night the Comte Mombello went missing, did you notice anything untoward happen, in the salon, or after?'

'This is all very indiscreet, Gracchus, perhaps you had better come into the garden where we can talk,' complained Berthier.

Outside in the kitchen garden, surrounded by raised beds of good green stuff, he began pacing up and down rapidly and proceeded to confidence. 'That evening played out as usual,' he began. 'After supper, there were amateur theatricals, the comte told a ghost story that displeased the General, and he went to work in his cabinet. I joined him, and we retired late, after the rest of the household. I checked that the villa was locked up before I went up and passed a quiet night.'

'Did you find Mombello in his library?'

'No. The lights were off; he must have just left the villa.'

'This would have been after two I suppose. Did you see anything untoward as you locked up? Anything out of the usual?'

Berthier hesitated, and Gracchus pursued the point. 'You must tell me, Berthier. Anything that happened may have significance. I can assure you that I serve the General's interests in this matter. I am as keen to clear up the comte's death as you yourself are.'

'Well, I don't see that it has anything to do with you. But I came across someone upstairs in her night things. On hearing the hard breathing, I conceived it to be a person that had walked thither in her sleep, with her eyes wide open, but fixed.

'I have heard of instances of striking those walking in their sleep by way of a cure. This I dared not do, and I gently awoke her, at which she would have fallen on the floor if I had not caught her in my arms; when she apologised for having disturbed me, saying that she was unfortunately accustomed to such nightly walks, and that she had been dreaming of calling her servant to dress her.'

'I can see that the matter is delicate,' suggested Gracchus discreetly, 'but it is imperative I have a name.'

'Impossible. There is a danger of her reputation being compromised. But there is no possibility that she left the villa anyway, I had locked the doors by then.' Berthier held up an admonitory finger to Gracchus. 'You will remain silent on this matter.'

They turned at the end of the garden, and began to walk back through the trellised fruit trees. 'Nobody has slept well at Mombello this June,' began Berthier again in a more confidential tone. 'Perhaps this was the start of the problems we have had. Myself, it is not that I sleep badly as you sometimes do when the weather is oppressive and a storm is expected, it is the opposite; I sleep too well. Everyone on the staff and in the household has been suffering from sleep problems except the General. Some sleep too much, some too little, and everybody is plagued by dreams. They blame it on the hot water system. Bonaparte refuses to move to another villa because he loves the baths. You may have noticed the water for the baths is piped into the house. It is possible that this modern affectation disturbs the humours.'

'I haven't noticed it in the lofts, I must admit,' said Gracchus.

'Of course not,' said Berthier smugly. 'It doesn't come into basins in each room as the ancients tell us happened in Nero's Golden Palace,' he continued, 'but arrives in a closet on each landing, from which the servants take it, and carry it, still warm, to each room. So, it is very much available on demand. In the General's room he has a chamber bath, made of copper well tinned within, and raised on four legs, so that a chafing dish may be placed underneath to warm it further. Sometimes the water is made salt, like that of the sea; and when he feels the need of it, he has vinegar, brimstone, iron filings and sometimes aromatic herbs put in the water. Perhaps that's why he sleeps so beautifully while the rest of us suffer.'

'The General does not complain of bad dreams then?' asked Gracchus.

'Him, dream? Corsicans dream of their villages,' snorted Berthier, and then, realising he had been guilty of an indiscreet lack of loyalty, he visibly pulled himself together.

'I slept badly myself last night,' Gracchus hurriedly suggested in an attempt to encourage the flow of confidences to resume.

'I expect you did,' observed Berthier archly, 'you sleep badly because you eat too much. This cook is making everybody ill, and the ladies are all getting fat. I will give orders to Leonardi to produce simpler food and all of this nonsense about dreams will end.'

—

Vanderville had proudly adopted the habit of walking with Paolette in the gardens. On this morning, however, he tarried in the stables until he was sure one of the other officers, who habitually competed for this obligation, would have supplied his place. He tried and failed to convince himself that it was his duty that required him to check the horses, and not his suspicion that it had been her he had glimpsed locked in a stranger's embrace under the stands in the stable yard.

Well, he would not condemn her for her frivolity, and although he disapproved of her betraying Leclerc, he would not censure her. She was too young to be married, he told himself, and perhaps she had felt the need of a fling before the wedding. *Then why not with me?* The unwelcome question asserted itself unbidden and he shook his head to rid it of these troubling thoughts.

After sufficient time had passed, he made his way to the terrace, determined to ask Paolette's sister, Elisa, to walk with him instead. She accepted with alacrity and taking his arm suggested they stroll to the chapel to admire its adornments.

'I hear that you are another of the conquests of my vivacious sister, Lieutenant Vanderville.'

'Your soon-to-be-married sister,' said Vanderville.

Elisa nodded. 'Just as well. When every eye in the room is upon her, she feels impelled to misbehave. My brother indulges her, so she believes there will never be any consequences. It's time she learnt to live up to her position.'

Vanderville guided the conversation onto the surer ground of the preparations for the upcoming nuptials, and Elisa expressed a hope that Vanderville would form a part of the honeymoon party expedition planned for Lake Como. He conveyed the belief that duty would prevent this, while secretly forming a resolve to avoid Paolette until after the wedding. His resolution was in vain though, for scarcely had they arrived before the chapel when a pleased voice interrupted them.

'Ah! There you are,' exclaimed Paolette, seizing Vanderville's other arm as if by right. 'It's time you saw the corbeilles, they are divine!'

Vanderville felt Elisa stiffen as she relinquished him, and he managed a mute shrug of apology. Elisa rolled her eyes and walked away towards the villa. Vanderville found his shame promptly yielded to the satisfying comfort of Paolette's familiar arm in his as she led him into the chapel, and down into the nymphaeum.

'Mine is the blue one of course,' she said, 'Elisa's is rather vulgar, don't you think?'

She dismissed the pink basket with a wrinkle of her nose. Vanderville picked up the lid of Paolette's corbeille. He felt strange, as if something were out of place. His stomach was troubling him again, it did not occur to him that he was sick of an emotion that was older than the chapel itself. Although Paolette was undoubtably charming beyond description, he told himself that he could not resent Leclerc's good fortune. He sensed instinctively that marriage to Paolette could not bring Leclerc any real happiness, and yet he felt discomposed when he imagined their imminent wedding. He felt ashamed of himself, and small-spirited, and felt a sudden wish that campaigning against the Austrians would resume so that he could leave the villa and return to the certainties of the front.

Paolette was listing the contents of her trousseau on her fingers, but she soon ran out of digits, and resorted to pointing at the myriad of packages tied with pink and blue ribbons and squealing with delight instead. He had to admit the trousseau in the corbeille was magnificent.

'Embroidered chemises, chiffon bathrobes and muslin camisoles from India, cashmere shawls, veils, and dresses of all colours and shapes,' she squealed with delight. 'A dress for the wedding, presentation dresses, dresses embroidered in silver lamés. And then ribbons of all widths, and of all colours, bags, fans, gloves…' she barely paused for breath; Vanderville was exhausted just listening to her.

As she took the fragile lid from him, he noticed the split in the blue leather that had attracted Gracchus's attention. He traced it.

'Vanderville, please don't damage that any more than it already is.'

'Did somebody drop it?' he asked.

Paolette smugly replaced the corbeille lid, and asked, 'Do you really believe in this story Vanderville? That the ghoul shoved Mombello down the well?'

'I'm not really sure,' he answered. 'Gracchus doesn't want to talk about it, he says he has seen an awful lot of dead men over the last three years, and this would be the first one who reached that unhappy state through the intervention of a ghoul.'

'I ask,' she said, 'because of a funny thing that happened. I didn't want to tell Gracchus. He has such a confounded insinu-ating way of saying nothing, while you find yourself almost unaware telling him the most surprising things.'

'You can tell me,' he said.

She brushed his arm, and he found her suddenly too close. 'Yes, I think we could have secrets together,' she said. 'It was the morning after Mombello disappeared, and the corbeilles were here in the chapel already. I liked to come and look at them whenever I had a chance. But when I got here that morning, mine had been thrown on the floor by the spring and was broken, with all the packages spilling out. It had to be repaired. Of course, Elisa did it to spite me. I feel sorry for her. Her Corbeille looks like a fat pink pumpkin, which is appropriate as her husband reminds me of one.' She frowned. 'He is not clever at all, certainly not dashing, and probably too stupid ever to be a general, even if my brother made him one, which he hasn't, and there must be a reason for that, mustn't there?'

Gracchus had also been waylaid. While walking in the formal gardens, Josephine overtook him. He realised that this was the first time he had seen her without any of her companions, and he resolved to ask her about her night excursion with Charles.

'*Citoyen* Gracchus, may I speak with you a moment?' she asked.

'*Citoyenne*,' he bowed.

'Please. Call me Josephine. We are almost friends after all. It's about Fortune.'

'A terrible thing,' said Gracchus. 'A most unfortunate accident.'

'Let us not pretend, Gracchus. Bonaparte has already tried to convince me that the cook's dog was responsible, but we know differently, don't we?'

'I'm not sure I quite understand, *citoyenne*...'

'It was him, wasn't it?' she said. 'The ghoul. No, do not interrupt. Whatever killed the geese and poor Mombello also did this thing to dear Fortune. The horrible things happening in this villa cannot be explained away by natural means.'

'Is there something you know about this, um, creature, *citoyenne*? Something you wish to tell me?' probed Gracchus.

'Oh, I should have said something sooner. It is so difficult. Dear Bonaparte wants us all to pretend that this is not happening, to act as if everything was perfectly normal, but he knows, Gracchus. He knows that someone, one of us, is behind it all.'

Gracchus considered carefully. He very much wanted to hear Josephine's thoughts on the matter but receiving confidences from the General's adored wife was not something he had counted on. He glanced around the grove. 'Are you referring to the ghost story Letizia told us?'

Josephine nodded gently. 'It was her way of bringing hidden things into the open.'

Gracchus sighed. 'Your husband was right to want to ban these silly stories.'

She looked at him perplexed. 'But it's the fashion, Gracchus,' she said, as if that explained everything.

'*Citoyenne*,' he began carefully, 'If you are so worried about the ghoul, why did you venture outside in the garden the night that the comte was killed?'

She stared at him blankly. '*I* go outside in the night? You must be mistaken, Gracchus. Whoever told you that?'

'It does not matter, it was just a theory of my own.'

'You can confirm my whereabouts with Berthier, or Bonaparte, come to that, if it will help you to concentrate on catching the ghoul.'

Pondering this, Gracchus asked her, 'You believe the ghoul might be real, then. A warped monster stalking the villa?'

She drew a little closer to him. She smelt expensive and she smelt Parisian. The unbidden, unwelcome evocation of the Palais Royale crashed like a flood tide over the bastion Gracchus maintained against his exile's sentiment, and he was utterly disarmed when she flashed her violet eyes large for effect. Smiling faintly she whispered, 'There are more things under heaven than natural philosophy can explain, Gracchus. The ghoul *is* real, and it is stalking us. You must catch it before it hurts anyone else.' She squeezed a tear from one eye, and dabbed it expertly. 'They talk about it amongst themselves, the Bonapartes, they all know about it, and that is the point. This is a Corsican ghoul – it comes from there, and so it stands to reason that only a Corsican can be the monster.'

Gracchus was stunned; this was dangerous territory. 'The Corsicans here are all of the General's family!' he exclaimed.

She abruptly stopped crying. 'Then you know where you should be looking. Do not waste any more time. Fortune has already been made a sacrifice, next time it could be one of us.'

There was a sound of a servant exiting the kitchen, and she flitted out onto the terrace as if she had never been there, save for her scent lingering in the air.

Gracchus headed straight for the kitchen, blinking after the sun-drenched garden. He dimly made out Leonardi at the range contemplating a huge steaming vat.

'Today is no day in this kitchen for sightseers!' bristled Leonardi, as Gracchus joined him and sniffed the bouquet emanating from the vat Leonardi was stirring.

'Zuppa di Erbe di Primavera?' said Gracchus, taking the long spoon from him. 'Thickening nicely,' he tasted it, 'not ready yet, though.' He pondered a moment, with a faraway look in his eyes, and then dropped the spoon into the soup. 'Leonardi, have you dredged the well for crabs yet?'

'Berthier has closed the well,' said Leonardi glumly, 'they sealed it this morning with boards.'

Gracchus rubbed his brow. 'I see. How does one access the cellars?'

'They are forbidden. Bonaparte only may enter. But also Piotr has keys. For making the ices. Maybe the young master, too.'

'Many thanks,' said Gracchus. 'Where *is* Piotr?'

'He was up all night working on his ices. Maybe he is sleeping now. Maybe his laundry. He had his arms full of sheets and was annoyed.'

Gracchus scaled the kitchen stair as fast as his uncertain gait permitted and set out for the stables. He found Vanderville just outside that place talking to one of the Bonaparte girls. 'Where are you going?' asked Vanderville, abandoning her with indecent alacrity.

'You wanted action, Vanderville, now you shall have your chance. Find Alexandre for me. I will meet you here in five minutes.'

Vanderville said a hasty farewell to Elisa and hastened into the stable yard where the Polish Legion were drawn up for inspection by their officers. From the galleries Hercule was bellowing out a song about a peasant girl negotiating her virtue, while shaving from a bowl. He waved companionably. 'We are going hunting for boar tonight,' he shouted down at Vanderville. 'Will you come?'

'I can't,' Vanderville shouted back. 'Have you seen Alexandre?'

'He said not to disturb him, he's sleeping before going on duty.'

—

It was hot and the noon hour had gone by when Gracchus called out to Piotr, barging open the door of the stable bunk room he shared with Alexandre none too gently, 'My apologies for disturbing you, but...'

One half of the window was open, the other closed. The light admitted caressed the spectacle of glistening limbs bound in delight. The far bed was empty but for clothes discarded in haste and a pair of Guides' scarlet *pantalons* were slung across a chair's back.

Amid the clinging sheets, a pair of arms wound about his neck, Piotr stirred. 'I do beg your pardon,' uttered Gracchus, reversing his steps awkwardly. At that moment, the door slapped open again, and Vanderville cannoned into the back of Gracchus, precipitating him headlong onto the foot of the bed, where he recoiled in distress from thigh pressed to thigh and mingled damp hair.

Vanderville pulled up short behind Gracchus, who was floundering to his feet. Vanderville's eyes glazed at the half obscured tangle. He flushed to the same shade as the red *pantalons*, his worst fears confirmed. '*Paolette*,' he mouthed involuntarily to himself, seized by some atavistic fear.

The second figure in the bed sat up, his brow wreathed in the aftermath of ardour. 'The devil take you Gracchus, is that everyone, or are Dumas and the commander-in-chief coming up too?' asked Alexandre.

'Oh! So sorry,' mumbled Gracchus, backing out of the room and colliding with Vanderville in the doorway. They paused on the stair outside the room, and Gracchus stuck his head back round the door. 'By the way, Piotr, can I get the keys to the cellars?'

'In my coat, back of the door,' came the muffled voice from beneath the bed clothes. 'I'll meet you there as soon as I'm up.'

Vanderville's head was churning with shifting reference points. 'I should have known,' he muttered to himself. 'All perfectly straightforward. In the Greek tradition, the Greek *military* tradition after all.'

Chapter Ten

'I will not pretend the death of the pug is entirely unwelcome, Berthier,' Bonaparte was saying below in his cabinet. 'However, the domestic repercussions are disruptive. I have passed a disagreeable morning. We must consider the rending of that damned dog as a challenge to my authority here.'

'Would you like to have Gracchus shot?' asked Berthier hopefully.

'I'm not positive that that would be helpful. I retain some measure of confidence in him, although I agree his efforts as editor of *The Courier of the Army of Italy* justify your suggestion. He has requested that we extend his authority to interview suspects, and I am inclined to agree. It is imperative that this matter is resolved immediately; the discreet approach has been ineffective.'

'And if results are not forthcoming and he continues with his transgressions of the ordinances?'

'Then we will revisit your idea.'

'Rank ingratitude,' muttered Gracchus, smiling to himself. He disengaged from the hearing trumpet and rolled over on the floor to look up at the ceiling. Certain details of the case had resolved themselves, but the pattern was still obscure. Shortly, it occurred to him that his newfound passion for the ear trumpet was vying with his love of conversing in the kitchen with Leonardi, so that one pursuit was sometimes missing out to the other. He resolved to correct that imbalance at the first opportunity, but first he had to conduct some interviews in his press office.

Blueskin was a dark chestnut. He had a beautiful shoulder and racing hindquarters, with a showy blood tail. His back was a bad point but, with a high cavalry saddle well forward, he was a delight to ride. He had great spirit and Vanderville had a real liking for him. His care was in the hands of a groom, but Vanderville often found an excuse to superintend his work, and on a morning such as this he found the horse's company preferable to that of anyone else.

Vanderville's thoughts strayed again to Paolette as he brushed the horse. They had met earlier that morning in a secluded summerhouse, and remembering certain liberties she had granted him, Vanderville was imbued with a piquant sense of guilt that was only exacerbated by his realisation that he was powerless to prevent himself from behaving in the same manner again at the earliest possible opportunity. It was as if he was mounted on Blueskin in a dream and the horse was wildly out of control, and despite the imminent threat of terrible danger, he was enjoying the savage thrilling sensation that made him feel more alive than he could ever recall being. Could he stop if he wanted to, he asked himself? The point was moot. He did not want to stop. He shrugged and resigned himself to the maelstrom. Better to think of matters he could affect. He turned back to the business of the horse resignedly.

He consoled himself that he had at least accumulated some information to relay to Gracchus. When he had mentioned the awkward moment in Piotr and Alexandre's bedchamber, Paolette had greeted the news with a surprising equanimity. 'I know, it seems such a waste of Alexandre, doesn't it?' she had said. 'Caroline will be so disappointed.'

'Your sister?' Vanderville had replied. 'But Caroline is ten years old!'

'Yes, but she fancies marrying a duke when she grows up, or whatever Alexandre is, now his father is dead. Which is better, a duke, or a general, do you think?'

'Depends on whether the general is republican or not,' said Vanderville.

'It's weird with Piotr, though. He is old enough to be Alexandre's father,' she suggested.

Vanderville frowned. This was an exaggeration. Although Alexandre was young, Piotr could not have been past thirty himself. 'Everyone is old to you, Paolette.'

Paolette turned her back to him and made some adjustments to her toilette, and then apropos of nothing, she said over her shoulder, 'I think he's one of them. A ghoul.'

'Hold fast a minute, what makes you say that?' exclaimed Vanderville.

'You agree we have a monster on our hands?' she explained. 'A Corsican dream ghoul who is bumping off the villa guests one by one?'

'Sort of...' he began.

'Well, your ancient friend, Piotr. He isn't Polish, he's Corsican,' she announced triumphantly.

'What? How do you know?'

'I heard him talking to Mamma yesterday. I don't know what they were saying exactly, because they were speaking fervently and very quickly, but I have yet to meet anyone who can speak the dialect of the mountain fastness of Corte save they were born there.'

Vanderville turned this new information over in his head, and before he could ask for further explanation, she excused herself.

'I have to go back to the house, my brother is letting me use his bath. They are putting jasmine in it. He wants to tell me about the names too.'

'The names?' asked a bewildered Vanderville, who was struggling manfully under the weight of accumulated revelation.

'Yes, we all have to discard our Corsican names. Since Napoleon changed Buonaparte to Bonaparte, he is so pleased with the sound of our French family name that we all have to be frenchified officially now. There is a problem, because the law says we have to use our baptism names on the marriage certificates. Then of course we keep our real name, Bonaparte, but we have the right to use our husband's name instead. Josephine doesn't always though, does she? She is still *Citoyenne* Beauharnais sometimes, which was her first husband's name. I think the smart thing, the Parisian thing is to stay a Buonaparte— I mean Bonaparte! You see how hard it is.' She frowned. 'Anyway, Napoleon insisted Mamma send for copies of everyone's baptism certificates, from Ajaccio. It took ages, and guess what? Guess who my brother Louis's godfather is on the baptism certificate? The Marquis de Marbeuf! So Alexandre Marbeuf is a sort of honorary brother to us I suppose.'

'Listen, Paolette,' Vanderville had told her. 'This might be important, and I think Gracchus would like to know. Can you possibly borrow those birth certificates from your mother for me to show him?'

'I don't think so, she is very careful with her things. I can write it down for you though I think. By the way, you probably shouldn't call me Paolette now that I'm getting married. Pauline is better unless you prefer Paolina. Why aren't you hunting this evening?'

'The boar hunt was Berthier's idea,' said Vanderville. 'He is a passionate hunter, and conceived that the chestnut woods harbour boar who may be responsible for the attacks attributed to the ghoul. Gracchus thinks it's a waste of time.'

'He's right. No boar tracks have been found outside the woods,' said Paolette, laughing. 'Everyone knows that. My brother had men check for wolves and every sort of wild beast.'

'It can't hurt to count out his theory, and at least they are doing something,' said Vanderville defensively.

'Rampaging around the woods will achieve nothing. If I were a man, I would lay a trap and let the ghoul come to me. The creature seems to attack in the vicinity of the chapel or latterly the kitchen garden, much closer to the house. Here is my idea. Tonight, there is a moon at last. I shall establish a vantage point from my window in the villa. You will be stationed in the chapel which we will bait to attract the ghoul.'

Vanderville nodded emphatically; this was the sort of direct action of which he approved.

'You will be stationed behind the altar. If you start falling asleep again, get up and patrol the outside of the chapel, but do not leave the immediate environs. If the creature takes the bait, make as much noise as possible and hopefully I will hear you and come to your assistance.'

'That's your plan?' asked Vanderville sceptically. 'It seems a little light in a few areas.'

'I have never set out for a general, or a genius of strategy. I am a simple girl. But it seems to me that simple combinations are the best.'

'Very well,' sighed Vanderville, considering that he had his sabre and could probably handle one ghoul by himself, armed or not, even a homicidal one. 'What are we using for bait?'

'Here we enter into the beauty of simplicity. *You* are the bait.'

'I am the bait, and the trap? I fear you may be confusing simplicity with stupidity. The creature has so far struck at animals and old men, it may not fancy its chances against an armed man.'

'I have considered that,' she nodded. 'You must conceal your weapon somewhere in the chapel, so that you appear to be alone and undefended. Perhaps you can feign sleep.'

'I see. I think I understand the simplicity of this plan. You had better go now before I conceal my sabre in some unspeakable part of you.'

'*Bonne chance mon ami.* Remember to shout loudly.'

–

Dumas was in the stable yard in his shirt, baring his face and arms to the sun.

'Glorious morning,' he said with his easy grin. 'Will you two be joining us for the hunt this evening? A chance for you to earn your spurs, eh Gracchus?' he said, digging him in the ribs.

'I regret that this display of princely skill is not my metier,' answered Gracchus. 'I do hope that the boar will not take you away early? I believe there is a feast of some sort today.'

'I doubt it,' said Dumas, his head askance. 'We depart at dusk. This is more an exercise in vermin control than a sporting occasion. Are you sure you won't come? I daresay we could mount you on a carthorse or something.'

'I fear I shall not hunt,' said Gracchus, 'and I must detain Vanderville here too, but I wish you joy of it. Chasing boar must make a pleasant change from hunting rebel insurgents?'

'They squeal just the same,' said Dumas, and he turned on his heel and stomped up the gallery stairs.

—

Imagining that Vanderville was at a loose end, Gracchus had proposed a few errands for him. These were concerned with finding people with whom Gracchus required to speak and then directing or escorting them to the press office in the stables, where Gracchus was conducting his interrogations with a smug disregard for both propriety and the social or military status of his guests.

'You haven't got very far with your reading, then?' said Vanderville brightly, as they entered the press office. He was a profound, though not an avid reader, confining himself to study in military technical works.

'You could help me instead of making observations that are as unhelpful as they are fatuous. I have in fact completed a great deal of my preliminary sorting and evaluation. I don't have your eyes,' said Gracchus, indicating his spectacles. 'There are volumes and volumes of bound diaries,' he grunted, rifling through the cases, 'and what looks like business papers. I will wager we find his will in here somewhere too.

'This is interesting. Mombello corresponded with Corsican friends who could shed light on Corsican folklore. There is one here that is pertinent to Paolette's strange remarks about a Corsican dream monster. Listen to this:

> The dream hunters, or mazzere, are unknown outside Corsica, and probably date from prehistoric times. They are people possessed of a particular faculty for foreseeing death. At night they go hunting – or dream they do so – and kill an animal, in whom they recognise a human face. The person recognised in the dream invariably dies, which always takes place within a year.'

Vanderville nodded. 'The bit about killing animals seems to fit...' but Gracchus was still holding forth.

'There are some annotations here, over his own earlier research, Mombello has made a note to the effect here that he was careful to preserve any knowledge of the tradition from Alexandre himself, for fear of exasperating his condition, which indicates that he had not identified Alexandre's malady as a kind of sleeping sickness. Then he mentions these mazzere again,

> The common people believe that they are persons at whose baptism some words of the ceremony were omitted or garbled by the priest, or incorrectly repeated by the godparents. Thereafter they live a life apart, linked with the forces of darkness and death. In fact, they are intermediaries between death and the living, or what one might describe as death's heralds.'

'Didn't Alexandre say that he was helping his father to write his memoirs?' asked Vanderville. 'Might he have come across this study of mazzerisme and made some conclusions of his own?'

'That is one possibility,' said Gracchus, sucking his pen. He shoved away the papers and grasped a pile of leatherbound journals, opening the first one. 'Now we come to Mombello's old diaries. This section has been definitely worked over by Alexandre in compiling the memoirs. I presume this other pen is his hand.'

He shuffled feverishly through the journals. 'The relevant point in this one is that the dates of Marbeuf's relations with Letizia are laid bare. I had two questions – could Mombello's brother be the father of Napoleon? The answer is no, the dates of the movements of Marbeuf and Letizia do not coincide. There is no convenient sofa, as it were. The second question concerns the paternity of one of the General's brothers, Louis. In that case, the evidence is damning if not conclusive I'm afraid.'

He sighed. 'I have just the baptism records Paolette promised to recite, and I'm done. It occurred to me that when Mombello told his valet he needed to talk to Alexandre about the tree, it was not the liberty tree he was referring to, but a genealogical one.

'Imagine the scene. Mombello, out after dark and unable to locate his son, comes across someone in the chapel. A woman according to Charles. Their conversation is overheard by a third party eavesdropping up a ladder. Who was that person, Vanderville?'

'It could have been Alexandre or Piotr. Or Charles could have lied, maybe it was him up the ladder? How else could he know who was talking inside the chapel? I don't believe he could have heard from the door.'

'There is another possibility. Someone who was outside that night who we have not yet identified.'

They were interrupted by a new arrival. Vanderville nodded to Gracchus and left.

'Thank you for coming,' said Gracchus, moving out from behind his editor's desk to greet Commissary Fesch.

'Not at all,' replied Fesch, 'I had been meaning to come and see what you were getting up to in the print office. I may have a few things that would be useful to you to include in the *Courier*, so when I received your summons, it was not unwelcome.'

'You must be very busy preparing for your nieces' wedding mass?' said Gracchus, indicating for Fesch to join him in sitting down.

'Not really. I did help the priest a little with some of the republican forms that he needs to incorporate to assuage the misgivings of the more anticlerical elements of the Army of Italy.'

'I believe in the French Republic, one and indivisible, creator of equality, and in General Bonaparte its sole defender?' suggested Gracchus.

'Be good Christians, and you will all be excellent democrats. Be good democrats and you will make a successful marriage,' sighed Fesch. 'It's not really rousing stuff, but that is weddings for you. Banality reigns supreme.'

'A person very dear to me once said that marriage is the tomb of trust and love,' said Gracchus ruefully.

'Which sounds very fine and permits the utterer to gather a modest basketful of Rousseau's laurels, but I am belatedly finding that marriage is not all bad. There may even be some faint, very faint benefit in it for the man,' mused Fesch.

'And for the bride?' asked Gracchus.

'I see none whatsoever,' said Fesch, leaning back in his chair. 'Her family sign away her procreative and amatory rights with the bride price. She is entered into a contract loaded against her before she is old enough to know what she is in for.'

'One of the great benefits of the new republic's laws is that one can now exit such an unequal contract. Man has rent asunder the bonds formed by god,' observed Gracchus.

Fesch surprised Gracchus with the orthodoxy of his reply. 'No power can break a marriage when it has been validly contracted; for god himself having formed the bond of matrimony, no human power can dissolve it.'

'An unfashionable position in republican Paris,' countered Gracchus.

'Perhaps. I do believe that the republican form of matrimony *is* an improvement,' said Fesch. 'Marriage is no longer a yoke, a chain, it is no more than it should be, the accomplishment of nature's great plan, the receipt of an agreeable debt that each citizen owes to the fatherland.'

'I suppose that the proof of this is that since the revolutionary tribunal instituted the law of divorce, women have pursued divorces almost twice as often as men,' observed Gracchus.

The two men sat back in their chairs and regarded each other with some liking. Fesch broke the agreeable silence first. 'I had understood from your previous victims that you were breaking all the conventions of polite discourse in your interrogations this morning,' he said.

'Sadly, not everybody appreciates my efforts to clear up the mystery surrounding Mombello's unfortunate demise,' agreed Gracchus. 'Nor are they all equally helpful.' He leant back in his chair. 'You, for instance, Commissary Fesch, told me that you were absent from the villa the night of the comte's murder, because the supply convoy was thought to be arriving and you went with General Dumas to arrange its reception and passage through the village.'

'Ah,' said Fesch, 'now we come to the rub. That is correct.'

'And yet the supply convoy did not arrive here until several days later,' said Gracchus.

Fesch sat back in his chair and spread his hands expansively. 'Indeed. I believe that is a matter of public record. The fact of the matter is transport is notoriously unreliable in these sad times of war. Upon arriving in the village that evening we discovered that the reports of the convoy's imminent arrival were somewhat exaggerated. The waggons had been halted on the road when an importunate artillery officer requisitioned their draught cattle, causing an involuntary halt to their progress until replacement animals could be pressed into service.

Without authority, I might add. This is, in some ways, an occupational hazard of life in a war, where the priority of the military functionaries follows a hierarchy of needs. My own waggons, those under my command, that is, have been involved in similar incidents. Several that I had despatched to Paris carrying works of art have been delayed by orders for the requisition of their animals signed by my own nephew. On complaining I was brusquely informed that all available transport has been reserved for the army in a strict order of priority: first, ammunition; secondly, food and forage, third, the transport of the wounded; and lastly, transport of other stores, namely uniforms and equipment for the soldiers at the front.'

'Your presence in the village earlier in the evening has been confirmed by General Dumas,' continued Gracchus smoothly. 'After meeting with disappointment there, where did you proceed?'

'I spent the rest of the night in the company of a friend in the village,' replied the ex-priest evasively. 'She will be prepared to confirm that if pressed.'

'Was this friend an amateur, or a professional?' asked Gracchus.

'Well, if you must know, she tends more towards the latter,' said Fesch, 'but who is casting stones?'

'Thank you,' said Gracchus. He knew that testimony of this sort was easily bought and would be as difficult to disprove.

'Now if that is everything, I will be on my way.' Fesch rose from his chair. 'I must say though Gracchus,' he said as a parting shot, 'you are really grown into quite the tyrant. There is scarce a gnat's hair between you and my nephew in terms of dogmatism.'

As Fesch opened the door, Gracchus cleared his throat. 'One more thing, *Citoyen* Commissary,' said Gracchus. 'You are perhaps the person closest to *Citoyenne* Buonaparte here. How would you describe her relations with the Comte Mombello since this jolly house party began?'

Fesch paused in the doorway. 'Letizia is not an ardent woman,' he began. 'Her warmth is as a matter of good form reserved primarily for the members of her family. But in some ways, the Comte Mombello, as an old friend, transcended her coolness. It is my belief that the renewal of their acquaintance reminded her of happier days, and therefore of her much-regretted husband too. Consequentially her feelings towards Mombello I would describe as warm.'

'Too warm for her son, Bonaparte's liking?' asked Gracchus.

'You would do better to ask him about that,' said Fesch, and he let the door clang abruptly behind him.

Vanderville was on his way in as Fesch left. 'He didn't look too happy,' he said to Gracchus, as he unloaded a copper pot of coffee and two cups down on the desk. 'What's up? Did you prove one of his stolen paintings a fake?'

'Possibly,' said Gracchus, absently, steepling his fingers, and lost in thought.

'I must say,' said Vanderville, pouring the coffee, 'it has been most instructive to observe your interrogation technique this morning. But I can't see that we are really getting much further on with this business.'

'No?' said Gracchus, through narrow eyes. 'How would you characterise our progress, my young protegee?'

'We have established that there is a general fear of some supernatural being stalking the villa grounds at night, ripping up animals, and pushing people down wells,' began Vanderville.

'I am quite prepared to discount the ghoul,' said Gracchus, 'but somebody wants us to believe in it. I am inclined to view the animal killings as an attempt to spread terror or doubt, but as regards the murder of the Comte Mombello, I place the supernatural aside. It is at best a distraction, and quite possibly a deliberate piece of misdirection on the murderer's part.'

'Which leaves us with those present in the villa that evening who had both opportunity and motive,' said Vanderville. 'I suppose we may exclude the children, and those who had almost no connection with the murdered scion. Also, the servants who universally adored their master. That leaves us with any of the house guests that evening, especially those we know left the villa.'

Gracchus's eyes lit up, 'Bravo, Lieutenant. And if our dear departed friend the Comte Mombello made it to the chapel that evening we have a much briefer list of suspects.'

Gracchus stroked his waistcoat, and managed to get ink on it. 'Foremost of whom is one Alexandre Marbeuf, the dead man's nephew who stood to inherit, and has admitted to being outside the house at the same time as his uncle apparently met his fate. He had both motive and opportunity.'

'So, we arrest Alexandre,' said Vanderville disconsolately into his coffee. 'We have sufficient proof. The will gives the motive, he admits to night forays. The evening of the murder he was abroad, and he is the only one who admits to having been in the chapel that night.'

Gracchus stared at the ceiling. 'It is not enough to hang a man, Vanderville, and his motive is weak, he did not need to kill his uncle to inherit, merely to wait. If we could but catch him in the act of ramshackling a pug I would feel better about it.'

'I don't like it either. He is my friend, and I feel sorry for it, but he is in the frame.'

'Let us consider those of our fellow guests we can be reasonably certain were in the vicinity of the chapel that night.'

'Fesch is out, then,' said Vanderville.

'Actually,' corrected Gracchus, 'I spoke to Dumas this morning, and his reaction – I quote – was, "Fesch helped with the supply recce? That reprobate didn't hang around to help. He was with us for fifteen minutes, no more. We didn't see him again. Probably went back to bed in the villa with an altar boy," so Fesch's whereabouts aren't really clear. His alibi is, shall we say, more gut than gilt.'

'So Fesch is still with us?' said Vanderville.

'Yes. He is demoniacally unscrupulous, and he had a strong financial motive. We have seen that there is a complicated web of vultures competing for the immensely lucrative army supply contracts here. Access to Mombello provided an opportunity to gobble up those new contracts related to the new republic Bonaparte has established here.'

Vanderville considered this. It seemed unlikely that the parsing of a few scraps of cloth and a purloined sack or two of bread was much of an incentive to murder, and he said so.

Gracchus shook his head. 'Not only are the sums involved enormous, but it does not finish here. As the network of new republics expands to include Genova, Venice and the other territories Bonaparte threatens to overrun, an established contractor with a proven reputation could establish a fortune to rival Croesus. Mombello held the key to this, so Josephine and Lieutenant Charles, Fesch and Piotr; they all had reason to seek his favour, and if it had turned out that they realised Mombello himself wanted the contracts instead of a mere consideration, Mombello would have instantly transformed himself from a potential ally to a certain liability.'

'We can narrow our list further to include any of those we have demonstrated were both at the reception and abroad that evening.' Vanderville counted them off on his fingers, 'Charles and Josephine, Alexandre, who were all at the reception too, and whoever was up the ladder.'

'Yes, and you have missed out one,' said Gracchus. 'The General himself. He has told me that the comte had become an embarrassment to him, and he is one person who can traverse the entire grounds, even Berthier's sentries, with entire ease.'

Vanderville sucked in his breath, and glanced at the open window. 'Careful Gracchus...'

He got up and closed the window. 'But if it comes to that, Gracchus' he went on, 'Why not Berthier? He can also bypass the sentinels and the liberty of movement applies equally to him.'

'He lacks motive,' sighed Gracchus, 'his only interests are *Citoyenne* Visconti and his work, and Mombello was a threat to neither, as far as we know.'

He decided to broach an even less promising subject. 'Let us not forget that according to Charles that roll call at the chapel includes the Bonaparte sister, Paolette.'

'Surely not,' said Vanderville. 'Charles is a decent fellow, but you can't take anything he says too seriously, and the sentries didn't see any women abroad.'

'The sentries missed Josephine if she *was* with Charles,' said Gracchus sternly. 'Why not Paolette? Berthier said that one of the Bonaparte women is a sleepwalker.'

'Speaking of Paolette, did you see her at breakfast?' Vanderville asked with an air of unconcern, wandering over to the stable door to glance outside.

'She was in excellent spirits,' said Gracchus carelessly, 'babbling on about her trousseau.'

Vanderville shot home the stable door bolt with a bang. 'The corbeilles *are* impressive,' he said. 'They must have cost a fortune.'

'Hmm,' said Gracchus. 'For people completely ruined four years ago, it's a pretty success.'

'The family is on their way up,' observed Vanderville glumly. 'No wonder Bonaparte was unimpressed with the Baciocchi mesalliance.'

'The Bonaparte girls are too good for captains now. Which reminds me, did you bring the things from the kitchen bins I asked you for?'

Vanderville pulled out his handkerchief and upended it on the table. A number of cracked empty crab shells fell out. 'They are all empty,' he said. 'You will have to wait 'til tonight to indulge yourself.'

Gracchus picked one up on the end of a pencil and peered at it, then he carried it to the corner of the room and raising it above his head inserted it into a spider's web. Rotating the pencil until it was thoroughly bound in dusty cobwebs, he looked at it closely again in the light by the window. He regarded Vanderville over his spectacles. 'I am almost certain, I have something at last,' he said.

'Congratulations,' snorted Vanderville, 'does it make our task easier?'

Gracchus shook his head. 'We are about to find that out.' He picked up his papers and stashed them haphazardly in a manger. 'We had better get to the kitchens, we have an appointment, and Piotr will be waiting.'

They found Piotr in the cold larder adjoining the kitchen, and as he unlocked the door there, he explained, 'These cellars are older than the villa. They are in a sorry state, but the temperature down here is perfect for making ices.' He pushed the door open. 'Not that Bonaparte eats them, but his wife is crazy for them, which keeps me busy creating new flavours.'

'But isn't the water down there hot?' asked Gracchus.

'That water comes from lower down in a separate pipe and doesn't need a pump. You will see the pipes for the hot water travelling through the lower cellars and the old baths. Watch your step, there is a lot of decaying masonry and the floors are cracked.'

A cement spiral staircase led downwards from the cold larder. Below, they followed the bobbing lantern of Piotr through vaults crammed with cobwebbed wine barrels and decayed olive presses. He talked over his shoulder as they went. 'Bonaparte took possession of the keys on the pretext that the children may get down here. I suspect he just wants to explore it himself and learn the engineering secrets. He chose Villa Mombello for his headquarters because he loves having hot baths on demand, and the hydraulic installation here is the last word in refinement.' The passage opened up into a chamber, and he held his lantern high. 'Welcome to my kingdom,' he said, laughing. 'There are more lanterns on your right, have a look around.'

By the light cast from the lanterns they saw the baths. They were built on the roman basilica plan, with a wide central hypogeum, two lateral aisles divided by the stumps of arches, and a third intact aisle at the end shading three niches. They lit a lantern each and explored. Here and there were some faint traces of stucco decoration, while in the corners there were still some coloured tesserae, giving a hint of the former polychrome mosaic floor, which was now just beaten dirt. From these humble traces it appeared that the baths must have been truly impressive. A few remnants of a ceiling of shells and pumice stone were inside the niches themselves, which still had carved spouts where water once gushed out. It was cooler there, and Piotr's buckets and equipment for making ices were clustered around.

'I suppose the baths themselves were filled in when the piping system was put in, sometime in the last fifty years,' explained Piotr. 'There are some fragments of marble basins in the garden that may have come from here. Sad for the antiquarian, but it gives me more space to work.'

'So, this is the ancient bath complex,' breathed Vanderville. 'It must have been beautiful.'

'There must be more rooms,' said Gracchus. 'This would have been the baths, but if you follow the pipes, they pass through the end wall. How do you get in there, Piotr?'

'Come and see.' Beside the niches he placed his lantern on a hook jutting from the wall. With his fingers he traced the outline of a stone door set flush in the wall behind his buckets. It would have been difficult to find were it not for the head of some grinning satyr carved into the surface, and the fact that the whole door and the floor before it was scrubbed clean.

'This must be the entrance to the reservoirs,' said Piotr. 'Nobody has the key to this one though. It must have disappeared in the paraphernalia of some long-departed major-domo. Bonaparte was quite angry about it, and he talked about having it blown open with gunpowder. Berthier dissuaded him.' He gestured at the roof and crumbling walls. 'Look at this place, an explosion in here could bring the whole villa down. They wanted a mason to open it up, but there isn't one in the village, and the one who came from Milan looked at the door for about three hours, declared he didn't have the right tools with him, and disappeared never to be seen again.' Vanderville tripped over a wooden bucket, almost spilling it. 'Careful with that, it's pistachio with citrons,' said Piotr, checking the brown paper and lard seal was not broken.

Gracchus looked at the other buckets. Each was labelled, and he peered more closely. 'Burnt filbert, parmesan, bergamot – I perceive we are in the presence of a master. Please explain your method.'

Piotr smiled. 'An adept perhaps. I use a syrup of sugar dissolved in water, then work the various flavours in with eggs and cream. The mixture goes in one of these pewter *sorbetières* which goes in a wooden bucket filled with ice and salt. When it has congealed it goes into the moulds, then I seal it with brown paper and lard and freeze it hard in the salt and ice mixture. They keep for a while down here.'

'You have to keep your preparation area very clean?' asked Gracchus, indicating a set of brooms and brushes propped by the niches.

'Yes,' agreed Piotr, 'dust in the air will affect the freezing process and ruin everything.'

Gracchus shivered. 'We had better get back upstairs to eat,' he said. As they left, he whispered to Vanderville, 'We ought to see inside the rest of the complex. Find a way to get that door open.'

Vanderville shrugged; if the combined efforts of Berthier and Bonaparte had failed to open the door, he did not see what he could do, but he bit his tongue. He too was hungry, and he was looking forward to seeing the hunting party leave, after which his unwelcome vigil at the chapel could commence. 'No one has passed through that door in centuries,' he asked Gracchus. 'Why bother?'

'If they had, we would not know,' whispered Gracchus. 'Piotr keeps the whole area so neat, a demi-brigade could pass through and leave no trace.'

When they exited the kitchens, they heard the merry sounds of a family party on the terrace to celebrate the first anniversary of the Transpadane Republic. Gracchus went off to make himself presentable, and Vanderville made his way to the stable yard, where tables had been laid out for the junior officers. Feasting continued until it grew towards dusk when the hunting party began to assemble. Its numbers were much diminished from the promised crowd, as drunkenness had wrought sad carnage among the hunters and the hunt followers alike. Some of the generals passed through the yard on unsteady legs on their way back to the inn to sleep and announced their belief that the salvos of gunfire and loud rejoicing from the camp had ruined the possibility of a good hunt. As they tottered off to bed, only a few die-hards mounted up with Dumas, Hercule and the other passionate hunters.

As the junior officers peeled off one by one, Vanderville was the last one left smoking on the gallery. When all had left, he made his way wearily to the chapel, to begin his lonely vigil. and there he dozed in the nave on a chair under a blanket, his sabre neatly concealed under his seat, and the doors carefully pulled to.

It must have been past midnight when he nodded awake with a start, brought to sudden alertness by some primeval sense that he was no longer alone. He opened his eyes to reveal the roof, one spacious vault of brown timber, casting a solemn gloom, which was still increased by the lateness of the hour, and not diminished by the wan light of the moon, admitted through the windows of blue glass. He strained his ears into the shaded depths of the chapel, but heard nothing, so he eased himself up in his seat as silently as he was able, pushing back his cover to retrieve his sabre. The scrape of the scabbard on the moon-dappled chapel flagstones sounded too loud, amplified by the size and shape of this colossal chamber, and he froze a moment. The arching of the roof, with great rafters stretching across it, and the sickly gleams that glanced through the dull casements, possessed his fancy with ideas that he was inside the bowels of some ship adrift on a vapour of unwelcoming dreams.

Then he heard it again, the tread of a foot on the stone chapel steps, and he saw the chapel door already stood ajar. Steeped in lethargy, he covered the distance to it as swiftly as he was able, and took post behind the open door as he buckled on his sword belt, girding himself for action with a growing seed of foreboding churning his stomach.

From outside came the muffled sound of an urgently whispering voice; the words were indistinct until he heard the unmistakeable rich voice of Fesch say, 'We are in agreement until then, that is all that matters.' Vanderville stretched out an arm and then his scabbard scraped again on the floor, and he heard footsteps receding.

The door creaked open, and his poised sabre arrested the silhouette of Lieutenant Charles on the threshold. His countenance was ash coloured and forbidding, and his staring eyes were far removed from anything like cordiality.

'What the blazes are you doing here?' He took in Vanderville's unsheathed sabre with a frown, before his voice recovered its habitual velvet grace, 'Ah, hunting the goose-killer? Not bothered about geese myself. I'm more partial to pork, if you know what I mean.'

The chapel air, still perfumed by incense, was refreshing with the crisp nocturnal breeze from the door, and Vanderville lowered his sabre.

'Not tonight, you're not. I am on duty here I'm afraid,' answered Vanderville. 'What brings you out in the middle of the night?' He tried to see over Charles's shoulder.

'More or less the same as you. From the villa I thought I saw figures in the garden, so I shinned out of the window and followed them down here.' He ran his fingers through his hair, and with assumed weariness resumed, 'Probably nothing. You know how when you have the hammer of suspicion in your hand, everything starts to look like a nail. Damnably tiresome. Now I know you are here on watch, I shall leave you to it. Good hunting, and good night.'

Vanderville watched Charles traverse the lawns, and he was almost at the stables before it occurred to Vanderville that Charles had said he was coming from the house, where he had no business at this hour.

Settling himself back down under his covers, nothing further occurred to disturb his repose, but when sleep finally overcame him, it was a troubled, rather than restful, realm of repose that greeted him. He dreamt that he was with the crowd of village people who after the feast had made a din outside of the villa windows with saucepans, whistles and cowbells until Berthier paid them off. As they shouted and hooted, he heard a thrumming of feet behind him, and down the carriage drive trotted a procession of phantasmal pigs. It began as a trickle, but finally tens and then hundreds of the wild creatures came in great waves, and at they ran between the legs of the villagers they buffeted and pushed until people started to fall under their trotters, and the boar trampled and gashed them as they passed.

He woke with a jolt from the dream and realised he was cold. While he slept his blanket had slipped off, and his limbs were rigid, his feet dead in his boots. He eased himself carefully up and hobbled to the chapel door. It was almost dawn now, and outside grey light bathed the villa, while the last tendrils of night mists were eddying under the trees. From his vantage point the whole gardens were open before him, and he watched some tired hunters tying up horses below the terrace. The hunting party must be drifting in only now, but why had they chosen to ignore the regulations about horses in the gardens? Watching the men dismount, he detected a fatigue in their movements that was not accounted for merely by hard riding; they moved like men half asleep, or rather like unseeing phantoms. He rubbed his weary eyes. Even in the part-light the distinctive figure of Hercule was discernible where he was leading his unsaddled horse to water at a trough. He had just made up his mind to join his friend when his attention was distracted by new arrivals.

Two files of mounted Guides on tired horses paced under the arch from the stables forming an escort square. There was a morose slumped figure in the midst of them on a led horse. His horse's bridle was held by one of the Guides, and the dismounted men under the terrace turned their heads away as this forlorn-looking group approached. The riders of the Guides did not halt with the others but moved slowly down the garden towards the chapel road, and as they came nearer Vanderville saw that the hunched figure was slumped under a great coat; his naked pale legs, streaked with blood, were hanging limply against the flanks of his steed. The man swaying gently as if in a dream and did not stir as his exhausted horse stumbled. His hair was wet from the dew and matted with a sinister dark hue that could only be gore. Vanderville saw his face, and called out to him, but Piotr was deaf to his enquiry, and stared dazedly ahead, as the party passed by Vanderville and up the track to the villa without acknowledging him.

Chapter Eleven

By the time Hercule had stabled his horse, washed up and arrived on the stable gallery, Vanderville had roused Charles, and they waited tensely as Hercule clumped slowly up the stair, took a seat, and running his hand over his fatigued brow, began to relate his tale. 'We roused a drift of boar in the woods at first light and began a long chase. The roaming hounds with bells around their necks were sent ahead to bring the boar to bay, which we eventually managed after a long run, coming in at the death to a blocked gorge covered in heavy thickets. The gorge floor was obscured by low light and undergrowth, so the huntsmen formed a ring around its crest with the bay dogs, and three of us dismounted and began to beat through the bushes at the bottom of the cranny. Ahead of us bounded the catch dogs, who worry the boar so that the hunters can come up with their swords without being gored.' He paused, and drew the brandy bottle to his elbow.

'What happened then?' asked Charles impatiently, pulling his coat a little tighter around him, for the morning was still chill.

'It was cold, and a mist filled the gorge,' resumed Hercule, taking a nip of brandy. 'I could see my breath in front of me, and the mist dulled the sounds of the dogs, the whippers-in above me and the other hunters making their way through the dense bushes as we beat our way up. I could see almost nothing ahead, but I could hear the low growling of the catch dogs, and the occasional rapid skittering of boars' feet on the dead leaves.' He stopped again and stared cold-eyed out over the deserted stable yard. A few chickens had started a desultory pecking by the troughs, and their consort was preparing to salute the dawn from his post on a cart.

'I kept moving towards the sound of the dogs, who were crashing about the covert with eager yelps. I caught flashes of them bounding among some sharp slabs of fallen rock, and made haste to come up, but it was hard going with brambles tearing at my coat and face, and then of a sudden a small fox sprang out from between the rocks, startling me. She froze, quivering, and stared at me with her yellow eyes for a moment, and I looked back at her, and then as quick as she arrived, she streaked between my legs and away. A bad omen, I thought to myself, and it was then I saw the boar.' He took another bump of brandy, and Vanderville swallowed nervously and leant in to catch his next words.

'He was a magnificent brute, with a heaving great shaggy shield of muscle on his shoulders. Cornered at the gorge head, he stood defying the ring of barking dogs. He struck at the boldest with his tusks, and made a short plunging run at another. As he caught one dog and tossed it over his cape like it was a leaf, I saw a man moving in the shadows behind him. I parted the brush to see better and took a firmer grip on my sword.

'The dogs were circling and were barking fit to wake the dead. They too were alarmed by the unexpected appearance of the man, who suddenly leapt upon the boar from behind. I saw that he was in his nightshirt, and he sawed wildly at the boar's throat with a knife. It was over in a few seconds, and I approached him with my heart in my mouth. The naked man was hunched over the animal, working at it in a frenzy, his shoulders and arms shuddering. Although he had the body of a man, there was something in the way he moved that was not like any man or animal that I know.

'Trembling with horror I held out my sword at arm's length. I don't mind telling you that I was regretting my sabre – that pokey little hunting sword felt a mere table knife to me. Just as I was about to make contact, he spun around, and fixed me with glaring eyes, and I stepped back. His shirt was all streaked with blood, his hands and arms soaked in gore, but what was more horrible was his face. His eyes were glazed, like an actor devoured by his part, and he made odd jerking movements with his hands. I recognised him instantly even though it seemed to me, as I calmed him down, that he wasn't really there, and hadn't noticed me, or any of us at all. The other hunters had come up by then and I said, "Come on, old fellow, let's get you back," and covered him with my coat, and we helped him to stumble out. All the way back in, he didn't say a word, but sometimes talked to himself, as if he were asleep and dreaming.' Hercule sat back in his chair exhausted and shuddered. He closed his eyes briefly. 'It's a bad business, an awfully bad business,' he said, and he stood up wearily. 'I think I shall turn in now.'

Vanderville was not surprised when a Guide arrived with a message from the villa before he and Charles had even finished their coffee. The man bore a terse note from Berthier, summoning him to report immediately with Gracchus to the bureau. Charles had been a dour breakfast companion and Vanderville was glad to leave him.

An oblivious and peevish Gracchus greeted Vanderville in his night robe, and on hearing the revelations it appeared that he proposed to descend to meet Bonaparte and Berthier in that state of undress, and Vanderville had to waste time persuading him otherwise. When they did arrive at the doors of the bureau a stony-faced Guide of the bulkiest variety was stationed there, and he wordlessly ushered them in.

Expecting a scene of bloody horror, Vanderville was greeted instead by the sight of Piotr in a chair by the fire, with Berthier stood behind him in avuncular manner. Someone had cleaned Piotr up a bit and brought him some clothes, and even his sword, and he was listening to Berthier and drinking coffee while General Bonaparte paced agitatedly up and down beside the billiard table. A haggard secretary sat meekly at one desk.

'*Salut*, Vanderville, Gracchus,' said a pale-faced Piotr. 'Have you heard? I am under arrest.'

'Good morning *Citoyen* Gracchus,' said Berthier, tight-lipped. 'As you can see, while you slept others have accomplished what you proved reluctant or unable to do.' Gracchus cocked one eyebrow calmly and held his peace. Vanderville stood to attention, and Bonaparte continued pacing, ignoring them all, his head bent in concentration.

'As you may have heard,' Berthier resumed, 'Piotr is arrested for the murder of Comte Mombello. I have had my suspicions for some time about the identity of the ghoul, and when it became apparent to me that the efforts of the designated investigator were hopelessly mired in gluttony and distractions, I opened my own parallel approach I am pleased to announce that the walls of ignorance have fallen, and now I am able to lay out the chain of evidence that led to my success.' He placed his back to the fire with his arms folded, and Piotr leant forward with an anguished groan and put his head in his hands to stare at the floor.

'Just the bare points, Berthier,' said Bonaparte from where he stalked behind the table, 'the *pertinent* points.'

'The day of his disappearance, you overheard Mombello have an argument with his nephew,' commenced Berthier, addressing his remarks to Piotr's bowed head. 'Suspicious of something the comte had said, you returned to his cabinet later, and found there on his desk some papers that were of peculiar interest to you.'

Bonaparte stopped pacing. 'Yes, Berthier,' he said, gesturing to the secretary to stop writing. 'The intricacies of those documents are of less interest here than the evidence of a crime.' He turned to the secretary. 'Leave the record of this with me for review and make yourself scarce.'

Piotr looked up at Berthier. 'Where are these papers I am alleged to have seen?'

Berthier waved a hand dismissively. 'They disappeared before I could make a full examination. We will doubtless find them when we make a search of your quarters. My suspicion is that you found something that inspired you to blackmail Mombello. When the papers turn up, it will be sufficient to incriminate you.' Berthier held up a finger for effect; he was clearly enjoying his role. 'You arranged a meeting at the chapel, where Mombello's dignified refusal to be blackmailed frustrated your hopes of ill gain. And after arguing violently with him, you fought. In the process of the struggle, you knocked over and damaged one of the bridal corbeilles. At some point, you drew your sabre and struck him dead. After murdering him you manhandled his body out of the chapel to the newly exposed wellhead and hurled him down it. He was a frail old man, and it would not have taken much.

'You hoped of course that his death would be concealed, or if he were found, taken for an accident. Something, incidentally, that did not deceive me for a moment. But even if by some flash of brilliance foul play was suspected, you were aware that everyone had heard the quarrel between uncle and nephew over republican principles, and you cynically hoped that Alexandre Marbeuf would be framed for the cold-blooded murder.'

Piotr shook his head wearily, and Berthier crowed, 'Perhaps, even, you had read far enough in Mombello's papers to know that a motive would be ascribed because he planned to disinherit his—'

'That's enough, Berthier!' warned Bonaparte, bringing his hand down sharply on the billiard table.

Berthier swallowed awkwardly, and continued, 'On these grounds you are to be tried for murder. The punishment will be dire I'm afraid, if not quite on the ancient Roman level of barbarism.' Piotr gazed up at him coolly, and Berthier deftly manoeuvred from the fireplace to join Bonaparte at the billiard table. 'As for the unnatural massacring of animals that was some sort of preparation for your crime, or a symptom of some sort of brain-fever, we can pass over all of that. Presumably it will cease now that you are to be deprived of your liberty.'

Bonaparte leant over the table. 'Thank you, Berthier, that appears to be adequate. Now, Lieutenant Vanderville, you will escort Lieutenant Piotr to the crypt beneath the chapel. It is secure enough to serve as a brig until he can be dealt with. And no one need go in there until the weddings. Any idea who the proper authorities are, Berthier?'

'He is an officer of the Polish Legion, so technically we ought to try him under martial law, but I think it is better we hand him over to the Transpadane Republic civil power. It will bolster their authority and be a useful test of their interim judicial system.'

Bonaparte nodded. 'Put a file of Guides on the chapel, Vanderville, and have the wedding things in the crypt rearranged. Piotr, anything to say? No? Leave your sword with Berthier then, and off you go.' Vanderville stared at the floor of the bureau. It was an attractive herringbone pattern, and he wished he could remain looking at it forever. His meditations were interrupted by a scrape as a wan-faced Piotr pushed back his chair and stood uncertainly as if he wanted to speak.

'Yes?' said Bonaparte, impatiently. 'Do you have something to say after all?'

Piotr mumbled indistinctly, his eyes on the floor, and Berthier snapped, 'Out with it, man!'

Piotr looked up then, and addressing Bonaparte he said, 'Only when you learn to question your happiness will the truth be known to you, General.'

Bonaparte averted his eyes, and Berthier sighed with exasperation. 'Enough of this,' he said, and dismissed them with a wave. Vanderville saluted and left the room, with Piotr trudging behind him.

Berthier smiled at Gracchus who said, 'Is this matter resolved to your satisfaction, *Citoyen* General?'

'Oh, I think so,' said Berthier, looking at Bonaparte for confirmation, who nodded absent-mindedly. He had already turned his attention to the maps on the table and seemed little disposed to pay further attention to Berthier and Gracchus, who moved away to the windows.

'I will leave in the morning,' said Gracchus, cautiously lowering his voice. 'I have business in Milan, and now you have your suspect confined there is little for me to do here.'

Berthier was peering out of the window at the usual confusion under the awning in the courtyard. It was compounded by the pioneers of the Polish Legion, who had commenced construction of a wooden scaffolding directly outside on the carriage drive. 'Yes, having the murderer locked up is useful,' he said. 'However, there is still the matter of the newsletter.'

'If you designate my successor on the *Courier*, I can hand over the work this afternoon,' said Gracchus.

'I think it better you continue for now,' said Berthier. 'There will be the wedding, and the ball afterwards, then we depart Mombello for the lakes at Como. At that point you may take your leave of us, to resume your career as a rabble rouser, or a bookseller, or whatever you call yourself now that the matter of police work is apparently beneath you.'

'I begin to fear that you intend to delay me indefinitely,' said Gracchus, 'yet have you considered that my very disposition renders me unsuited to working here with you? I admit you are managing great things here under that man,' he indicated Bonaparte with his thumb, 'and your reforms of Lombardy are inspiring, but,' he sighed, 'the society here has started to resemble nothing so much as a court, and I am not a courtier, *citoyen*.'

'We do not want court people, Gracchus, but men who are devoted to the Republic,' said Berthier with equanimity, opening the creaking window. The clerks under the awning looked up, and seeing his surveillance, redoubled their bustle.

'Do you relish working under him?' said Gracchus, indicating Bonaparte again. 'Suffering his intolerable fits of temper?'

'You are astute, my dear Gracchus. But remember that one day it will be a fine thing to be second to that man.' He smiled.

'Very well, if you must go, have the next issue of the *Courier* ready for me after the wedding and you will have your conge and passports.'

–

'I hope you are not going to bind me,' Piotr said to Vanderville as they crossed the terrace.

Vanderville did not meet his eyes. 'There are horses in the stables,' he said flatly, 'and nightfall is far away. You could be in Milan in two hours, and halfway to Bologna before the morning. Once you enter the Papal States you will be outside of the Republic's reach. Even without passports you might win through.'

'I don't think I want to run, Vanderville,' said Piotr quietly. They stopped at the terrace balustrade and leant on it, looking out over the distant hazy plain.

'Let me tell you of my curse,' he said. 'It begins with a dream.'

'What happens, in these dreams?' asked Vanderville quietly.

'It only occurs on certain nights. I dream that I am hunting an animal, and when I close in for the kill, the animal has the face of a human. The person whose face I have seen will always die soon afterwards.'

'And did you see Mombello's face in a dream?'

'Yes,' he swallowed guiltily, 'yes, I did.' He took a deep breath and turned to look at Vanderville, 'So, you see, I did it all.'

Vanderville looked at the church towers on the plain. Suddenly the view seemed bleak and drained of colour, despite the rising sun.

Chapter Twelve

After the arrest a palpable breeze of relief blew through the villa. There was some sadness at the terrible fall of Piotr of course, especially among the *citoyennes*, but they were compensated by the ongoing preparations for the marriages. A promised excursion was keenly awaited, and rumour had it that despite the war, a delightful pleasure cruise on the local lake itself was entirely probable, that watery element being declared neutral territory under the terms of the armistice.

It was not just the female portion of the villa that anticipated this imminent interlude with pleasure. Bonaparte began to run the officers ragged to expunge from their minds the expulsion of their comrade. The Guides were made a sacrifice to their commander's tireless energy and stretched skin thin by continuous escort duty, while the Polish Legion were kept busy erecting a series of pavilions on the lawns of the villa for the weddings. These last had been demanded by the visiting Imperial Austrian peace plenipotentiaries. Although their *ancien regime* suavity was a welcome novelty and distraction for the republicans, Bonaparte found them to be great sticklers in the matter of etiquette. They had insisted that a pavilion be moved to the centre of the garden, where the deliberations would take place after the wedding, this bower being declared a non-partisan oasis. Bonaparte had consented to this fiction, confining his scepticism to the observation that, 'This neutral point is nonetheless surrounded on all sides by the French army, and is in the midst of our bivouacs.'

Mombello's front awning was under siege from patrician Milanese jostling for access to the General who was feverishly striving to translate the preliminary armistice between the French Republic and the Austrian Empire into a lasting peace treaty. Gracchus enjoyed the company of a whole host of new diplomatic arrivals, and the intense and complicated political questions were a welcome puzzle for him diverting his attention from the questions he still had concerning Piotr's forthcoming trial.

The republicans and progressives who flocked to Mombello from the mosaic of heterogenous micro-states and bloated foreign fiefdoms that riddled the peninsula exhibited the ardour of apostles, the inexperience of theorists, the rancour of true believers, and a total disdain for the ideas and customs that they claimed to transform. In almost every town, mused Gracchus, there were a certain number of intellectuals who aspired to something a little above the ordinary level of ignorance. Their usefulness was balanced by an army of meddling priests, more like characters from an opera buffa than anyone in reality had any right to be.

Although ostensibly friends of the new Italian republics, the French found the homegrown Jacobins almost as troublesome as the old order and Bonaparte spent much time doing what he described as 'regulating the public impulse towards liberty'.

The succeeding afternoon found Gracchus listening to the orators in the gardens, or on the terrace where Josephine was coquetting away with Melzi, her elderly Milanese aspiring paramour, who was a most melancholy object. A tall emaciated figure who hobbled with the gout and had a complexion as yellow as a frog. Gracchus also enjoyed the company of this skilled negotiator. He found Melzi to have a clear and subtle intellect and a prodigious memory. 'See how eagerly they clamour to encumber themselves with the shackles of a court,' Melzi described the supplicant republicans at Mombello to Gracchus, and with a sweep of his arm he indicated the assembled ambassadors on the lawn trailing forlornly in Bonaparte's wake as he marched from tent to tent.

'All of the shackles of a court, with none of its advantages,' agreed Gracchus. Melzi was one of the few enjoying open access to Bonaparte, but he was discreet, and in answer to Gracchus's enquiries as to his negotiations with the General he would say only, 'He suffers from an admirable lack of tact, which is much to his benefit.'

Berthier was confined by Bonaparte to the cabinet all day. They worked hand in hand, like an old married couple, and Bonaparte had started insisting Berthier sleep downstairs in case he needed him to work in the night. He was insensitive to Berthier's sleeping arrangements, and to his remonstrances, Bonaparte bridled, 'Oh, very well, erect a cot in the cabinet if you are going to be an old woman about it.'

The prospect of peace had cast a shadow over the daily life of the junior officers. Bonaparte was taking the opportunity the armistice gave him to reorganise his demi-brigades. Those battalions that were too weak were to be returned to France to raise new recruits. This was the anticipated nightmare for all of the officers realised. As Charles explained to Vanderville over breakfast, 'Because Bonaparte is the rising star of the Republic, and the sun shines out of his arse. If we are removed from his orbit, even for a short period of time, we might lose our place among the Hetairoi and our chance of advancement.' He sat back in his chair and frowned.

'This is why those sent to Paris with despatches and trophies hurry back to the front, instead of staying in Paris to coddle their wives,' added Hercule, spinning an apple on his knifepoint.

'The junior regimental officers whose battalions are decimated are so keen not to be reassigned that they will stay on in Italy without a command,' added Charles. 'The desperate bastards would serve as privates rather than be returned to man the Parisian depots.'

Paolette and Elisa was busy training their husbands to be, and Paolette had been too much disappointed at the failure of her plan to trap the ghoul. She was inclined to apportion Vanderville the blame for this and avoided him for some time as a consequence. To fill the gap in his day left by her absence Vanderville went to see Piotr in his makeshift cell under the chapel, but he was withdrawn and uncommunicative after his unexpected confidences on the terrace. After Piotr's arrest, Alexandre spent as little time as possible at the stables and maintained a distance from the other officers. He had reclaimed his room at the villa despite Berthier's objection. At first his self-ostracisation harmed the happy group, but being young, and busily overworked, they soon resumed their easy existence and the wounds left by the loss of two of their comrades formed up smoothly enough with a tacit agreement not to pick at the scars.

Leonardi felt Piotr's absence from the kitchen more keenly and was constantly hailing Vanderville and Gracchus when they passed. 'If you see that skink Piotr, tell him we are all working like the devil here, and the ices are sorely missed.'

Vanderville and Charles seldom spoke of Piotr, but when they did touch on the subject Charles drawled, 'It is my opinion that Alexandre knew about Piotr's sleep sickness all along. Who do you think cleaned him up when he found him all bloody after a night's goose-hunting?'

Vanderville nodded. He watched the camp women washing the officers' shirts at the water troughs below and remembered seeing Piotr furtively carrying what had looked like sheets to the laundry.

'Was that when they started...?' he left the subject hanging in the air.

'Perhaps,' mused Charles. 'Those two? If we are termed the Hetairoi of Alexander, then those two are the Hetarae.' He puffed at his pipe. 'I think they began sharing a room so Alexandre could restrain Piotr and stop him from dream hunting. And then one thing led to another.' He leant forward to look over the gallery railing at the washerwomen, and grunted appreciatively. 'Nature will take its course.'

'Ah,' said Vanderville in a worldly tone. 'Gracchus says Piotr is a subject of the malign gossip and eternal curiosity inflicted on those who refuse to fulfil the ordinary purposes of nature. That is why the Polish Legion had a problem with him.'

'A problem?' said Charles. 'Are you joking? Have you tasted his iced cream? Look, Vanderville, the Poles didn't beat him because he is an invert, they did it because he's pretending to be a Pole when he isn't a Pole, and because he was a blackmailing the General's wife, whom they adore to a man.'

'What do you mean, Piotr was blackmailing the General's wife?' spluttered Vanderville.

'Well not directly,' said Charles, smirking and tapping out his pipe bowl on the railing, 'but he dropped some pretty heavy hints to Fesch, who was advising Josephine in her financial transactions. Josephine is a child in these financial affairs and leaves herself wide open to allegations of misconduct. Fesch is pushing her to use her influence to help a large concern secure the contracts. Now Mombello is out of the way there is a lot of money to be made by brokering deals.'

'Is that what you and Fesch were discussing outside the chapel when I surprised you?'

Charles looked startled. 'Yes, that's right,' he said cautiously. He sighed. 'Look, I love Piotr, and his burnt caramel and all, but he was in a hurry to get rich quick, and he didn't care who knew it. No wonder it ended badly.'

Vanderville had expected that Gracchus would move on when the investigation was closed. He was equally outspoken on the subjects of the occupation of the Italian states, and his detention at Mombello. To his surprise it appeared that Gracchus intended to finish his work on the establishment of a newsletter for the Army of Italy. He spent the afternoon buried in his stable office feverishly working, or reading through Mombello's papers, which he had hidden from Berthier in a cradle of horse feed, and his leisure usually found him foraging in the hedgerows and kitchen garden, or discussing recipes with

Leonardi. Vanderville sighed, and took up his book, a rather dry discourse on cavalry tactics. He had just begun to read when he heard voices below.

'Say Berthier!' hailed Gracchus heartily. He was sauntering across the stable yard, clutching a bottle and two glasses under his arm with the latest edition of his pointless newsletter, smiling broadly, and holding out his hand.

'*Salut et fraternite citoyen*,' responded Berthier coldly, ignoring the proffered hand. 'If you must "hail fellow well met" me in this way before the men, Gracchus, I will have you enlisted. What do you want? Why aren't you working on the *Courier*?'

'I have finished for today,' announced Gracchus, waving a copy of the news sheet.

Berthier glanced at the tower clock. It was barely half past three in the afternoon. He opened his mouth to respond, but Gracchus cut in quickly, 'Have you heard this copy?' he asked, reading from the paper. 'Bonaparte flies like lightning, and strikes like thunder. He is everywhere. He sees everything. Like a comet cleaving the clouds, he appears at the same moment on the astonished banks of two separate rivers.'

'Heard it? I dictated it,' sniffed Berthier.

'Stirring stuff, eh?' said Gracchus. 'I was just wondering if the mason arrived this morning to open the cellar door.'

Vanderville put down his book and leant over the gallery rail to watch Gracchus curiously. He knew that an exploration of the well complex was the one aspect of the affair that both intrigued and confounded the investigating magistrate. When pressed on the subject, he had confessed to an academic interest in a few minor details of the case, as well as a more general enthusiasm for the hydraulic engineering miracles that he was keen to explore.

'That's no business of yours,' said Berthier. 'The matter is closed. You have no further authority to pursue it.'

'I was merely worried about the mason, he seems to be having a torrid time of it,' continued Gracchus. 'I have spoken with your clerk at the bureau every day, and he has kept me fully informed of the poor fellow's movements. Let me enumerate—'

'Please don't bother,' said Berthier, moving to leave, but finding Gracchus blocking his path.

'First he forgot his tools and had to retrace his steps to Milan to retrieve them. Then his cart was apparently fatally damaged on the road, and he was replaced by a more active fellow. The new mason was discovered to be insufficiently skilled and dismissed to be replaced by a *third* workman, who actually arrived here, but went away because he couldn't do the job, didn't have the right tools, or needed advice or an assistant. The clerk was unsure as to which was the correct or official explanation. Yesterday, we heard that this elusive *citoyen* went to visit his aunt, and although the assistant has arrived, he hasn't returned himself yet.'

'Apparently it has escaped your attention that we are engaged on matters of momentous consequence here,' said Berthier acidly. 'Neither the General, myself, nor my bureau have the time, nor the inclination, to engage in domestic matters.' He placed his hand on Gracchus's chest and propelled him aside.

Looking up at Vanderville he said, 'Since you clearly have nothing better to do either Lieutenant, you can return to duty with your General Dumas. Report to him immediately on his arrival back here tomorrow. And try to sit up straight when you read. All hunched up like that you look like a peasant taking a dump in the fields.'

The following morning Vanderville was breakfasting alone in the gallery watching Hercule teach the village girls how to wash his horses. Vanderville had been pondering the grotesque satyr head in the well complex which had been figuring largely in his dreams, and it was a welcome distraction. The village girls were scrubbing enthusiastically, and Hercule commented jocosely on the merits of the various techniques and practitioners.

'I have been inspecting the Guides' necessaries,' shouted up Hercule, companionably. 'It's a regular rag fair down there.

There's a girl in the village who lets out her fore room in exchange for regimental shirts, and there's hardly a decently dressed soldier in the company. If we stay here much longer, they will ride out naked.' He kicked a bucket. 'What are you going to do now that your charge has gone? Is there anyone else to nursemaid, or are you going back to duty with Dumas?'

'What do you mean? Gone?' said Vanderville, looking up sharply. 'What does *gone* mean?'

'Gone. As in last seen belting through the village on one of the miller's donkeys. Say, was it a donkey, or was it one of your General Dumas's horses?'

Vanderville sat bolt upright. 'Honestly?'

Hercule helped himself generously to butter. 'As the day is long. If he has taken Dutch leave, you had better hustle to get after him. See if you can find Piotr on the road too, it seems to be the season for deserters. He has escaped from the chapel.'

Chapter Thirteen

Vanderville cantered to the top of the next rise and despairingly scanned the road to Milan snaking through apple orchards as far as the eye could see. He shook his head disconsolately. He had borrowed Dumas's mount Blueskin, his favourite, from the stables, and they had thundered down the road, but despite that, there was still no sign of Gracchus on the route.

Vanderville was a superb officer. He was aware of this, not just as his own happy intuition, but because it had seemed to him to have been the universal opinion of each of his superiors prior to Dumas, who was so surrounded and smothered by the cream of the officer corps that he had yet to appreciate Vanderville's merits. He brooded on this, allowing Blueskin his head on the road while he pondered.

The orchards along the road were substantial but ill-tended and the trees had been left to grow unfettered. The result was that the stunted stumps jutting from the ground like angry clenched wooden fists had sprouted a verdant new growth that softened the outlines of their gnarled knuckles. Many Lombardy farms had been deserted by the farmers who had either been swept up into the armies traversing the plains or had fled before that prospect overtook them. That closest to him looked to have been abandoned for more than one season though, and beneath the fresh foliage springing from the old load-bearing branches Vanderville spotted a familiar horse stood in the shadows.

The shade of the trees had also attracted the attention of the field's other occupant. The recumbent figure had chosen the leaf litter under one of the most venerable trees for his couch and, wrapped in a pilgrim's cloak, he was stretched out under the trees asleep.

–

Gracchus had napped for some time; the previous night had not been kind and sleep had been a stranger to him lately. When he woke it was to squint up through the sun-dappled silver under-leaves of the tree and consider his situation with more contentment than he had experienced for a long time. He reflected that the years since the Revolution had been peculiarly unkind to him.

Beyond France's borders a fear of the spread of the infection of revolution had led to an unnatural alliance of natural enemies pledged to reinstate the faltering House of Bourbon on its foundations of Seine sand. But after three years of desultory campaigning on the traditional battlegrounds of the low countries in the north and Piedmont in the south, it had become obvious to all that whereas the new French Republic lacked the funds to sustain armies in the lengthy sieges necessary to break the belt of border fortresses that hemmed them in, the unwieldy alliance of counter-revolutionary powers were too busy squabbling over slithers of French territory to find the will to actually conquer them. Occupying France would have meant making a decision about what to do about the Revolution. So ultimately little had happened. Little, that is, beyond the rapine of the traditionally disputed border territories, and the dismemberment of any smaller principalities that happened to attract the notice of their grosser fellows.

In '96 of course, things had started to change in Piedmont, with the French Army of Italy swathing through Austrian armies like they were nothing. In this rapidly changing situation, with Bonaparte heaving aside old kingdoms and timeworn duchies like a barnacled behemoth rising from the briny deep below a fleet of cockleshell boats, Gracchus had unfortunately found himself found himself bobbing on the tide of refugees ahead of the flood of war.

He drank in the day drowsily with his eyes half open. The birds were hopping and twittering among the trees and an eagle was wheeling aloft, breasting the pure breeze. He was gathering his straying thoughts when a shadow passed over him and a familiar voice rang out a greeting.

Vanderville sat down clumsily next to Gracchus. 'I thought you said this business wasn't finished?'

'It is for me,' replied Gracchus, sitting up. 'You have arrested Piotr, you will probably hang him by the end of the week.'

'I personally haven't arrested anyone,' corrected Vanderville, 'and being a soldier, he will be shot, not hanged.'

'That is of little concern to me. My business is finished, and I'm getting out while I can. Berthier was becoming a bore.'

Vanderville was about to point out that the consequences of stealing one of General Dumas's horses was likely to prove more than a bore but forbore from comment. Instead, he said, 'Have you considered that your absconding in this way will place me in a difficult position?'

'I see that your spirits are oppressed; your humours unbalanced,' observed Gracchus. 'I have not suffered myself from this malady, and so unfortunately am not in a position to proffer advice.'

'There is something else,' Vanderville admitted. 'You said you were not happy with the case. I am not content with Piotr in the role of murderer either, and there are parts of this puzzle that seem still ill-fitting to me. What did Piotr mean when he told us, "Only when you learn to question your happiness will the truth be known to you"? But I suppose I must reconcile myself to the fact that these problems rarely benefit from an elegant solution.' He sighed extravagantly. 'Perhaps it requires a greater power of thought than I am capable of.'

'Piotr's ravings puzzled me too, but perhaps we attach too much significance to them. The discrepancies of the case have absorbed my attention to an uncomradely degree, and I am heartily sorry for it,' said Gracchus. 'I have not considered your interests sufficiently, and it appears that Berthier too has erred in overlooking your services in the matter, and your ambitions to join the precious Guides have suffered a setback. I regret my part in that.' He got up from the ground, dusted himself down, and started replacing the saddle on his horse. 'Don't expect too much from people, Vanderville, life is a sorry business at best, and your friends will invariably disappoint you. Go back to the villa, enjoy the wedding parties, and kiss Berthier's arse at every opportunity. Your rewards will come in the fullness of time.'

It is sometimes said of the hard-bitten men of the light cavalry that they never apologise or admit fault, but that is a brute's philosophy, not worthy of a man whether he was born to the barracks or the ballroom. So Vanderville closed his mouth against the protest gestating there, bowed in the exact proportion that an officer of the Republic ought to bow to a fellow who although in this instance in the right, was after all only a civilian, and proffered his hand in a comradely fashion. 'You are quite right, Gracchus. I had better be getting back,' he said, handing him the saddle's trailing girth to buckle. 'There is so much to do before the wedding, especially with Leonardi distraught over the loss of Piotr.'

'Just so,' said Gracchus, checking the girth.

'We will probably find him soon, though.'

Gracchus stiffened, and paused his buckling. 'Piotr has disappeared?'

'Nobody has seen him,' said Vanderville. 'Absconded without a word. The chapel is empty.'

–

When they returned to the villa in late morning, most of the household service had departed for the promised lake trip with luggage in carts, and the family were getting ready to follow in the coaches. At the stables, Dumas's groom accepted

Vanderville's tale of exercising the exhausted horses with an ill grace, and Vanderville was compelled to a sordid means to make good. His purse was at absolutely its last resort, having taken an unparalleled beating recently, and now, along with his uniform and sword, his own horse represented his last possessions of value. He had expended every coin in his sabretache, and to pay off the groom he was forced to part with a heron-feather plume that had been the gift of his sole conquest before leaving Paris, a compensation for the unpleasant itch that he later discovered formed the accompanying half of her parting present.

Reporting to Dumas to explain his unauthorised absence, Vanderville found him unexpectedly understanding, perhaps owing to his suspicion that Vanderville's absence related to a romantic intrigue, a form of diversion dear to the general's own heart. He took the opportunity to unburden himself of a tediously paraphrased lecture to Vanderville. 'I have always considered that paying tribute to the wives of civilians is allowed, in fact it can be considered a compliment to the territory, and an important source of comfort to occupied persons, but the wives of brother officers are absolutely *verboten*. It's a silly distinction, but there you go, it's one I expect my officers to follow.'

Vanderville maintained a respectful and dignified silence during this sermon, standing to attention with his eyes respectfully over Dumas's head. It was a head distinguished for its leonine proportions and the fringe of glistening hair surrounding the ebony dome. It was said in Lombardy that one could always tell when Dumas had called, because his hair oil left a grease on the furniture. Leaving this trace on pillows and sofas was a strange oversight in a man so addicted to visiting other men's' wives; but then Dumas's vanity was as exuberant as his pomade, and even if he had seen fit to discard the latter, he would still have found it necessary to leave some indication of his passing, much as a dog will urinate on a gatepost.

As Gracchus ruefully hung up his pilgrim's garb in the wardrobe and put the finishing touches to his toilette there was an unexpected rap at the door and Letizia entered his room. She nodded gravely, and strode past him to stand at the window, her upright figure framed in the light. Gracchus joined her as he adjusted his cravat. They silently watched a number of overdressed little beings disport themselves in the gardens.

'The wonder is that children can play so freely when they are so overdressed,' he eventually said.

'The dressing of children is carried too far in all French towns. It seems as if they were little dolls for milliners to try expensive experiments upon. You have no children, Gracchus?'

'No. I am not sure that matrimony is compatible with the rational being,' he said, sitting in a chair and beginning with his shoes.

Her gaze did not leave the window. 'I am not so sure. A rational mind must be a wonderful thing to have in a husband.'

'In the absence of your husband, it must be agreeable to have all of your children here at Mombello,' he suggested.

'My word, no! This is not all of them. I have eight children, not counting those we lost. I was married at thirteen, Gracchus, and I bore thirteen children before my husband's death.'

Gracchus considered this. 'You will forgive me for pointing out that many of the young officers here, some of them very young indeed, look upon you as a proxy mother in some way.'

'I have not observed anything of that kind,' she said stiffly.

'Oh, come, come, young Marbeuf, for example – Alexandre – he seems to idolise you.'

'That is different, he is the son of an old friend, and needs guidance. An exceptional case.'

'You don't take the same interest in, say, poor Piotr, our incarcerated ghoul?'

'He is not a mazzere but an imposter. He knows nothing.' Letizia stared out of the window again. 'I do not have either the time or the inclination to play mother to every waif and stray who appeals to me, Gracchus. Understand I am now a widow of forty-six, and content to live for my own children, most especially the one who requires me to fulfil the role of the old provincial widow.'

'Caesar's mother must be above suspicion?' suggested Gracchus.

'Especially when his wife is not so.' She turned away from the window to face him. 'I am not a prude, Gracchus. One must be practical about these things. Adultery is just a matter of a sofa. I do not dislike her for that. Being poor, extravagant and of indifferent character, all of these things are drawbacks in a wife. But for a marriage to beget children requires youth. Can you expect a mother to rejoice in her son marrying a woman almost as old as herself? To a Corsican, such a marriage is nothing less than a crime.'

'It has been suggested that the *Citoyenne* Bonaparte brought a considerable dowry, the command of the army of Italy,' said Gracchus, considering his shoes miserably.

'If that were so, my son has still embarked on a fruitless marriage. Worse, he is attached, whereas his wife finds him ridiculous and undesirable in the pose of a lover. Her own romantic inclinations are directed at Lieutenant Hippolyte Charles, of course, and she hopes that Bonaparte will eventually settle down into the role of convenient husband and let her continue her pleasures as she sees fit.'

'Many marriages have endured with fewer accommodations than that,' said Gracchus sadly.

She drew a finger along the dust on the windowsill disapprovingly. 'Fesch says marriage can be likened to entering a monastic order. If the novices were permitted a year of probation, as in the cloisters, it would have fewer devotees.'

'It strikes me that Bonaparte's passion is genuine, if faintly histrionic,' said Gracchus.

'My son plays the role of adoring husband because he is inculcated in that tradition from an early overindulgence in novels. This is extraordinary in someone usually so self-aware, but love makes fools of us all. He will grow out of it quite rapidly eventually, when he realises she has adopted a different role for herself.'

'Your masterpiece has feet of clay; I can understand why that distresses you,' said Gracchus, going to retrieve his coat from the wardrobe.

Letizia turned from the window. 'Do not try and lure me into further indiscretions, Gracchus. I have already over-indulged your curiosity. This weakness where women are concerned is merely something he will outgrow. It will temper the steel in his character, and she will be discarded after she has served her purpose. The Revolution has made divorce as common as marital misery used to be.' She swept past him, pausing at the doorway to say, 'I am glad to see you returned. Rest assured your absence has attracted little notice.'

Vanderville stepped smartly aside on the staircase to let Letizia pass down and entered Gracchus's attic. He lifted his fob watch and raised his eyebrows. 'What did she want?'

Gracchus rubbed his hat, thoughtfully. 'I have no idea,' he said. 'Tell me something, who benefits from Piotr's disappearance? Surely not Alexandre?'

'In one week, he has lost and buried his uncle, his beau companion has been arrested, and now disappeared. I don't think we can pin this on him. Paolette says that Letizia went to visit Piotr. Fesch encouraged her; it seems that he thought she could help him with his malady. Perhaps she took him a file in her basket.'

'I'm not sure that convincing him there was a supernatural element to his malady would have been helpful. If his senses are disordered, he needs a doctor, not a witch. Her tales may be an attempt to convince him and others that his ailment is not harmful, but consider this – was Piotr killing animals before she put this silly idea in his head? Or was he merely suffering from delusions and insomnia?'

'Well, wherever he is, he's out of it now. You had better hurry up and get ready, we are already behind the main party for the boats.'

Gracchus straightened himself in the mirror. 'I shall not join you. Today, while the household undertakes this pleasure trip, I shall remain here in Piotr's place to help Leonardi and devote myself to finding his erstwhile assistant. I cannot help thinking that the key to his disappearance lies inside the villa. If the opportunity presents itself for a tête-à-tête with your soon-to-be-married young friend,' he said to Vanderville, 'ask her again about what the Corsicans call the mazzere. I want to know everything about this disorder of the senses.'

Leonardi was more than content to have Gracchus's company and help in the kitchen and they were in the larder cellar inspecting tanks of water filled with crabs. 'These little fellows, each enclosed in his own sarcophagus, are touchy, and eat one other when offended, so we have taken care to uncrowd them,' said Leonardi. He poked one with the tip of his knife and lifted a discarded shell from the tank, peering at it dubiously before licking its extremity speculatively. 'I had hoped to recover more of them by dredging the well with a basket before that *coglione* Berthier had it closed.'

Gracchus stirred the warm water with his hand and watched the little crabs bristle aggressively, their tiny claws held aloft as they scuttled up and down the tank. 'Did the asphodels not poison the water?'

'The gardeners must have prevented them from falling down the well,' said Leonardi. He swirled the water speculatively. 'I could have prepared him in broth,' he pondered, 'but in the August heat he strips off his tunic crustacea and it occurred to me to provoke him to do that by filling his tanks with the warm water. Now, without shells, the frying is the simplest for him. I will let him steep in milk. Then drain, coat in beaten eggs, dust with flour or breadcrumbs, and deep fried he will eat beautiful with chopped parsley, salt, crushed pepper, and lemon juice.'

'You will serve him— I mean them today then?' pled Gracchus. 'Because *Citoyenne* Visconti has suggested they are a favourite of Berthier's, and as the meat provokes urine and purges the kidneys, I hope the dish will cure his choler, and render him more amenable.'

'The meat is heavy on the stomach and difficult to digest, especially when fried,' mused Leonardi. 'Perhaps it is not quite the thing for an al fresco repast.'

Gracchus shrugged. 'I shall not join any such barbarous pursuit; I am staying here, and hope to eat long before Berthier enters his coach. It is my hope to find where Piotr went. Do you have any ideas who could have released him?'

Leonardi smiled, and nodded ponderously. 'If he has sense he has disappeared into the country, and good luck go with him. Now the animal killing has stopped, hopefully he will be forgotten and show them all the clean heels.' He revealed to Gracchus that he too had refused to go on the jaunt, pleading his preparations for the wedding. The entire villa ground floor was to be upended and rearranged for the ball that would follow the day after the weddings, and while the bridal parties picnicked, everyone left behind to work at the villa would be stretched pretty thin. He poked the crabs thoughtfully. 'I will serve him on the terrace then, before they depart.'

—

Gracchus reported to Berthier in his bureau with a proof of the *Courier*. Both secretaries were scurrying to and fro, and aides de camp were coming and going at a clip. Berthier waved Gracchus to one of the armchairs by the fireplace where he would be out of the way and then ignored him.

Gracchus was just settling down to nap when Berthier leant over the back of his chair. 'The bridal parties have gone on to the lake,' he announced, 'but as usual, the General and I are delayed by work, and will follow on after eating. I have something for you to insert in the *Courier*.'

Gracchus crabbed himself out of the chair, and Berthier led the way to a secretary furiously scribbling at one of the desks who handed over a sheet, then returned to his pen. Berthier blew on the ink and read with a flourish, 'General Bonaparte has rendered the most important services. Advanced by you to his present glorious post, he shows himself worthy of it. He is the man of the Republic. Several times the fate of Italy has hung on his masterly planning. There is no one here but looks on him as a man of genius, as indeed he is. He is feared, loved, and respected in Italy. All the petty resources of intrigue are foiled by his penetration. He has a great ascendency over the individuals composing the republican army, because he divines or understands from the first their very ideas or temper, and directs them skilfully to the point where they can be most useful.'

Gracchus nodded without enthusiasm, as Berthier droned on.

'Do not imagine, Citizen Directors, that I speak from enthusiasm. I am writing calmly, and have no object but to acquaint you with the truth. Bonaparte will be ranked by posterity with the greatest men.' Berthier paused for breath, dipped a pen, sucked it, and struck out a few lines. He read on, 'I have ascertained here that he is too careful of his glory, too careless of party matters to have thought of enriching himself. The persons I have consulted, such as General Berthier and *Citoyen* Felix Gracchus, confirm this view.' Berthier nodded happily at Gracchus, and clapped him on the back. 'Commissary Fesch, whose probity is here regarded as strict, gave me a similar assurance. Marvellous stuff, eh?' said Berthier ardently. 'Take that copy to your print shed, Gracchus. Anything to add?'

Gracchus removed his spectacles and polished them on his waistcoat. 'It may be laid on a bit thick. Try this.' He took up a pen and scribbled, 'Nevertheless, General Bonaparte has his faults. He drives men too hard. He does not always address members of the army who approach him with the restraint befitting his character. He is sometimes harsh, impatient, precipitate or imperious. Often, he is too hasty in requiring difficult things. And his manner of requiring what may be good in itself debars those in contact with him from suggesting a better way to carry out his intention.'

Berthier considered, 'Yes, I like that for balance. Take this to print now, Gracchus. General Bonaparte has asked you to dine with us on the terrace. Until then...'

Vanderville had departed with Dumas, and when Gracchus emerged onto the terrace, the table there was laid just for the rear party who would be travelling on with Bonaparte. It consisted of Bonaparte himself, Letizia, and Berthier. Gracchus joined Berthier at the laden table and they discussed the merits of crabs, and presently Bonaparte and Letizia emerged from the villa. Gracchus went to rise, but Bonaparte restrained him with a hand on the shoulder. 'No fuss, *citoyen*, please do not let me interrupt your conversation. But perhaps you are expecting company?' he said, eying the profusion of dishes upon the table. 'Ah, but of course, you are both heroes of the table. For me, you understand, I cannot be led by my appetites, except where love is concerned! A simple spring chicken poached or roasted suffices, and guards against the excess that slows a man down.'

He arranged a seat for his mother, and with work laid temporarily aside, and the pleasure trip looming large, they ate well. At the far end of the terrace the detachment of Guides who would escort them were eating at another table, and their pleasant comradely noise was agreeable at such a remove.

One of the dishes was composed of young pumpkins about the size and shape of a cucumber cut in quarters, some fried in good oil, others stewed, and it was cool and wholesome with the crabs. The stewing in milk had rendered their fresh new shells like a jelly, and Berthier and Gracchus applied themselves diligently to do justice to Leonardi's creation. Bonaparte had his preferred dish, three trimmed pin poults. He ate sparingly, saying that the remnants would serve for a carriage supper in napkins later. While he and Letizia contented themselves with the chicken, he observed, 'The crab is similar to the land turtle, which is much esteemed for weak people, but as they are amphibious, I do not much relish them.'

Letizia said dryly, 'I do not eat the crab. He disgusts me. My husband died of a cancer of the stomach, and ever since I have been unable to view the crab with equanimity.'

After eating, Bonaparte and Letizia went to the balustrade to admire the view, and Berthier moved back his plate with a contented smack of the lips, and considered, 'Now the gloom over the villa has lifted, I am almost looking forward to this trip. Certainly, we cannot complain about the kitchens here.'

Gracchus shovelled peas into his mouth. 'Leonardi is a prodigy,' he agreed. He leant forward and tapped the table with his knife. 'But the wedding banquet may suffer from the loss of the iced cream maker, no?'

Berthier slid some peas around his plate with a fork. 'What are you talking about, Gracchus?'

'Hmm,' said Gracchus, 'doubtless you are right. I suppose young officers in positions on the staff turn renegade or run away all of the time.'

'If you mean the Polish fellow who has escaped – well, what of it? He has probably taken himself off to Milan. He will be picked up presently.'

Gracchus continued toying with his plate moodily. 'What?' said Berthier, exasperated. 'What is it now? If you are worried about him, ask Leonardi, I am sure he knows where he went.'

'It seems to me,' said Gracchus, 'that I was brought here to enquire after a person missing in mysterious circumstances, and here I find myself with another missing person. A murderer however, who has apparently disappeared into thin air.' He gestured again carelessly with his fork and propelled the peas across the table where they came to a rest in Berthier's lap like so many spent cannon balls. 'Now tell me this, *citoyen* general, isn't investigating this latest disappearance that, I should remind you, has occurred after the suspect was placed in custody, more important than producing your news rag? I say it is.'

Berthier gathered the errant projectiles in his napkin. 'Under the circumstances, yes, you may amuse yourself finding the absconder. At least it will take you away from my bureau. On one proviso, no fuss, no disruption of the weddings whatsoever, do you understand? Nothing must happen to embarrass the General or his guests.' He discarded the peas onto the terrace.

Letizia was returning to them, leaving Bonaparte at the rail, and she picked up Gracchus's napkin from the terrace where it had fallen and rolled it up. 'Am I to understand you are thinking of leaving us soon?' she chided him.

Gracchus swallowed nervously. 'It is my understanding that your son is soon to gird on his gaudy harness, and take up the ashen spear shaft again,' he said lightly. 'And not being cut of the heroic cloth myself, I must occupy pastures elsewhere.'

She placed the napkin beside his plate, and chanted rhythmically, 'His captain's heart, which in the scuffles of great fights hath burst, The buckles on his breast, reneges all temper, and is become the bellows and the fan to cool a gipsy's lust.' Gracchus looked at her puzzled, and sitting down as Bonaparte approached, she said softly, 'In those circumstances he may linger a while yet.'

As Bonaparte sat, she said in a more conversational tone, 'Your leaving will be a shame for all of us *citoyennes* here. You must console us by joining us today on the lake.'

She looked up expectantly at Bonaparte, and gathering the threads of the conversation he responded, 'Certainly you must give us the pleasure of your company. There is room in the second carriage if you don't mind sharing with him, madame. We leave in thirty minutes.'

Berthier gave instructions for the remaining crab and other dishes to be distributed to the Guides with orders to mount up in twenty minutes. For his part, Gracchus conceded defeat, and went to change yet again.

–

Berthier travelled with Bonaparte so that they could work on the journey, and so Gracchus was alone with Letizia. Under the republican regime, the ponderous coaches of the nobles had given way to the lighter Berlin, or even the rapid Phaeton with its jingling bells; Madame Buonaparte favoured comfort over style though, and her carriage was of the massive sort. Its varnished panels had neither arms nor cyphers, giving an air of solidity without elegance. Cut square and mounted high, it rolled sumptuously, and the coachman was perched so far up that he resembled a stork on a chimney pot. This had the advantage of isolating the occupants from curious ears.

After they set off, Letizia sat back in her padded seat and stared resolutely through the window glass lost in some private reflection. Gracchus too turned his attention to the view. The road was fair, and the sun breathed warmth over the plains, while in the distance the corn swayed luxuriantly in answer to the soft breeze. The vines were sweating, and goats brayed merrily under the trees as they clattered down the highway.

'*Citoyenne* Letizia,' said Gracchus, 'it appears that the tumultuous events of these last days have their root in Corsican folklore, and it occurred to me that you would understand that tradition better than anyone else. Can you relate a few tales to me, so I can understand the tenor of these stories?'

'If you don't mind, I prefer to converse in Italian,' she said, smoothing down her black dress. 'It is good that someone is taking seriously these matters. The young people like to mock, but there are many old practices, and yes, even now there are those who believe in these traditions, which only the church can counter. Or those in the church who understand the power that these beliefs hold, and do not dismiss them merely as ghost stories.'

'You conceive it possible that a man can become a ghoul and stalk the grounds of the villa at night, murdering those who stray from their beds?'

She stared out of the window, frowning at the goats. 'I do not assert one thing or another, Gracchus. It strikes me that it is *your* calling to discover whether or not these things are so. You will not get very far without a proper understanding of what you appear so eager to dismiss.'

'The night that Comte Mombello disappeared, he organised a ghost story for the evening's entertainment. I believe you disapproved of his choice of subject matter. That story concerned a phenomenon known as mazzerisme. And you disapproved of it, did you not?'

She looked out of the window. 'The mazzere are not monsters from the imagination of a child, with horns and dragon's feet, but people like you or I. Not supernatural, as some would have it, but perhaps you could say unnatural. But they exist, and so they must form some part of the creator's plan.' She fixed him with her strange blue eyes, and he was struck again with the feeling that he was staring into an icy clear mountain pool, where fish flittered half seen in the depths. He spread his hands in conciliatory fashion.

'I can see that I have enough to learn, and I am grateful to have found somebody capable of illuminating me. May I ask you why the people in the stables and in the kitchens speak of this as a Corsican phenomenon? The curse of the island people, they are calling it.'

'I suppose it is natural enough that the common people are scared of what they cannot hope to understand. There are things one must learn when one is very young, otherwise one may not come to understand them until it is too late. And there are enough Corsicans amongst them here, that some ideas and half-truths may have been whispered about the place and spread to the local people. They are right to call mazzerisme a curse, but it is a curse for the mazzere, not for those around him. If you are interested, I can tell you a little and you will see how ridiculous it is to believe a mazzere capable of indiscriminate slaughter.'

'I am at your disposal. All ears, madame.'

She seemed to turn the matter in her mind for some minutes while gazing at the passing country, then began. 'Some believe one is born a mazzere, and some that they are people who have been improperly baptised. The mazzere are not personally responsible for what they do. They act as if under hypnosis, they are called by an unseen imperious power. Yet they may develop a taste for their night hunting. Some take to it like a vice, just as others take to gambling or alcohol.'

The carriage lurched, and Gracchus steadied himself against her facing seat with his leg. 'Did you suspect that there was a mazzere here when Mombello told the story that night?'

'The senseless killing of animals is one of the signs of a mazzere being in the area. Possibly I drew a connection without realising, but I did not know then that that man was unbalanced, nor that he was Corsican.'

'It seems, though, a reasonable explanation of events to you?'

She half smiled. 'I am afraid our island is rife with these superstitions, and I am a creature of my island, Gracchus. Sometimes it seems that everything is an *auspicio*, an omen. If wild pigs are seen passing a house at night, it must be the *mubba*, a procession of phantasmal pigs passing the house at night. The hooting of an owl in a house where someone is ill, a bird tapping at the window – there are so many of these tales it is hard to keep count of them all. If Fesch was here, he would tell you more, he collects these stories.'

Gracchus settled himself back into his seat and adjusted his posture to the motion of the carriage. 'Thank you, madame. I leave you better informed than when I began. There is one more thing – do you know a Corsican proverb that states, "Only when you learn to question your happiness will the truth be known to you"?'

'There is no such expression in our country,' she said shortly. 'Where did you hear it?'

'Oh, from someone who worked in the kitchens,' said Gracchus. She smiled and began to arrange herself for repose.

Letizia proved an agreeably silent travelling companion, and a comfortable stillness pervaded the interior of their conveyance. The fresh warmth of the spring sun, and gentle buzzing of bees lazily foraging in the heather verges of the lanes soon contrived to instil a sleepiness in them both. The road was sandy, and the going was still soft under hoof, so the gentle motion of the carriage proved an enticement, rather than an impediment, to repose.

–

On their arrival at the lake, the north lavished other wonders, the vista being considerably more extended than it had been from the carriage. The water bathed the footing of the slope where they stopped, and the neighbouring banks clothed in myrtle and willow overhung the waters. Beyond the water, chestnut forests chased from the shore to the mountains. The creased canopy was pierced here and there with the exalted spires of dark cypresses, and in the far distance loomed the noble summits of the alpine giants, commanding the skies.

It transpired that there would be a picnic beside the lake before embarking, because the view was judged exquisite from the tip of the headland which was reached by a short walk. Unfortunately, the way was inadequately chosen and the walk towards the water's edge was a damp and dirty path without a guide or attendant of any kind to show the various parties the way. As the guests had chosen to arrive in dribs and drabs rather than together, many had, therefore, to grope it out as best they could at the hazard of leaving a shoe behind in the mire and Gracchus regretted his lack of boots; until at length they reached in safety a truly rustic prepared encampment, one portion of which was actually under tents, which thrilled the younger portion of the company.

They were accommodated with seats under the shady bower of some large trees whose branches swept the ground. The soldiers accepted it without thinking as yet another bivouac, and the *citoyennes* were very much amused with this picturesque camp. From the deep shadow thrown upon them from the overhanging trees, they could admire the bright, sparkling wood fire, and the steaming apparatus of the boiling coppers, as staff prepared food. It was a romantic and charming situation, perfect for a bridal party. Gracchus was not in a mood to put himself out agreeably among the company, and he confided to Vanderville, 'I am bloating most uncontrollably. This is the consequence of an excess of politeness. This morning, after eating on the terrace, Berthier insisted I take a glass of sweet wine with him, and Marsala wine following on from fried crabs is sure to bring on a bilious attack. I knew it, but I could not hold myself back from doing honour to him, and we went on to do honour to the Republic, and the General, and the Army of Italy, and so on, and this is the result. Politeness will kill me. An excess of manners is fatal to the feeling man.'

Vanderville ignored him with a studied lack of sympathy and stared without interest at the meandering chattering throng. The locals invited along were a poorly dressed lot on the whole he thought, and unlikely to hold the staff's interest for long. 'I am fair clammed,' he ventured. 'Two hours in that infernal nuisance of a carriage, and nothing but watered wine and a slipper of bread between me and ruin. What did you do with the leftover crab, Gracchus?'

'We gave it to the Guides,' recalled Gracchus, taking Vanderville's arm to steer him away from Dumas, who seemed inclined to be sociable.

'I rather thought that you might have. I have come from the carriages, where Berthier was dressing them down. He was in the most awful mood, and the Guides were puling and squeamish.'

Gracchus smiled broadly. 'Berthier is old womanish about his health. He is indulged in this by *Citoyenne* Visconti, who encourages him, and uses her feigned concern as a tool for controlling him and making herself indispensable. In fact, anyone with a quack remedy to suggest can achieve a temporary ascendancy over General Berthier. Look at him now.'

They both adjusted their gaze to where Berthier sat under a gracefully drooping willow by the water's edge. Visconti was hovering around him with a handkerchief, and he was waving her away irritably.

'I shall go and ask him if he knows when we eat,' announced Gracchus, and he departed with alacrity. Watching him wend through the party, Vanderville considered that Gracchus moved adroitly when he wanted to make mischief, his limp only exhibiting itself when his spirits were depressed.

'I have no idea, Gracchus,' Berthier said testily. 'They seem inclined to keep us here making small talk until it gets dark.' To Visconti he added peevishly, 'Why did you sit me here in the cold? You know that draughts are death to me.' Visconti trotted off to fetch him a glass of water, and wincing, Berthier turned his posterior to the lake and vented furiously.

'I was wondering,' Gracchus asked, 'if you could spare some time to go through something with me?'

'I have been prostrate, Gracchus, literally prostrate,' answered Berthier, shifting uncomfortably on his bench, 'with the most disagreeable stomach complaint. My evacuations have been dramatic, and profound.' He waved an arm pathetically. 'I am done for. I do not believe I shall see tomorrow, but if I do, we will discuss it then.'

Gracchus left him, not without satisfaction, and made his way towards the kitchens.

–

Vanderville caught up with Gracchus, where he was surveying the cooking arrangements. 'It occurred to me that we should have put Piotr in irons,' he said.

'Ah, you think so? Because there may be some way out of the chapel, and I needed to prevent him using it?' A cook batted him away from the broth he was trying to taste. 'Listen, there is something of greater import,' said Gracchus. 'The girl who was providing Fesch's alibi asked to see me. She is working in the kitchens, having found Fesch insufficiently open handed to support her, and she has withdrawn her assertion that she passed that night with him.'

'So what?' asked Vanderville, passing him his spectacles. 'I thought we had our murderer. Even if he has escaped. You aren't telling me Fesch is in the frame again?'

'I do not believe Fesch the murderer of Mombello, no, venal as a fox though he may be.'

'Why not?'

'You may call it an intuition. He is not the type we are looking for. One develops a nose for these things.'

'You told me not to trust my intuitions,' said Vanderville exasperatedly.

'Quite correct. I maintain that assertion. You have given me no reason to revise my opinion. My own, however, are sound. I have a certain feeling in my stomach.'

Vanderville examined Gracchus's paunch sceptically. 'Could it be the crab?'

'I find you are pleased to be jocular this afternoon.'

'I am also pleased to keep a close eye on Fesch, whatever you may say about your stomach.'

'Make time to speak to Paolette as well. Ask her about Piotr's damnable riddle about happiness, and see if you can get anything from her on the relations between Fesch and Charles. Invent some excuse for getting her alone.'

–

After eating, much of the company rested at the small tables which enabled them to gather privately in twos or threes, the seclusion being presumably for the benefit of the bridal couples, who were alone under a bower, away from the other guests. Gracchus was sharing with Charles at a table by the waterside when he saw Bonaparte and Berthier approaching. The various officers moved to rise as they passed, but Bonaparte waved at them to continue sitting. The General was in a good mood, and so the staff looked up and smiled, and reapplied themselves to their conversation with renewed vigour and good cheer.

'I do hope the boat trip finds you better equipped for society?' Gracchus asked of Berthier as the latter passed his table in the wake of the General.

'My digestion is ruined,' moaned Berthier, pausing beside them, and wrinkling his nose at the sight of Gracchus's groaning plate. 'I dare not trust my arse with a fart.'

'Is there a doctor who can attend to you?' asked Gracchus solicitously, applying butter lavishly to a bread roll.

'Doctors are no use to me. I have studied medicine and know that it is only by a miracle that I have seen the day out,' said Berthier, grimacing. 'I shall be compelled to remain here on shore to rest.'

Bonaparte had retraced his steps and grasped Berthier by the arm. 'Good,' he said to him. 'Before you expire, complete the army returns, and the surveillance reports. I need the Austrian returns yesterday. If you must die, do it tomorrow, or better next week. It is very well to be ill, Berthier, but do it at your desk.' He nodded to Gracchus and moved on.

Vanderville joined Gracchus and Charles presently with his plate. The perpetual murmur of the waves lapping at the moorings appeared to have lulled Gracchus into a reverie, and he sat with his eyes closed and his hands folded on his lap. Charles, inspired by the sublime view, seemed inclined to wax lyrical to a more receptive audience and gratefully seized on Vanderville to inform him, 'Seeing any celebrated water for the first time is always to me, an event. This lake exceeds anything I ever beheld in beauty. I am greatly looking forward to the boat trip.'

Vanderville rearranged the chairs to obscure his view of the bridal bower, and sat down, merely nodding at Charles's observation. Gracchus slowly opened his eyes. 'I confess to a certain indisposition in the carriage,' he announced to the table at large. 'I shall be most thankful for my modest chest of medicines when we return. I don't know where I would be without my most sanative elixir of julep, my truly comfortable cordial of hartshorn tincture of rhubarb and marsh mallows paste, and purgative senna tea.'

Charles excused himself with a smile to seek more amusing company, and Vanderville maintained a diplomatic silence. It was lamentable, he thought, to see poor Gracchus overgorging himself as he did, and falling into a lethargic sleep immediately after, from which he had not power to preserve himself two minutes together. This was truly a piteous sight, for Gracchus was a man of genuine talents and gifted by nature with a firm constitution which he was destroying by gluttony.

Vanderville swallowed awkwardly and Gracchus removed his spectacles. 'I regret my indisposition will not allow me to embark on the pleasure cruise this afternoon. You will be my eyes and ears on that boat. I want you to particularly pay attention to Charles. Try to draw him out on the subject of the supply contracts. He has implicated several people now, and I suppose he himself has something to hide. It is difficult with that one because he is the most suave, the most charming swan on the lake, but underneath his little legs are pumping furiously to keep his head above the water. And be careful, Vanderville, do not goad him past his endurance yet. Remember, the Greeks said that a swan can break your arm, though I do not know of that ever having occurred. Make the most of your opportunities, because we will depart this place immediately that you berth. I want to arrive back at Mombello ahead of our compatriots.'

'But what will you do here alone?' asked Vanderville.

'I shall stay here on the shore and rest myself. I need to clear a few matters up with Berthier, and I also want to speak to Fesch, who is arriving later according to the Guides captain on the gate.'

The embarkation was not effected without difficulty and danger. To the accompaniment of squealing, *Citoyennes* Hamelin and Gherardi were handed up two loosely fixed planks which connected the first vessel with the shore. When it came to the turn of the brides to be, their fiancés handed Elisa and Paolette up the plank to the boat, where laughing officers vied to offer them help. At this point a practical joke was enacted, and the gang plank was unceremoniously cast adrift, leaving the two protesting men on the bank. With ribald jests, the first boat pulled away, leaving Leclerc and Baciocchi wryly shaking their heads, and they were compelled to embark on the second boat with the staider party of Bonaparte. Josephine was also left on the bank, divorced from her friends. She turned away to cover her discomposure with good grace and Paolette stuck out her tongue at her back.

Dumas, Charles, and Vanderville had secured their places on board the first boat, and as a soft breeze carried them off from the vine-studded shore, one of the sailors escorted them all to the cabin, where silk cushions and mattresses were arrayed. A cloth was spread there, and there was a basket of provisions; one of the dishes was a cold pigeon pie, with macaroni, oysters and truffles, and there were also flasks of turbot soup, kept miraculously hot in a basket padded with straw.

Each boat was powered by two great oars and a mast equipped with a sail bearing the town arms. They had a long shallow bow, with one adorned by a swan and the other a painted tiger, and each had a cabin towards the stern. The grated structure of the cabin roof was partially covered with an awning to protect the more fortunate part of the boating party from the sun. A pennant fluttered from the roof, and the mast, the stern and prow posts were adorned with festoons of vine leaves and flowering myrtle. The rear of the cabin was supported by a pair of caryatids supporting a platform on which reclined a reluctant naiad. Three grinning barefooted boat men in short yellow *pantalons* and sky-blue short jackets and caps manned each vessel, and a third boat followed with the music.

As the boats reached the centre of the lake, the breeze fell off and two of the sailors went to sleep on the prow, while the other watched from the tiller. The hills around were elegant, the mountains at a distance venerable, while such a glow of blossoms ornamented the rising banks that their scent carried across the water to bathe the pleasure seekers. Charles was in his element entertaining the young *citoyennes*. His dimpled chin was constantly wrinkled with laughter, and his jests and infectious good humour pervaded the boat. Vanderville reclined on a cushion and watched Paolette when he was able to do so unobserved.

Charles was waving to the occupants of the other boat, where Josephine and Letizia were studiously ignoring him while some of the local *citoyennes* and their *cicisbeos* pointed out the sights to the generals. Paolette pouted. 'We don't need that silly old woman, Charles, this boat is the fun one.' Charles made a face, and Paolette nudged Vanderville and said to him carelessly, 'I can do everything *she* does, she's just had more experience than me. Where's Alexandre, he doesn't seem to be on their boat either?'

'He has returned to Mombello, a passing indisposition,' said Charles.

The time passed pleasantly enough, but Vanderville found no opportunity to be alone with Charles, who was as much in demand by the young *citoyennes* as Paolette was with the officers. He was surprised, then, when Charles took him aside and walked him to the prow of the boat to point out some of the sights. Vanderville could not think of a way to broach the subject of the supply contracts, and he was wracking his wits when Charles abruptly stopped extolling the view, and said to him in a low voice, 'I would like you to do something for me, Vanderville.'

Vanderville, taken aback, must have gaped a little. Charles was staring ahead and appeared not to have noticed his consternation. 'I have friends, powerful friends in Paris who have asked me to carry out a commission for them here, but things have become complicated, and I need some help.'

'Powerful friends? General Leclerc, you mean?' asked Vanderville, struggling for composure.

'Much better than a general,' said Charles absently. 'Perhaps better even than a commander-in-chief,' he added. 'These friends asked me to keep my eyes open for an opportunity to learn more about the supply situation for the Army of Italy. Apparently, it is being very badly run by the Compagnie Flachat who have the contract, and they, my friends that is, want to help out. I tried talking to Piotr about it, his position in the house meant that very little escaped him, and he might have been able to advise me a little. It so happened that Piotr had already had the same idea, but driven by rank considerations of profit rather than being motivated by the good of the Republic, he had engaged himself to supply information to Compagnie Flachat.' He turned and lent on the prow, looking back to the cabin, where the company were playing cards, and Paolette was exerting herself to win the admiration of the boatmen.

'You had better tell me everything from the beginning,' said Vanderville. 'There is still much that is not clear to me about this business of supply contracts. We have time to spare with these boatmen so inclined to amble. What is it you want me to do for you?'

Charles rubbed his temples, and wrinkled his handsome brow into a frown. 'It's hard to know where to start,' he said. 'Beginnings are such arbitrary things.'

–

From their vantage point at a table on the moorings, Fesch, Berthier, and Gracchus watched the pleasure boats tacking their way up the lake.

'What I don't understand,' Gracchus was saying, 'is why there is so much fuss about the uniforms of the Guides and the Polish Legion.'

Berthier shuffled his papers and arranged them neatly in piles.

'Contracts for army clothing on the grand scale are open to competitive bidding, but given the urgency, potential suppliers were given only two days to place a bid in this case. The losing bidders tended to place their bids based on an accurate assessment of the availability of the cloth. Winning bidders just lie about their production capability, and then when the designated cloth runs out, ask for permission to substitute an "equivalent", and use a substandard product. This "accidental" graft can be institutionalised by having people working as commissaries or clothing inspectors who are bought off to rubber stamp defective products.'

'It is a racket then,' said Gracchus, watching the boats in the distance.

'Say a cut-throat business rather,' quibbled Berthier. 'This sort of thing multiplies when contracts are being sorted locally. So, on a microcosmic scale it can be inflicted on the clothing for the Guides and Poles. In theory, the city of Milan is to find the necessary cloth. They have to buy it from their own merchants, so have an interest in buying cheaply. The merchants have an interest in selling substandard stuff. These abuses can only happen if a commissary is involved in signing it all off as acceptable in exchange for a consideration.'

Fesch cleared his throat. 'Which is why so many army commanders need a person they can trust in that important position.'

'Just so,' agreed Berthier. 'The sums involved with the Guides are petty. However, where the contracts are extended to the whole army they are not. Then you must consider that the army needs not just clothing and shoes, but food, forage, transport, supplies and stores of every kind, and the Republic has dozens of armies in the field fighting on multiple fronts for its very survival.'

'The sums must be very great,' mused Gracchus, standing and walking to the water's edge.

'Colossal,' said Berthier.

'Millions,' added Fesch smugly.

'The large fees inevitably attract the attention of merchants or private *citoyens* or various levels of probity looking to make money fast,' continued Berthier. 'The danger is that speculators on a small scale start to find themselves stalked in these lush financial pastures by the great wolves of the Parisian banking concerns. And those wolves make our local jackals look very tame indeed.'

Gracchus removed his hat, and scratched his head ruminatively. 'The Comte Mombello had a part to play in these machinations?'

Berthier nodded slowly. 'He was going to be responsible for the administration of the new army of the Transpadane Republic. Naturally he was besieged by suitors anxious to resolve the substantial contracts involved. It would be an opportunity for a correct man to immensely enrich himself by distributing favours.'

Fesch spoke up from his seat by Berthier. 'This sort of corruption is despicable. I abhor it, make no doubt about that. I see my role as ensuring that the inevitable corruption is kept to an absolute minimum. Where a less scrupulous individual would make an immense fortune, I endeavour to suppress the profiteering and to keep it within reasonable compass.'

'How very public spirited,' said Gracchus dryly, watching Berthier stare fixedly at the lake.

'You judge, Gracchus, which is scarcely your prerogative. Let me tell you, these merchants expect corruption, and if they didn't find the faintest trace of it to reassure them, they would worry that they are were being robbed in some other fashion that they were unaware of, and they would back off from the deal, and probably end up in the hands of some very unscrupulous people indeed.'

'Thus is the Republic served,' considered Berthier, placing his hat on his head.

'Amen,' said Fesch, nodding.

In the prow of the pleasure boat Vanderville's tête-à-tête with Hippolyte Charles was reaching a critical juncture. Charles was finally reaching his point. 'Now, I am not so welcome at the villa as I was on account of Bonaparte's insistence that his wife be at his side all of the time.' He sighed. 'There is nothing more tedious than a husband who also wants to play the lover. Anyway, my opportunities to hear what is going forward have been curtailed.'

'Have you not formed an alliance with Fesch?' began Vanderville.

Charles let out a dry laugh. 'Now Mombello is out of the running, a lot of pressure is on Josephine to use her influence to have contracts awarded, and frankly she cannot sustain it. You remember I told you that Fesch proposed to her letting a larger concern handle business rather than meddling herself? Well, I was on the other side, I had been helping Josephine speculate, but eventually I reached the same conclusion as Fesch, it is time for us to hand the reins over. Fesch and I differ only in the firm we represent. Fesch, like Piotr, is with Compagnie Flachat. He has the use of their waggons to transport his artistic plunder back to France. I fear he too is putting profit over the good of the army.' He turned to look Vanderville in the eye. 'Will you help me, Vanderville? I know I have not been entirely straight with you, but the army matters to you, and it must be well supplied. The Compagnie Flachat are not efficient. They might mean well enough, but they are a long way away from us here, and by the time their contacts have been passed through subcontractors and sub-subcontractors all that is left for the army is mouldy forage and shoes with cardboard soles.' He glanced at Vanderville, who was turning the matter in his mind, his eyes on the cabin.

'Then there is Paolette,' continued Charles, following his gaze. 'She likes you. I know you like her. It will be difficult, her natural goodness and generous inclinations are belied by a character that lacks the strength of purpose or constancy to see them through. I can help you with her.'

'Perhaps,' said Vanderville, his throat dry. He had never heard Charles so serious. Nor, for that matter, had he ever heard anyone talk of Paolette's goodness of character, and he realised he was being flannelled.

'And Gracchus,' persisted Charles. 'He is inclined to be awkward, but I know he just wants to get on with his travels and put this ugly situation at Mombello behind him. How much easier his voyages would be with his expenses taken care of. Do you think he would be approachable? My friends in Paris pay. They pay very well, and Gracchus has a remarkable set of talents that could be made use of.'

'It is impossible…' began Vanderville, his hackles rising, but at that moment, Paolette looked up and saw them in the prow, and when they did not immediately respond to her beckoning, she bounded up to them. Charles just had time to whisper, 'Consider these matters, we will talk tomorrow,' before she arrived.

'If you are going to be tiresome, Vanderville, better that you change and travel on the other boat,' she said petulantly, taking a bite of a bread roll.

'I shan't be able to reach it now,' he said, and indeed Bonaparte's boat had passed them while he and Charles were speaking, and was surging ahead chasing the onshore wind, leaving both the music boat and their own in its wake. They heard Josephine's laugh and Bonaparte's answering voice as it passed by, and Charles's head swung round to follow the sound.

'Why is he hurrying?' carped Charles. 'He always has to ride further and faster than everyone else.'

'You think he is comparing himself to you lot?' said Paolette with her brilliant smile. 'When he was a boy, he compared

himself to Caesar and Alexander. Now he is aiming higher.'
She leant over the prow and waved fervently at her brother,
who turned his grey eyes on them and smiled gravely. 'He is
comparing himself with his own imagination now,' she said, her
face glowing with pride.

On the stern of Bonaparte's boat sat a glum-faced General
Leclerc, and Paolette waved even harder. When he did not
respond she threw a bread roll after the departing vessel.

'You are not a child now, Paolette,' said Charles. 'Perhaps it
is time you stopped acting like one.'

'I don't see why I have to pretend to feel something that I
don't just to make you feel more comfortable,' she said angrily.
Charles smiled indulgently, and her rage increased in proportion. She shook loose her black hair, which until now had
flowed in graceful ringlets over her neck. 'I like you better when
you aren't mounted on your high horse,' she advised Charles.
He ignored her, increasing her aggravation, and she struck her
left breast, where usually the Italian virago hides her stiletto.
'A lieutenant should not talk to the wife of a general in that
way,' she commanded him heatedly. Vanderville raised a hand
to intervene and took her wrist gently.

'Don't touch me,' she said without taking her blazing eyes
off Charles's mocking face. Reasoning with this fury was like
throwing chaff before the wind, and Vanderville dropped her
hand.

Charles allowed an exquisite pause before he drawled, 'And
a general's wife with the morals of a mattress should learn to
conceal it, my dear.' He turned his back on her to walk towards
the cabin, and with a step and a swift push she precipitated him
into the water.

There were shrieks of laughter from the stern cabin, and
Dumas moved to the starboard rail and peered over it into the
water. 'Are you playing the fool again, Charles?' he sighed, and
a boatman casually hooked Charles with a long pole and drew
him spluttering back into the boat.

Vanderville walked back from the boat moorings with Paolette in a roundabout way and found Gracchus waiting with horses beyond the bivouac, and the two horsemen made good time on their journey back to Mombello in the lowering sun. They expected to far outpace the carriages, which were not near ready to being assembled when they set out, they being under the custody of the malodorously indisposed Guides.

'I asked Paolette about Fesch,' said Vanderville as they trotted. 'You said that Letizia suggested he was the repository of the mazzerisme tales.'

'Yes,' said Gracchus, 'apparently he wants to write some sort of collection of Corsican folklore. It would be an interesting project if he manages to complete it. These old traditions are dying away in our modern age. What did she say?'

Vanderville tried to recall the pertinent points of their conversation. He had extracted the information from her during a hurried assignation in the bower, certain cherished details of which he wished to draw a veil of discretion over. 'When I mentioned his name she laughed and said, "Fesch? Fesch collects them from her. She is an encyclopaedia of superstition! You should hear them talking together about the Squadra d'Arozza. They pretend to be very devout, but they are both crazy for these tales." That was the gist of it.'

He did not repeat to Gracchus her next remark, which had been, 'Anyway, why are you so interested in this nonsense, I thought you had brought me here so that you could try to kiss me, and now you are going to be boring again.' He recalled her wriggling deliciously in his arms.

'Was that all?' asked Gracchus.

Vanderville rubbed his horse's neck thoughtfully, content that the gathering dusk hid his face. 'We didn't talk any more about it.'

Gracchus explained that he had been through the supply and inspection returns with Berthier and reached some conclusions.

'The cloth for the Guides is absolutely first rate, which is important because they are immediately under the General's eye. That for the Polish Legion looks superficially well, but the garments themselves are poorly made, because the Poles will be re-posted soon. And probably to garrison Mantua, a long way away from the front. Out of sight, out of mind. This was Piotr's part in the speculation; having the freedom to come and go in the villa he knew that the Poles were to be moved and that information enabled Fesch to tailor their clothing contract to a precise extent. And not just the Poles, Piotr must have provided information on each and every demi-brigade in the army of Italy to Fesch. Those soldiers being sent back to France? Give them cardboard shoes. They will fall apart on the march anyway, so what difference does it make if it happens in the first week, or the last week. Going to the freezing encampments of the Army of the Rhine? Have some greatcoats made of paper-thin crepe, who cares.' Gracchus shifted in his saddle. 'The information Piotr supplied to the speculators must have been invaluable.'

Vanderville considered this as they wended their way down the last rise towards Mombello. 'So Piotr was rather important to Fesch, but he also knew a lot of dirt which could get Fesch into trouble with his nephew if he felt inclined to try his hand at blackmail. And Charles has hinted that he was doing just that.'

'Yes. But Charles also has an angle; he represents a bigger concern that wants to edge Fesch and Compagnie Flachat out,' said Gracchus, 'and everyone either wanted the dead Comte Mombello's favour or wanted him out of the way. I still cannot make sense of that evening,' he went on. 'Let us assume that Mombello was indeed in the chapel. Perhaps he was meeting someone to award the supply contracts?'

'Talking to Piotr,' said Vanderville.

'Talking to someone,' corrected Gracchus, 'a woman if Charles is to be believed. But if the faction of Fesch were with Mombello it would have been Fesch himself who negotiated.

Piotr is too menial for that task. Further, I do not believe that Charles and Josephine went there to conduct an intrigue of an amorous nature but to engage in their own negotiation with Mombello, and were surprised to find the door locked against them.'

'It makes sense,' said Vanderville, knitting his brow, 'but which faction was invited by Mombello, or were both?'

'We don't know who, but I have a theory. When Alexandre and his uncle argued at the reception they agreed to continue their discussion outside in the garden. Anyone present could have overheard them and resolved to intercept Mombello to force their own discussion on him. Fesch was absent from the reception of course.'

'But Piotr was there, unobserved, quietly serving drinks, unseen by the guests,' breathed Vanderville with growing hope.

'I am also curious about the mysterious eavesdropper on the ladder.'

'I have an idea who was up the ladder,' said Vanderville. 'Someone who was outside in the garden looking for Mombello and not involved in any of the speculator factions...'

'And now might be a good time to talk to him alone,' Gracchus smiled, 'and quite possibly find his elusive companion, too.'

Chapter Fourteen

Alexandre was not at the villa. The stable hand thought he might have gone to the chapel. Gracchus agreed that Vanderville should go there to question his friend alone first and they arranged to meet at the villa afterwards, and parted in the gardens.

Descending into the chapel nymphaeum with a hearty bang of the trapdoor, Vanderville found that Alexandre had dismantled Piotr's bunk, and was stowing it neatly. They greeted each other cordially, and Vanderville saw that Alexandre looked better than he had for days and was almost cheerful despite the near proximity of his deceased uncle. He even had a small basket of provisions.

'Pardon my enthusiasm,' said Alexandre. 'This is the first evening that I have really had an appetite.' He paused to swallow.

Buoyed by this evidence of improved mood, Vanderville launched straight after his hare. 'I am glad to catch you here alone, there are some things, important things, which we must discuss.'

'Are you come in a *gendarme*'s hat then, Vanderville?' said Alexandre with surprise.

'Say rather I am your friend, and Piotr's, and have your interests and his both in my heart.' Vanderville was relieved that Gracchus had primed him on the art of questioning without giving offence. He was acutely aware that Alexandre was about to become his social superior as he inherited his uncle's title and estates.

'I see. Listen, having had time to think quietly here has done me a great deal of good. When Piotr was confined, I admit frankly I was in a world of confusion, and I didn't know black from white. I had half convinced myself that he had actually done what they accused him of. After reflection I start to have confidence that all of this can be sorted out, and that when he turns up Bonaparte will have him bounced out of here.' He stuffed another small handful of bread and ham into his mouth, and offered Vanderville the basket.

'I think the main barrier to his release would have been the circumstances in which he was found during the hunt,' suggested Vanderville tactfully, folding some salted olives into a piece of omelette. 'If there was some explanation that could convince Berthier or Bonaparte, he would occupy a much stronger position. The evidence that he is the ghoul is strong, but tying him to your uncle's murder is a much harder prospect. There is no solid proof.'

'That's the thing,' exclaimed Alexandre through a mouthful of crumbs, 'I can explain it, and I have the best possible advocate for persuading the General. It needs a woman's touch.'

'His wife?' asked Vanderville, surprised.

'Even better. His mother!' burped Alexandre triumphantly. He swilled a little wine and water into beakers for them both. 'It's a long and disturbing story, so brace yourself my dear fellow, but I think I can offer you full satisfaction.'

Vanderville watched him carefully; he seemed elated, as if a great weight had been lifted, and although pleased at this change in his friend's mood, he had begun to have his doubts about Alexandre's mental stability.

'Piotr has assumed the role of the ghoul, I believe he told you about it,' Alexandre began.

'He told me that he was a mazzere,' recalled Vanderville. '"Let me tell you of my curse," he said, right before he admitted killing your uncle.'

'There is a curse, yes. But it is not his.'

He began to explain in a great flood of words, and Vanderville, hungry after the ride from the lake, contented himself with the occasional nod and grunt of encouragement to stimulate the flow as he applied himself diligently to the heaped viands.

'I believe it is no secret that my uncle moved me from France because of my ill health. I told you once before about my weakness of brain fevers, and how it had gradually cleared up when my uncle brought me to live here. He had always said I had had this problem since his brother adopted me as a youngster, but it had almost completely stopped over the last few years. He thought the change would help to cure me. And it did, for a while, it did! But then when all these people came here, the dreams began again, and it began to get worse, with the geese going missing. I would wake up in the morning dishevelled and covered with scratches, not knowing what horrors I had visited on the house in the night. My uncle sent the servants away then, except for the ones we could not do without.

'Anyway, I had an incident shortly after everyone arrived here. It was much like the one the other day. I woke up and found myself in the stables with the horses. That was before the officers moved into the stables, and it was still quite quiet. I was completely naked, scratched all over, as if I had been wrestling with a bramble bush, and covered, as you would expect, in mud and blood. I had woken because Letizia, *Citoyenne* Buonaparte, that is, had come into the stables and discovered me there. I was hugely embarrassed of course, but she was very matter of fact. She put down her basket of mushrooms and used a napkin and bottle of spring water to clean me up a bit. It was a warm morning, and with her help and a stable boy's jacket I managed to get back into the villa without anyone noticing.'

He paused to observe the effect of his story on Vanderville, who was listening keenly.

'She came to talk to me later that day and was very kind. It turns out that she knew all about my problem, because she had grown up in Corsica with a little girl who suffered in the same way. I can't tell you what a relief it was to be able to talk without reserve to someone who really understood. She helped me a lot. Just knowing that there are other people who have had the same experience was a revelation to me, and she also made me understand that there is nothing wrong in it. It is just a sort of dreaming, and even when one leaves the house and goes on these sort of nocturnal jaunts, it is nothing wrong. I mean, killing the geese is wrong, I have never done that before, and I probably ought to pay for them, but it doesn't actually harm anybody, any actual person I mean, whatever I see or imagine. And there's nothing sinister, nothing harmful in it.'

Vanderville chose his words carefully. He knew that Gracchus would expect a full report from him, and he wanted to ask the questions that Gracchus would have asked, and to remember the answers clearly. In his mind he could already hear Gracchus's exasperated tone expressing his annoyance that Vanderville had forgotten to press some vital point.

'Did she give a name for it, this affliction, a curse you called it before?'

'Well, that's the thing, she said only people who don't understand it properly consider it a curse. She didn't actually go so far as to call it a blessing, but she said that in Corsica it wasn't considered anything too far out of the ordinary, or anything to be scared of, and many, if not most villages, had someone of this sort living among them.'

'A mazzere,' said Vanderville quietly.

'That was her name for it, yes, she called it mazzerisme. The people who dream are called mazzere in their language. The night killers.' He added hurriedly, 'Because they kill animals you understand, not people. She did say that they normally hunt wild animals and not domestic ones, but that might just be a perversion of mine, because I wasn't brought up in the country.'

Vanderville pondered this news. If there was a natural explanation for Alexandre's night forays, then they were no more sinister than sleepwalking – except for the decapitation of the various courtyard animals, he quickly correctly himself. But even so, that was a small matter compared to murdering a person, and he still found it hard to believe his friend would have killed his own uncle, even if he was technically asleep at the time.

'But what about Piotr? He was found by the hunters. Do you mean to tell me you both suffer from this affliction? I don't suppose it is possible that you are both mazzere,' asked Vanderville doubtfully.

'Oh no, I asked Letizia that, and she said I would know if there was another one here. She said mazzere are solitary, and that if two of them are in the same place, they will stalk and fight one another in their dreams until one of them dies.'

'But Piotr...' began Vanderville helplessly, feeling utterly at sea in this unforeseen new realm.

'I have an explanation for that too, but I would rather leave telling it to when I can see the General. Do you think when he comes back, I could speak to him?'

'I don't know, Alexandre,' said Vanderville cautiously. 'If you keep changing your song it won't help your case with Gracchus.'

'Gracchus is a salt bitch. Did you hear he wanted Piotr put in irons? It's the General who counts.' He pushed away his plate contentedly.

They were interrupted by a clattering in the chapel above, followed by the crash of the trapdoor, as someone opened the hatch clumsily. Alexandre rose from his chair as Gracchus came down the stairs with his hearing trumpet under his arm.

'I apologise for the intrusion,' said Gracchus, 'but it was necessary.' He waved Vanderville's imminent protest away and turned to address Alexandre directly. He pointed an imperious finger at the niche opposite that in which Mombello was interred. 'You have spun a most remarkable story, *Citoyen* Marbeuf, to a credulous audience, but now you will sit down and answer some questions.'

To Vanderville's amazement, Alexandre meekly did as he was bid. Gracchus commenced stalking up and down the chapel like a tiger, his hands clasped behind his back. 'We have something in common, you and I,' he began. 'We have both been reading from the same library, you while you worked on your uncle's memoirs, and me regretfully not as fast or far as I could wish. I did, however, make some use of my time in the carriage today to advance my studies, and would appreciate your candid opinion on my conclusions.'

Vanderville discreetly perched himself on the dry spring-head, watching Alexandre's face, which on Gracchus's arrival had instantly reassumed the mask of anxiety that seemed habitual to him. He found himself clutching the rim of the spring basin tighter than necessary.

'Firstly,' said Gracchus, tabulating on his fingers, 'your uncle, the Comte Mombello, recorded in his private papers his intention to recognise an illegitimate son of his brother, by the "Marvel of Ajaccio", which would mean his Italian estate would pass away from you. The proof that Mombello was considering changing the disposal of his estate in favour of another, I'm afraid constitutes a motive for you.'

'I didn't know,' said Alexandre weakly.

'You have had every opportunity to find out,' said Gracchus, 'as did your friend Piotr, who I foolishly despatched to collect these documents for me. However, let us assume for the sake of argument that despite your denial, you had in fact become aware of the contents of your uncle's will. The afternoon preceding his disappearance he learnt of your discovery, and this led to a rupture in your relations, which up until that point had been as close as everyone has related to us.

'Being a person of nervous and frail mind, you could not contain your displeasure, and you prolonged the argument with him over supper on spurious grounds because you were in public, so that afterwards everyone thought you had been quarrelling over republican principles: about a *liberty* tree, rather than your own murky *family* tree.

'Then, because of the presence of guests in the villa, you agreed to continue your discussion that night at the chapel, which would afford you the necessary privacy.

'Later, at the chapel, Mombello sought to appease and calm you. His attempts were mistaken however, and after arguing violently with him, you fought, with the bloody consequences of which we have become acquainted.'

Alexandre shook his head again, but Gracchus held up his hand and continued, 'As for the night of the boar hunt, that is swiftly disposed of. Piotr, cognisant of your affliction, and motivated by affection, had followed you on your nocturnal assignment. Knowing the hunters were about to discover you in the gorge he sacrificed himself, assuming the mantle of ghoul and murderer to draw them away from you. After his confinement, he revealed to you that he had witnessed your foul work in the chapel by means of ascending one of the workmen's ladders and peering through the windows in the dome. Desperately enamoured of you, he promised he would die without revealing your secret, but you, not being under the same spell of attraction, decided to silence him. He must be concealed somewhere here, or perhaps he followed your uncle down into the well.'

'No,' said Alexandre, 'no. You have it all wrong. Piotr is alive. He is here in the villa somewhere.'

'Prove it!' commanded Gracchus with a roar. He appeared to have grown in stature, and Vanderville blanched almost as deeply as Alexandre, who appeared to want to shrink into the cold niche on which he perched.

'I cannot,' he said in a whisper. 'Not in a way that will satisfy you.'

'I will hear you,' said Gracchus, more quietly, but with a firm gaze on the young man.

'I dreamt of him last night,' said Alexandre. 'Not as you dream, but as we do. And it is impossible for me to experience the mazzere dream of one who is already departed.'

'More nonsense!' exploded Gracchus, throwing his arms in the air. 'And tell me, did you also see your uncle's face in a dream before he was killed?'

Alexandre nodded meekly. 'I warned him, but he just smiled, and told me that he was a very old man, and that he too dreamed of his own death all the time. He wasn't afraid at all.' He breathed out long and slow. 'I don't think I killed him. I dream, and I kill the animals while I sleep, but I have not harmed a person before. But I don't know. I am confused, and I'm tired, and if I did do it, I deserve to be tried and hanged or shot. Maybe it is for the best anyway. Even if it wasn't me, I feel that one day soon I shall do something worse than I do to the geese, or dogs. I might harm someone, a child, or a woman, it would be better for everyone if I was destroyed.'

It was dark when they opened the chapel doors. 'Well that went well,' said Vanderville morosely, as they left. 'Do you think he told the truth about Piotr?'

Gracchus strode ahead in that peculiar way he had of forgetting his weak leg in times of great mental agitation, 'I have no idea,' he said, 'but we will find out tomorrow. I shall spend the morning endeavouring to find out more about Josephine's role in this. I shall also ask Letizia if there is some way of restraining Alexandre at night that won't harm him. It might help that he is sleeping at the villa now and can't get out so easily. We don't want the wedding party to be ruined by the discovery of a dead goose nailed to the front door of the villa.'

Chapter Fifteen

Dawn on the day of the weddings crept over the Mombello rooves and dappled them with late spring light. On the roof above the terrace a figure was poised awkwardly, half in, half out of one of the upper windows.

Gracchus was hanging precariously out of his garret casement. Not fully trusting to the impromptu safety anchor he had furnished from his breeches braces, he also took the precaution of having one hand clamped to the sill, while the other supported the hearing trumpet to his ear. He was craning the device to the terrace below, where *Citoyennes* Visconti, Hamelin, and Bonaparte were reclining on chairs chatting. He had not caught the beginning of their conversation, and was struggling to catch up, their meaning being obscure. They appeared to be discussing table cutlery.

'Let us return to the subjects of forks,' Josephine was saying, 'Giuseppa, you opened the subject last night with a vigorous paeon in admiration of The Good Fork.'

Gracchus smiled complacently to himself. He had recently been complimented by Leonardi on his table skills, and he was no more averse to compliments than other men. Hoping to catch some snippet of gossip, he pressed the trumpet nib a little further into his ear, and gained a few more inches more on his braces. Certainly, this charmingly anodyne domestic conversation was a pleasant antidote to Bonaparte and Berthier's incessant power political diatribes.

'Forks,' reiterated Josephine. 'The subject of a good fork. The fork is the means of transporting food to one's mouth to give pleasure. In this context, "food" may be considered both literally, and as a metaphor.'

'As can "mouth",' chortled the husky voice of Hamelin to general mirth from the assembly.

Josephine's voice came again, 'Thank you, Fortunée. Now, forks come in many different kinds, but we are generally in agreement here that we prefer the silver sort to the pewter or wooden kinds.'

'I like mine with a coronet on them,' said Hamelin, and the others trilled with laughter.

'I am indifferent to the details of the design, or the expense of the material, as long as it has a thick handle,' said Visconti, and they all collapsed in laughter again. Gracchus gave up, reflecting that gossip was more baffling than missing murderers. He withdrew his trumpet and regained the safety of the windowsill. He decided it was time to explain his plan to Vanderville.

–

Vanderville was tending to Dumas's horses in the stables. He rubbed some dirt from a window to let in the sunshine, surveyed the rosy courtyard scene with a disgruntled air, and went back to his one-sided conversation with Blueskin, who listened patiently as long as the brush kept moving.

Vanderville's thoughts were just about to return with mixed chagrin and pleasure to the moment of his last parting with Paolette when he was recalled to the present by a hearty greeting. 'I thought I might find you sulking here,' said Gracchus cheerfully, limping up. 'Do you often talk to the horses?'

'*Salut* Gracchus, you are up early.'

'Everyone was today,' said Gracchus, who was keeping a respectful distance from Blueskin's stall. 'Have you forgotten that delightfully pagan young woman is getting married to Leclerc today? Not to mention her more sensible sister, although that union appears less favoured by our resident deity.'

'Technically, yes,' said Vanderville. He commenced a vigorous final brushing of the horse. 'Bonaparte forbade Elisa's marriage to Bacciochi, but Letizia pretended that the letter arrived too late to prevent the arrangements. There were squalls when she arrived here.'

'Paolette is keeping you well informed. Did she tell you why he disapproves of Baciocchi?'

'The Baciocchi family were Ajaccio rivals to the Bonapartes. In his opinion this is his mother looking backward to Corsica and aiming low. Everything Corsican and provincial about his mother disappoints him now.'

'I have noticed that,' said Gracchus. 'Leonardi said Letizia insisted on baking castagnaccio for the girls to eat this morning, chestnut flour cake, it being a Corsican wedding tradition. Bonaparte refused to eat it.' He pulled a greasy package from his pocket. 'It's actually quite good. Do you want some?'

Vanderville shook his head and lifted a horse's hoof to peer speculatively at the shoeing.

'So, tell me what happened when Letizia and the girls first arrived here at Mombello,' mumbled Gracchus indistinctly through a mouthful of cake.

'Bonaparte accepted the coup of Elisa's marriage calmly,' said Vanderville. 'He was not pleased, but he arranged the dowry and secured a military post for Baciocchi at Ajaccio, and promotion to a rank more fitting to a brother-in-law of the conqueror of Italy. He then announced that it would be a double ceremony, with that of Paolette and Leclerc. A fait accompli of his own, and counter blow against his mother.' He poked around in the feed basket, and started refilling it with oats from a sack.

'That ought to be a lesson to Letizia not to manoeuvre against the new Caesar with her flanks uncovered,' laughed Gracchus. 'Mind you, at least one of the bridegrooms doesn't appear in good humour this morning. At the breakfast Baciocchi broke his glass and a plate, and for equality's sake,

I suppose, while he threw wine upon the lady to his left, the lady on his right was inundated with sauces.'

'Baciocchi's talents seem to be confined to the violin,' admitted Vanderville. 'It is well known in the army that when under Jourdan in Germany he was ordered to retreat his demi-brigade towards the Rhine, and while pointing out the route to his subordinates, mistook upon the map the River Main for a turnpike road and commenced the retreat accordingly. Ever since, the army have called that river Baciocchi's Turnpike.'

'After breakfast,' continued Gracchus, applying himself mercilessly to the castagnaccio, 'we all went into the salon where the contents of the trousseaus had been laid out on very long tables. The brides' clothes were arranged from the shoes to the head dress. The matrimonial shifts were conspicuously placed, they were of very fine linen, open from the neck to the feet, fastened only at the centre with a single coloured ribbon, on which the company displayed their jocund talents, and the young couples were merrily jested with.'

'People always drink too much, and talk too much at weddings,' observed Vanderville glumly. He tossed the brush into a basket. 'Anyway, I am bored of listening to endless chatter, I need to go for a ride and blow away the cobwebs.'

'Listen,' urged Gracchus, taking a step closer to him, 'I think I know what is at the bottom of your choler today, but it is something that it is impossible for us to speak of as one man to another.' Seeing Vanderville's expression lower he hurriedly went on, 'Please, I beg no confidences of you, I just wish to say that whatever there is growing inside you, let it die today. This is a natural end of it, and to continue can only cause grief for you, and for the... others involved. Stay here, miss the wedding and be with your horses, but then let it be. There must be an end to it.'

'I think you must have misunderstood something I said,' Vanderville said carefully, his eyes intent on Blueskin. 'I will come and find you when I am done here, and we can dress for the weddings together, if nobody else dies in the meantime.'

Oh, I understand all right, thought Gracchus, taking his leave. I could tell you how it was for me, but I think it would not help you. He said quietly, 'I'm going to the chapel, and then I shall be in the kitchens to help Leonardi. If you meet me there in one hour, you may find something that will surprise you.'

As he walked away from the stables across the yard, he collected his satchel from the print office, and chided himself. Better to have said nothing, he reflected; these matters are so delicate, especially for the young, and an offensive remark is so hard to retrieve once uttered. I was a fool to broach the matter.

In the event Gracchus didn't get to the chapel; he wandered disconsolately in the gardens by himself and eventually fetched up in the clearing surrounded by high hedges, in the centre of which stood the fine statue of Medusa and Perseus locked in their eternal struggle. The day promised glorious weather, and the morning light showed him the statue anew. It demanded his attention and he paused to admire the effect. After a while, he sat down on the pedestal bench below the statue and let his thoughts wander unchecked. The result was not a happy one, and he sank a little into melancholy, closed his eyes, and leant back upon the strong thigh of Medusa.

'Why, what are you dreaming of, Gracchus?' came the voice of Letizia suddenly. 'You look as if the sky were upon your shoulders.'

Gracchus opened his eyes. The mother of the brides was looking remarkably distinguished in an aubergine-coloured silk round gown.

'I was thinking about love,' he said.

'Well today is the day for that,' she replied briskly, coming closer. 'Though I cannot see it is much use to you at your age. Or I, for that matter. Whatever put such a foolish notion in your head?'

'Watching a young man make the same mistakes I once did, and being powerless to stop him,' he said sadly.

'And what turn did this philosophical digression of yours take?' she asked, moving his satchel, and sitting down beside him companionably.

'Reminiscences of a time long ago and far away.' He patted her knee absentmindedly. 'A young man of my acquaintance once fell in love with one of his companions. It all went on the usual way and plans and promises were made and broken in the usual way, and to all appearances it was the same old story that the fortunate live through and then more or less forget several times in any one life.'

'It all sounds perfectly commonplace and rather tedious,' she said, but she allowed her hand to brush his lightly. 'How did the story end?'

'Well,' he said gently. 'Little did my friend suspect when what was after all a mere transitory matter came to the irrevocable end, that the day they parted there would begin a hunger in him for her company that would outlast everything that came afterwards. Even when he was past the temptations of youth, and immune to her from long disillusionment and even distaste. Unfortunately, on her part despair matured into hatred, and finally faded to indifference. But he found, on the contrary, that even where others passed later, and trod more heavily, they passed in her footsteps. And after they too, in their turn were gone, she was still there, or rather the idea of who she was, or of what the two of them could have been if it had ever come to anything.'

After a few moments, Letizia sighed. 'It seems that regret is an intrinsic part of this particular affliction,' she said, and took his hand in hers. She held it for a brief moment and then softly placed it back on his leg. 'We didn't have anything like that when I was young,' she said. 'Where I grew up, one was never alone with a man before being married. Marriages were nearly always the outcome of long, careful negotiations between fathers, and the children were rarely consulted. Few people in Corsica were rich, so the power and prestige of the families were the important motives for marriage. Land came into it, too, especially when it involved neighbouring plots. Of course, that meant that most people married their cousins to keep property in the family.'

She patted the back of his hand firmly. 'We were not children of course, and affairs were not unheard of among what passed for the metropolitan elite in Ajaccio. But even in such matters the wife was essentially the property of her husband, and he disposed of her in that, as in other matters.'

She stood up and smoothed her apron. He saw that she had been gathering flowers in a basket. 'For my daughters today,' she explained. 'That idiot Baciocchi has been having bouquets delivered to me from Milan every day for the last week, as if there wasn't everything we needed already here in the gardens. Another one who has learnt nothing and forgotten everything in his haste to become a Parisian.'

'He has forgotten the asphodel?' asked Gracchus.

'Yes, that's how we put it. How sweet, are you learning Corsican?'

'I'm picking it up here and there. By the way, did Alexandre pass the night securely?'

'I detailed a maid to sit outside his room as you suggested. She says he didn't stir.' She bobbed. 'I hope that I will see you later at the wedding, *Citoyen* Gracchus. Be sure to change yourself, and do something with your hair,' she said, and she was gone as quietly as she had arrived.

–

Gracchus heard noises of celebration from the terrace and caught the raised voices of Elisa and Paolette laughing. A Guide blocked the chapel steps up. 'Bridal party,' he informed Gracchus politely, saluting. '*Citoyennes* only.'

Reaching the front of the villa by means of the stable steps he found Fesch there under the awning, admiring the almost completed triumphal arch. Despite being dressed for the grand occasion in silk stockings and dress shoes he appeared to be tidying the workman's tools abandoned under the arch.

'Are you not dressed yet, Gracchus?' he said. 'Be careful Madame Buonaparte doesn't start fussing over you.' Gracchus looked over his shoulder with a start, and Fesch laughed. He hung a coil of rope on a nail protruding from the arch's face, and put his arm companionably around Gracchus's shoulders. 'My sister has conceived a fondness for you, you know,' he confided, conspiratorially.

Gracchus stiffened. 'She unnerves me with that basilisk stare of hers,' he said, 'and then she always seems so disapproving of me, and the way I am clothed.'

Fesch stifled a smirk. 'Yes, that's how I can tell she likes you. Better go and get yourself ready,' he said, checking his watch. 'See you at the chapel later, Gracchus.'

Ignoring this suggestion, Gracchus watched him disappear into the house. Then he picked up the coil of rope, and weighed it in his hands. Beneath the nail on the arch was a fresh slaughterhouse stain, as if something had recently been hanging there, bleeding out.

Vanderville glided up next to him. 'Berthier was at the stables simpering like a young girl going to the church to meet her admirer. The thought of spending a few days away from his bureau at the lakeside with *Citoyenne* Visconti has reduced him to a babbling idiot.' He smiled. 'It is strange to think of Berthier in love, he only has eyes for the General normally, they are like an old married couple together and anyway he is so old.'

'It is certainly true that Berthier guards access to his master like a shrewish wife, or say rather a faithful dog,' agreed Gracchus. 'I'm sure he would kill to protect him from any unwarranted trouble or interruption when they are busy planning how to dismantle some republic, or knock off a few thousand Imperialist Austrian soldiers. But you are wrong when you imagine that love is just for the young.' He indicated the stain on the arch. 'What does that look like to you?'

Vanderville peered more closely. 'Like someone ruined the arch by gutting a goose on it?'

Gracchus nodded. 'I am worried, Vanderville, really worried now,' he said, handing Vanderville the rope as he led them under the awning. 'I don't think we can wait before we open the well complex. I have been looking again at the ground in front of the satyr door, and I am convinced that someone else has been passing through it. We need to find Piotr again, and we need to open that door. I feel the key to this whole mystery is on the other side, and it is intolerable that we are being prevented from arriving at the facts. It is tantamount to obstruction on Berthier's part and hinders our investigation to a criminal extent.'

Vanderville considered that disobeying the General's second in command in order to satisfy Gracchus's curiosity was probably a heap of trouble he could do without, and prepared himself to say so. He slung the rope over one shoulder.

'Anyway, I have decided to exert those powers bestowed on me by Bonaparte, and I am going to ask you to extend your military authority in turn. That door must be opened, and it must be done today. Now, in the camp there are some large, bearded men in pinafores who I saw performing various engineering tasks when the wedding festival was being prepared.'

'The pioneers of the Polish Legion,' said Vanderville primly, 'a sort of military demolition and construction unit. The *aprons* are to protect their uniforms.'

'Just so. I spoke to their corporal earlier and asked him to meet us at the kitchen door with one of his minions, and as many crowbars, axes, mallets and hammers as they can marshal.'

'And he took orders from you?' asked Vanderville incredulously.

'Certainly he did. Why would he not?' bristled Gracchus. 'Sometimes an assumed air of blunt authority is enough to overawe these fellows. You do, after all, train them up to act as mere mindless automatons.'

They hustled under the deserted awning and into the villa proper, from whence they proceeded cautiously to the back hall before the kitchen door. On turning the corner to the back hall, they were confronted with the backs of Letizia and Elisa Buonaparte, amid a great profusion of grounded baskets filled with flowers. They appeared to be bartering with a Guide outside the terrace door. The two men drew up short, Vanderville painfully aware of the rope worn saltirewise across his chest. Gracchus slid his satchel discreetly behind him. 'Good day to you madame, *citoyenne*,' he managed to utter, gracefully uncovering his head.

Letizia fixed him with her basilisk eye. 'As you can see there are an embarrassment of presents for the mother-in-law. Each day Madame Bernard, the famous florist of l'Opera in Milan, sends to this house a magnificent bouquet of flowers.' She turned to her daughter. 'Some of these can go the chapel, Elisa, the rest you can let him have at the agreed price.' She glared at Gracchus, who wilted a little. 'What are you doing here, Gracchus, have you forgotten the wedding begins in an hour?'

'Not at all, madame. I just wished to give the *citoyenne* my best wishes in person,' he bowed to Elisa. 'My commiserations to you and your sister.'

'Congratulations...' murmured Vanderville, out of the corner of his mouth.

'You are babbling, Gracchus, whatever is the matter with you?' asked Letizia.

'My commemorations?' he attempted, and cleared his throat. 'Little matter, the meaning should be clear. Will there be a buffet?'

'I daresay you will know better than us what we are to eat,' said Letizia, dryly, 'you spend more time in these kitchens than the cook. Are you two going to scale a mountain?' she asked, indicating Vanderville's impedimenta archly.

'You are right to be amused, madame,' covered Gracchus. 'Let me tell you my secret. I intend to mark this millstone, that is to say, milestone with a cake! And its construction requires my most immediate supervision, so if you will excuse us?'

Under the disapproving gazes of the two flower sellers, they edged their way past the baskets of blooms into the safety of the kitchen.

'Oh, *Citoyen* Gracchus,' trilled Elisa behind them, 'you have forgotten your candle.' Under Letizia's eye, Gracchus retrieved the dropped article. 'Candles,' he murmured, 'no cake without candles,' and he gratefully closed the door on them.

They made their way across the busy kitchen under Leonardi's disapproving eye. The cook was upset and grumbling about the plans for the wedding banquet. He explained to Gracchus, 'Because I know the General, he has simple tastes, I conceived of a table of fourteen covers, in two services, with two soups. But in case he wanted to mark the occasion in a fitting manner I planned also the grand *opzione* of fifty covers, with four soups, and you know what he did?'

He waved his knife under Gracchus's nose for emphasis. 'He struck out both of my schemes and wrote his own menu instead. I'm finished, Gracchus. I can't work here. He may be the new Caesar, but he is not a *buongustaio*. I want to work for a man who is a good hand with a fork. You know what he wants to eat? Chicken. Choking froth of the devil, every day, chicken. Roasted, always roasted! You know how many ways I know how to cook chicken? I can tell you! I wrote the book on chicken! One hundred and thirty-five. And that's before I get started on the capons!'

Gracchus tentatively tried, 'About the cellars, Leonardi…'

'I used to love cooking chicken,' continued the cook, ignoring him. 'May a cock's bone stick in his blood ass neck and choke him. *Enough!* Enough chicken!'

'I have the utmost sympathy,' tried Gracchus again. 'I can see that you are very busy and will be out of your way as soon as I can.'

Vandeville had his doubts regarding Gracchus's powers of persuasion over the Polish Legion's finest, but sure enough, as Gracchus bustled him through the kitchen to the back garden door and propped it ajar, he heard the tread of hobnailed boots on the gravel in the kitchen garden.

'We will not be disturbed for at least an hour,' murmured Gracchus. 'Ample time before the wedding begins.'

The figure of a colossus with a great beard appeared at the kitchen door. 'General Vanderville?' he asked as he stepped inside. 'The man you ordered is outside with the torches and tools. Please sign the requisition form.' He thrust a pen and inkpot at Vanderville.

'General Vanderville is not here,' replied Vanderville, signing the proffered receipt of orders with a sour stare at Gracchus, who had descended the stair and was labouring at a loaf with a knife in a rather mannered fashion. 'I am *Lieutenant* Vanderville, and I will sign for him.'

The two pioneers battered at the satyr door for twenty of their precious minutes while Vanderville and Gracchus looked on anxiously holding the torches. 'Roman engineering,' volunteered the corporal to Vanderville. 'Nothing like it. We had to blow up one of their old aqueducts during the third siege of Genova. Took us three days, and six waggon loads of black powder. Incredible masonry, irreplaceable you might say.'

In the end, they hollowed out part of the stonework to expose the keyhole and used a small charge to blow out part of the lock, allowing them to wrench the heavy door open with a crowbar. Vanderville dismissed the soldiers with profound misgivings, and they stood facing the black void in the wall. A cool breeze blew out of the mocking darkness, daring them to enter, and they paused on the threshold irresolute.

Gracchus looked at Vanderville for reassurance. Leonardi's remarks on the terror the bath complex inspired were in both of their minds, 'We should have kept the pioneers, for carrying torches,' said Vanderville. In answer Gracchus removed two large oil lamps from his satchel and lit them.

'These will be ample, they have reflecting plates that throw more light,' explained Gracchus.

'Where did you find them?' demanded Vanderville, worriedly.

'They are Berthier's,' said Gracchus breezily. 'Don't worry, we shall return them before he has even realised they are absent!' He placed the bread and cheese from the kitchen in the small satchel round his waist. 'Shall we waltz?' he suggested and strode boldly through the door, leaving Vanderville spluttering in his wake.

There was a startled cry from beyond the portal, and Gracchus disappeared. Hurrying forward Vanderville found that his companion had stumbled down a short flight of steps and was stricken on the floor below, his oil lamp spilled beside him. One of his legs was tangled in a writhing snakelike mass, at which he was kicking and yelping. With a horrified oath, Vanderville half drew his sabre from its scabbard, before the light of Gracchus's lamp revealed that the serpents gripping his leg were not vipers but some sort of vine. Helping him up, Vanderville raised his own lamp and turned up the flame to better illuminate their surroundings.

The light revealed that they were at the portal of a long brick-lined chamber. Around the entrance of the door behind them were the remains of a plaster coating on the brick, much of which was now dust and debris piled on the floor, and in which Gracchus now lay, mired in dirt, and coughing pathetically. Above them soared a great barrel vault, and from the vault dangled a myriad more of the vines, which gradually revealed themselves to Vanderville's bewildered gaze as great fibrous tree roots which had protruded through the ceiling like stalactites. Those Gracchus had disturbed in his tumble were swaying, casting grotesque shadows on the walls, and where they had grasped and carried down parts of bricks and exfoliated plaster, they bulged like engorged serpents digesting their prey.

Close against Gracchus's recumbent form were three short waist-high walls, which formed the short ends of three parallel cisterns. These stretched out ahead of them beyond the reach of the lamps, and in two of them gleamed water darkly at the bottom, but the central basin was dry, and cluttered with debris and abandoned junk. From the wet cisterns mossy iron pipes rose and wormed up the steps to pass through crude holes rent in the wall behind them. The air was eerily still but warm, and somewhere in the darkness falling water gurgled and tinkled.

Each cistern was separated from its neighbour or the side walls by a narrow walkway between the lips and these passages were fouled by lateral rootlets running down the sides and along the floor of the chamber. 'We have begun,' said Gracchus with hollow bravado, 'let us continue,' and he tenderly got to his feet and began groping his way in between the cisterns, stepping over discarded barrels and stacked timber in dusty piles until they began to be able to make out the far end of the chamber. Each cistern must have been ten metres long, and as they passed the quiet water, above which the roots so ominously swayed, Vanderville had to force himself not to think fancifully of shapes gliding in the depths.

Inching their way carefully down the very centre of the walkway they found that gradually their flickering lamps illuminated a fine brick arch on the rear wall. Parts of it were still fully plastered and as they grew closer, they saw it was extensively muralled in the Roman style. In the heart of the arch, water passed from a large hole in the wall trickling over a marble slab modelled to resemble a cascade, from which three narrow channels led to the cisterns. Two of these channels were flowing, but the third, leading to the central cistern was closed by a stone sluice gate, which prevented all but a few briny drips from passing.

As Vanderville focussed his lamp on the cascade, the still vivid colours of the mural surrounding revealed to them a scene showing the hunter goddess Diana, placing an arrow in her bow. Two frightened deer gambolled around her in a verdant forest of immaculately rendered plants and trees. To the other side of the cascade facing Diana there was a nymph wearing a curious bandeau crown of shells, picked out in mother of pearl. She appeared to be leading a deer towards a spring, parts of which were missing, the decayed plaster having crumbled around a central niche, in which must have stood a statue, now lost.

Gracchus traced the design with his fingers. 'Marvellous,' he breathed in the humid air. 'At least we know Fesch hasn't been down here, or he would have found a way to hack this from the wall.'

'Perhaps he took the statue,' suggested Vanderville, and they smiled weakly together, too nervous to laugh in the hallowed vault. Gracchus turned his attention to the dry cistern behind them, and placed his hand on its lip. He raised his lamp to examine it. 'Regard this,' he whispered urgently. 'Someone has been here recently.' Vanderville joined him, and indeed the soft green surface of the stone lip was scored with bright gashes where the dry algae had been removed by the passage of some cumbersome object. Gracchus shone his light over the edge, and they saw that the deep bottom of the cistern was reachable by means of a very inconvenient and partially eroded iron ladder propped inside. There were further signs of disturbance on the floor of the cistern, and as they followed these traces across the surface with the narrow focus of the lamps they illuminated a great obstruction in the centre of the basin. It was composed of chunks of masonry and other debris piled on top of one another in desultory fashion. The tumbledown cistern walls were propped up with occasional transverse lengths of timber, and strands of rope were coiled on the floor, amid what looked like scattered bones.

'Good god!' Vanderville uttered, and he might have crossed himself if his hands were not full of his own lantern, and the second one which Gracchus thrust into his chest at that instant. 'What are you doing?' he croaked, as Gracchus thrust one leg over the parapet of the cistern and heaved himself down onto the ladder. Gracchus answered him by commencing the descent; the ladder creaked ominously as he made his way down it.

'Shine the light down,' complained Gracchus, 'I can't see my feet.'

Vanderville placed one lamp on the lip, shining on the nest, and followed Gracchus's stumbling progress across the bottom of the cistern with the other. Gracchus stooped over the pile and leant on one of the timber stilts.

'Bring one of the lights down here so that I can see better,' he said excitedly, tugging at a piece of timber. By the time Vanderville had forced himself down the perilous ladder and reached him, Gracchus was kneeling down and furiously rifling the rubbish. Vanderville held the flickering lamp over his shoulder so as to shine on his labours. Here were packets of paper, some discarded clothing and an old shoe, all tumbling out in mazy fashion. Gracchus brandished the shoe. 'Mombello's I believe!' he hissed triumphantly. Vanderville leant in to look more closely.

His foot tapped against something solid by the cistern where the ladder descended. Looking down he saw three of Piotr's ice cream flasks. He rolled one speculatively with his boot and it clinked. It was too heavy. He knelt and unscrewed the lid. It was full of coin of small denominations glinting dully. Bundled up in an oilskin cloth beside the buckets was a sabre in its silver scabbard. Gracchus smiled. 'Piotr's pathetic stash, he must have hidden it here. We are on the right track. I'll warrant our elusive friend is not far away.'

He took the torch from Vanderville and flashed it over the packets of documents, and Vanderville shuddered and flinched as something wet swayed against his neck. By the low light of the lamp he saw that it was a tree rootlet tumbling from way above up in the roofs of the vault; many of these faint tendrils descended from there and swayed in the shadows around them. He turned his lamp upwards to where the roots descended from and froze. 'Gracchus,' he tried to whisper, but no sound came out, and then louder he croaked, 'Gracchus!' Turning from his probing of the wreckage Gracchus saw the lieutenant rigid and pale, his petrified face gazing directly over their heads, and slowly, an icy grip tightening in his vitals, he raised his head too.

Above them, suspended in the void, loomed a sort of cocoon slung from the ceiling above the basin floor. Parts of the plunging roots were woven into the precarious structure above them, lending it an obscenely organic and disgusting appearance, like some great bubbling spider's womb, and Gracchus recoiled involuntarily from the sinister construction, gripped by an irrational deluge of fear. He struggled to conquer his repugnance and submit the grotesque apparition to rational light.

'Vanderville,' whispered Gracchus, his finger to his lips, 'I think someone is coming.'

Vanderville peered up at the lip of the cistern dubiously just in time to see the lamp he had left above them swept from the lip. It crashed to the floor of the basin and guttered out. Vanderville sprang up in alarm, straining to pierce the darkness with his eyes, but as Gracchus pivoted, the beam of his lantern throwing wild shadows on the looming cistern sides, he missed his footing and slid over, spilling the second lamp with an ominous crack which echoed around the chamber. They were thrown into complete darkness.

Vanderville stood poised, his arms outstretched in the blackness, and listened as the echoes of disaster ebbed away. There was something out there in the dark above them. A hand grasped his leg and he recoiled in horror before realising it was Gracchus, who had started muttering and fumbling for the lamp at his feet. He shushed him and bent every ounce of his ears into the darkness. He was rewarded by the sound of stone grating on stone, and he realised the satyr's door was being pulled to, leaving them alone in the black night of the well complex.

Chapter Sixteen

'Here,' hissed Gracchus, 'the wall parts, there is a junction, or an opening at least.' Vanderville stumbled and swore extravagantly. After an eon of floundering around in near darkness his patience was almost as exhausted as his spirit and his legs. He could feel that he was filthy, his uniform ruined, and the passage they had just passed through was clogged with the dangling tree roots and the rusty remains of lantern hooks set in the walls that had torn and scraped at his exposed face and hands. Ahead of him Gracchus was on his hands and knees yet again, like some great bumbling mastiff, and the feeble glimmer shed by the last drops of burning oil in their battered stub of a lamp showed that if Vanderville was dishevelled, Gracchus had descended into some grimy subhuman state.

'There is a slight flow of air from this side passage, whereas it is stale ahead,' croaked his wild-eyed companion. 'Courage, my friend! We have yet some chances of seeing the day again. Follow me towards the light.' Vanderville grunted despondently. At least they had left that sinister womb in the cistern far behind them in their dizzying descent into the depths of the earth, he thought, and he bent his shoulders to the side passage.

After the disaster in the cistern chamber, they had managed to retrieve Gracchus's lamp and rekindle its flame. The reflector plates were damaged beyond retrieval, but there was enough light to make their way out of the cistern without further accident. By the lamp's dull glow, they had examined the rear of the door that had closed them off from the world, and found that it had a satyr's head, corresponding to that on the front, but instead of a laughing face it showed the satyr in dreamy repose. The door was firmly closed or wedged and could not be moved. Relieved to have escaped unscathed apart from barked knees and scraped hands, Vanderville had suggested that they await the inevitable relief that must occur when the wedding party noticed their absence. Gracchus had been more pessimistic.

'Our presence or absence is hardly worthy of note,' he said, 'everyone will be looking at the bridal couples, not at the spectators. And if you think that girl will notice you are missing, you are developing an exaggerated idea of your importance to her.'

'I don't have to listen to these insults from some cloth-buttoned civilian, you know,' said Vanderville.

'I am insulting her, not you,' asserted Gracchus. 'Let us not argue, for pity's sake, we have not the luxury of time nor oil to burn.'

Vanderville sighed; the tepid air of the cisterns combined with the reek of the oil lamp was beginning to wreak unpleasant sensations in his lungs. With the activity and prospect of adventure his perspective had returned, and with it his customary equanimity. 'Speaking of burning,' he coughed, 'this lamp is almost out of oil. The idiot who stole it must have forgotten to top up the reservoir.'

'I could have sworn it was full,' replied Gracchus sadly. 'It must have lost some of its juice when it fell.'

'When you dropped it, you mean, you cack-handed fool,' muttered Vanderville, fiddling with the oil distributor to ration the flow to the bare minimum. 'If someone talks to the pioneers about General Vanderville, the corporal will lead them straight here,' he reasoned, torn between relief and dread at the trouble from Berthier that foolish subterfuge was likely to bring upon their heads.

'We cannot afford to wait here for rescue,' pondered Gracchus grimly. 'Who knows what mischief our would-be imprisoner will wreak while we linger here. I have flint and steel in my satchel. Let the lamp go out, we must conserve the oil. We can sit here in the dark and contemplate. Some solution must arise.'

They sat for what seemed an eternity in the dark. Neither had thought to equip themselves for their expedition with a pocket watch, and the only noises were the movement of water and their occasional shifting of position where they reclined on the cold dry floor. After a while Gracchus closed his eyes, let his mind beat to work like a mill race wheel under a torrent, and listened to Vanderville's breathing. Presently, he broke the silence.

'It is a curious thing, Vanderville, that your spirits are so depressed by our circumstances. Forgive me the licence of noting that you have passed some years in the armies of the Republic in near constant discomfort and peril of being at any moment deprived of your life by our nation's myriad enemies. I have observed also that you young men live constantly on edge, ready to interpret any insult as impugning your honour, which stains can only be expunged in blood apparently. Blood, blood, always blood, as if your names or family honour were so precious a commodity that they could be shattered by words, and yet from your agitated breathing I infer your profound distress.'

Vanderville's voice answered him from the gloom, 'I have the honour of being an orphan, Gracchus. Or at least, I have the fortune, for better or worse, to have no recognised ancestors. It may be that my birth was on the wrong side of strict morality, though I do not pretend to any exact knowledge on the subject. Further than this, I was a foundling. The only name I possess was given to me by the good sisters of the foundling hospital, and in honouring it, I honour them.'

'They are the great ones of this earth who serve others,' agreed Gracchus quietly.

'The truth is that I have a distaste for confined and dark spaces. I have often reflected on the source of this affliction which amounts to a terror, and I believe that it derives from my earliest days at the foundling hospital. I have been told that for lack of space, the cribs of the youngest children, or those expected not to live, were in the drawers of a linen chest, and I have witnessed myself that those children who cried too long or too loud provoked the sisters to close the drawers of the chest to stifle them – to stifle their noise, I mean.' He was interrupted in his sad digressions by a ridiculous flopping noise. 'Is that your stomach, Gracchus?' he asked. 'Are you hungry already?'

'No. I am greedy, but it amounts to much the same thing,' said the other. 'The flapping is the sole of my boot, which has come loose on that damned ladder. Finding myself without strong boots yesterday, I accepted these soldier's shoes from Fesch, and the sole has detached already.'

There followed a series of peculiar squelching noise and grunts emitting from the darkness as Gracchus apparently released his feet from their confines. Vanderville heard him shiver, 'The floor is wet here under my feet.' A moment later he offered, 'Vanderville, I have just trodden on something unpleasant. Strike us a light, so that I may see what it is.' Vanderville busied himself with his flint and steel and by the glow of the lamp they found that under Gracchus's feet was the desiccated carapace of a river crab. Gracchus picked it up and tapped the hollow shell.

'How did you come here my friend? Unless...' he pondered. 'I had already come to the conclusion that the well communicated with the chapel in some way. Vanderville, there must be a passage from here to the chapel,' he added excitedly. 'Search the sidewall on the west.'

Their subsequent investigations had revealed, hidden behind a stack of crates in one of the corners by the door, an opening to a brick-lined passage heading away from the cisterns. It was partially blocked by a wooden hand trolley and a pile of rope.

Beyond the entrance lay the tunnel in which they now found themselves groping along in the murk. 'Wait, turn down the lamp for a second,' said Gracchus, 'I think I just trod on another old crab shell.'

'And if it won't re-light?' said Vanderville angrily, but he complied.

'I thought so,' breathed Gracchus at his side. 'There is a faint light from the tunnel, and I think I detect the passage of air upwards.

-

The two troglodytes were unaware that their subterranean meanderings were taking place mere metres beneath a charming bucolic scene in the gardens of the Villa Mombello. The wedding party were assembled on the lawns and Leonardi, with his customary panache, had arrayed the wedding feast in pavilions there. There was music from the Guides band, and tables groaning with every dish imaginable except crab. The company had congregated there to eat, and the younger part played at battledore and shuttlecock on the lawn, while the older ones rested at the tables or strolled in the gardens.

No considerations of delicacy had prevented the well from being pressed into service as a table from which drinks were being served, by means of a board laid across the structure covering the well head itself. It was from underneath that board, which was dislodged with an almighty crash and much commotion, that two slimed creatures emerged, shattering the idyll of the garden party.

A resolute Gracchus marched up to Bonaparte's white-draped table, with a reluctant and bedraggled Vanderville hovering behind him. Gracchus went to uncover his head before realising that he had mislaid his hat at some point, and his hand came away from his head trailing a string of green algae. The effect was not an elegant one. '*Salut et fraternitie,*' he said, dripping slime on the pristine tablecloth.

'You are forgetting yourself, Gracchus,' bristled Berthier.

Bonaparte raised a hand to admonish his companion. 'I will hear him,' he said levelly, his unsmiling eyes on the two dripping forms.

'There is something you need to see, Bonaparte,' announced Gracchus. 'We,' his sweeping gesture encompassed Vanderville, who wished that it had not, 'have made an extraordinary discovery in the cisterns beneath the villa.'

'I thought it was common knowledge that that area is off limits,' interjected Berthier. 'And in any case, the door is impass-able.'

'And yet I have passed it,' countered Gracchus, his eyes settling on the chicken *al sultano* occupying Bonaparte's neglected plate.

'Am I to understand that you have forced your way into the well complex?' said Bonaparte, cleaning his fingers carefully and discarding his napkin over the chicken. In reply, Gracchus ushered forward Vanderville, who hesitantly placed the bundle he bore on the table before the generals.

Bonaparte poked the grimy wrapping open with his knife. Inside was the silver sabre. 'Show me where you found this,' he said, his face even paler than usual.

He has beautiful fingers, thought Vanderville, whose immediate future was shrivelling into a pale nothing encompassed in the General's slender hands.

'If you will accompany us to the cisterns,' said Gracchus, 'you will see something even more remarkable.'

'Go and clean yourself up,' said Berthier. 'We do not have time for your party-games, Gracchus.'

'One moment, Berthier,' said Bonaparte decisively. 'I will see what they have to show me before passing judgement on this fiasco. I hope for their sake it is worth the seeing.'

An uncomfortable Gracchus and a downright pessimistic Vanderville escorted Generals Bonaparte and Berthier through the kitchens into the cellars. Two Guides accompanied them with lamps. On arriving at the satyr door Gracchus pulled up short. The door that had been closed on them was hanging open, leaving the entrance to the cistern chamber clear once more. He exchanged a worried look with Vanderville, who shrugged bemusedly.

Bonaparte gestured at the door. 'Who opened this?'

'The Polish sappers, General,' mumbled Vanderville, before Gracchus could speak.

'Berthier, go and place the corporal of sappers under arrest,' said Bonaparte. 'I will continue with these two.'

The brick vault was much better lit on their second visit by the combined lamps of the Guides, and from the top of the satyr's steps the whole complex could be made out. The roots of trees dangling from the heights were clearer, and the rude mass of the suspended cocoon was silhouetted against the plastered end wall like a giant tumour infecting the root system. The light revealed more of the green lichen on the brick surface of the vault, and with the masses of roots hanging from above them like an inverted forest the chamber looked less like something made by men and more like a cavern or the mossy entrance to a grotto cave.

General Bonaparte sucked in his breath as they contemplated the scene, and then he strode forward towards the creature's nest, drawing the others behind him.

'Whoever, or whatever, has been stalking the villa appears to have been using this chamber as its retreat,' explained Gracchus, 'compelled by its twisted mind to create this extraordinary perch. Below the construction, as well as the sabre, we discovered a shoe which I expect to find is one of those that the Comte Mombello was wearing when he disappeared.'

Bonaparte twisted his head on one side, and looked at the tangle. 'It seems to be hollow in the middle, like a cage.'

'Or a crib,' said Vanderville, shuddering.

There was a gross noise behind them, and Vanderville turned frowning to raise an eyebrow at Gracchus, but discovered his friend's gaze fixed rigidly on one of the wet cisterns. Bubbles were ascending from the depths, popping on the surface of the dark water, and he heard Bonaparte's sharp intake of breath as the Guides stood forward, their free hands moving to their weapons.

With a final watery belch, the cistern delivered up its obscene contents. A bobbing mass composed of sticks and bundled rags. Then, with mounting horror, Vanderville realised that the sticks were not sticks, but legs, and from the unruly mass, one pale white arm floated clear of the old clothes. As one of the Guides reached out his sabre to snag it, Vanderville saw among the tangled mess was a smudge of dull red that provoked some recollection – with a jolt he recognised it was a sodden cap, and he knew whose remains floated there.

–

'Is this your first prison cell, Vanderville?' asked Gracchus brightly, looking around the chapel's nave from the table at which he sat. Before him were the papers recovered from the cistern vaults, and they were spread out to dry, while he rearranged the less wet ones into piles and sub-piles.

'Yes, and the last, I hope.'

'It is not mine,' said Gracchus blithely. 'You will find that the misfortune of incarceration has one beneficial effect; all of your acquaintance will visit you once to express their sympathy. Which is useful, because I want to talk to some of them.' He screwed up a paper from the table and bounced it off the stone head of an effigy. 'The fact that they then forget you as if you had dropped from the edge of the world is the corresponding unwelcome effect, but that too may work to our advantage in this case.'

'I don't really see how that can help us,' said Vanderville, running his hands over the effigy's features hopefully, looking for some secret stud to press.

'Everyone will forget us,' resumed Gracchus, 'and then Piotr's murderer may take advantage of our absence and in doing so make a mistake.' He rummaged among the great mound of papers before him. 'I wonder why they didn't put us downstairs? Not that I'm complaining,' he hurriedly added. 'At least we have time to reflect and study.' He indicated a tall pile of papers he had impaled with a table fork. 'Now in these papers I have found enough information to buy our release from Bonaparte. I have enclosed enough hints of that useful stuff in this letter,' he waved it, 'which I am sending to the General now by one of the Guides. Unfortunately, most of our acquaintance here are potential murderers so cannot be entrusted with it.' He smiled encouragingly, but Vanderville was upside down groping behind the effigy, and could not return it. 'On receiving my intimations, Bonaparte will either release us to buy our silence, or immediately arrange for a fatal accident to befall us, and ensure his secrets remain buried by that means. I am inclined to think he will do the former. I rely on him not being yet so corrupted by power as to kill indiscriminately.'

'I hope you are right, Gracchus,' came Vanderville's dry voice from the rear of the tomb.

The other gave his belly a hearty slap. 'I told you formerly, I trust in my intuition. But just in case, keep looking for that tunnel. We may need to use it ourselves if our luck takes a grim turn.'

'Watching Paolette push Charles off that boat yesterday it occurred to me that a woman could have pushed Mombello down that well as easily as a man,' suggested Vanderville.

'Yes,' mused Gracchus, 'it could have been done like that. But I wonder what force must have been needed to finish off poor Piotr.'

'Once he was in the cistern, he would have drowned swiftly enough,' said Vanderville, with a shiver, 'and a quick shove from the dark would have sufficed to topple him in.'

'Piotr had managed to make himself eminently disposable,' reasoned Gracchus. 'His machinations in the financial concerns of all and sundry had left him with few friends.

'Anyway,' he said, as Vanderville shuddered anew, 'I'm inclining to the conclusion that Mombello may not have reached his watery end from the well head. Assuming the unexplored section of the tunnel does exit somewhere here in the chapel, Mombello may have been placed in the water from there. The window into the well is on a downward slope, and it would have been simple to bundle him into the well from there. Which explains why none of the trysters saw his body being moved. In fact, he need never have been at the chapel at all.'

'Perhaps,' answered Vanderville slowly, 'but you are forgetting that Charles heard him arguing with someone inside.'

'We have only Charles's word for that. He said he heard arguing in the chapel, but did not enter, and recognised Mombello's voice, but did not identify the second person.' Gracchus reapplied himself to his documents.

'And then there's the tunnel,' said Vanderville, bracing himself against the tomb and pushing against it with his back. 'It continued after the window into the well; where does that go if not here?' He pushed harder and grunted. 'Nothing.' He stared at the tomb in disgust.

'Naturally,' said Gracchus, peering over his spectacles at him. 'If there was a way to move it, either Piotr would have found it during his incarceration, or you would have moved it on one of your fourteen or so previous attempts. Now listen, our investigation has entered an exciting phase. A most stimulating passage of events is about to begin.'

'I admit I am at a loss to see what brings you to that conclusion,' said Vanderville, and he sat down with his head in his hands. 'Our prime suspect in the first murder has been most horribly deprived of his existence. We are locked up in his stead on charges of the most serious nature, which will almost certainly see me shot for impersonating a general. The situation is bleak. I confess to feeling most abominably underwhelmed by your promise of an imminent turn of events.'

Gracchus drew back the rickety church chair on which he sat. 'It is possible,' he remarked, 'that some of the facts have temporarily eluded you, owing to your quite understandable depression of spirits. I will summarise them for you, and you will share my sense that a resolution is imminent. Indeed,' he patted the damp documents, and peered over his spectacles again, 'I believe the answers to my remaining questions will be contained in these, and I intend to complete my study of them if I have to work all night.'

He swept up a small pile of crab cases, which he had pocketed in the tunnel, and poked them thoughtfully. 'Let us begin with Piotr: a reconstruction of his last moments. Having either proved more astute than you in the matter of discovering a tunnel, or assisted by someone, he makes his escape from the chapel. He traverses the cisterns, past the horrible cocoon or nest, looking for a place to bury his humble hoard of copper, unaware that something is waiting for him in the dark. What was it Leonardi said to me? "It's not nice down there. You wouldn't like it." So, he hurries a bit as he reaches the nest, you can see from his footprints there that his pace quickened. And then he stops – dead. He hears a whisper in his ear, "Petru…", his secret Corsican name, and he knows he has been found out. Then bang! A clout behind the ear with one of the empty ice buckets, and while on the floor unconscious he is bundled into the cistern.'

'But why Piotr? Why now?' said Vanderville, pacing like a caged chicken, his long hat plume bobbing.

At that moment, they heard the voice of one of the Guides stationed outside, and the sound of the key turning in the chapel door.

'Ah,' said Gracchus, pushing back his chair. 'If I am not mistaken these must be the first of our visitors come to gloat.'

One door grated open, and they saw the faces of Letizia and Fesch peek in from the sunny world outside, blinking in the relative gloom. 'A family visiting party, how charming,' said Gracchus. 'Lieutenant, please show the first of our visitors in, and ask Commissary Fesch to pause outside for a moment.'

Letizia entered, placed a basket covered with a napkin on the floor, and looked around herself blankly, as if expecting to see the chapel transformed by bars on the windows. 'We have not been incarcerated in durance vile,' said Gracchus. 'Either we have been adjudged a minor risk, or we will be moved at some point to the crypt so that the chapel can accommodate another arrival.'

'That poor young man,' said Letizia, accepting the chair opposite Gracchus that Vanderville provided, before he discreetly moved off to the far end of the chapel to inspect the carvings behind the altar. 'I suppose he hid somewhere here at the villa while the depredations continued, hoping that my son would be forced to release him. How sad that this should happen to him now.'

'Naturally,' Gracchus replied dryly. 'Perhaps he had found out something about Mombello's killer that meant he must be silenced. What do you think, madame?'

'I do not concern myself with the servant's business, *Citoyen* Gracchus,' she said primly, smoothing down her dress.

He picked up one of the dried flower stalks he had on the table and twirled it between his fingers. 'I wonder,' he said. 'When you told me that for the Corsican people the asphodels symbolise their island you forgot to tell me of another signific-ance the asphodels hold for you. When were you going to tell me about the importance of the asphodel to the mazzere?'

Letizia favoured him with a frown. 'Providing a full litany of the superstitions of our benighted people would keep us here for days,' she said, 'and it's chilly in here,' she added.

Gracchus nodded, and pushed his spectacles up his nose. 'There is another thing you neglected to tell me when you explained the essentially passive role that mazzere occupy in their turbulent dreams and in the subsequent deaths of those around them. There is another type of mazzere, is there not? The mal-mazzere, whose role in their dreams is not innocent, and whose role in the subsequent events is not passive at all? In fact, you may well say that it is a fulfilment of their morbid imaginings that they bring to pass. They are the mazzere who kill men as well as animals.'

'It is you who says so?' she said quietly. 'Or is it the Comte Mombello speaking from beyond his grave?' and she indicated the papers surrounding Gracchus.

Gracchus picked up a volume from the table, and turned a few pages speculatively, then slammed it shut. He looked up at her and asked, 'Your reticence in these matters has seriously hindered my attempt to shed light on the comte's death. And yet you, madame, were fond of him, were you not?'

'In a way, yes, I was once. You have to understand, our friendship was transactional. His brother was the most important man in Corsica, the governor of the whole island. And my husband, our family, were ambitious. I had a part to act, and as far as he was able, Marbeuf made that part pleasant for me to play. He was a not unattractive man: urbane, courtly, and charming.'

'A transaction, madame?' queried Gracchus.

'Yes. You heard correctly. Like a marriage in fact. Nothing more or less.'

Vanderville was maintaining perfect immobility, craning his ears, yet afraid to twitch a muscle lest he break the spell between the two at the table.

'Oh don't be so shocked,' said Letizia, getting to her feet. She indicated the basket on the floor. 'I have brought you something to eat. I do hope there is enough for both of you,' and she smiled faintly, and left.

'This is rather awkward, Commissary Fesch,' beamed Gracchus to the seated figure opposite him. 'Among the papers of Comte Mombello is a very detailed record of transactions made between himself, and a commissary of the Army of Italy. It appears that exemptions from financial requisition to support the army were exchanged for various valuable works of art. Worse, the comte, having acted as a go-between to give access to this opportunity to many nobles of his acquaintance, appears to have become distressed to find that in the event the agreements have not been honoured, and the requisitions were in many cases made upon their estates anyway, leaving many of these people in a regrettable state of relative penury.'

Fesch examined his fingernails complacently. 'I see,' he said. 'I am rather at a loss to know what you intend to achieve by relating these distressing circumstances to me. You must realise that the General is unlikely to permit the exposure of his own uncle as one of the army's despised vultures. At best, your revelation will result in my reprimand and reassignment, and I can assure you it will create a great deal of unpleasantness for yourself.'

'And if these papers can be construed as a motive for murder, then there will be rather a lot of unpleasantness for you too, Commissary.'

'I rather think you cannot pin that one on me. Mombello proved intractable in financial negotiations, it is true, and I can't pretend I don't hope things will be easier with his successor, but as I have explained, I was not at the villa the night the comte disappeared.'

'Nonetheless, the removal of your spy must have caused you some embarrassment, eh?' suggested Gracchus. 'Or perhaps it was convenient to have a loose end tied off?'

'Not only have I paid for a cast iron alibi for this latest tragedy that justly proves I had nothing to do with it, it also happens to be true. Piotr had a great number of enemies, one of them must have discovered where he was hiding.'

Gracchus slid the basket that Letizia had left towards him, and sniffed it. 'I will not pretend that I will take you at your word, as we are discovering just what that might be worth, but nevertheless. I believe that to spare yourself exposure you will be willing to do something for me.'

'Oh,' said Fesch, smiling, 'how elegantly you plot, Gracchus. Are you sure you never trained for the church? You have more than a hint of the Jesuit about you.'

'I think, Commissary,' said Gracchus, lifting a corner of the napkin from the basket to peek inside, 'you knew the Comte Mombello rather better than you have pretended up to now. And I also have reason to believe you know more about his brother's relations with your half-sister than you have been willing to offer. Tell me what you know, and I will give you back your contracts.'

Fesch considered one of the documents on his side of the table, turning it carefully to and fro in his hands to peer at each side, holding it gingerly as if it were smeared in excrement. He sat back in his chair and half closed his heavy-lidded eyes. Then he spoke. 'Marbeuf's first marriage nearly fifty years ago was contracted with an ancient relic of a widow who brought him castles, but naturally no children. In fact, she declined even to live with him. She died unrepented in the 1780s, and in the same year of her death, he remarried.' He clasped his hands and peered at the chapel roof. 'His new wife, Catherine Salinguerra Antoinette Gaillardon de Fenoyl, was a twenty-year milch cow, who swiftly squirted forth a girl whelp on the next Christmas Eve, and a boy two years after that. She and her children reside on one of his estates in France, having also declined the pleasure of his company.' He leant forward, and grinned broadly at Gracchus. 'Our mutual friend Alexandre must have come along between those two marriages.'

Gracchus speared a document with his finger. 'When Marbeuf was resident in Ajaccio, Corsica, with his brother Mombello acting as his secretary, was Alexandre the only apple who fell from the comte's bounteous tree on that island? Was there also a golden apple?' he jabbed again at the paper for emphasis.

Fesch sighed. 'I know what you are driving at. As for the absurd thesis of Napoleon's paternity being mistaken, the simple verification of dates is enough to make it absurd. Napoleon was born on 15 August 1769, and therefore conceived around the November of the preceding year. At precisely this time, Marbeuf was busy settling his troops into winter quarters, during a campaign to pacify the rebels in the Nebbio, some fifty kilometres over the mountains away. Of all Letizia's children, Napoleon is the least likely to have been born from Marbeuf. Anyway, Marbeuf was busy with another Corsican, a certain Madame Varese, at this time. Living with her, in fact. It was not until later that he threw her over for Letizia.'

He looked at Vanderville, transfixed at the altar. 'I hope you have a malleable memory, young man,' he smirked. 'You have placed your neck in a noose by eavesdropping here.' Vanderville turned away to cover his consternation, and unabashed, Fesch continued, 'The arrangement with the Bonapartes was a mutually advantageous alliance. Marbeuf and Mombello were cultivating supporters in Ajaccio, and the Bonapartes were climbing the social ladder of that new French regime. Marbeuf happily used my brother-in-law Carlo Buonaparte's abilities as informer, propagandist, and go-between. As for Letizia, in accepting Marbeuf's attentions, she was doing no more than what was required of her as a good Corsican wife. It was expected of her by her husband and other relatives. Even her brother-in-law, a priest at that time, you might say connived in the friendship.' He paused, and took out a snuff box, then stood up, walking towards the tombs with his hands clasped behind his back.

'You want to ask me if she was in love with Marbeuf?' He frowned, taking a pinch of snuff. 'She was fond of him. Letizia might well reminisce that Marbeuf's sponsorship enabled the Bonapartes to add another storey to their house. A not inconsiderable undertaking, and a gesture of increased status. You must understand that my half-sister is a woman of iron will, Gracchus. To bring up a family of eight children thoroughly well on less than one hundred pounds a year in a revolution-torn country like Corsica is in itself a remarkable feat. To do it when handicapped by a husband like Carlo Bonaparte was more remarkable still. Our own genius commander-in-chief is her masterpiece; none of the other children responded so well to her teaching.'

He placed one leg on a tomb, and stretched his hands along his boot with his back to them. When he spoke he was looking at the tomb wistfully. 'But passion? Her passion is first for her children, and second for money. Having lived on the widow's mite, she is now a miser. If you give her a dinner, she will eat a quarter, save a quarter for tomorrow, pocket the other half and sell it back to the grocer.' He turned back to them and lent over the table. 'Naturally, my nephew wants none of this scurrilous speculation known. Napoleon requires his mother to adopt the role of the prematurely old provincial widow. His ideal woman is the staid Roman matron.'

'Letizia may not yet be prepared to play that role,' commented Gracchus thoughtfully.

'She had better learn quickly,' added Fesch dryly. He straightened up. 'Now about those papers, Gracchus...'

'One more question first. Your spy Piotr had informed you that Mombello was about to award the army supply contracts to himself rather than the concerns represented either by your-self, or by Josephine and Lieutenant Charles. That night, after leaving the supply waggons in the village, you hurried to the chapel where you knew Mombello would be to confront him. What happened next?'

Fesch shot a furious glance at Vanderville, then took out a handkerchief and mopped his face. 'You have been talking to that village girl,' he observed. 'The trouble with whores...'

'Is that they require paying,' interrupted Gracchus. 'Answer the question.'

'Very well. You are right that I was irritated that Mombello had reneged on our agreement. Even Josephine's impending discomfiture at also missing out didn't soften that blow. My intention was to confront him and persuade him to change his mind.'

'And when he did not?'

'There's the rub. When I arrived at the chapel it was later than I thought, and I found it deserted. The doors were locked from the inside, and there was no trace of Mombello or anyone else. I walked the perimeter of the chapel, but seeing and hearing nothing, I returned to the villa and turned in.'

Vanderville coughed from his post by the tomb, and Fesch spun round to address him. 'Still here, young man? If either of you think I am capable of committing murder on hallowed ground you are very much mistaken. Luckily for both of you,' he added. 'Now give me those papers, Gracchus.'

Gracchus looked up from his contemplation of his belly. 'Hmm? Oh, I seem to have misplaced them temporarily. But they will be yours when I have checked the veracity of your latest assertions.'

'Jesuit,' snarled Fesch, banging his fist on the table.

'Atheist,' parried Gracchus, rising to his feet and returning Fesch's glare as he made for the door.

'Until tomorrow then,' said Gracchus, grimacing as the door slammed shut.

Chapter Seventeen

Gracchus unbuttoned his coat and arranged the last soggy packet of papers. He had been driving Vanderville to distraction bustling around his table, moving piles of documents from one spot to another according to some arcane filing system of his own, which apparently had included the rejection of a significant portion, which were discarded carelessly across the chapel floor.

'Is that the last?' asked Vanderville. 'Have you found them all?'

'Not all of them! But I have arrived at the end for now,' he announced triumphantly. 'Some of the documents are water damaged and illegible, but there are sufficiently intact to draw some conclusions.'

'What have you found, a plan of the tunnels?' Vanderville asked hopefully, rubbing his temples.

'Better than that. I will tell you where the tunnel is presently. There is only one, and it's all quite straightforward. This labyrinth on the other hand,' he tapped the table significantly, 'took some unravelling.

'The pertinent papers I have arrayed under two main headings. Look here, and I shall summarise for you, as Mombello's writing has the common failing of the over-educated – a mere spider's scrawl.'

Gracchus held up a finger. 'This last of the journals records the further research that Mombello conducted into mazzerisme in an attempt to understand and cure his nephew's condition. Mombello understood the mazzere concept profoundly. We

257

are indebted to his enlightened views, and for the information on cultural traditions he collected. His interest in this subject deepened as he came to suspect it was the source of his nephew's afflictions, and listen, this one is particularly interesting, the name of Mombello's correspondent is noted, dated several years ago. It is one Fesch, archdeacon of Ajaccio, Corsica. Sound familiar? Let us see what he had to say:

> *Also known as culpadori (from culpo, a blow). The mazzere are not personally responsible for the deaths they foresee. Yet they may become addicted to the practice with solitude and time. The women are the worst. They may become passionate hunters at any age.'*

Gracchus looked up to see if Vanderville was following, and stabbed the papers with his finger for emphasis. 'There are several later entries, which chronicle Mombello's increasing concern for the boy, and desperate search for a cure. These include,

> *Possibly a mal-mazzere can provoke his dreams by means of narcotic substances: mandrake, Datura or belladonna.*

This is a reference to the mal-mazzere again. A mythical deviation, or perversion rather, from the accepted tradition. The mal-mazzere do actually kill, or bring about the deaths of those whose end is foreshadowed in their dreams. Mombello notes that most authorities deny their existence, considering the known examples mere charlatans using an honest, if slightly sinister, tradition to cover their malfeasance.

> *Mazzere can be exorcised by priests. There is an occult ceremony.*
> *The creation of a mazzere can be provoked by evil rather than being hereditary.*

'The end is quite sad; Mombello appears to have succumbed to despair,

> *A mazzere cannot be called one of Lucifer's, but neither does he belong to Christ. Not that they are wicked, but only empty of good, as if all of the righteousness had been scoured away.*

The section on the innocence of the mazzere has been struck through by another pen.'

Gracchus closed the journal and pushed it away, drawing the last sheave of documents towards him. 'Vanderville, this last pile is more curious. It is a selection of entries copied out from Parish baptism registers in Corsica and supplements the information Paolette furnished us with. Someone, probably Mombello, has compiled a list of those relating to the Bonapartes. Most of these occurred at home; we have already seen how prolific Letizia was in this period.

'It begins with the sad record of some of the children who did not survive. She recycled their names for the later children, so let us jump to our own dear General who was born in 1769 and baptised at home two years later. Most of the children were baptised at home in batches, waiting for the arrival of a sibling before the sacrament was performed. When we arrive in 1778, the year before Alexandre's reported date of birth, we find the birth and baptism of Louis, one event following quickly on the other. Unusually for Letizia, Louis was baptised in church with three powerful sponsors, including the Comte Marbeuf. At this time, Lucien, born in 1775, and Elisa, born in 1777, were still waiting for the ceremony, which eventually took place in 1779, at home, with undistinguished godparents.

'Less than a year after Louis's birth, Letizia was delivered of a stillborn child, in August 1779. Going back to Mombello's journal we find that he records that Marbeuf was travelling with her at the time and they were present at the birth. He wrote, "Madame Buonaparte exhausted after being delivered of a child, not breathing, whom I took away.'"

Gracchus paused, and pushed his spectacles up his nose, peering up at Vanderville and prodding the paper before him. 'The stillborn child was not baptised of course, so there is no record of that event elsewhere. Here there is a page missing. If we had it, that would conclude my research. I rather suspect that—'

'Good news!' boomed Hercule, throwing the chapel doors open. 'You are to have a companion in distress.' He perched his bulk on one of the tombs, and related, 'What we have heard in the stables is that Charles has been arrested, and Bonaparte is going to have him shot.' He adjusted his sabre and grunted, 'The Guides say that he was interrupted courting the General's wife; Leonardi says that he was seen stringing Piotr up in the cellars; whereas the camp women, who have a soft spot for Charles, say that he was caught stark naked on the stable roof worrying a dead goose.'

Vanderville rubbed his chin. 'If you play with the tiger's tail, you are going to get burnt.'

'And this particular fire has a nasty bite,' agreed Gracchus from his work at the table. 'Why has Bonaparte arrested him now? Was he surprised *en flagrante*?'

'Ask him yourself,' said Hercule, stepping away from the tomb, 'he's outside with the Guides now.' He opened the chapel door and Charles stepped inside, flashing his easy smile.

'*Salut* comrades in peril, is there a bunk spare?'

'I think the idea is that you go downstairs where we store the murderers,' said Hercule, indicating the trapdoor to the nymphaeum. 'These two are under voluntary confinement so get to stay upstairs.'

'Good morning, Charles,' said Gracchus affably. 'What brings you amidst our band of desperate men?'

A cloud passed over Charles's face. 'They have taken dear Piotr up from his watery sepulchre. Whoever perpetuated this atrocity has put me as squarely in the frame as if Gros had painted me there. You remember my silver sabre of honour?'

'The one you awarded yourself?' asked Hercule sarcastically.

'It was a gift from a friend,' smarted Charles, waving a hand dismissively. 'Well, anyway, it was discovered in the cistern chamber beside what was left of Piotr, daubed in gore by all accounts, and that was all the excuse Bonaparte needed to quit himself of me.'

Gracchus shifted uneasily in his chair and frowned and Vanderville asked, 'They think you used the sabre on him?'

'That's what I don't understand. It's impossible for my sabre to have got there. It doesn't make any sense.'

'When did you last see it?' asked Gracchus gravely.

'It was in the stable yard after I was pulled off the cart. There was a bit of a scene, and Berthier made me remove it. In a rather childish fit of pique, I abandoned it on the stands.' He removed his hat and ran his fingers through his dark hair.

Gracchus looked up keenly. It was not unexpected. Given the choice of exposing his collaborator in speculation, or otherwise impugning the good name of Josephine, Charles had decided to hold his peace. That reticence, compounded by the General's irritation at Charles involving Josephine in his financial peculations, had brought the majesty of his wrath down upon him. The sabre was surely a convenient gambit for Bonaparte. Gracchus snorted. 'This is becoming very complicated indeed, and I like less and less what is unfolding here. Hercule, would you and Vanderville settle Charles in downstairs please, I need all of the air of the chapel to think in.'

'Not me,' said Hercule, 'I'm off.' He threw Vanderville the trapdoor key. 'Sort yourselves out. I have to arrange the Guides detail for tomorrow's ball. Berthier doesn't want any more trouble, and has ordered a ring of sabres around the villa.'

As they descended into the nymphaeum Charles expounded to Vanderville on his fate. 'Naturally, I have been painted as the filthy hound after lucre, better that than admit that his beloved wife has been not quite correct in the observance of fidelity, or that she is involved in contract speculation up to her magnificent neck. I do believe he has even convinced himself it is true that I have inveigled her pretty unwitting head. Our General has no sense where Josephine is concerned.'

'She does not love her husband then?' asked Vanderville, showing Charles where to bunk down, and dusting off the tabletop.

'Not as he loves her,' said Charles, throwing down his meagre belongings. 'I mean she is just bored by his blandishments; she prefers amusements and the gay life. And shopping.' He paused. 'Actually, everything wearies her… often she weeps, several times a day for very trivial reasons. At the same time Josephine is happy to receive presents from everybody and takes great delight in them. The King of Naples sent her a string of perfect pearls, the Pope a set of antique cameos.' He knelt down and began rifling his portmanteau. 'It's a bit rich that Bonaparte is threatening to dismiss me from the army owing to the usual financial irregularities committed with army supply contractors, whereas everyone is involved in the same game, including Josephine herself. And now I am to be accused of murdering my own friend. On what grounds?' He thumped the portmanteau angrily. 'The General has been vaguely jealous since he heard I was with Josephine in Genoa last month. Reinforced by Paolette's tattling, he now feels able to take action, and this business with the sabre is very convenient for him.'

'Perhaps if Josephine was more attentive, more loving, the General would love her less?' suggested Vanderville.

'There could be something in that,' considered Charles. 'We are talking of a conqueror after all. He may prefer a variable sky, one minute splendid, then black and vexed by lightning, to love's unclouded blue.' He sat down on the lip of the dried fountain. 'It's a fine calculation on her part, but then she makes love as he makes war, and is no less adept in the use of her weapons.' He indicated the cold chamber with a wave of his hand. 'One thing is certain, trying to play their game has brought me to this.'

Vanderville poked the water grate under the springhead speculatively, and pondered, 'Dumas told me that his aides de camp are expected to treat love like war. A necessary evil, and also glorious and exciting. The revolting parts he considers or justifies as a hangover. To experience the highs of the intoxicant glory, you have also to grovel in the lows. It is the contrast that enhances the savour.'

Charles pithily cut him off. 'I can do without glorious highs in matters of love. One should write one's feelings on water, and not engrave them in stone.' He pulled a sheath of paper out of a coat pocket. 'Here is my dilemma, Vanderville. I can reveal Josephine's interventions and advice in supply contracts on my behalf to the General and make her unhappy – something I am loathe to do – and secure my own release. Or I can expose my own connections with Compagnie Bodin, who have asked me to secure those contracts for them, and lose at the very least my army career and commission.'

'Which will you do?' asked Vanderville.

He sighed. 'I don't know. I don't care about the army like you. If only I could find a middle way...' He sat down wearily. 'Give me a pen, I am going to write to the General and get myself out of here. Now that fool Mombello has gone, all of the contracts are back on the table, and once I am free, nothing and no one will stop me getting my hands on them.'

While Charles wrote and scratched out his lines to Bona-parte, Vanderville prodded around the masonry surrounding the springhead. Charles put his head on one side. 'What are you looking for, Vanderville?'

'Gracchus and I found a tunnel leading from the cisterns under the house. We were in a bit of a hurry to get out, so used an opening from the tunnel to get into the gardener's well and climbed up... well, rather, I climbed up, and hauled him up with rope. The well entrance was for maintenance, I suppose, but the main tunnel lead in this direction, and we thought it might have been used by the family to get to the chapel when the house was built. It might also have been used by Mombello's murderer to pass to and from the chapel that night.'

He gave up on the fountainhead and sat down with Charles, who thought a bit, then said, 'The problem is that you are running up and down poking around everywhere trying to find it. Use your head. One of the wedding Corbeilles was found down here disordered the next day, am I right?'

Vanderville nodded. 'It was Paolette's, which was in the second niche here on the left. I've looked all over the platform it was on and found nothing.'

Charles frowned. 'Your memory is in error. Paolette's corbeille was in the last space by the spring, where Mombello now lies,' he pointed, 'and Elisa's was opposite. I distinctly remember, because I was forced to listen to Paolette enunciate the contents of the wedding baskets at great length. I was almost tempted to force a kiss on her to make her shut up.'

Vanderville considered this combination of welcome and unwelcome news. 'Why would the position of the corbeilles have been changed?' he asked.

'Because Mombello was interred in the last niche,' reasoned Charles. 'Rather bad taste to leave a wedding basket on top of him, don't you think? If you are looking for secret passages, I'd start there.'

Vanderville nodded again, and paced over to the tomb of Mombello to resume his search.

'Look,' said Charles, 'passages and caves are all very well, but I will tell you one thing. At the root of all of this trouble are the Corsicans. And since the only Corsicans here are the General's family, you really want to find a way to leave the whole thing alone.'

'Piotr was a Corsican,' said Vanderville.

'Yes,' countered Charles, 'and look where it got him. I wish we could bring him back, but we can't. Take my advice, go back to duty with Dumas, and leave Gracchus to this delving in dark places. It will bring you nothing but ill fortune. Or worse.'

He finished his letter to Bonaparte with a flourishing signature. 'There, that ought to do the job, better disgrace and dishonour than a firing squad. Give it to the sentry on the door please.'

—

'Leonardi is a most extraordinary man, Vanderville,' Gracchus said as Vanderville came back up through the trapdoor. 'While you were messing around down there, he has brought me a trembling cheese.' He pointed out that article, which had displaced the remaining papers on the table and sat there proudly. It was indeed quivering.

'He honoured me with a discourse on the science of guzzling, delivered with magisterial gravity and demeanour as if he had been expounding some great point of theology. He spelled out to me the difference in appetites: the one we have before eating, the one we have after the second and third course; the means of simply gratifying it, then of arousing and stimulating it; the organisation of his sauces, first in general, and then in particularising the quality of the ingredients and their effects; the difference in salads according to the season, which ones should be warmed up, and which served cold, the way of adorning and embellishing them to make them also pleasant to the sight. After that he entered on the order of serving, full of beautiful and important considerations. And all of this swollen with rich and magnificent words, like the way we used to talk about the government of an empire.'

'Wonderful,' said Vanderville sourly. 'Would you mind moving your table away from that tomb, I have a new theory to test.'

'Your tunnel, you mean?' asked Gracchus. 'I have given it some thought, and decided it must be under Mombello's tomb. Its position corresponds to the odd shape of the nymphaeum on that side. There must be a cavity behind the nymphaeum wall that comes up under the tomb. It probably swings round in some way to expose the opening, but I imagine it only opens from below. I examined it while you were asleep and couldn't find a way to move it.'

'I have spent some hours searching for this opening,' said Vanderville. 'Did you not think to tell me this before now?'

'I did consider it,' replied Graçchus, 'but judged it was beneficial for you to have occupation to keep your spirits up.' Vanderville threw his hands up in despair and started tidying the table. 'You can lead a horse to water, but you can't make it drink,' sighed Gracchus sadly, rescuing his cheese.

'A horse can tell when water is contaminated better than the rider can,' snapped Vanderville.

After despatching his letter Charles resigned himself to a moody wait in the nymphaeum, and Vanderville sulked in the chapel while Gracchus continued alternately working on his papers and prostrating himself in silent thought. Hours passed before the chapel door ground open and Dumas strode in. His feather plume caught on the door jamb, and he whipped the hat off and examined the damage regretfully, 'Orders for Charles's release,' he announced to the chapel generally. Vanderville leapt to his feet respectfully, but Gracchus was stretched out on the altar asleep or meditating and did not look up. Charles poked his head out of the open trapdoor.

'From the General or his wife?' he chirruped.

'Don't talk to me about that woman,' grumbled Dumas, striding round the chapel waving his hat. 'She has been hurling break tooth words at me all morning.'

'How remarkably dear of her,' said Charles. 'Nothing like friends in high places, eh?' he winked at Vanderville.

'She looks as if butter would not melt in her mouth, though I warrant cheese would not choke her,' offered Dumas obscurely, peering behind the altar as if he expected to find a renegade priest crouching there.

'I doubt you will have the chance to find out, my dear General,' said Charles, 'unless you fancy exchanging your place for mine.'

Dumas glared at him. 'By the way, Vanderville,' he said, 'you and your bacon-faced friend are free to leave too. Bonaparte thinks you will be more use at liberty.'

'Thank you, General,' said Charles equably, climbing out into the nave. 'And how is our cherished General Bonaparte this fine day?'

Dumas grunted, and started pressing his hat feathers out on Gracchus's table. 'His wife has been breaking his balls. There was a squall over shawls this morning before their carriage ride, but the General must have applied the matrimonial peacemaker during the carriage ride, and by the time we returned, all was well, and they were both napping like dormice.'

'What bliss,' grimaced Charles. 'I'll collect my things.' He bobbed out of sight like a jack-in-the-box.

'I'm taking the sentries with me,' said Dumas over his shoulder as he made his way out. 'I need you tonight, Vanderville, so don't make any plans.' He paused. 'And tomorrow it's the ball at last, and then we can finally leave this backwater and get back to work, if those damn Austrian fools don't sign the peace treaty first.' He exited with a bang.

Chapter Eighteen

Gracchus and Vanderville left the chapel at a lollop. Vanderville hoisted his neat bedroll bundle on one shoulder, clutched Gracchus's squalid loose blanket under his arm, and made for the stables, while Gracchus ambled towards the house. As he passed through the gardens, he came across two workmen measuring the statue of Perseus and Medusa. They were being directed by Fesch.

'*Salut* Gracchus,' said Fesch affably. He indicated the statue group. 'We need to leave these up for the ball guests tonight, but then we are all leaving, so I'm preparing everything for a quick operation.' He surveyed the statues critically. 'Do you think they would look better on the terrace? It would save time tomorrow if we could get them halfway to the waggons. Berthier won't let me bring carts through the garden.'

'Aren't these technically the property of Alexandre, the new Comte Mombello?' queried Gracchus, frowning.

'Yes, but he has seen fit to present these to the Republic. He doesn't like them anyway; he says they give him bad dreams. It is useful for him to have his disorder hushed up and this sort of donation to the Republic helps to foster good will; his estate would have been under requisition anyway. We cannot make any exceptions, or the General would doubtless be accused of favouritism.'

'Will there be any works of art left in Lombardy after the Army of Italy have looted their way on to Austria?' asked Gracchus.

Fesch took him by the arm and led him towards the terrace steps. 'Listen, what we take they will replace. You wouldn't believe some of these young sculptors like Canova and Bartolini, they are doing wonderful work. What you unjustly malign, I regard as a harvest. I compare my role to that of a farmer. As much as we farm, as many eggs as we collect, the chickens will replace them multi-fold. In fact, without the harvest of the eggs, the chickens will feel little need to produce more. So the farmer stimulates the chickens to realise their potential. Within ten years, all these empty pedestals will be filled up again, probably with better stuff than we are buying, the moderns are surpassing the antique.'

'*Buying* is a euphemism?' asked Gracchus acidly.

Fesch dismissed this with a wave. 'If you had seen Canova at work as I have, his studio lit only by a guttering lamp, the great man, tool in hand, labouring over some nymph, the sweat dripping from his brow... Magnificent.' He gripped Gracchus's arm more tightly and looked earnestly into his face. 'You would understand, is what I mean.' He strode out of the garden clearing and indicated to Gracchus to follow him.

'Speaking of young artists, have you met the painter Gros? He is on the terrace painting Bonaparte now. I will take you there.' As he led the way through the gardens, he patted Gracchus's arm. 'By the way, while you were under a cloud in the chapel, I took the liberty of securing Bonaparte's agreement that you reinstate to me the supply contracts you had found in Mombello's papers. I will send a man to the chapel to pick them up. They are of no interest to anyone except myself and the Comte Mombello, so I thought it best to take them into my custody. The Comte, of course, no longer has any need of them.'

'Yes, that is remarkably convenient for you,' said Gracchus, who had pocketed the key to the chapel. He fingered that object carefully where it was secreted in his coat and removed the commissary's hand from his arm. Fesch was still waxing enthusiastically. 'Naturally, I will still help you with any of your questions, Gracchus. Although I understand that the official line on the deaths has been resolved now.'

'Has it?' said Gracchus, raising a quizzical eyebrow. 'And what has been decided?'

'The sad death of Comte Mombello has been assigned to Piotr, who overcome with remorse, or feeling the Republic's net of justice closing in on him, then destroyed himself in the cisterns.'

'Did he also disembowel himself with a sabre?' asked Gracchus dryly.

'I don't know all of the details,' admitted Fesch. 'Bonaparte has resealed the cistern complex, which is a shame, because apparently the deranged man had constructed a sort of cocoon for himself down there, incorporating the grotesque catafalque cloth from the comte's funeral, and all sorts of bones. Apparently it is so horrible that Bonaparte wouldn't let anyone else down there.' He stroked his chin thoughtfully. 'It would have been of great interest to the natural philosopher in me to see these productions of his warped mind. And I wanted to secure that textile.'

Gracchus paused at the foot of the steps to the terrace. 'I did not know about the catafalque cloth,' he uttered.

'No. Well even you cannot know everything, my dear fellow,' said Fesch, leading the way up the flights, 'especially if you keep getting yourself locked up. Anyway,' he said, as they arrived at the terrace, 'here is everybody, they can fill you in on the details. I had better get back to my workman to supervise.'

'And Lieutenant Charles?'

'Has agreed to resign his commission after admitting trading in army contracts. He chose business over honour, which will rebound on him when Mombello's successor at the ministry of war awards them to me. We were all worried it would be Alexandre, who is uncorruptible, but apparently it will be Melzi, and he is a reasonable man.'

He paused, and then took Gracchus's hand, and whispered urgently, 'Look, I will tell you one thing. I have done you a good turn having you released, but in return it is implicit that you stop poking around in the supply contracts. That comes from the top,' and with a greasy smile he scampered back down the steps.

—

Gracchus flung open the doors to the salon, which was in the process of being transformed into a ballroom by servants busily rearranging furniture. 'A word, Berthier!' Gracchus hailed at his bustling back.

'The bureau is closed to you, the commander-in-chief is closed to you, everything is closed to you,' said Berthier. 'If I weren't so ill, I would have you put on a charge. Go away and stop bothering me.' He continued moving purposefully through the salon without breaking stride. 'It is well for you that I am too unwell to argue with Bonaparte about your release. We are all too busy. Come back tomorrow, and if, as I fully expect, I am on my deathbed by then, you may attempt your circumnavigations on my successor.'

Gracchus followed him, persisting, 'Fesch tells me that you have arrived at an explanation of the murders. Are you dispensing with my services then?'

Berthier stopped and fixed him with a gimlet eye. 'These gods of cloth! Fesch is just what he always was, building castles in the air and writing me six-page letters on some meticulous point of speculation. The present means no more to him than the past, the future is all.' He turned to one of the workmen and barked instruction, then back to Gracchus, and said more reasonably, 'Thank you for the resolution of the army supply contract situation, I don't know what you said to him in the chapel, but we now have a full confession from Lieutenant Charles. Apparently, he was involved in contract speculation on behalf of one Compagnie Bodin of Paris. He has absolved that person whom rumour may have linked to his name of any involvement, and that matter can be considered closed.'

He lifted one finger to silence Gracchus's riposte. 'Piotr's demise has been deemed a suicide, provoked by his guilt at having murdered the Comte Mombello. Unfortunately, that young officer, always prone to influence, had his head turned by the talk of ghosts and phantoms, and influenced unduly by these thoughts his fevered brain had led him to consider himself a monster, and to commit the depredations on the animals.'

'His drowning was surely not self-inflicted, General,' protested Gracchus.

'We will never know,' agreed Berthier, nodding, 'but that is immaterial. The new Comte Mombello has agreed to leave the army to seek treatment for his own malady, and is desirous that this matter be considered at an end.' He went to pass out of the salon but Gracchus stretched out his arm to prevent him.

'There was one more thing. Now that it doesn't matter anymore, perhaps you would reveal to me who the sleepwalker is among the General's family?'

Berthier removed his hat and scratched his head, 'You sometimes overthink these things, Gracchus, and perhaps let yourself become a bit deranged in pursuit of a perfect solution.' He regarded him steadily. 'You have very nearly got thin in consequence.'

'My concern,' began Gracchus, keeping his voice low for the benefit of the servants passing behind them with a sofa, 'is that we have not apprehended the incubus who has committed these outrages. I may be mistaken, but if I am not, there may be more trouble ahead.'

'I understand your intentions, Gracchus, and am not insensible to them. Just in case we still have a problem here, I have made out a brevet commission for Lieutenant Vanderville as an officer of the Guides, filling the vacancy created by Alexandre's imminent departure. This is temporary, and he is to understand that this is not yet a full commission. It will enable him to organise a discreet security this evening. Most of the officers will be at the ball, and there will be the corresponding jollification for the private soldiers at the stables, so manpower will be limited. The Polish Legion will throw an iron cordon around the villa, but Vanderville and you will be responsible for ensuring there is no disruption inside that cordon. It is on your head. Enjoy yourself, but don't get in the way, or address me or the General in public. Now let me pass before I have you sent back to the chapel in irons.'

—

At the stables Vanderville had deposited his bed roll and was walking in the yard with Hercule, who handed him a docket. 'You are to become one of us at last!' he smiled. 'There is no time to have you fitted for a Guides uniform I'm afraid, so you will not have the advantage of our red *pantalons* to help you with the *citoyennes* tonight. You must continue in your miserable rags for now.'

'It's only a temporary appointment anyway,' grinned Vanderville. 'Tell me what is going forward with the ball preparations.'

Hercule kicked a chicken out of his path. 'Alexandre is host. His father planned the ball, and he has taken over his duties. He says he is going to resign from the army, and go into politics in place of his uncle! The Poles are organised to provide external security by Dumas. All of the Guides officers are invited to the ball, so the Guides themselves will be at the stables standing by in case they are needed.'

Vanderville nodded seriously. 'This is all pointless, each of our suspects will be inside the house. We must organise and arm ourselves, so that you and I will deal with any incidents.' They turned and walked back down the yard.

Hercule waved in the direction of their quarters. 'We had better include Charles too,' he murmured, and then stifling

Vanderville's protest added, 'Yes, I know what you are thinking, Vanderville, but he is still one of us.'

Vanderville considered. 'Very well, if there is trouble, we may need him, and if he causes any trouble at least we will be near to restrain him.' They stopped under the gallery, and Hercule asked if Vanderville was coming up.

'I have no time to spare, Hercule. I'm back to Gracchus, who doubtless will be in the vicinity of the kitchen after his confinement.'

Vanderville caught up with Gracchus in the kitchen garden where he was strolling moodily. He looked up when Vanderville joined him and said, 'Look at this paradise. It's hard to recall all of the subterranean horrors in the light of a perfect day like this.' Vanderville cast an eye over the garden; a lazy midday sun was bathing the flowers among which bees were hustling greedily.

'Yes, it's idyllic. Anyway, have you heard the news? It has some relevance for us. Now that Alexandre is to become the new Comte Mombello, Melzi has announced that all of his uncle's posts and perquisites accrue to him. Including his role in the Transpadane ministry of war.'

'I rather thought he might announce that tonight,' said Gracchus.

Vanderville shot him a pointed look. 'You had a hand in this, didn't you? Don't you realise it makes him a target in all of the same ways as the old Comte? Alexandre is incorruptible, he is more of an obstacle than his uncle ever was. It's as good as a death warrant.' He strode up and down the garden in between towering rows of staked bean plants in agitation. The great face of the house above them was encased in shadows and the air was oppressively hot.

'Be calm,' said Gracchus, 'nervousness is contagious.'

'Alexandre spoke of a dream,' fretted Vanderville, ignoring him. 'He said he dreamed that he died and turned to stone like the fellow in that story. How can we defend him tonight, it will be chaos with the ball-goers milling all over the villa?'

'It is the perfect combination. His would-be assassins will all be present tonight. And when one of them strikes, we shall be on hand to expose that person.'

Vanderville clasped his hands together and remonstrated, 'But what if the mazzere comes out to play?'

Gracchus examined his sandal-clad feet. The sun was warm on them, and he grunted contentedly, 'Which one?'

'Alexandre Marbeuf! Who do you think I mean!' exclaimed Vanderville. 'We can't have him in here tonight. If he didn't kill his father, he certainly murdered the geese, not to mention the bloody dogs.'

Gracchus considered him dubiously, and pushed some dust around with his toes. 'You are right. We had better have Leonardi locked up too, he has accounted for a great deal of goose lately. And your General Bonaparte, he has a chicken ramshackled for his stomach every day.'

'You are pleased to be perverse, Gracchus,' expostulated Vanderville, 'but what about Alexandre, or Fesch, or Charles too, come to that? Both Charles and Fesch went to the chapel to confront the Comte Mombello that night, and he did not leave it alive. One of them is a murderer and has been set at liberty to stalk their way through the villa.'

Gracchus removed his hat, stretched his arms out, and turned to feel the sun on the back of his head. 'What would you have me do? If nobody who has taken a life is allowed to dance tonight, we exclude the entire staff of the army. A pretty ball it will be without the officers. What about your General Dumas, how is his counter-insurgency campaign going? The man stinks of burning villages. What about you, Vanderville?'

Vanderville frowned. 'That is different, and you know it.'

'Is it? Is it though?' said Gracchus, dropping his arms to his sides, and examining his deteriorating hat lining. 'Is not all Lombardy one great goose pen that your army is rampaging through?' He adjusted the offending hat on his head, and walked towards the kitchen door. 'Why am I responsible for preventing a death or two here, while those orchestrating it on the grand scale are to escape my notice?'

Vanderville followed him towards the kitchen door. He struggled and then failed to repress his irritation, and was as equally ashamed as angry when he erupted, 'It is all very well for you to skate across the thin ice of the moral high ground! If this war is a mess, and the Revolution a farce, it's you and the other old men who are responsible for it. It is you lot who made it so. It could have been beautiful. Damn it, you began it!' He looked around for something to slam his fist down on, and settled on a bean pole. The impact set off a chain reaction, and the entire supporting apparatus of poles and nets came down on their heads.

Floundering around under the net, Gracchus growled back, 'What does youth ever achieve? Wiser heads could yet retrieve this mess.' He pounded at the entangling net in exasperation, but succeeded only in further binding his arms. 'If it wasn't for your bloody *genius* General who refuses to lose a battle like a decent person ought, we would have a stalemate, and that leads to peace! But no, you are all too busy with your feckless grand adventure. As long as you are enjoying your stupid war, the whole world can go to hell, and damn the consequences.' He lunged at Vanderville, who responded in kind, but caught in the nets, they were suspended metres apart, each unable to advance or retreat, and they spent their passion on struggling futilely. Unable to come to blows, their remonstrances reached a critical level of foul epithets and extreme volume.

'Do either of you require any help?' asked Paolette, entering from the terrace and interrupting their affray. 'It's only that we are trying to take tea on the terrace, and it sounded as if the Austrians had arrived. Mamma says thank you for expanding her French vocabulary though, Lieutenant Vanderville, and begs you to accept the loan of her clasp-knife.' She held out that article, and then seeing him unable to make use of it, proceeded to cut away one of his hands until he was capable of taking it himself.

Under her civilising presence and ministrations they began to cool, and discreetly avoiding each other's eyes regained some scant semblance of dignity as they emerged from the netting.

'*Citoyenne* Bonaparte,' said Gracchus hesitatingly, as he examined the clasp-knife, 'would you help us tonight? We have reason to keep a close eye on certain of the ball guests so as to avoid any…' he was almost about to say unseemly scuffles, but mercifully averted the unfortunate reference. '…Any uncomfortable scenes? Would you undertake to help us keep watch?'

'As long as you assign me the murderer, and not the ghoul. I can handle any number of angry uncomfortable men, but I'm not sure I can stand a ghost.'

'I am thinking in particular of Lieutenants Charles and Mombello, the others concerned will be under my especial care.'

'Meaning I must not watch anyone I am related to? That certainly cuts the field down a bit. But Charles? That buffoon?!' She made a face something between a scowl and a pout. 'I would prefer Mamma to *him*. No! Vanderville, I'm joking!' she laughed. 'You take her!'

Vanderville frowned. 'I think it better that I keep an eye on Alexandre, not because he will make mischief, but because he is the aim for our unknown assassin's rancour.'

'Who will marshal the guard in your absence?' said Gracchus.

'Hercule, I can rely on him like my own right arm.'

'I shall adopt Letizia then,' said Gracchus. 'Unlike the rest of you I am neither intimidated by her, nor vulnerable to her charms.'

'Did he really say charms?' whispered Paolette, grimacing at Vanderville, and clutching his arm.

–

Leonardi was below in the kitchen, supervising a skeleton staff, who seemed mainly to be concentrating on sugar confections.

He looked up from his chopping as they entered, and sipped dolefully from a glass of wine, while indicating the cakes with his knife.

'*Salut* Gracchus,' he nodded at Vanderville, 'I hope you two haven't destroyed *all* of my garden. I can tell you; I am very much feeling the loss of Piotr. He was wasted in the army. If he hadn't been sucked up in its great hungry maw, he might have made a beautiful pâtissier of repute in five or six years.' He took a swig of wine. 'And now they are saying he is the murderer. It's a foul piece of the banditry, Gracchus, that's what it is.' He resumed his rapid chopping at a pile of chicken breasts. 'He was only Corsican on his mother's side anyway.' He waggled his knife in Gracchus's face. 'It's one of them, Gracchus. This monster, it came here with them, and now it's living down there – under my kitchen!' He bristled with outrage and pointed at the larder door which led to the cellars. 'And another thing, the young master, him, he never harmed a goose until this lot arrived here. Then suddenly the goose pens are turned into a charnel house. It stinks. They provoked him to it.'

Gracchus shook his head, slowly. 'Alexandre said that he was helped with his condition by the arrival of the staff circus, and particularly by talking to the Corsicans.'

Leonardi swept his arms out expansively. 'They are as slippery as the river crabs, those ones.' The effect was marred by his precipitating his glass from the table. It expired in a burst of shards on the kitchen floor. Gracchus wondered if his friend's evident inebriation would impact the ball supper, and Leonardi read his mind. 'Better drunk on wine than ink like you Gracchus, it is less morbid. Come here and see what I have prepared for the General's last supper. I am leaving this house, it is a death to me now with the comte and now Piotr gone. But I have one final parting shot for the General.'

Gracchus saw that Leonardi's last word to General Bonaparte was to cook an entire menu for him composed of chicken. Leonardi enumerated the dishes. 'A pâté of chicken breast and partridge minced with tiny white onions, creamed with sauce remoulade,' he announced, 'then we have the crest of chickens stuffed with chicken livers, lard, beef marrow, truffles and walnut wine. I have prepared also the head spikes of a rooster, his kidney, liver and heart in a beautiful broth.

'I haven't found a way to make the feathers edible yet,' he said mournfully, 'but given time, it might be done.' He indicated the cellars again. 'If Piotr was still here, we might have made the ice of a chicken, but who wants to go down *there* now,' he shuddered. 'You get the whole idea, we finish with a pudding made of shredded chicken breast cooked in milk with vanilla sugar, and Marsala, all heightened with spices.'

'A trenchant comment,' observed Gracchus, trying a sugared biscuit. 'You say you are leaving Mombello's employ, where will you go next?'

Leonardi shrugged. 'For my talents, there is no shortage of friends waiting, Gracchus. And you?'

Gracchus grimaced. 'I haven't decided yet. Away from the army.' He took the cheese Leonardi offered.

'Cheese is the biscuit for a drunkard,' Leonardi muttered through a mouthful, offering some to Vanderville. 'He stimulates appetite without satisfying. I can never get enough cheese.'

'*Citoyen* Leonardi,' said Vanderville, refusing the proffered cheese, 'I would like to post a man on the cellar door tonight. It ought to be two,' he mused, 'but we are short. Can he be here in the kitchen so he can keep an eye on the back hall too?'

'I can't have him in the kitchen,' said Leonardi, shaking his head, 'it's a distraction for the village girls.' He considered a moment. 'He can go in the back hall outside the kitchen door for now, and when I dismiss the girls before the ball he can go into the larder. I will be alone down here, and it will be the comfort to have the cellars watched.' He cocked his head on one side. 'I might even send him down there to see if Piotr left any ices in his buckets.'

'Sorry,' said Vanderville quickly, 'no one is allowed down, the General's orders. I will post the sentry immediately.' He turned to Gracchus. 'Shall we go over the rest of the villa now? We can discuss the other posts.'

As they went from the other kitchen stair into the back hall a breathless Letizia entered from the terrace. 'Madame Buonaparte,' said Gracchus courteously, sweeping off his hat, and tucking the lining back in. It appeared to have become disarrayed during their combat in the bean vines. She surveyed his figure, from his head to his sandalled feet.

She nodded to Vanderville, and addressed Gracchus seriously in a low voice. 'I am pleased to see you both restored to us. We have need of your protection, Gracchus, more than ever tonight.'

'I thought that you might be of one opinion with your son, madame, that our problems are resolved,' offered Gracchus. 'If he is right, there is nothing to be done tonight except enjoy the ball and prepare for our departures on the morrow.'

Letizia moved closer to him, with a sideways glance at Vanderville that sent him tactfully retracing his steps towards the front hall and grand staircase. Like many her age, she underestimated the strength of young ears when he was removed a step or two away. She leant in to Gracchus's ear and urged, 'Your favourable impression of your own abilities blinds you to the truth, Gracchus. You have made a complete fanfaronade of this whole business.'

'It appears that the gap between what you know and what you choose to reveal to me is widening into a veritable chasm, madame,' thought Gracchus aloud.

She considered him a moment with her strange gaze, and he found her eyes shamefully back on his disgraceful hat. 'I will see you tonight, Gracchus,' she whispered, 'when the children are dancing. Be ready.'

She brushed past Vanderville, who had been listening discreetly, and mounted the stair with a rustle of black skirts. Gracchus knitted his brow. 'Who the devil is she talking about?' he hissed. 'She is talking in riddles.'

'Scarcely a novelty where she is concerned,' whispered Vanderville.

'You are so caught up in your own cleverness that you haven't even the wit to see what is in front of your eyes,' came her sonorous voice from above them. She was encased in the shadows of the staircase, and neither of them could see her face. 'Why do you think the mazzere has carried the catafalque cloth to the cisterns?'

Gracchus opened his mouth and then pulled up short, struck by a sudden revelation. 'It is not a nest, it's a sepulchre,' he breathed.

Letizia nodded. 'Exactly. The mazzere has constructed a mausoleum. The dreamworld has revealed that destruction is imminent.'

Chapter Nineteen

The villa courtyard under the awning had been cleared of the clerks' tables and clutter, and the triumphal arch standing before it had been completed by the masons, ready to welcome the ball guests. The canvas stretched over its wooden frame was bedaubed with republican symbols and trophies of arms. The new Comte Alexandre Mombello had insisted on the Transpadane flag being given parity with the French, so there were twinned tricolours crossed on its summit. Bonaparte was beneath the arch, surveying the carriage drive with a calm and satisfied eye while Gracchus watched him thoughtfully from his post under the awning.

Bonaparte was tranquil, and Gracchus wondered if this was the same mood he displayed on the eve of a battle with his dispositions made and his troops arrayed. He was in a similar position himself and as he turned his own thoughts to his fears and worries for the evening ahead he brooded. Letizia's uttered prophecy preoccupied him. Her motives were as usual obscure, but he was in full accord with her insinuation that trouble was ahead. Nor had he solved that last riddle Piotr uttered to Bonaparte, 'Only when you learn to question your happiness will the truth be revealed'. That Piotr had found answers in the cisterns he was sure, and that the same answers evaded him was a source of frustration.

Bonaparte at least seemed utterly unconcerned. He had never mentioned the riddle again, and Gracchus envied him his imperturbability. He was riven with doubt. Had he been too blasé in exposing Alexandre to the blades of potential assassins?

Was that cavalier approach dictated by his own distrust of Alexandre?

No, he told himself, he had confidence in his own perspicacity, and should the night conclude in a trial of arms, he had a growing faith in the young officer who had shared the ordeal of Mombello with him. Vanderville, at least, would not let him down.

He thought also of Mombello, cut down by one of his friends or loved ones, almost certainly by one of the guests who had shared his table, and laughed at his parlour games; and of poor miserable Piotr, who had found love and obliteration at this place, then been ostracised by his regiment, shunned by his peers during his captivity, and squalidly drowned in a subterranean hell. Perhaps Vanderville had been right after all, and he wanted this resolved tonight, with justice for the victims, or at least the truth that Voltaire had required for the dead.

The whole villa and camp were alive with excitement, and spirits soared as eagerly as the first few fireflies that were dancing over the gardens in the dusk. The tedious staccato rhythm of the cicadas had started under the trees; their rustic frenzy Gracchus felt as a vaunting ambition floating in the evening air. After all, Bonaparte had delivered everything he had promised with an imminent peace won by force of arms. The staff had delivered with a new cadre of inspirational leaders. The soldiers themselves had delivered with a string of extraordinary victories that had set the whole world talking, so why not start to dream? Can it be called swagger when the laurels were so justified? Was it the prospect of peace with Austria and freedom for Lombardy filling the Milanese with hope? Was it the chance of a welcome return to arms and fresh triumphs for the French soldiers? Perhaps it was all and none of these things, and merely the prospect of a wedding ball as the ultimate punctuation to the sojourn at Mombello. For everybody present, the night crackled with anticipation, and the morrow brimmed with promise, and that was enough to render the atmosphere thrilling.

Gracchus took a deep breath of the fresh air and reflected on Josephine's promise to him, 'A ball is a splendid spectacle, but a military ball is to die for.' The ball did indeed promise to be as brilliant as splendid uniforms, beauty, and fashion could make it. As the sun began to set the female guests appeared all together upon the paths before the villa. The serene sky, the mild and equal temperature, the cleanness of the newly swept paths justified the wearing of their Athenian muslin gowns, with white pendent folds drawn up on their arms to reveal their pretty ankles, and as they swayed and posed in the twilight, the approach to the house seemed to be one great gallery of the antique brought to miraculous life.

The generals, staff officers, and the merry officers of the Guides and Poles arrived preceded by their own bands of music, who halted under the awning. They wore their formal square coats of an impractical length, blazing with embroidery, and reaching the knees. Their hats they wore under their arms to better display the teased and dressed hair that fell to their shoulders and many sported clumsy and exuberantly embroidered sword belts over the shoulder.

Some of the younger officers had evidently launched their celebrations early, and among these, marching up the path with their arms around one another with an air of great conviviality, Gracchus saw the lieutenants Alexandre, Charles, Hercule and Vanderville. He wondered whether they would enjoy the same brotherhood on the morrow. Charles was singing tunefully, and Hercule lustily. Alexandre was in breeches with tiny shoes as thin as pasteboard stuck onto the point of his foot, but the others proudly wore snug white *pantalons* with their new buskin boots. Their chins reposed on the cushion of their vast cravats, and they bowed stiffly as they greeted the women and disposed themselves in couples before the arch. How quickly the young put aside the loss of a beloved uncle, a friend, a lover... thought Gracchus; he envied them.

The whiskered bandmasters of the Guides and Polish Legion glared at each other from their posts on either side of the awning. Their bands, in harmony for once, took up a lively tune, then the company passed through to present themselves at the villa doors. Bonaparte took Josephine by the arm, and all followed them through the hall to the grand salons at the rear of the villa. The loftiest chamber had been transformed into a ballroom decorated with festoons of vines, flowers, and lamps, so that the whole apartment resembled an illuminated arbour. In the centre of the ceiling hung a lustre filled with dozens of candles. It was composed of such light materials that every puff of breeze from the open terrace doors gave it motion; indeed it had the appearance of being turned round by an invisible hand. The evening flooded in through the terrace doors and windows, bringing the air of the night inside, and the candles of the ballroom were complemented by torches illuminating the terrace.

On the arrival of the Polish band, the dances began with the formal quadrille, which would have been admired on any opera stage, especially as the dresses of the female dancers were in some cases better adapted to the stage than respectable society. From the walls, full-length portraits of Lombard nobles glared down at the froth in timeless disapproval.

Gracchus had been swept inside with the throng and as the entrance dance reached its conclusion there was a crescendo of delighted applause from the onlookers and Bonaparte, beaming with pleasure from his seat on the dais, received a parade of veteran soldiers ushered in as examples of republican virtue. These grey-haired worthies achieved a mixed success with the impatient dancers, who appreciated the last to be presented most emphatically. Especially as he met Bonaparte's republican platitudes with a heartfelt impromptu acclamation, 'In Italy we have neither law nor government, the generals are the sovereigns!'

Bonaparte riposted adeptly to this unwelcome adage with a smile. 'Never a sovereign. But a republic can perhaps admit of a proconsul.'

Dumas usefully interposed and ushered the elated soldier and his companions towards the hall. 'Dear Grognard. You are yet a terrorist at heart I see. Take this coin and get thee to the stables before you give the ladies the vapours. That's my job.'

With the inconveniently virtuous republicans ejected by their handler with gifted bottles and indecent haste, the dancing recommenced. Bonaparte noticed Gracchus evading the dancers with his adroit hobble and indicated to him to join the party sat on and around the dais.

'Thank you General,' said Gracchus gratefully, with an inelegant bow to the *citoyennes* who surrounded Bonaparte.

'The leg troubles you?' asked Josephine solicitously from her seat of honour.

Gracchus nodded with a grimace, and she murmured, 'Sit here with the family where you can see everything.'

Gracchus perched next to her and scanned the room for the older Bonaparte girls. 'Where are they?' he asked.

Bonaparte replied, 'They are changing for their display dance, so that they may make a fine entrance. They have it in mind to outshine the Parisians tonight. Am I right?' he asked Josephine, smacking her lap affectionately. She nodded, smiling her sphinx's smile, and took his hand in hers. 'Our fair *citoyennes* pursuing the fantasies of Greco-Roman dress are of more consequence than all five armies on five fronts, you see,' he said. He was in high spirits and caressed his wife with an almost improper abandon. For a moment Gracchus was reminded of how young he still was. Letizia, who sat at his other hand, studied a dance card with affected concentration that betrayed not the slightest waft of annoyance until a very strong scent of attar of roses pervaded the dais. It emanated from *Citoyenne* Hamelin who was dancing in the set in front of them, surrounded by admirers, in a charming dress in the French national colours, shedding her fragrance with each bobbing step. Letizia wrinkled her nose and shifted pointedly in her seat, saying to no one in particular, 'I think it must be a

Milanese perfumier's wife, or his daughter, it's enough to make the strongest man faint.' Gracchus inclined his head towards her in agreement.

Dancing in the same figure as Hamelin were three other *citoyennes* in classical gowns each composed of three colours. Josephine was pointing out to Bonaparte that each of the women represented one of the new republics. There was Genoa, Venice, the Transpadane, and France of course. They paraded down the centre of the ballroom and came to rest in front of Bonaparte, who they hailed as the protector and founder of the freedom of Italy to general applause and acclamation. The band's triumphant peal segued into a martial quadrille, and the combinations began again with grace.

Gracchus regarded his own borrowed shoes balefully; they were pinching him even now. What would they be like later if he was called to action? He regretted his oh so practical sandals ruefully. He leant towards Josephine and begged, '*Citoyenne*, please explain to me the costume of the women. The vagaries of fashion are a mystery to me. I have felt that I should understand something of the mode at Paris, but it all passes in a blur, and just when I feel I have acquired a handle on the thing, it whirls off again like a goblin in some maniac dance.'

As Josephine rambled on delightfully, Charles took a break from the dancing and approached the dais uninvited, placing his hand on Gracchus's shoulder. Josephine smiled dryly at him, and ignoring him Bonaparte interjected to his wife, 'Whereas a soldier, without regard to fashion or taste, should be dressed in the most comfortable and least embarrassing manner possible. The opposite of what the Parisian boutiques of *Citoyennes* Leroi and Despaux indicate for our women.'

Charles rolled his eyes at Josephine, who affected not to notice as Bonaparte continued unrelenting, 'However ambitious of conquest the fair sex may be, they cannot expect to attain their object by inspiring beholders with terror at their extravagance. The only anxiety of the *citoyennes* ought to be to choose those forms and colours in dress which assimilate with the sentiment of loveliness, and which will add to their native softness and attractive grace.'

'I am a decided friend to extravagance,' sighed Charles complacently, just loudly enough for all to overhear.

Watching an apparently exhausted and red-eyed Alexandre dance, Gracchus observed that he and the other officers of the Guides had all apparently shopped for their ball dress together and looked like ornamental monkeys in their red breeches with gold fringe, and yellow boots. One of the dancers slipped at that point and almost fell, being caught at the last minute by her partner, from whom she disentangled herself blushing, and they were all distracted. Charles murmured,

> '"Forbid it heaven", young Alex cried
> and clasped her to his breast,
> The wondering fair one turned to chide,
> 'Twas Alex's self that prest.'

While glad of having Charles under his direct observation, Gracchus felt he ought to get that young maniac away from the General. He rubbed his leg dolefully and stood up.

Josephine giggled gleefully. 'Look,' she said, 'wait a moment, Gracchus, here they come.' A party was entering from the terrace, and attention was diverted from the Parisian and Milanaise cohort at the critical moment of their dance.

Those coming from the gardens had the advantage of youth and were led by the incomparable Paolette and stately Elisa. Their dress was daring; they had come as nymphs, all in white muslin. In contrast to the silver and gold ribbons and jewels of the Milanese and Parisian party they were accessorised with garlands of flowers, and in many cases their bare arms glistened with pearl and coral. The greatest ornament was Paolette's dazzling appearance as a faithful copy of a bacchante, her bronze ornaments repeating the golden glints in her brown eyes. On her head she wore a chequerboard bandeau adorned with mother of pearl shells. The band, which had been playing a triumphal march for Hamelin, abruptly collapsed their theme, ending on a jarringly unfortunate musical fart, and the bandmaster who was tall and ill-shaped, having limbs like those of a field spider and a small nervous head, quickly raised his baton and began a lively air for one of the latest modern quadrilles.

'Time for you to fulfil your obligations to me, *citoyen* spymaster,' said Josephine, rising to offer Gracchus her hand, as the dancers filling the floor reorganised their sets. It was impossible to pass across the dance floor without being pulled into a combination, and Gracchus and Josephine found themselves cajoled into a group almost immediately. Bonaparte smiled down at them from his lonely dais, and waved his hand affably as Josephine pushed Gracchus into place despite his feeble protests.

Each set was made up of eight couples facing each other in a square, two couples to each side. The other couple on their side was formed of Charles and *Citoyenne* Hamelin. The couples opposite with whom they would combine and exchange partners were Letizia with Dumas, and Paolette with Gros. Gracchus saw that the latter had exchanged his usual paint-spattered clothes for a marginally cleaner version, but apparently not found his comb.

In answer to Gracchus's protests about his leg, Josephine commanded, 'You can dance a little at least? Then simply follow me.' The music began again. As they danced, Josephine smilingly guided him, and squeezed his hand, and he began to find himself at ease. The movements were repetitive, and his feet protested a little when he went to his toes, but as he relaxed into the music, he found himself essaying a flourish or two and at one point he alarmed himself by seriously considering an impromptu pirouette.

The next combination twirl found him exchanging partners, and unexpectedly face to face with Paolette. She bestowed a dazzling smile upon him, and he weakly complimented her on her exquisite toilette. 'Do you like it?' She flashed her smile again. 'It was my mamma's idea to come as nymphs.'

They exchanged partners again and Gracchus found himself once again with Josephine who murmured to him, 'I am worried for Alexandre, Gracchus, make sure nothing happens tonight. There are too many people in this villa tonight, it is dangerous.'

Gracchus nodded sagely and bumped against a woman behind him. As he recovered his balance Josephine span him around again to a new partner. He felt hot and a little dizzy, the music seemed to be speeding up and the lights were too bright. His next partner was Letizia, who gave him her gloved hand and allowed him to turn her carefully. 'I need to speak to you,' she whispered. 'Alone.'

He swallowed nervously, and mumbled about the mingling crowds.

'In the garden then,' she said, as they exchanged partners again. Gros was beside him now with Paolette, and a flustered Gracchus realised he had inadvertently changed places with his partner Josephine, and was now in the woman's place.

Gros looked at Paolette approvingly. 'Your head dress is admirably in the antique style.'

'It is the true head dress of a Roman nymph, taken from the antique,' she said proudly.

'From a painting, or a cameo? I would dearly like to see the original,' answered Gros, licking his thin artist's lips.

'Mamma made it for me,' she whispered, staring at Gracchus over the artist's shoulder. Everyone came into the centre of the figure together, and the nimble Charles bounced on his toes.

'Yes, where did you see it, *Citoyenne* Buonaparte?' asked Charles mischievously. 'In one of Fesch's waggons of stores?'

Letizia raised one elegant eyebrow. 'You are more amusing when you are less advanced in your cups, Lieutenant,' she riposted as the dancers raised their arms in unison.

'Yes, but do tell,' said Josephine. 'Do you have a secret album of curious etchings you are keeping from us?'

The dancers dispersed to their respective positions again, cutting short the possibility of reply. Gracchus was searching his head. He had seen that curious chequerboard effect of the bandeau adorned with shells before, but where? He was exchanging places with Josephine, and she laughed at his puzzled frown as they passed one another. He was thinking so hard he missed his step, and when the next crossover began, he turned the wrong way and collided with another dancer. He stared at his feet, trying to remember which was which, and weaved left then right, and failed to pass. Aware he was holding up the dance he looked up with a mumbled apology into the face of Letizia. She was neither smiling nor frowning, and her clear eyes looked straight through him. And suddenly he realised where he had seen Paolette's bandeau before, and what it meant as clearly as if he had spotted a cloven hoof on the dance floor. He removed his handkerchief from his coat pocket, mopping his brow to cover his consternation, and proffering muttered apologies to his dance partners bent his head to the terrace windows and the safety of the terrace. As he went, he spotted Vanderville talking to the Guides officers, and attracting his attention gestured urgently to him to join him.

'There is sure mischief afoot tonight,' he said, as they met at the terrace doors. 'Are all of your men in place?'

Vanderville nodded. 'Be secure,' he said seriously, 'they are everywhere.'

Gracchus shook his head distractedly, and pushed past him onto the terrace.

After the quadrilles, there were to be waltzes, and Charles was practising his gliding step to general admiration. 'Come shake a shoe with me, young spider-shanks,' he called to Vanderville, who noticed with a start that Charles's shoes were the heroic buskin boots that Bonaparte had rejected as a present from his wife. Charles was obviously intent on demonstrating against his persecutor. He shook his head, his experience of the Parisian fad was even less than his grasp of the finer evolutions of the quadrilles, and he yielded his place to the first of an eager coterie of nymphs.

Bonaparte and Berthier had left their eyrie on the plinth, and their small court was dispersing among the revellers. Pushing through the excited crowd in search of refreshment, Vanderville found himself suddenly face to face with a beaming Paolette. She had drunk too deeply from the cup of social success and her gestures were prouder and more thoughtless than usual. Her arm was entwined with the disappointingly turned-out artist Gros, who appeared to have come as a stable hand. She thrust him forward, gushing, 'Gros is painting me! There is a picture of me doing full length, Vanderville. You would steal if you could get a peek of it; Mamma commissioned it, she said never was anything more beautiful or more cheap.'

'It must be an extraordinary likeness then,' observed Vanderville drily. 'Might I ask if you intend to dance with your husband all night, or will you be free at some point?'

She placed her head on one side and looked at him through her eyelashes. 'I prefer being sheltered under the wing of an eagle to hanging from the bill of a goose. Good evening, Lieutenant.'

As she turned away, Gros grinned offensively at Vanderville, who sighed. He was not the only disappointed one, the generals had descended en masse to monopolise the dancing partners to the consternation of the junior officers. Charles appeared at his elbow. 'Let us go, my friend, this battle is lost, but there is still time to win another. To the stables, where we may fare better against a more amiable enemy.'

Vanderville shook him off. 'I have to do my rounds of the cordon first. I will catch you up.'

The long glass doors in the ballroom were all open, allowing the music and the blazing light of the chandeliers to flood the terrace, which was filling up with groups of officers and *citoyennes* talking and laughing. As Vanderville stepped out, Hercule handed him his sword and hat, and he buckled on his sword belt. There was no sight of Gracchus. Many of the younger officers were drinking there, forming clusters of tribute around those citoyennes who were not dancing. The evening was warm and balmy after the heat of the day, and the scent of flowers drifted on the breeze. A few early fireflies were leaping in the gardens below, and the chirrup of cicadas could be heard from the terrace edge. Warmed by wine, the officers were attentively passing shawls to the *citoyennes* on the terrace to ward off any chills provoked by their scant attire.

Hercule led Vanderville to the corner by the stable stair where the throng was sparser. A Guide was stationed there in the shadows leaning on a statue plinth, and he straightened up and saluted them as they approached. Looming above him was the large figure of Medusa that had formerly stood in the gardens, now temporarily installed on a vacant terrace plinth. Apparently Perseus had become detached from his foe during their translocation to the terrace, and he was ignominiously face-down on the paving behind her. The moonlight reflected from his backside in a startling descent from grandeur. Medusa, liberated from his combative embrace, seemed a prouder gorgon altogether.

Hercule chuckled. 'Fesch keeps his workmen going through the night. Pillage by torchlight.'

Vanderville inclined his head. 'Is the cordon secure?'

'There are men patrolling the gardens as you demanded, with orders to report here every fifteen minutes.' He adjusted his sword belt. 'Almost everyone has been out here at one point or another. The guard on the staircase will prevent anyone from going upstairs. He is loitering in the back hall by the kitchen pretending to help with the drinks.'

'He will be plastered by midnight,' asserted Vanderville.

'Yes,' agreed Hercule, 'and there is no relief in sight unless we can organise one from the stables.' He grimaced. 'Some guests are in the gardens. Berthier took a walk by the ornamentals with *Citoyenne* Grassini, but they were surprised by *Citoyenne* Visconti and there was an eruption.'

Vanderville smiled; Gracchus would enjoy that one, he thought, but where was he? He cast his eyes up and down the terrace again. 'Anyone else?'

Hercule continued his resumé of movements. 'General Dumas escorted *Citoyenne* Gherardi twice, once in the rose garden, and once by the composting bins.' He counted off on his fingers. '*Citoyennes* Elisa and Paolette both went for a walk with their husbands. The latter returned with other officers of the staff.' Vanderville turned to the balustrade and leant out over the gardens, breathing in the clean air. Hercule persevered with his litany behind him, 'General Leclerc was sick in the asphodel bushes. Charles and…' he coughed, '…a companion, are down there now in the sculpture garden if you want to take a look.'

'I don't think I'll bother, thanks,' said Vanderville. He turned back to the terrace and straightened himself up. With relief, he recognised a shape limping down the terrace towards them as the familiar gait of Gracchus, and he and Hercule went to greet him.

'Look at that young woman,' said Gracchus as they came up, pointing at a young woman laughing in the middle of a circle of Polish Legion officers. It was *Citoyenne* Gherardi, whose sylvan grace was somewhat spoilt by a broad grass stain on the backside of her muslin round gown.

'She has been pigging in the bushes,' concluded Vanderville, who had noticed over Gracchus's shoulder Leonardi making his way towards them with a tray piled high with cakes in the form of balls. As he passed the group of Legion officers one called out to him. 'Where are the ices, Leonardi?' chided the officer. 'We miss them.'

Leonardi, his way blocked by two of the Poles, interrupted his progress. 'The icemaker is gone,' he said quietly. 'You know what happened to him.'

'Didn't he leave us anything?' said one of the bolder and more offensive Polish officers. Vanderville stepped forward to usher Leonardi away, looking sternly at the offender as he pushed past. The officer looked inclined to be argumentative, and moved his hand towards his sword, while his companions peeled away from the group to surround Vanderville.

Suddenly Hercule was there, rising like a giant from the gloom, and as the troublemaker squared up to Vanderville, Hercule swept him contemptuously over the balustrade with one great haymaker from his strong right arm. The effect was so immediately impressive as to dissuade anyone from further altercation, and Vanderville got Leonardi away from danger and into the ball salon with no further ado, Hercule covering their retreat with his peacemaker's glower. 'What's all the fuss?' asked Gracchus, bustling in behind them. Upon hearing about the ices he unhelpfully also seemed inclined to lament the lack of the popular treat.

'Come with me,' Leonardi said, putting down his tray on a table just inside the ballroom. 'I'm alone in the kitchens, but if you can man the top of my rotating delivery apparatus then I'll go downstairs to the kitchens to load it.' Gracchus popped one of the round balls from the tray Leonardi bore into his mouth; it was a sort of artificial peach glazed with sugar, and extraordinarily good. He smacked his lips with relish, and heartily concurred with Leonardi's suggestion. They wandered off together around the fringes of the laughing whirling mass in the ballroom.

Vanderville looked around at the dancers and sighing turned back to Hercule. 'Where is Fesch?' he demanded, peering back through the terrace doors. 'At the stables?'

'Fesch?' said Hercule absently. He had removed a bottle from the ballroom, and was replenishing his glass. 'He finished supervising the statues on the terrace, then disappeared. I think he wants to get into the cisterns, he is consumed at the thought that some antique treasures down there are escaping his net.'

Vanderville swore under his breath. 'And the merry Lieutenant Charles? Isn't Paolette supposed to be tracking him?'

'Well, she could hardly follow him into the bushes. Anyway he was looking for Fesch. He said something about scores to settle.'

'That's all we need,' said Vanderville, shaking his head at Hercule's offer of a glass. He had already had one too many.

'Fuck Fesch,' grunted Hercule, draining his own glass, and picking up the bottle again. 'He has it coming.'

'And Alexandre?' asked Vanderville.

'With *Citoyenne* Paolette. He said he was going to show her the real nymph I think,' said Hercule, checking the level of his bottle regretfully. Vanderville blinked; at least Letizia wasn't with Alexandre, dripping more of her nonsense into his ears.

'They went into the house together?' asked Vanderville.

'No, the other way. I suppose they went to the stables, which is where we ought to be, that's where the real party is.' Hercule winked. 'Shall we go?' He indicated the terrace doors with an expansive gesture, but Vanderville paused on the threshold, his hand on the door frame. His head was whirling with the champagne, and ceaseless thoughts and suspicions. He cursed the wine, and bidding Hercule wait for him, he rudely shouldered his way back through the crowds in the ballroom. It was crammed with dancers, and pausing to gauge their movements, he darted across the room in between the milling couples to their annoyed shouts and ribald comments. He brusquely shoved open the door leading to the hall and staircase. It was dark there by comparison, and the staircase was laden with shadow. The Guide stationed in the dark behind the staircase straightened up apprehensively when he perceived Vanderville, who nodded and waved for him to relax. He stood in the centre of the cool hall for a moment staring up into the darkness at the top of the stairs. The only sounds came from the ballroom, music and muffled enthusiastic voices. He shook his head again and walked across the hall to the candlelit room where meals were served.

Gracchus placed his tray down beside the speaking tube. He was finding the role of replenisher of tables a mixed blessing. The constant circulation from the delivery apparatus to the ballroom enabled him to keep an eye on the hall, all the more useful as the Guide stationed there appeared to have slunk off. He could also eavesdrop on a number of conversations, his presence ignored as if the menial business of transporting of cakes had rendered him invisible. On the downside his feet were killing him. There was no sign of Vanderville yet, and he wondered whether he was still at the stables organising a relief of Guides, or whether he had been distracted by his own concerns. He reflected that Vanderville was becoming an amatory martyr, constantly distracted by the inappropriate young Bonaparte girl. He bent down and rubbed his stocking leg where it was tender.

'We have a problem,' said Vanderville, pushing the door open with a bang. 'Too many people to watch, and not enough men.' He closed the door quietly behind him. 'Half the guards have slipped off to get drunk, and half of our suspects, let alone those we are supposed to be looking after, have gone to the stables to get pissed.' Gracchus nodded in understanding. 'I'm going to the stables to round up more Guides,' said Vanderville. 'Will you be all right here?'

Putting down his book, Gracchus pointed out a fully laden plate, a pile of napkins, and a bottle. 'Yes, yes, Leonardi will keep me busy supplying the thirsty guests.'

'Very well,' said Vanderville. 'The Guide in the hall will keep an eye on you. Have you seen Charles?'

'He passed through the hall earlier. I don't think he is as drunk as he pretends to be. He poured his drink into one of the vases.'

'Was he alone?'

Gracchus nodded. 'Yes, quite alone.'

Vanderville moved to the hall door. He paused with his hand on it. 'I will be back before you notice I'm gone,' he said, his jaw firmly set against the apprehension rising inside him, and he strode purposefully through the door.

There was a muffled noise from the uncapped speaking tube, and Gracchus picked his end up irritably and spoke into the brass cook's head, then pressed it to his ear. 'I found something in the ice buckets,' came Leonardi's muffled voice. 'Go and enjoy the party a bit, I'll bring it up with the ices.'

'Wait,' began Gracchus, fumbling the tube, which he promptly dropped. But there was no reply from Leonardi, and as he picked it up and strained his ear to the hole, he heard a stealthy tread behind him and turned to see Letizia stood wordlessly there watching him. Alexandre hovered in the doorway behind her with Paolette at his side.

'You promised me a turn in the gardens,' she said gently.

'Letizia, may I beg a moment to speak to you,' said Alexandre in a hollow voice.

'You may,' she said, looking at him, distastefully. 'Afterwards.'

Letizia and Gracchus had become in the habit of sharing a postprandial turn in the gardens. Gracchus was often in need of exercise after overindulgence at table, and Letizia, who hardly ate at all, enjoyed surveying the progress of the garden remodelling. The gardeners soon learnt to vacate the groves as they passed through, so as better to avoid her critical eye. It suited them both to be alone together. They walked now by the moonlight among a miasma of dancing fireflies and by degrees arrived in the clearing where the statue of Medusa had previously stood. It was warm still, and the air was fragrant where the sleeping flowers breathed. Gracchus leant on the empty pedestal. The faint sound of drunken song drifted to them from the terrace above, mingled with the distant barking of a dog, and they both smiled indulgently. Gracchus indicated the space where the statue had stood. The remains of an iron bolt and crumbling remnants of mortar marked where the statue had been. 'Our little retreat has been bereaved,' he said sadly, picking up one of the little insects on his finger to admire its glow.

'Let us not cry for mere garden ornaments for all mercy,' said Letizia.

'Perhaps you are right,' answered Gracchus carefully. He shrugged. 'Our times have seen so much loss and sudden death that we are all become inured to grief and suffering. The soldiers shrug it off with a drink and a song, and perhaps we should do the same.' He circled the empty pedestal thoughtfully. 'Tell me,' he asked quietly. 'It was you who took the sabre of Lieutenant Charles and placed it in the cisterns, was it not?'

She kept her eyes steadily on him, until he was forced to lower his. 'Why would you think that?' she asked.

'The sabre was recovered by one of your daughters, and you saw an opportunity to implicate Charles in the death of Piotr. This would distract attention and suspicion from Alexandre, for whom you have conceived a, shall we say, maternal fondness, and rid you of an enemy, a supporter of your rival, Josephine.' He paused, running his hand over the cool stone of the statue's base.

'What a dangerous conclusion you have arrived at, Gracchus,' she said, and smiled. She was about to speak further when they were disturbed by a moan and a rustling in the bushes, Gracchus held a finger to his lips and moved swiftly towards the sound. He parted the branches and saw a prostate figure on the ground. He touched him gently and saw that it was General Leclerc, dead drunk. He was without his coat or hat and looked young without his accoutrements of office.

Letizia said, 'He is not…?'

'No,' said Gracchus, 'a surfeit of wine is all.' He noticed that the general's sword and sword belt were under his head as a makeshift pillow folded around his ridiculous little white buskin boots. 'Someone has made him comfortable,' he remarked.

'Let him sleep,' said Letizia, looking over his shoulder at the recumbent general. 'He looks so peaceful there devoid of care. These young men won't have much rest ahead of them if my son has anything to do with it, and god knows, this one will get little respite from my daughter.'

Gracchus looked around the clearing and behind the pedestal for the general's clothes, but of them there was no sign. Letizia arranged herself on the empty plinth and summoned him. 'Stop being so busy, Gracchus. Come and sit.' She patted the pedestal. He sat awkwardly on the perch, which was insufficient for two. His borrowed ball shoes pinched his feet. Another clamour of laughter and shouts from the terrace reached them, and Letizia suggested the vacant space above the plinth with a gesture.

'I saw Medusa here alone earlier when they had removed Perseus, and felt sorry for her. My own husband died young, leaving an empty space like this. He did not see forty. I was a widow at thirty-five. He left me with eight children, the last just four months old. You live for them of course, and your own hopes and torments become centred entirely around them. And yet, it is hard to be resolved to live only *through* them at the age of thirty-five. Besides the material loss of a protector and provider one misses also the companionship and comfort. You must feel the same sometimes; my son told me you are a widower.'

Gracchus glanced around the clearing. The absence of the blue general's coat was needling him. He adjusted his seat uncomfortably; she had left him just the corner, and he was struggling not to lean against her. He rubbed one foot absently against the back of his leg and said, 'I feel the loss only rarely now.' He paused, this didn't seem sufficient, and he added cautiously, 'I sometimes ask myself, is this it? Or rather, was that it? Everything that two people can experience on their journey together was imminent and promised and then in the blink of an eye, was lost and passed away. Now, when I think of my wife, the feeling is only an echo in an empty room. That time has gone.' He sighed, uncomfortably aware of her cool skin too close to him, and moved away. 'Now I welcome a life without the distraction of intense feeling.' He stared listlessly at his dangling feet and uncomfortable borrowed shoes and added sadly, 'But sometimes I am weakened.' He slipped off his shoes and rubbed his feet dolefully.

'Is this one of those times?' she said, turning her face to look at him. He felt her gaze and was afraid to raise his eyes to hers. She slipped from the pedestal, and he too stood, slowly, and warily. The grass tickled his feet through his stockings. Behind her a million fireflies spotted the sky. Gracchus was almost dizzy, as if some drug suffused his veins. His reason felt dull, subordinated to something else in his stomach. These were unfamiliar, and worrying, feelings.

They were silent for a moment, and then Gracchus, feeling like an imposter, took a clumsy step towards her. They were interrupted by the panting of Leonardi's huge bandog trotting into the clearing, shaking its head at the bobbing insects which surrounded them.

The animal froze when it noticed them, and gave Gracchus a baleful look, before noiselessly padding past and out into the gardens. Letizia turned her eyes expectantly on him again, but Gracchus's mind was elsewhere. 'The dog should be closed in the kitchen garden,' he said with a frown, and then, grateful for the breaking of the spell, he bowed. 'Excuse me, I must get back to the kitchens now,' and leaving her alone by the empty pedestal, he stalked off in the direction from which the dog had come.

Chapter Twenty

As Vanderville passed into the hall, his arm was grasped by an unseen hand. He disengaged with a sharp spring, forcing a blade's measure of space as he drew his sabre. Hercule grinned at him, and waggled two bottles. 'Be calm! Iced wine – drink cold and piss warm! We can begin them on the way to the stables.' He held out his hand for Vanderville's sabre, and tucking one under his arm, he cleanly smacked the top from the neck of the other bottle. They tumbled out of the hall front door into the night air under the awning. Pushing a protesting Guide out of the way, Hercule thrust the open bottle into Vanderville's hand, and suggested they take the long route around the house to avoid passing through the ballroom again.

'While our betters dance the night away the soldiers shall have a rougher jollification,' announced Hercule, taking him by the arm. They strode along the side terrace which was dotted with courting couples, and Hercule reminisced, 'At Milan last year, the prefect organised a grand ball and didn't invite the Guides who were billeted there. So we marched in and trashed the place. All of the food went out of the windows followed by the *citoyens*. The *citoyennes* we kept. So now we always have a band and party organised for the soldiers too. At a suitable distance naturally!'

Indeed, the scene at the stables was one grand bacchanal. Lanterns had been strung along lines passed from gallery to gallery. Musicians were belting out popular airs under the liberty tree, and the whole band of the Guides were dancing naked but for their hats and bright red shawls borrowed from the village girls, slung from their shoulders like hussars.

Hercule marched Vanderville straight up to the punchbowl. Behind it, stripped to the waist, General Dumas was wrestling good-naturedly with a huge Polish soldier whose beard identified him as the corporal of the sappers. As they arrived, Dumas threw him to the ground, giving him a slap on the behind as he passed, to the admiration of the onlookers. 'Ah, there you are,' Dumas said, getting up panting. 'Have you seen the Bonaparte girls? They have run away of course to have fun with the soldiers.' He fished a piece of fruit out from the punchbowl and sucked it vigorously. 'Their brother is furious.'

Vanderville surveyed the stable yard scene. There was no chance of rousing any sober reinforcement here, nor was there any sign of Paolette or Alexandre. Dumas launched into the telling of a laborious and infinitely vulgar story to Hercule.

Vanderville grimaced. He could raise no help here, instead he was losing Hercule, and he knew he should be back at the villa. He asked Hercule incredulously, 'Alexandre really said he was going to show Paolette the nymph?' There was a cheer from the dancers, as their combinations were interrupted by the ponderous progress across the dancing area of a horse. Asleep on its back was a man, dead drunk and completely naked.

'Did he say nymph? He might have done?' said Hercule, swigging deeply.

'The nymph in the cisterns?' persisted Vanderville. 'Are you sure that's what he said, Hercule?'

Hercule considered this a moment. 'They were tipsy,' he said, 'talking all sorts of nonsense.'

'Anyway,' slurred Dumas, reaching the finale of his anecdote, which concluded by insulting the mother of every Pole present. He roared with laughter. Vanderville stared blankly at him, and saw the face of the bested Polish wrestler as he drew himself up cracking his knuckles ominously. 'What happened?' said Dumas petulantly. 'Everyone is grizzling at each other. Alexandre is glumping around like a sour-faced nag, Charles is sullen and chunting at anyone in his path. We are brothers under Mars, have you forgotten?'

At that moment the sapper launched himself onto Dumas's back and the pair of them went through the table, splintering the wood and upsetting the punchbowl over Vanderville and Hercule. Dumas was on the floor, convulsed with laughter, and pummelling ineffectually at the sapper's head with a table leg.

Vanderville eased himself down by Hercule, who had sat down on a bench under the pine to swab his *pantalons*. 'Are you drunk?' he asked him.

'No,' responded Hercule morosely, swilling at a bottle neck, 'but I'm trying.'

'Come with me then, we have to scour the villa.'

Hercule shook his head. 'That's that,' he said. 'You can't fight this ghoul with swords. Time to let it go, Vanderville, what could go wrong tonight? We leave tomorrow, anyhow, have another drink…'

But Vanderville was already gone.

–

As Vanderville vaulted up the last steps to the terrace he ran into a crowd of revellers dispersing from the ballroom doors. The musicians were taking a break, and the dancers were moving to the terrace. The nearest generals were joking ribaldly that Bonaparte had gone to bed early with Josephine. Further down the terrace he was relieved to spot Charles. A bit elevated in spirits, he had decided to serenade one of the balconies above. He had marshalled two musicians of the band and they struck up a concert under the window. Josephine, smiling palely, appeared at the balcony's edge with General Bonaparte who graciously acknowledged what he imagined was a fanfaronade in his honour. Charles leapt onto the balustrade, almost over-balancing as he did so. He steadied himself against the Medusa statue and cried hoarsely, 'It is not for you, my General, that we serenade, it's for the *citoyenne*.' Vanderville yanked him away from his indiscretion, and they fled the terrace, afflicted variously with laughter and misgivings. Charles halted at the ballroom's doors, his sides stricken with laughter, and he leant heavily on Vanderville, who said, 'Listen, Charles, where's Paolette?'

Charles was wheezing, he straightened up and clapped Vanderville on the shoulder. 'That bird has flown, brother,' he said. 'Let her go.' Through the open doors on the other side of the ballroom Vanderville saw a flash of white moving like a wraith in the gloom of the stair hall. He pushed Charles off and raced after the apparition.

–

Gracchus arrived in the kitchen garden by the terrace gate that was swinging open. The garden was deserted, but as he tried the door to Leonardi's domain, a wet whimpering announced the dog, who shoved impatiently at his legs as he warily entered. The creature preceded him down the steps into the gloom of the empty kitchen and stood at its post by the dying fire quivering suspiciously. Gracchus eyed the dim shape of the large beast cautiously, and he groped for one of Leonardi's knives from the table as a precaution. He called Leonardi's name softly at the black cellar entrance but there was no reply, so he felt his way down the steps keeping one wary eye on the dog. Away from the party, everything was strangely silent and deserted, except for the whining of the animal whose shadow announced he had moved to block the doorway. In the cold cellar, all of the sweet magnificence of the cook's invention was laid out. Various spun sugar centrepieces were awaiting the attention of the last revellers, ghostly white in the gloom. Gracchus put down the knife and lifted a sugared peach to his lips, calling again through the creamy mouthful. As he stuffed the last remnant guiltily into his mouth, there came a whisper and he whirled around. There was nothing there but shadow. But he saw the silhouette of the trapdoor to the spiral staircase ajar. He advanced stealthily towards the black gap in the floor.

He descended cautiously, calling as he went, 'Leonardi? Is anybody there?' He bumped his foot against the ice buckets all stacked by the satyr door, which yawned open. The air from the cisterns was creeping up through the entrance and he was cold in his stockings and ball shoes. Beyond the satyr's grinning face was a glimmer of faint light, and he poked his head carefully through the door, resting his free hand on the satyr for luck. The cistern vault was lit by a single flaming torch abandoned on the lip of the dry cistern at the far end by the fresco of Diana. There was nobody in sight, but again he heard a faint rustling and footsteps. He shivered; it was difficult to gauge the source of the noise. The echoes in the cisterns played tricks with sound. He glanced towards where the tunnel entrance lay to his right, but could make nothing out. He started threading his way down the central aisle of the chamber, the dry and wet cisterns to each side of him as he advanced step by measured step towards the lone flickering torch.

Vanderville slammed through the doors into hallway and darted to the bottom of the main stair. The pursued wraith was on the first flight and span to confront him. 'Paolette,' he gasped. 'I thought you were watching Charles, then I heard you were with Alexandre.'

'Alexandre?' she called down to him. 'I lost him. He was impudent with me. Completely crazy, and ranting about my family and his uncle, so I left him at the stables. He looked exhausted and I told him to go and get some sleep.' She started up the stairs.

Vanderville caught his breath. 'Wait! Sleep is the last thing he needs. When was that?'

'Oh! Earlier,' she replied airily. 'You know how time flies at a ball.' She started up the stairs again. 'I'm getting my shawl,' she shouted, and disappeared round the stair head. Vanderville looked around in frustration; there was no sight of the guard who was supposed to have been posted in the hall. Gone to join the party. He had one thought: Alexandre mustn't sleep, not now, he must stop him from sleeping! He raced up the stairs after the disappearing Paolette.

Gracchus paused and polished his spectacles to see better. The fresco of Diana emerged from the shadows as he advanced; the white of her mother of pearl bandeau shone out of the gloom and gave him pause for thought. If Letizia was familiar with it, then she must know the cisterns better than she had pretended. As he approached the fresco, he saw the frightful catafalque draped over the cocoon, as if it was garnished with bones. In the shimmering light the dreadful shape seemed to rustle and tremble, and Gracchus shivered. He picked up a pole from the debris on the floor and poked it tentatively. A hoarse whisper answered his probing touch. 'Don't leave me, Gracchus!' It was Leonardi, cowering behind the other side of the dry cistern.

Vanderville was running up the stairs after Paolette. She looked back, laughed, and tripped up the next flight faster. He caught her on the landing of the last floor before the attics and took her by the arm. 'Go to your room and lock yourself inside,' he urged her breathlessly.

She shook his grasp off angrily. 'Are you drunk? You are behaving like a husband. Leave me alone.'

'But it's not safe in the house alone.' He pulled her back towards him.

'Stay with me then,' she whispered, wriggling into his arms, driving all thought of Alexandre and Fesch and Charles from his mind. He bent his lips to her mouth, and she kissed him back feverishly. The sound of revellers spilling into the hall drove them upstairs again to the tower rooms that looked out over the roof at the very pinnacle of the villa. There were windows on three sides of the bare tower space; one stood idly ajar, and the moonlight flooded through to paint their conjoined bodies in limpid light as they kissed and bit, tearing at each other's clothes in a frenzy of yearning, the potential of desire fulfilled at last.

Leonardi's eyes flickered and blinked. 'Gracchus!' he moaned, his eyes struggling to focus with dread. 'Be careful, there's something out there in the dark.' Gracchus advanced towards him, gripping the knife point down at his side.

'What did you find in Piotr's bucket?' he hissed urgently, crouching over the cook. Leonardi fumbled inside his apron, and Gracchus flinched away despite himself. But Leonardi merely thrust a crumpled piece of paper at him. Gracchus put the knife on the cistern lip beside the lantern and took it from him. He recognised Mombello's writing. It was the page torn from Mombello's journal, but in this light even with his spectacles, he could hardly make anything out.

With a gasp, Leonardi's face went rigid with terror, his eyes bulged frantically clear out of his head. Every hair on Gracchus's own head stood on end as he realised Leonardi's petrified gaze was not on him, but on something behind. His heart stood still; and slowly he swivelled his head. A figure was silently materialising out of the darkness behind them. Indistinct in the shadows, its face half covered by a cloth, only the eyes, inhuman, demonic, reflected the light. Only the eyes... and a knife glittering in its grip.

Leonardi moaned piteously, and stuffing the journal pages into his breast, Gracchus fled. All thought of his ruined feet dissipated; his dancing shoes lent him speed and he went through the cellars as if all the shades of hell were on his heels. Behind him he heard something moving faster. He was first up the spiral staircase, but as he cleared the stair head, a hand slipped through the murk and grasped his ankle in a vice-like grip, bringing him down. Gracchus squealed, and kicked himself clear, losing one shoe in the process. He scrambled towards the tables, but the creature had leapt up the remaining stairs with unimaginable speed and was upon him. Gracchus, shrieking and flailing his arms like a banshee, shot towards the pastries table but the creature had a hold of him, and began pummelling him furiously. Gracchus battered ineffectually at the top of its head and shoulders, but it was hopeless. It was stronger, and it began pulling him towards the stairs. Stretching out in a final spasm of effort, his flailing hands encountered the hanging edge of the tablecloth. He pulled hard and brought the whole mess of table, cakes and tablecloth down on top of them both. The beast was shrouded by the cloth and Gracchus struck down hard at the shape with bone-crunching force. The grip on his legs was released, and Gracchus found his feet startlingly quickly and streaked up the stair into the dark kitchen.

As his pursuer emerged into the after him, Gracchus met it with a veritable fusillade of missiles snatched from the kitchen tables and its advance was checked as it beat away the projectiles, covering its face to protect itself. Scrambling between the laden tables Gracchus deployed the full battery of cuisine in his defence. Onions, the herb pots, a chicken carcass, a jar of frogs, the dog's bone and bowls; he snatched each up heedlessly in the gloom, and flung them all in futile terror. As his weapons become sequentially less effective, he found himself cornered by the rotating apparatus. Arming himself with a roasting spit, with three poulet still attached to it, he prepared to sell them and himself dearly.

His assailant advanced on him, masked incongruously in a napkin, and Gracchus, backed helplessly up against Leonardi's apparatus, began to fumble at the catch of the doors.

A low growl sounded further into the kitchen and Gracchus and his assailant were alerted to the presence of the dog. Unwilling to suffer the attentions of either dog or fiend, Gracchus finally found the catch of the doors and felt them give way behind him. He gratefully eased himself seat first into the confines of the rotating apparatus as his pursuer was distracted by the deep padding of paws crossing the kitchen.

The doors mercifully drew a veil over the scene in the kitchen as they closed behind him, and cramped inside he was imbued with unexpected strength as he pulled urgently at the cables that began creaking him upwards to safety.

He tumbled breathlessly out of the rotating apparatus on all fours, gibbering to himself. The dining salon was deserted, and he lay panting on the floor, recovering his scrambled wits to sense. He must make order of events! He forced himself to think. Had the ghoul been wearing a uniform? He could not be sure at first, he recalled only a dark coat, and the napkin covered its face, but as his memory coalesced he thought that yes, surely he had seen the glint of gold buttons on the cuff of the sleeve holding the knife. It was not conclusive, and of course Fesch, Alexandre, and Charles would all be in uniform, among any number of others...

Gracchus hauled himself to his feet and streaked through the door to the main stair, where he entered a different world. Several tired couples were refreshing themselves there in the cool of the hall, relishing the music that leaked through from the ball. They recoiled as a wild-eyed Gracchus burst forth, and without blurting out any explanation glared at them. Either his disarrayed appearance or the arrival of the dog from the kitchen had the desired effect; the hall rapidly emptied, and the dog departed chasing retreating heels through the front doors of the villa. Gracchus ignored its departure, for in the dim light he saw a figure skulking stealthily on the landing above. Without pausing, he stumbled his way to the staircase and limped up it.

The door of the tower room was flung open, and a dishevelled figure burst in.

'He is after me!' said Alexandre. 'Help me.'

Vanderville seized his coat, and Paolette gasped, clutching up her dress.

'Alexandre, quick, hide on the roof,' said Vanderville, pointing at the open window. The wild-eyed youth gave them barely a glance; his eyes were intent on the beams of moonlight streaming through the windows. He strode past them as if in a dream and seizing the sill, sprang onto the ledge and passed out onto the roof.

Vanderville drew his sword and prepared to defend access to the roof with his life. 'Paolette! Run downstairs, find Gracchus and bring him here. Now.'

Recalled to herself, she scooped up her sandals and bolted through the door. On the landing she ran round the corner head on into Fesch. 'Calm yourself niece, what is all the hurry?' he said, his bloodless face straining into a smile.

'Vanderville is on the roof with Alexandre,' she said breathlessly. 'Have you seen Gracchus?'

'Not for hours,' lied Fesch sweetly, and as he watched her career down the landing towards the stairs, his smile faded, and he set his jaw. Unseen behind him, a third figure who had been watching them talk from the shadows slipped out and followed him quietly.

Gracchus crashed into the turret room, and narrowly avoided being impaled by Vanderville as he came through the door. 'Where is he?' he wheezed.

'Alexandre? On the roof. Where's Paolette?'

'She is coming. No wait,' he said as Vanderville seized the window frame and prepared to mount the sill. 'There is still something I don't comprehend.' Gracchus stuck his hand in his breast, and his exhausted face lit up with pallid concern. He swapped hands and tried the other side, then with a sigh of relief pulled out the creased sheet of paper Leonardi had given him. He then commenced patting his pockets in a vain search for his spectacles.

'What is it?' asked Vanderville, and Gracchus held it out to him. 'It is the missing entry from Mombello's journal in Corsica. It will say something about the stillborn child.' He looked at Vanderville again. 'If the child *was* stillborn…'

Vanderville scanned it quickly. 'Mombello returned to France to take up a new post after Corsica. He employs a wet nurse for the voyage, and again after he returns to France.' He turned the page over. 'Later he mentions a dangerous malady for the child, who "suffers from the sleeping sickness".'

Gracchus stared at him wordlessly, then he too read the sheet by the moonlight. He finished, folded the paper, and put it back in his breast. He peered through the window at the sky, where the stars mirrored the fireflies flickering on the earth below.

Vanderville was the first to speak. 'Marbeuf was the father of one of the Bonapartes, then? No wonder Piotr hid this.'

'It is worse than that. If this is all true, then Letizia Buonaparte is the mother of Alexandre.'

Vanderville met Gracchus's eyes, and then followed their gaze to the gaping window. He sheathed his sabre smartly and vaulted over the windowsill onto the roof. Striking the tiles with a clatter he caught his breath in the sudden cool night air. He was poised uncomfortably close to the edge of the terracotta tiles, and just below him were the lead gutters beyond which was a drop to the stones of the terrace three stories below. Alexandre was plunging crazily, jerkily across the roof ahead of him, dislodging tiles with a rattle as he careered towards the stack of chimneys that provided the only handhold between this tower and the other. There was a yelp as Gracchus rolled gracelessly over the window ledge behind him and thumped onto the tiles, scrabbling for a fingerhold. Vanderville steadied him, then set out precariously across the roof after Alexandre.

Alexandre clung by one hand to the chimney stack. He held out a warning hand to Vanderville. 'Go back,' he said desperately. 'You don't know these roofs as I do.'

Beyond him Vanderville saw one of the windows of the other tower ease open, and two shadowy figures started to emerge. He started to move forward, step by agonising step towards Alexandre.

'I read my uncle's journals where he related the obscene details of my birth, and how my parents abandoned me for dead, as well they might, provoked by their shame. He I still loved, for hadn't he saved me, and brought me up like a father, but she, who had been so kind to me since she discovered my condition, she was my mother! But when I spoke of it to him, he was angry that I had explored his private papers and we quarrelled bitterly. Better to be a Mombello, he said, than a bastard Buonaparte. But I insisted that he reveal the truth to Letizia, I was sure she would accept me, and reluctantly he agreed, asking her to meet him in the chapel that evening. He reached it by the tunnel as usual, and he told me to wait in the bushes unseen and watch Letizia arrive, then lock the doors after she entered so they would not be disturbed, and return to my quarters. I did as he commanded, but consumed by curiosity to see how my mother received the news of her child's survival and my true parentage, I scaled the workman's ladder to listen at the windows while they spoke.

'I wish I had not had that unhappy inspiration. She did not take it well. She thought that he wanted money, and as their words grew more heated, they withdrew to the nymphaeum so I couldn't hear any more. I had heard enough. I knew now she didn't want me.

'Then I was interrupted by voices. I recognised them at once, it was Charles and Fesch. They were conferring by the chapel door, everything in their figures and the scattered snatches of their conversation I could make out bespoke evil intent, and I knew they meant my uncle mischief. I concealed myself from them and watched them prowl the exterior of the chapel like the murderous greedy wretches they are.'

Vanderville saw that the two figures at the other end of the roof had stopped to remove their boots, and now they fanned out to make their way towards them, probing the tiles with their stockinged feet.

'When at last they left, I hastened to unlock the door, but I found the nymphaeum empty. The tunnel door lay open, and there were signs of a struggle. My path was clear, I rushed down into the darkness of the tunnel after them. Halfway down, beside the entrance to the well, I came across his body. He had suffered a congestion of the heart and was struggling for breath. There was no sign of her, but a lantern stood beside him. As I cradled him, he confessed to me that when she refused to acknowledge me, he had threatened her with exposure, and she had fled. Pursuing her, he became overwrought and collapsed. His health was not good. He had bungled everything and turned her against me. Overcome with disappointment, I pushed him away from me. You know how the ground slopes down there. He slid instantly into the well. There was a horrible sound as he met the stanchion, and a splash, nothing more.'

Vanderville blanched. 'Come back, Alexandre, for pity's sake,' he whispered hoarsely. 'You can stop all of this now. You don't have to go through with it.'

'You still don't understand,' said Alexandre, untying a napkin from around his neck. He feinted behind the chimneys and emerged over the upper range of tiles. Vanderville matched his movements as best he could, his feet unsure and his head spinning as he arrived gratefully at the chimneys. 'Piotr was a different matter. He knew too much, of course,' uttered Alexandre, over his shoulder, scampering away. 'I see that now. He was working for Fesch all along, while simultaneously hoping to blackmail him, or Josephine.

'It was I who told him about the tunnel and allowed him to escape. I loved him, you see, especially after he put his head in a noose for me, and I didn't want him to take the responsibility for a crime. Neither could I have him lose his nerve and expose me.

'It must have been when he was hiding in the cisterns that he decided that the General's family was too dangerous a target, and that he could use those papers he had got hold of to target me instead. So he had to go too.'

'Alexandre,' came Gracchus's voice, imploring him. 'Please. Not like this. We can burn the sepulchre you built...'

'I built?' Alexandre said with a strange laugh. 'Oh, you are still so far from the truth. Do be quiet, Gracchus, I need to concentrate.'

He resumed his narrative, more quickly now. 'Uncle's mistake was trying to blackmail her, and he paid for that. But I had a mother at last! Even though I knew that she didn't want me At first I thought she wanted to help me. I believed that she would come round in time, but primed with her tales I have allowed myself to become a puppet in her hands.'

Vanderville glanced behind. Gracchus was inching along the roof on his belly, his feet trailing in the guttering. His mouth was working furiously, as he muttered to himself. Turning back towards Alexandre he saw further away, but making rapid progress, the faces of Charles and Fesch apparent as they edged closer.

Alexandre followed his gaze and flinched when he saw Fesch. 'He is the worst of that family,' he gasped, 'a ravening vulture come to feast on the carcass of Mombello. Better for Uncle and I that none of their accursed clan had come here!'

Vanderville forced himself to focus on Alexandre and skipped forward in a crouch. As he did so, the tiles slid under him and he lost his feet. He twisted frantically, clutching at the chimneys as he fell, but missed. Landing with a crash on the roof, he slithered down to the gutter, unable to arrest his slide. His feet bumped over the lead drain but he caught it with one palm at his waist. He was prostrate, and capable of nothing but maintaining his ground spreadeagled on the very edge of the roof facing the crest far above. His weak left hand was above his chest clutching a thin sliver of lead that ran from the chimney to the gutter, and his right was at his waist braced hard against a flat tile. His legs were in thin air. He squinted down and regretted it instantly. Below them, the music had begun again, and the sound of couples strolling and laughing on the terrace reached them. He could hear Gracchus and the others still some way off, but couldn't bear to turn his head to look, and then Alexandre appeared behind the chimney and crept down towards him. He reached down towards Vanderville's handhold where two fingers gripped the lead sheet precariously and Vanderville closed his eyes and tensed every fibre of his being, trying to press himself into the tiles, and blot out his horrible predicament. Then a hand grasped his wrist, and he opened his eyes and looked into those of Alexandre, who was balancing backwards against the roof and pulling with all his strength to haul Vanderville up, up to the safety of the chimney. He grimaced with pain as he pulled, and Vanderville edged his feet back onto the roof. They huddled below the chimney together, clutching each other, and leaning against the bricks. Alexandre held Vanderville's hand tightly. It was a poor position just above the precipice, but it felt like security to Vanderville after his near fall.

Alexandre was laughing. It was not a pleasant sound. 'This does nothing for my credentials as a ghoul,' he spluttered.

'It was you?' said Vanderville. 'Both of them?'

Gracchus covered the last part of the edge of the roof towards them, dislodging tiles with his groping feet. 'You still don't understand, Vanderville, he is not the only one. He is not alone. The problem here is not that there is a mazzere, the problem is that Mombello harbours two.'

'No, Gracchus, it was me. It was all me,' hissed Alexandre urgently.

'I don't believe you,' shouted Gracchus. 'There were no animals killed before the army arrived here, because this does not form part of your condition. That began when the staff moved in. Therefore, there is a second mazzere. A mal-mazzere, who acts on their impulses and destroys in life as in dreams. Name her!' He was just metres from them now, and Vanderville felt the strength in his arm around the chimney ebbing away.

Fesch loomed out of the dark, reaching out for the chimney on which Vanderville's shoulders were braced. Taking hold of it, he swung one stockinged foot towards them.

Alexandre untied Vanderville's desperate grasp of his hand, finger by tired finger.

'No!' cried Vanderville, comprehending as Fesch clutched for Alexandre's shoulder.

Alexandre turned to stare into Vanderville's face, so close he felt his hot breath on his face.

'I know what Mother wants,' he said. 'I can play my part,' and he launched himself the few steps to the roof edge and off he went.

He plummeted with arms outstretched and circled twice, before his body was flung horribly upon the statue of Medusa on the terrace's edge. The statue tottered on its pedestal, then collapsed over the edge of the parapet, the whole whirling tumbling mass of stone and body disappearing into the garden below.

Gracchus slumped down beside Vanderville, blotting out the startled shouts and screams from the terrace.

'And the second mazzere? What did you mean by that?' asked Vanderville, listening to the sounds of distress drifting up from the world below.

'Only Alexandre could answer that,' said Gracchus. He shook his head to clear it. 'I fear the secrets of Mombello have died with him.' He lay back against the chimney and closed his eyes against the night.

Epilogue

The villa was being packed up. The army was leaving, and the villagers were clearing up behind them. The Bonapartes were arranging their travelling equipage in front of the villa. Fesch was organising the waggons to follow on. 'We have so many more bags than when we arrived,' he sighed contentedly to the watching Vanderville.

Gracchus went rather sheepishly to return Mombello's papers to Bonaparte's cabinet. Berthier was waiting dourly outside the door.

'What on earth can you want, Gracchus?' he said peevishly. 'There is nothing for you here. The commander-in-chief does not believe in reinforcing failure. Good grief, three dead men, all of them despatched under your very eyes; the wedding ball disrupted by noble scions plunging from the sky. Some investigating magistrate you turned out to be. You have upset half of his family, and corrupted at least one of them. I think I shall come in with you, this ought to be worth seeing.' He knocked on the door and ushered Gracchus in. Bonaparte looked up enquiringly from his seat at the desk.

'I have some papers to return.'

'I see.' He summed up Gracchus at length, in silence, then scribbled something down, tore off the piece of paper and handed it to Berthier. 'Copy this before issue. And provide Citoyen Gracchus with a horse and a passport. Issue him a pair of boots too if you can find such a thing.'

Berthier blanched and complied with a furious glare at Gracchus. Bonaparte sighed and sat back in his chair.

'When you do something, do it with alacrity, Gracchus. You are too slow in your combinations.'

'Yes General.'

'However, your discretion is developed beyond that of most other men, and you have provided a conclusion of a sort.'

Gracchus inclined his head without answering.

'Under the circumstances, I think you are more useful in my service than left to your own devices. You would be a liability off the leash.' He bent his head back to his work. Gracchus waited what seemed to him an unconscionably long length of time.

'General. May I...'

'What is it now? Are you still here?' he reached for the bell.

'I want to ask you a question—'

Bonaparte shook his head. 'No.'

'—about your mother.'

Bonaparte paused, his pen poised above the paper. He did not look up, but he frowned.

'It is not that,' said Gracchus hurriedly. 'It is her name, Letizia. What does the name signify to a Corsican?'

Bonaparte wrinkled his brow further. 'It means gladness.'

'Or happiness?'

'Or happiness,' he agreed. 'You may go.'

Josephine was already sat in her travelling carriage. She leant from the window and beckoned to Gracchus as he emerged from the awning. He was grateful to leave Bonaparte, and determined to make it the last time. A new pug dog was wriggling impatiently in her grasp. 'A gift from an admirer,' she explained, holding it up to his face. It sniffed Gracchus warily. 'Bonaparte is already refusing to share the carriage with him,' she complained. 'He has expressed a wish that the new dog will meet the same fate as the old.'

Gracchus fondled the creature's head as it nuzzled his hand. Scratching behind its floppy ears, he saw that it wore a beautiful silver collar lined with velvet. The silver was rather rudely battered into shape as if it had been made in a hurry from something else and he saw that it was adorned with the *sabre d'honneur* emblems of the Army of Italy.

'The collar came with the dog,' she said, smiling enigmatically, and she put the creature down on the floor of the carriage, where it whined desolately. Josephine beamed down at him. 'We are going to the spa baths at Como, Gracchus, why don't you join us?'

'I regret, *citoyenne*, that I have had my fill of cisterns, baths and nymphaeums for now, perhaps for this lifetime.'

'My husband tells me that you are travelling on to Rome. You go with his brother Joseph then, to knock some sense into the Pope?'

'My passport is for Rome, yes,' said Gracchus. 'But at Milan I shall evade my watchers and strike out for territories the republican army has not reached.'

'You are unwise to tell this to General Bonaparte's wife, Gracchus!' she exclaimed in mock horror.

Gracchus considered this, head askance as he watched the dog scratching the white leather seats of the carriage. 'Bonaparte is General of the Army of Italy, not general in charge of waifs and strays, he has other matters to occupy his attention.' He shrugged. 'Anyway, I think we can keep each other's secrets, *citoyenne*, don't you?'

She beamed a rare smile. '*Au revoir* then, Gracchus.'

Bonaparte arrived at the other door of the carriage and mounted. His face was gloomy and abstracted. Gracchus moved away, but he heard Bonaparte lean out of his side of the carriage and ask Fesch, who was wandering past with a stack of canvases under his arm, 'Have you seen my mother?'

'Yes, I'm just loading her into an ox cart,' said Fesch, smirking, and he pulled the sack cloth from one of his acquisitions to show Bonaparte. Gracchus saw that it was the painting Gros had begun of Letizia. It was already blocked out, and the hands were accurately rendered, and parts of her dress.

The face was not yet worked up apart from the eyes, which had obviously captivated the artist, but the work begun had obliterated utterly the face of the Comte Mombello that had been there previously. And so it was, thought Gracchus, that the last trace of Mombello was obscured, and concealed behind the eyes of Letizia.

In fact, the General's mother was not with the carriages being loaded in front of the villa, and Gracchus realised he would be obliged to leave without a farewell. Bonaparte was hanging from his carriage door and haranguing a Guide to go and find her. Gracchus thought of his last conversation with her on the terrace the night before. 'Will you miss the villa, madame?' he had asked her.

'No,' she had replied, 'it is too big, and out of repair, and the garden is infested with serpents.'

Gracchus did not disagree with this assertion. 'And Alexandre Marbeuf?'

She had shrugged. 'He had his destiny to fulfil. He fooled us all.'

Gracchus was moved to reply that Alexandre had a different destiny before the arrival of his step-family, whose malevolent influence had brought nothing but horror to Mombello in their greedy passage, upsetting the ordered quiet life of the comte and his nephew and ruining them both. He wondered bitterly whether Alexandre's condition may have taken a different course, had he not been exposed to the Bonaparte brood. He held his tongue though, as she fixed him with those eyes: ageless, unveined and brilliant. Once more he had the impression that they looked through him, as though fixed on some private vision elsewhere.

Gracchus's recollections were dispelled by a crunching of gravel as Bonaparte's carriage lurched away, with the Guide escort hastily spurring their mounts to conform, and Gracchus waved fondly to Vanderville and Charles where they sat on their horses in the drive waiting to salute Bonaparte as he passed.

Vanderville and Charles drew their swords to salute as Bonaparte's carriage rattled past. Through the glass of the window Vanderville saw that Josephine stared straight ahead and on the other side of her Bonaparte may have been glaring at Charles, or he may simply have been talking to his wife. With a spurt of dust and the clatter of outriders they were gone. Charles stared after the carriage wistfully, and as it became obscured by dust, he turned to Vanderville and raised one quizzical eyebrow. 'As for me, I'm not leaving the cavalry after all. Off to the Army of the Rhine apparently.' He waved away Vanderville's commiserations. 'Oh, it's all right. I am not in the least discomforted. My position here has become untenable. Italy is Bonaparte territory, and Bonaparte is utterly dominant here. I will be safer in Germany. Outraged husbands are so much more amusing at a distance, don't you find?'

'I heard you were moving on,' said Vanderville. 'Congratulations on your promotion, by the way.'

'It was bad luck your own commission not being confirmed,' commiserated Charles.

Vanderville nodded absently, his eyes on Fesch and his waggons. 'I daresay the Guides will get by without me,' he said.

'Their loss, my friend.' He flicked dust from his shoulders. The last Guides passed, and Charles said wistfully, 'I liked Josephine in Paris, and I very much liked the possibility of getting army contracts and making money.'

'She liked you too,' offered Vanderville.

'Yes, she likes amusing young men,' said Charles. 'Perhaps it flattered her for a while. She may even have loved me a bit. But she is complacent enough now as wife of the conqueror of Italy. Basking in vain splendour suits her. Do you know, when she found that I was quite ready to surrender her affections in exchange for amnesty, she chided me as a coward.' He shrugged. 'In fact, I *am* scared of Bonaparte. I am a man more practical than honourable. Which, I reminded her, is how we came together in the first place.'

He smacked the carriage's dust from his *pantalons* with his riding gloves. 'Ultimately, she did all right for me, because Bonaparte can't have me shot without acknowledging that his wife had erred: financially or physically.' He patted his saddle holsters and smiled broadly. 'And anyway, she lent me a bit of tin for the journey to the Rhine.'

Vanderville said nothing; he was surveying the departing carriages with his hands folded on his saddle pommel. Charles watched him scan each heavily laden carriage as it lumbered past them and down the drive. He coughed and reached down to rummage in his saddle holster. Pulling out a fold of paper with no seal, he passed it to Vanderville. 'She left early with her husband and the advance guard,' he said. 'She said to give you this.' Vanderville turned the letter; it was light. One sheet. He unfolded it on his pommel and read it.

> *My Dear Vanderville,*
>   *Tomorrow, I set out for the country, and with no regret I assure you, but that of leaving you. The person I am going with will be no consolation to me, and therefore, if I receive any satisfaction in my journey, it will be entirely owing to your fidelity. Adieu, think of me, or forever forget what I promised you.*

It was not signed. He took a deep breath and slid the letter into his pocket. The dust from the carriages was settling. 'We had better get moving,' he told Charles, 'or we will get snarled up in that lot,' and he indicated Fesch's waggons with a thumb.

As the two riders drew clear of the park of Mombello they crept past the numerous train of horses and vehicles snarled in the village. The fiery victor, who had focussed the eyes of the world and the hope of nations, was going away, escorted by his officers, and by troopers ranged around him and his baggage train. There was now an end to the shouts and cheers, the cohort of blessings and acclamation, with which the people used to surround his laurel-strewn carriage. Silence reigned as the farmhand, the workman, turned away at the sight of the convoy, and fell back without a word. Their gestures and looks proclaimed the indignation and scorn their mouths dared not utter.

As Vanderville and Charles cleared the column, one of the waggons happened to overturn in the middle of the road, spilling a host of little gold pieces onto the dirt of the highway. Some of the escorting soldiers flung themselves avidly on the spoil. It was as though they had not moments enough to fill their pockets, and they would never satisfied, even when sinking under the weight of metal. Bonaparte's cold, immobile visage watched them from his carriage displaying neither remorse, nor grief, nor emotion. Insensibility was written on his brow in letters of ice.

After the very last waggons had departed the villa Gracchus was left alone under the abandoned awning, with Letizia's ill-favoured carriage standing there empty. He mounted his horse without haste and ambled along the road to Milan.

The golden Lombard plains were swollen with sun pink corn, and he was in no hurry. Stopping on the first rise before the village to admire the vista over the plains one last time, he saw black clouds, their breath heavy with promise, mingling in the distance. Below him, outside the chestnut forest surrounding the chapel of Mombello, he saw a figure in black clothes hurrying across the cloud-striped plain. Gracchus turned his horse off the road to intercept her path. Noticing him on the ridge, she hitched up her dew-heavy skirts and disappeared into the woods. Recognition loomed then fled unfulfilled, and before he could be sure, she was lost in the trees. He sighed and put his horse back to the road.

Outside the village, Gracchus heard a thudding of hooves on the road ahead of him, and he saw a rider coming and heard a voice calling his name. He drew his horse up on the brow of the hill and waited. The rider came up to him.

'I thought you were going to the front with Dumas,' said Gracchus.

'Bonaparte sent a change of orders,' said Vanderville. 'I'm reassigned to diplomatic escort, with passports for Rome.' He smiled, and added, 'And orders to ensure all essential non-military personnel assigned to the Rome mission arrive safely, and in good time.' He tapped his sabretache. 'We are to proceed with ultimate despatch.'

Gracchus sighed. 'I suppose that means we shall not stop for a good dinner between here and the eternal city.'

'Oh, between friends I think "ultimate despatch" is worthy of sensible interpretation, don't you?' grinned Vanderville. There was a low rolling rumble of thunder in the distance, and the first eager shadows of advancing clouds pushed over the plains.

'We might yet outrun them,' said Vanderville, and the two riders turned their horses' heads to the open road.

Historical notes on Mombello

Villa Mombello really was Napoleon's choice for a family reunion. To celebrate the marriages of his sisters and amuse his new wife he removed his headquarters from Milan to the country for a few weeks. In his memoirs, dictated on St Helena shortly before his death, he refers to Mombello as Montebello, and this error has been repeated by numerous biographers since. In my malicious hands Napoleon's excusable slip of the memory has become an attempt to obscure a regrettable episode.

Villa Mombello still exists, now known as Villa Crivelli-Pusterla after various subsequent owners. Its chequered twentieth-century history saw it repurposed as a sanitorium, which added a sinister frisson to its local reputation. The crumbling buildings became a haunt of urban explorers, but the thrill seekers have now been displaced as the villa itself has a welcome new role as an agricultural college. I moved the chapel's location from the front to the back of the villa, but the house and grounds were otherwise as the reader finds them here, and the bluff on which the house stands is indeed riddled with subterranean secrets.

Almost all of the inhabitants of the villa in the book are historical personages and it was unnecessary to take any but the lightest liberties to grant them new life. Gracchus and Vanderville are entirely my creations, each inspired by a mélange of period parallels. The term, 'investigating magistrate' is a free translation from comparable French period parlance. The cook Leonardi was a real person, and really a great chef, but I have exploited some gaps in his historical itinerary to insert him into the Bonaparte story; there is no evidence that they ever coincided. Comte Mombello is a partial invention, but his family, the Marbeufs, and their connections with the Bonapartes in Corsica are genuine. The precise nature of the relationship between Marbeuf and Letizia is still a source of contention and fascination to historians. The only recorded death at Mombello during this period was Josephine's pug Fortune, who probably fell victim to the cook's dog (to General Bonaparte's delight). The now almost extinct phenomenon of mazzerisme has been evocatively recorded by Dorothy Carrington, who wrote the most caressing accounts of Corsica it has been my pleasure to read.

For the other characters, it was necessary to prune many. I was sorry to lose the young Eugène Beauharnais, Josephine's son; Junot, Napoleon's friend and shadow; and Caroline Bonaparte, Paolette's competitive and fiery sister, but the reader will have the opportunity to meet these people in later editions of the series.

Acknowledgements

Thanks to Mike Bryan and Kit Nevile, without whose sage encouragement and guidance this book would still be languishing on the author's desktop.